FRET ME NOT

SARAH ESTEP

ISBN: 979-8-9880770-5-3 (print)

ISBN: 979-8-9880770-4-6 (e-book)

For Erin, who held my hand from across an ocean and refused to let me quit

And for the pets who give us a reason to get out of bed

CONTENT CAUTIONS

Before you begin Fret Me Not, I wanted to give those of you who appreciate them a few content points to be aware of. Keep in mind this is still a Sarah Estep book, so despite the nature of some of these points, Fret Me Not is still a warm, cozy read.

Content Cautions:

- Parental Death (past)
- Depression and anxiety
- Conversation about suicidal ideation (assumed intent)
- Undiagnosed ADHD
- Financial instability
- Explicit sexual content

EXTRA SPOILERS (turn away if you don't want to know)

Lacey's mom passed when she was 17. This book is not her grief journey.

Sam has depression and anxiety. He's been to therapy, but

doesn't do a great job keeping up with it. He is currently unmedicated.

Sam's friends have worried in the past that he would shuffle the mortal coil.

Sam and Lacey enjoy dom/sub play (both directions), impact play (spanking, paddling), choking, edging, and some public play.

I tried to take great care to treat these subjects with as much sensitivity as possible. Please take care of yourself.

CHAPTER ONE

IT WAS a truth universally acknowledged in Crane Cove that Edith Nelson knew everyone's business about a half hour before they did. The former school secretary was a fount of information. From first dates to divorces, new jobs and firings, births to deaths, Edith Nelson knew everything that happened in the sleepy coastal town and could spread information faster than the antiquated phone tree the town still used because cell phone service was too unreliable for an emergency alert system.

Sam Shoop was counting on this. He needed it to be true. Because if it wasn't, his next best option was to hole up in his cabin in the wooded hills outside of town and become a local myth. *The Musician Who Haunts The Hills.*

That wasn't a bad song title.

Sam stopped in the middle of the sidewalk, took out his phone—with its one glorious bar of service—and opened his notes.

For most people, the lack of service in Crane Cove was a deterrent. For Sam, it had been one of the main draws. Where else could he claim he hadn't responded to calls or texts due to lack of service and still get a great cup of coffee?

Nowhere.

Fuck, he wanted a cup of coffee. If he stopped at Stardust now, he could still catch Edith at Knot and Purl right as her mid-morning knitting circle ended. Knit Around And Find Out was, in his humble opinion, the best name ever given to a gossip circle pretending to make socks and hats.

Sam turned around quickly, tapping out the few spare lyrics rattling around his skull, and collided with another body. His phone popped out of his hand and fell to the sidewalk, clattering as a full iced coffee dropped on top of it. Dark brown liquid spread in a rapidly widening puddle.

"Fucking hell," they cursed in unison.

Sam stooped down and scooped up his phone, shaking some of the coffee off. "It's mostly waterproof. It should be fine."

"I can't say the same for me."

Sam looked up from trying to dry his phone with the hem of his shirt. The woman he'd collided with was trying—and failing —to brush spilled coffee off her sweater and leggings. Her white shoes were splattered brown and the liquid surrounded her feet like a river moved around rocks. Unease rolled through him.

Of all the people in Crane Cove, why did it have to be *this* woman?

It wasn't the first time he had collided with her. They couldn't seem to avoid each other. Every time he came to town, he ran into her. *Literally.* The last time had been Labor Day weekend when their grocery carts smacked into each other like bumper cars at a county fair in the canned goods aisle.

What was her name again? Mazey? Stacy? Casey? Lucy? Daisy? The answer sat on the tip of his tongue alongside the answer to why she looked so fucking familiar he wanted to scream.

The first time he'd met her, she had been leading a dance lesson for his friend Graham's wedding party. Or at least he thought that was the first time he'd met her. She'd said hi to him like she knew him, and the familiarity had grated on him. Because of his music career, people had a parasitic parasocial relationship with him, and he'd been coming off weeks of terrible creativity-induced insomnia. Sam had bristled, but instead of falling over herself to say she was a fan and felt like she knew him through his music, she'd rolled her eyes and gone back to her job. For the next thirty minutes of the lesson, Sam had stared at her, the feeling that he'd met her before only growing stronger, but he couldn't fathom from where. And now it had been months, and he was pretty sure it was too late to ask.

Sort of like how he was going to have to fumble through this interaction because he'd forgotten her name too many times.

She crouched down and picked up her quarter-full iced coffee.

She sighed, eyeing the mostly empty cup mournfully. "I was looking forward to this."

"You could get another one," he suggested, and the flash of ferocious annoyance that zipped across her pretty face zinged through his body.

"I don't have time." Her tone was clipped, like she was biting her tongue instead of letting him have it. Sam kind of wished she'd let him have it. And then she wrapped her lips around the straw and sucked, the rattle of too much air and too little liquid echoing down the street.

"Then why are you standing here talking to me?"

"Because you're such a sparkling conversationalist." She raised an eyebrow, inviting him to disagree with her. He did, but he wasn't going to give her the satisfaction.

Seconds of silence ticked away like hours.

She broke first. "Always great seeing you, Sam. We should run into each other again sometime."

"Wear a poncho next time," he said, and nearly fell over when she smiled, a single chuckle sneaking past her teeth. The eyeroll that accompanied the laugh sent a strangely pleasant tingle through his stomach.

"Right. Moisture-wicking clothing. I'll get right on that." She saluted him with her cup, then turned and walked away, ponytail bouncing as she did. There were streaks of faded purple and pink on the underside of her blonde hair, a hidden treasure of color.

Sam couldn't help but watch her go, his eyes sliding from her hair down her body to her hips, her ass, and finally her long legs. They held his attention like magnets. What would they look like draped over his shoulders? Or wrapped around his hips? How would they feel clenching around his head while he—

Sam squeezed his eyes shut. Apparently taking the summer off from sex had rotted his brain.

What had he been doing?

Coffee. Coffee, then Knot and Purl. Not standing on the sidewalk panting after the dance teacher.

When she reached the corner, she raised her hand and waved behind her head, like she knew he was still looking.

He really needed to get laid.

He really needed coffee.

Stardust looked blissfully empty as he walked past one of the large, street-facing windows on his way to the door. Sam wasn't sure if his need for coffee would have outweighed his desire to avoid crowds.

The bell over the door tinkled merrily as he entered, and the sound dovetailed nicely with a loud "God-fucking-dammit" from behind the espresso machine. Sybil Morgan, owner and operator of Stardust Coffee, appeared from behind the machine like a redheaded nightmare. It was easy to see why and also hard to believe that at some point in the last two years their mutual friends Graham and Eloise had tried to set them up. Eloise claimed they both had "black cat energy" while Graham said Sybil was "asshole proof." No matter the reason, the suggestion had gotten as far as a race car with four flat tires, and their one date—if sitting on opposite sides of Graham and Eloise at a movie could be called a date—had probably sparked his current predicament in town.

"Rough morning?" Sam asked, pretending to look at the menu like he didn't order the same drink every time.

"I burned myself on the fucking steam wand," she grumbled, shaking her right hand like it would fix the injury. "London Fog?"

It was on the tip of his tongue to say yes, but instead he asked, "The blonde that was just in here—what did she order?"

"An iced seafoam latte."

"What's that?"

"A caramel latte with a sea salt caramel whipped cream, heavy on the salt."

"Is it any good?" he asked.

Sybil fixed him with one of her sardonic stares. "Would I put something on the menu that wasn't good?"

"No, you would not." Sam reached for his wallet. "I'll take one of those and my usual."

She took his credit card and inserted it into her card reader. The thing looked ancient, and Sam remembered Graham shuddering when he said Sybil still had a flip phone.

"Thinking about switching things up?"

"The salt thing isn't for me," he clarified, then added, "It sounds good, though."

Sybil smirked and handed him back his card. "Who are you buying coffee for?"

A hot blush bloomed over Sam's face, radiating down his neck and up to the tips of his ears.

"No one."

"Uh-huh. Does no one have a name?" she asked, dropping a bag of Earl Grey tea into a cup of steaming water.

Sam glanced around, looking for something to change the subject. His eyes landed on a lavish arrangement of purple, orange, and pink flowers in an orange glass vase. It ate up a lot of real estate on the end of the bar.

"Who sent the flowers?"

Sybil's answer was the hiss of the steam wand. He got it. Not wanting people in his business was the genesis of his morning errands.

Sam rooted around for something else to talk about, but came up short. It wasn't that he didn't like Sybil; she terrified him, and he respected that about her. They weren't really friends, some strange shade of acquaintance, but he didn't feel the urge to make small talk with her. And she didn't try either, which was one of the things he did like about her. Sometimes he wondered what it was like to be like his friend Peter, who didn't understand small talk because he simply didn't believe in it. All conversation was valuable to Peter Green. The actor could have a meaningful conversation while going through a drive-thru.

"One seafoam, one London Fog latte," she announced when she placed them on the bar. "And be forewarned, the twins are trawling for donations for the Boo-wery."

Sam stared at her. "The what?"

"The Boo-wery. They're having a fundraiser for the county humane society the weekend before Halloween. Raising money to redo the dog yard or the kennels or something."

"And I care because..."

"Because they're going to ask you to donate something to the silent auction," Sybil explained, "and Chase and Cole have powerful puppy dog eyes." Her sigh was heavy and resigned.

"What did they get you for?"

"A gift basket," she grumbled.

Sam picked up his drinks. "Thanks for the heads-up."

He popped the door open with his hip, then he held it open for a couple about his age who were headed inside. The man said thank you without so much as a second glance, but the woman stared at Sam, her body moving forward while her head tried to stay in the same place. Sam knew that look of disbelief too well. She recognized him, but her brain couldn't reconcile seeing him in this setting. Sam let go of the door and walked away as quickly as he could without being obvious. The shock never lasted long, and he didn't want to be around when it wore off.

Knot and Purl was at the other end of the historic section of downtown Crane Cove, just before the street changed from brick to pavement. The store was stuffed to capacity with skeins upon skeins of yarn. Wool, alpaca, cotton, angora, silk, mohair, cotton, in all the colors of the rainbow were nestled into cubbies, sorted by type and weight. Sam took a deep breath, letting the smell of fibers fill his lungs. In a perfect world, his house would look like this, but he knew having that much yarn was called hoarding if he wasn't trying to sell it.

He'd timed his entrance perfectly. The knitting circle was packing their projects away into their bags, the cacophony of chatter at a gentle roar as everyone talked over each other. Plans for coffee or lunch were lobbed across the room, someone promised to share a recipe, and the entire thing was wholesomely overwhelming.

Delores, the owner, spotted him first. "Sam!" she chirped, smiling broadly at him, a pink sweater for either a baby or a doll clutched in her hands. "I was about to call you. Your order came in."

There were two beats of silence as his brain rearranged his haphazard thoughts and plucked the memory of ordering the custom yarn from the bottom of the pile. He hadn't been able to find the exact shade of green he wanted to make a hummingbird hat for Annie, his best friend's girlfriend. It was destined to be a Christmas present and his own weird way of signaling to Jordy that he was happy she was around. Sam hadn't exactly been receptive or supportive when Jordy had told him he'd fallen in love. There was a song forming in his notebook—more lines scratched out than actually written—about how strange atonement felt.

The funny thing was, he had a good feeling that if Annie knew what he'd said, she'd understand and forgive him. She was that kind of person. The kind of warm, kind-hearted, generous person he'd hoped if Jordy ever decided to settle down that he'd meet.

Of course, until Annie, Sam had never thought Jordy *would* settle down.

"Oh, good," Sam said, heading for the counter while keeping one eye on the knitters, searching for Edith Nelson. "I was wondering when that would come in."

"It's beautiful," Delores promised, "I'll go get it from the back."

She puttered off to her stockroom, and Sam tried to make himself look as bored as possible. Approachably bored. The kind of bored that made nosey old ladies inquire about his relationship status and would he like the phone number of one of their very single grandchildren?

That was another thing he appreciated about Crane Cove. The speed with which the older generation had adapted to his bisexuality. After he'd turned down a couple of granddaughters setups, someone had asked him if he was gay, because they had a very lovely grandson. Sam didn't know why he'd explained his sexuality, but he had, and that only doubled the number of offers.

They could understand that his preferences were fluid, but they couldn't understand that he wasn't interested in dating.

Edith Nelson sidled up to the counter, holding a skein of yarn that looked more like an excuse than a legitimate purchase.

"Good morning, Sam," she said cheerfully, smiling at him in the wide way that made him suspicious.

"Morning, Edith."

"How are you? I feel like I haven't seen you in weeks. We miss you in the knitting circle."

He couldn't understand why. He'd never said much.

"I was traveling," he explained, "for work."

"And how is your little music career?"

Sam bit down on a sigh. If he wanted the advantages of relative anonymity, he needed to accept the anonymity part. When he said he was a musician, the vast majority of Crane Cove senior citizens assumed he was of the struggling variety. That he toured in a van and was his own road crew. And Sam was perfectly happy not to correct those who didn't know the status of his career. Mostly.

"I'm working on a new album," he answered honestly. Working being a loose term for feeling like every word was blood squeezed from a boulder.

"Good for you," Edith said, patting his shoulder patronizingly. Her eye caught the two coffees on the counter. "Double-fisting it today?"

"The, uh, seafoam isn't for me. I'm dropping it off at the dance studio."

"Sybil has you doing deliveries?"

"No, I wanted to do it."

"That's very sweet of you." Edith nodded, and Sam could see the windup coming. "Speaking of sweet, my granddaughter, the one I told you about, the nurse, is coming to—"

"I'm seeing someone," Sam blurted. Not the calm, cool, collected, and slightly mysterious way he'd wanted to relay the information, but it was out there.

Edith blinked. "Oh? What's her name? Or his. No judgment here."

Sam said the first name that popped into his head. "Lacey."

Surprise, followed by a soft, wry smile, passed over Edith's face. "Isn't that nice," she commented. "Been going on for long?"

Delores reappeared just in time, placing a paper bag on the counter. "There you go, Sam. Edith, are you ready to check out?"

Edith blinked at her, then started, remembering the yarn in her hands. "Oh, right, this." She plopped the skein onto the counter, and Sam gathered his bag and two coffees.

"Have a good day, Edith, Delores."

The explosion of frantic whispering as he walked away buoyed his spirits. Sam inhaled deeply once he was outside, then exhaled slowly. With any luck, that was the most he'd have to do to stop the constant barrage of inquiries about his relationship status.

THE CRANE COVE PERFORMING ARTS STUDIO, which Sam thought could seriously benefit from a shorter name, was a short walk from Knot and Purl, just outside the historic section of downtown.

A large picture window showed...whatever-her-name-was laying down six orange circles in a neat line on the floor in front of a mirror that spanned the length of the room. She stepped back, examined the line, seemed to think better of it, and pushed every other circle back several feet into a second row. This earned a nod of approval, and Sam's mouth quirked up in the corner in response. She glanced up at a clock on the wall, and then out the window.

Right at him.

Sam froze. Even with a legitimate reason to be standing on the sidewalk outside of the dance studio, it was creepy as hell that he had been watching her through the window inside of walking directly inside like a normal fucking person.

Her hands rested on her hips as they stared at each other, her like they were having a staring contest, and he like a deer in the headlights of a midsize sedan driven by someone texting. Finally, she jerked her head toward the door and snapped the spell between them.

"I know I said we should run into each other again, but you following me to work wasn't what I had in mind," she said when she opened the door, her eyes flicking suspiciously to the coffee cups in his hand. "I didn't have time to get a poncho yet."

Sam opened his mouth to point out that the first cup hadn't been his fault, but then closed it. Arguing about earlier events probably negated the nice gesture he was trying to make.

He extended the coffee to her. "I promise to stay at least a foot away at all times."

She grinned and accepted the cup, stepping out of the doorway. Sam filled the empty space, and she let go of the door, letting it close behind him.

"Thanks for this," she said, and took a long sip. "Fuck, that's good." Another sip. "I don't think she likes me very much."

"Who?" Sam asked, looking around the empty small lobby-slash-waiting room. Chairs lined each wall, and if it weren't for the performance photos in cheap black frames, it could have doubled as a dentist's office. At least the dentist office he'd grown up going to. The one he went to in Los Angeles was more like an expensive spaceship.

"Sybil."

"She doesn't like anyone very much," he countered.

"Must like you. She made you a replacement coffee for me," she pointed out.

Sam snorted. "Sybil made it for me because I paid for it. If I showed up without my wallet, she'd kick me out."

"Hmm. I thought you were friends."

"Friends by marriage."

"The dreaded in-law." She wiggled her eyebrows in jest, then turned and went back into the mirror-lined room. Sam followed her.

"What are the orange circles for?"

"We're pretending to be pumpkins today." She handed him back her coffee, and he took it, purely by surprise. She grabbed a cardboard box from the corner and brought it back to him, tipping it forward to show him the green scarfs inside. "These are going to be their stems."

"Pumpkins?"

"It's fall. They're four and under. This is my best chance at getting half of them to stand still for more than twenty-five seconds." She put the box back then sidled back to Sam, plucking her coffee from his fingers.

He didn't know too many women who could sidle. Her movements were almost feline in their fluidity, and his brain whirred trying to find ways to describe her properly. The horrible, nagging hum of recognition buzzed at the back of his brain, like he'd been through this entire exercise before. Too little sex and too much deadline were playing tricks on his mind.

"Do you like kids?" Sam asked for no particular reason than

to keep the conversation going. It felt good to have his brain moving again.

She shrugged. "They're cute, but teaching them anything feels like an exercise in futility. Most of the time I think their parents are paying us so they can watch their kids torture someone else for half an hour."

"But they're cute," he reminded her.

"I understand how our species continues," she conceded, and then added, "Barely."

The door opened before Sam could fire off another question, and a couple of kids, trailed by their chatting mothers, burst inside. Organized chaos ensued, as shoes were changed and outer layers stripped off.

"I think that's my cue," Sam said, stepping out of the line of fire as small children tripped over themselves to look at the orange "pumpkins" on the dance room floor.

"Save yourself." She sighed as the circles became toys. "If we bump into each other again, can it be with lunch next time? Nothing with a red sauce, though."

"A dry salad," he promised, backing through the door into the lobby. He nodded at the seated mothers, who stared at him, mouths slightly agape, and exited the building before they could ask him for anything.

Not a bad morning, he decided as he walked back to his car that was parked at the other end of the downtown area. A peaceful, quiet life in Crane Cove was back on the horizon.

CHAPTER TWO

"LACEY!"

The shriek heard around the world made Lacey Finch jump just as she was lifting her water bottle to her mouth and almost half the contents spilled down her front.

Investing in that poncho was becoming less of a joke and more of a necessity.

"Indoor voices," Lacey reminded her intermediate jazz class as they rushed through the door. There were a lot of similarities between teens and toddlers. Times like this they reminded her of the toddler class, all excitement and limbs they weren't sure how to control, accompanied by the complete lack of volume awareness.

"Are you dating Sam Shoop?"

Lacey choked on her water, some invading her airway and some coming out her nose. It burned. She coughed, fighting for air and composure.

"What?" Lacey gasped, putting her water bottle on the floor before it killed her.

"You're dating Sam Shoop," Sydney repeated, less of a question and mostly a statement.

Sydney was not the ringleader of the small class of five—that was Aubrey. But her personality was larger than she was, and the other girls used her non-existent filter to their advantage. If an awkward question or outlandish request needed asking, Sydney was the one to do it.

"Where did you hear that?" Lacey's voice went up at the end with another cough.

"My aunt saw him here this morning," Mikayla said.

"That's not exactly proof of relationship," Lacey countered. "Sam was bringing me coffee because—"

"You're dating," Olivia interrupted. "My grandma heard him tell Edith Nelson this morning at her knitting circle. He said he was seeing someone named Lacey. And then he came here. With coffee. For you."

Lacey stared at the teenage girls who were staring at her, her cheeks heating up to a flame.

What the hell was his angle? Every time he saw her, Sam had a panic-stricken look on his face like he'd rather hide in a poison ivy bush than talk to her, and he'd never gotten her name correct. Every possible rhyming variation *but* Lacey, when he'd bothered to attempt it. It was truly amazing how far into a conversation a person could get without using a name. So why had he told anyone they were dating? Was it his idea of a sick joke?

It was on the tip of Lacey's tongue to deny it when Aubrey said, "Mr. Appleton said it couldn't be true. I heard him talking to Mr. McMahon in the office."

Fucking Mitchell.

Mitch Appleton wasn't her worst dating mistake. That award was bestowed upon Jace Kieffer, musician and professional vampire, both emotional and financial. But Mitch had managed, in one short summer, to land himself high on her list of mistakes. Not so much for what had happened while they were dating, but for what happened after she ended things.

To hear Mitch tell the story, she had pursued him (false), things had been good until they weren't (mostly true), and then when he'd broken things off (false), Lacey had become clingier than a barnacle superglued to a mega yacht (incredibly false).

Mitch had seemed like a safe bet. A high school PE teacher, he had a college degree, a job, and health insurance. Being with him didn't make her mind fuzzy or her blood fizz, but those reactions were overrated, right? Every time she'd had that, it had ended in disaster.

Except it turned out that without those things, she was bored. She'd broken up with him in August, explaining they weren't compatible, and she'd patted herself on a job well done. No screaming, crying, or throwing things. Mitch had tried to talk her out of it, but she'd remained resolute. They could be civil adults in a small town where they'd inevitably run into each other.

She never should have smiled and waved at him. That had been the springboard into the pool of rumors that surrounded her. She knew it was Mitch. But no amount of denial seemed to make a difference. Lacey was an outsider. Mitch had been the quarterback of the football team back in his day. His word carried more weight than hers in Crane Cove.

"We're not discussing my private life," Lacey said. "And Mr. Appleton doesn't know sh— anything."

She did not need these girls running around town telling everyone she'd said Mitch didn't know shit, even if it was true.

Lacey went to the sound system and turned on her warm-up playlist to drown out the chorus of pleading teenage girls begging for a scrap of information. Jenna Fox's "What Are Boys Good For?" filled the room, and she shouted over the chaos, "Find your spots! Warm up time."

It was one of those classes where she never fully got control. Any lapse in activity, and the girls would try and ask her about Sam.

Teenage girls should be allowed to run interrogations. The level of persistence alone made her want to agree that she was dating Sam just to get them to *stop*.

At the end of class, Lacey stood by the door, water bottle in one hand, the other raised to give high fives as the girls exited the studio. Gavin insisted she make herself "available" to parents after classes, even though no one ever really talked to her.

Which was why she was surprised when Aubrey's mom, Monica, walked up to her, the other moms watching expectantly from their seats, completely within earshot.

"So, Sam Shoop, huh?"

Lacey choked on her water again. "Umm..."

"Quite the upgrade from Mitch," Monica continued.

"I think the only way to go there was up," Lacey responded. "But, um—"

"How'd you meet?"

"It's kind of a long story," Lacey said truthfully. It was a long story. A long, sexy, sweaty story that ended in blank, panicked stares years later.

"Mom!" Aubrey snapped her fingers. "Come on. I've got play practice."

Monica laughed airily, giving Lacey a playful shove. "I don't know why I signed her up for so many extracurricular activities. Just call me Mom's Taxi Service."

Aubrey groaned. "Oh my god. Why are you like this?"

"Teenagers. We should hang out sometime. Maybe you could introduce me to Sam." Monica wiggled her eyebrows as Aubrey pulled her out of the building.

It was the friendliest any of the moms had been to her in

months. And it was because they thought she was dating Sam, which was objectively annoying but also somehow better than them thinking she was hung up on Mitch.

Too bad it wasn't true.

Not that she *wanted* to date Sam Shoop. No more musicians. But at least when people whispered behind her back it wouldn't be about *Mitch*.

Still, she needed to clear things up and nip this in the bud at the source. Where would Sam Shoop hang out? Where could she confront him without feeding the rumor mill anymore?

Graham and Eloise Thatcher's house came to mind first. But she couldn't knock on the door of Crane Cove's wealthiest couple and say "Hello. Remember me? I helped teach you to dance for your wedding? I'm looking for Sam. I promise I'm not a stalker." Because anyone who said they weren't a stalker was, unavoidably, a stalker.

Could this wait until Thursday? Sam usually made an appearance at barbeque night at Cranberry Brothers Brewing.

Lacey plopped herself down in Gavin's incredible ergonomic desk chair that was more comfortable than her bed and pulled off her jazz shoes.

No, this couldn't wait. If it had only taken a few hours for the story to get this far, it would be Godzilla-sized by Thursday. It could take out an entire city by tomorrow if she let it go.

Maybe he'd stop by Stardust again in the morning. That was a reasonable place to casually run into someone. Too bad she couldn't afford to casually run into people. Her coffee this morning had been a financially irresponsible splurge, and she deserved a medal for not crying or screaming at him when it spilled.

The unexpected replacement coffee had made her feel warm and gooey on the inside, like an underbaked brownie. It was why she'd let him in instead of slamming the door in his face.

Next time she would slam the door in his face.

After she took the coffee. Because only an idiot rejected a free coffee from Stardust.

Lacey finished tying her shoes, dug her earbuds from her bag to hopefully give the impression she Didn't Want To Be Bothered, and grabbed her coat from the hook on the wall.

Under her coat was a neon green note with "LACEY WRITE YOUR NEWSLETTER" in thick black marker.

She sighed and sank back down into Gavin's chair. The silly little admin things were her least favorite part of teaching. But Gavin insisted. And he'd been doing this successfully for so long that it was impossible to argue with him.

Forty-five minutes later she finally left the studio. The weekly newsletter wasn't hard, but it was boring, and she never remembered to write down what she'd actually taught in each class so she had to think really hard. And it forced her to make a mini lesson plan for the following week. And as much as she refused to admit it, that wasn't a bad thing, because her first few weeks had been...less than successful.

It wasn't a lack of knowledge. Lacey had been a professional dancer since she was eighteen years old. She was bursting at the seams with knowledge. But teaching was its own craft. She envied Gavin's ease and the way he always knew what to do. Lacey was pretty sure the only reason the teens hadn't rebelled against her was because she had a Cool Factor. Like a hip young wine aunt with a fast car, except Lacey didn't have a fast car.

Maybe she wasn't a bad teacher, but she didn't think she was necessarily a *good* teacher. It was hard to tell if the mistakes made were her fault or her students' fault.

But teaching wasn't forever. Crane Cove wasn't forever.

Teaching and Crane Cove were how she was going to get her feet back under her. Pay off her debts. Save money. Start over somewhere with a clean slate and slightly older joints.

Lacey wished she didn't care so much what people thought of her. That she hadn't enjoyed that tiny rush of acceptance when Monica had thought she was dating Sam.

She left her newsletter open on Gavin's computer so he could proofread it before it got sent out. The "as/ass" typo on the summer camp flyers haunted her. Then she picked up her bag and her keys, made it to the door before she realized her water bottle was still on the desk, turned around to get that, *then* left the studio for the day.

The repeating rain showers that had left puddles all over the street had let up for the time being, but gray clouds still loomed ominously overhead, so Lacey hurried to her car.

Even though she was up to her eyeballs in debt, particularly the credit card kind, she owned her car outright. Lacey was proud of that. She was a colossal fuck-up in so many ways, but she'd managed to make all of her car payments. It wasn't cute, fancy, or fast, but it was hers. The red Corolla had been her first purchase after she finished her last cruise ship gig three years ago, and when she'd decided to leave Los Angeles for Oregon, she'd stuffed it so full she couldn't look back at what she was leaving because she couldn't see out the back window.

That was eight months ago.

The rain started again as soon as she pulled out onto the street, coming down in sheets instead of drops. With her windshield wipers on full blast, Lacey cursed the rain and Sam Shoop. She was going to get soaked looking for him. Because most likely he was at Stardust Coffee or Cranberry Brothers Brewing, if he was in town at all.

Maybe she could let the rumor fester until the morning.

What was she supposed to do after she found him? Grab him by his ear and drag him to Edith Nelson's house to clear up the whole misunderstanding?

Lacey drummed her fingers on her steering wheel, the space behind her sternum constricting and twisting in a painful squeeze. Indecision was worse than indigestion.

"Fuck it," she muttered, flipping on her blinker at the stop sign, going right towards the grocery store instead of left towards the other end of downtown. Anyone who gave a damn had probably already heard. Rumor-squashing could happen in the morning.

THE PARKING LOT of Hudson's Grocery was blessedly deserted. Maybe she should buy a lottery ticket while she was inside.

Tampons. Pads. Ice cream. Hurricane Flow was on the horizon, according to her period tracking app, and Lacey was out of the essentials. Borrowing a tampon from an eighth grader was a humiliation she'd only wish on her worst enemy.

Lacey yanked one of the half-size carts out of the corral.

Tampons. Pads. Ice cream.

She repeated the list to herself like a mantra. Pay day was Friday, and she couldn't afford to wander the store buying whatever snacks caught her eye.

Her stomach grumbled.

There's leftovers at home, she reminded herself as she walked past an end cap full of cookies and crackers. Why did the last few days before her period turn her into a bear preparing for hibernation?

Tampons. Pads. Ice cream.

Luck was on her side because sanitary products were buy

one, get one 50% off. Which freed up a little money in her budget to get some nice ice cream, instead of the generic brand Hudson's carried. Not that it tasted bad, but the good stuff tasted *better.*

And in the frozen section, Lacey truly felt like the universe was apologizing for her shit day because she could see the little sale tags hanging under her favorite brand of ice cream. Yes, it looked picked over as hell, but she could see a solitary pink container left in the case.

Maybe today wasn't going to be so bad after all.

A slender man wearing a plain black sweatshirt and a base-ball hat stopped in front of the ice cream. He looked like a burglar escaped from a low-budget home security commercial. Lacey stopped her cart behind him on the other side of the aisle, a respectful distance away while she waited for him to make his selection.

She couldn't be held responsible for the sharp "No!" that escaped when he grabbed the last Tillamook strawberry ice cream. And she equally couldn't be held responsible for the defeated "Oh, for fuck's sake" when he turned and happened to be Sam Shoop.

Sam frowned. "It's not a liquid."

"It's the last strawberry," she snapped. "That's my favorite flavor."

"Grab a Neapolitan. It has strawberry."

"It's not the same," Lacey ground out. "Why don't you get the Neapolitan, and I'll take that strawberry? You owe me."

Sam held the ice cream closer to his chest. "I already bought you a replacement coffee. We're even."

"No, we're not. Because that coffee wasn't even an apology coffee. It was a Trojan horse."

"What the fuck are you talking about?"

Sam didn't sound mad, or even raise his voice. He sounded tired, laced with exasperation. It threw Lacey for a moment.

"You told Edith Nelson we're dating," she explained, half the wind out of her indignant sails.

"I did not," he responded sincerely.

"What name did you give to Edith this morning?"

And then she waited, arms crossed and eyes narrowed, for his response. The overhead music, which was usually unnoticed noise, seemed to blare in the silence between them.

Sam opened his mouth, and shut it with a deepening frown.

"Trouble in paradise?"

Lacey jumped. She hadn't heard Kiki Bowman sneak up behind them, which was impressive in her black platform boots. They made her almost as tall as Lacey.

Kiki smiled broadly at them, confusion growing on Sam's already befuddled face.

"Strawberry is a good choice," Kiki said, sliding around Sam to get access to the freezer case, "but I'm a mint chocolate chip person." She grabbed two cartons, and placed them in her cart. "Any fun plans tonight?"

"No," Sam answered, slowly lowering the strawberry ice cream into his cart like Lacey wouldn't notice. "Just getting some ice cream. What about you?"

"Horror movie marathon. It's like my only night off this week so I'm trying to make the most of it."

"I don't like horror movies," Sam and Lacey responded at the same time.

Kiki grinned. "I don't know if I would've put you two together, but it's cute."

"I'm dating Lacey," Sam said matter-of-factly.

Kiki quirked an eyebrow, and Lacey would've laughed if it wasn't so painfully embarrassing.

"Yeah, I know," Kiki said, backing up her cart since Sam and

Lacey were effectively blocking the aisle. "Have a good night, you two."

Lacey waited until Kiki was out of sight. "What's my name, Sam?"

"Umm..." He pursed his lips, looking up at the ceiling before answering. "Casey?"

"Lacey. My name is Lacey."

CHAPTER THREE

SAM COULD HEAR the sound of his blinks as his brain slowly took in and filtered information.

The dance teacher with the great ass and even better legs was named Lacey.

He'd named his fake girlfriend Lacey.

He'd told Edith Nelson he was dropping off coffee at the dance studio and then he'd told her he was seeing Lacey. Romantically.

Part of his plan had worked perfectly. He'd planted the seed of rumor with Edith, and she'd made it grow in a matter of hours. The spread and sprawl had gone far enough to come back and bite him in the ass.

Lacey.

Where had he even plucked that name from? It had floated to the top of his mind like an iridescent bubble. Why?

"Your name is Lacey?"

"Yes, it's Lacey. For fuck's sake, Sam. We've met *so* many times, and every time you stare at me like someone used that clicky thing from *Men In Black* on you."

"I do not," Sam protested, heat creeping across his face and down his neck. He did look at her exactly that way every time he ran into her, but he wasn't going to admit it to her. "And we haven't met *that* many times."

Lacey snorted, and Sam once again got the impression he was missing something.

"Can we talk about this somewhere else?" he asked, movement at the end of the aisle catching his eye.

"Where?"

"Your place?" he suggested hopefully.

"I live with Gavin and Leo," Lacey pointed out. "So if you want to hide out in my room like we're fifteen, yeah, let's go to my place."

"Fine, we'll go to mine," Sam grumbled.

"And I get the strawberry ice cream."

"Absolutely not."

Sam put his things on the conveyor belt, then put down the divider stick. Behind him, Lacey put the meager contents of her cart on the belt, then moved the divider to annex the ice cream.

He moved it back.

Lacey moved it again.

Rather than continue the ridiculous silent argument of ice cream ownership, Sam moved the divider behind Lacey's items, and silently dared her to argue.

Instead of rolling her eyes, sighing, or grumbling, she stuck her tongue out at him, then smiled. Warmth bloomed in his chest and spread down his limbs like a winter thaw. Sam turned his attention to the cashier who had been watching their interaction with a mixture of confusion and amusement.

"We're having a custody battle over the ice cream," Lacey explained.

"I'm winning," Sam said, taking his credit card from his wallet.

"No, I'm allowing you to win this battle so I can win the war."

"Over ice cream?"

"Don't think I won't fight you."

"Land wars in Asia," Sam muttered, hearing Peter's voice in his head religiously quoting *The Princess Bride*.

"Stop going against a Sicilian when death is on the line," Lacey retorted.

The cashier announced Sam's total and began to bag up his items, mixing Lacey's menstrual products in like they belonged there. Sam chose not to call out the assumption and inserted his card in the chip reader.

"You're Sicilian?" Sam asked while his payment processed.

"No, but I wasn't going to let the joke die."

"Anything for the bit?"

"I'm a natural-born performer."

Sam considered this as he loaded his bags—and Lacey's things—into the cart. His little white lie might benefit from some professional assistance.

"So, am I riding with you, or am I following?" Lacey asked as they stepped into the crisp night air.

"Following, obviously."

"Okay because you're holding my tampons hostage."

Sam opened his trunk. "I'm not holding them hostage. I'm transporting. And aren't they technically my tampons because I paid for them?"

"Do you need them? Because I'm happy to share if you do."

His face burned from his ears down. He'd walked right into that one.

"Don't lose me. My road isn't well marked," he said to change the subject.

"How fun and mysterious," Lacey said drolly, gently

bumping his hip with hers to get him to move over. Out of surprise, he did. She pulled out the ice cream.

"Hey, that's mine," he protested.

"Insurance so you don't try to lose *me*," she said.

"And how do I know you're not going to take the ice cream and buy new tampons?"

"Because," she said, looking him up and down like she was sizing him up, "I'm curious why you did it."

"I didn't do anything," Sam protested.

"Tell that to the Crane Cove rumor mill. Come on." Lacey patted the top of the ice cream carton. "This is going to melt."

Sam didn't have to worry about losing Lacey. After they left the grocery store parking lot, he had to worry about her ending up in his backseat if he tapped his brakes.

That his road wasn't well marked was an understatement. There was no mailbox at the end of the lane. The house number, required by the Crane Cove Fire Department, was tacked to a tree and easy to miss. A single reflective post sat at the mouth of his driveway so he knew when to turn. Sam couldn't decide if installing a gate was a good idea. It was a layer of security, but it also alerted passersby that there was something down the road worth protecting. He flipped on his bright lights to better illuminate the way for both of them. The little lanterns that lined the driveway didn't even start until half a mile down the mile-long road.

Was this the dumbest thing he'd ever done? Apparently his self-sabotage streak ran deeper than he thought. Because making up a girlfriend was all fun and games until said imaginary girlfriend turned out to be a real person with great legs and a fantastic—

Nope. Not going there.

Warm light filled the windows of his woodland home. The lights inside were on a timer because entering a dark house unnerved him. Anyone could be lurking in the dark, so he made sure it wasn't dark. The only kind of person that would wander up here was an ax murderer.

Sam parked in the driveway. The garage was still half full of boxes he needed to break down and haul to the recycling center, and there were a few more boxes in his trunk he'd picked up at his PO box earlier in the day. Plus he didn't like the idea of Lacey being able to block his car in completely if she parked behind the closed garage door.

"Holy Fortress of Solitude, Batman," Lacey said when they got out of their cars.

Sam frowned. "Superman has the fortress, not Batman."

"Yeah, but Superman could never afford this place." She followed him up the short walkway to the front door. "And I don't think Superman was quite so into security."

There was a keypad on the front door. On all of the exterior doors, actually. Two wrong answers set off the alarm and alerted the authorities. Not that Sam had a ton of faith in Crane Cove's small police force, but it was better than nothing. He tapped in the code, heard the whirr of machinery inside the door, and then opened it.

"I don't think Superman was worried about break-ins. He could just laser people."

"I think Batman enjoyed break-ins. Gave him a chance to test out his gadgets and gizmos. Like Kevin from *Home Alone*." Lacey slipped off her shoes by the door. "Poor, dumb criminals thinking they're breaking into lonely billionaire Bruce Wayne's house but instead they get Bat Justice."

Sam chuckled. "You have an active imagination."

"Keeps life interesting."

She followed him into the kitchen, and he pretended not to hear her small noises of surprise as she took in his private refuge. The high, vaulted ceilings were lined with the wood of the trees that had been cut down to make room for the house. And then there was the wall of windows from the floor to the ceiling. During the day, he could see the ocean from his spot in the tree line.

Sam put the grocery bags on the large island in the kitchen. The space was his particular pride and joy, the thing he'd cared the most about during the design process. Black cabinets and pale gray countertops gave it a sleek, moody feel that reminded him of the persistent coastal gloom. The double ovens, professional-grade range, and unreasonably large refrigerator made it look like a celebrity chef had moved in, not a musician.

"You've got a lot of groceries," Lacey observed, snooping through his bags. He was about to tell her to stop when she pulled out her menstrual products. "Planning on having a dinner party?"

"No," Sam answered, drumming his fingers on the counter while he waited for Lacey to move out of his way.

"You've got this big kitchen and all that food, and you're *not* entertaining?" She sounded skeptical as she boosted herself up onto an empty section of the counter. "I thought you had friends in town."

"I do."

"Do they ever come up here?"

"No." Sam unloaded his groceries onto the counter, separating the ingredients for his dinner from the rest of the pile. An uncomfortable silence formed between them, but when he glanced at her from the corner of his eye, Lacey was just watching him. So he was the uncomfortable one. "I like my privacy."

"I mean, I guess I get it," Lacey said, pulling a green grape from the bunch and popping it in her mouth. "It's much easier to leave someone else's house than it is to get people to leave yours."

"I wish it was acceptable to hang a sign that says 'Please leave by nine,'" Sam admitted, and Lacey laughed. The warmth bloomed behind his sternum again. It made him want to squirm.

"Did you eat yet?"

"No. I just left work."

There hadn't been any food in her cart, he remembered.

"Did you have plans?"

"Me and the microwave," she said, unabashedly eating his grapes. "Are you asking if I want to stay for dinner?"

The warmth from his chest spread to his face, so Sam quickly grabbed the freezer items, including the coveted strawberry ice cream, and restocked his freezer. The cold air felt good on his skin.

"They special-ordered my scallops, so I've got a pound to get through."

"Was that a statement or an invitation?" Lacey teased.

"You can stay if you want."

"I don't turn down free food, even though that philosophy has gotten me into a lot of trouble." Lacey broke off a stem of grapes, giving up the pretense of picking them off one by one. "I think I'd be pretty easy to kidnap. A sign that says 'Free cheese' would be enough."

Sam chuckled. The statement tickled something in the back of his brain, in roughly the same spot that bugged him whenever he looked at Lacey. That strange sense of familiarity, like he'd had this exact conversation with her before in another time and place.

"Do you have any allergies?" he asked, opening a low cupboard to grab his salad spinner to wash the greens he'd bought.

"I mean, dairy doesn't always like me as much as I like it, but it's not an allergy," she said. "Do you want any help?"

"Not really."

"I don't mind."

"You don't, but I do. I don't necessarily like people in my flow when I'm cooking."

This was true. Sam had rare exceptions to his "get the hell out of my kitchen" rule. Graham was one of them, because his friend was conscientious and excessively detail-oriented. And then there was Connor McMahon, a sort-of friend Sam had inherited through Graham. The lifelong Crane Cove resident was a fantastic baker and meticulous enough to satisfy Sam's high standards. Connor's brother Cole cleared the bar, too, but barely.

Lacey didn't seem too upset not to be helping. In fact, she seemed very content to sit on his counter and eat his grapes like she belonged there. Like her spot was a foregone conclusion to a question he hadn't asked.

Sam quickly wiped his wet palms on his pants and took his phone out of his pocket, opening his notes app and writing down the thought before it escaped him. These days he'd take any lyrical inspiration.

"I didn't realize you were such a control freak." The teasing edge was back in Lacey's voice, and Sam started to suspect that she liked seeing if she could make him blush. That prickly feeling in the back of his brain told him that there was a reason she could make him turn red as easily as tapping her feet.

"I like things just so," he deflected, putting his phone on the counter then handed her the full salad spinner. "Here. You can do this."

"Oooh. I get to push a button. So much responsibility."

"If you can handle that, maybe I'll upgrade you to can opener."

"That might be above my skill level." Lacey pressed the button on the lid of the salad spinner several times in quick succession until the inner bowl whirred. They both watched its quick revolutions until it slowed and stopped. She picked up the bowl and handed it to him with an overly exaggerated presentation. "Ta-da."

A wide smile broke across his face, so big it almost hurt. She was ridiculous. When she didn't seem vaguely angry with him, she was playful and silly. In some ways, she reminded him of Peter, but a little less chaotic. Peter was a bullet in a steel box, whereas Lacey felt more like a sleek race car with a few loose lug nuts. He was holding on for dear life because he didn't know when the wheels would fall off, but it was thrilling.

"If you're going to get cocky, I'm going to revoke your can opener promotion."

"Does it come with a raise? Because I can't accept more responsibility without a change in compensation."

Sam shook his head, biting down on a laugh that was building in his throat. If he laughed, it might break the strange, vibrating tension building between them. He hadn't had this feeling in years. "Are you angling for ice cream?"

A bright smile was his reward. A field of rainbow wildflowers filled his mind, with ethereal white and yellow butterflies fluttering near the flowers, kissing the petals with their delicate feet.

He wanted to reach for his phone to try and write this feeling down, but how to capture the multi-sensory moment he was having? Those butterflies lived in his mind and his stomach. He could hold on to this, right?

"Is it angling if I know I'm going to get it?"

"Scoop size is up for negotiation."

"Gimme that can opener so I can razzle-dazzle you," Lacey said, holding out her hand.

Whatever magic had been building between them that made her easy for him to talk to her even though he barely knew her popped like a soap bubble. There was no can involved in the meal. And Sam couldn't begin to think of a witty comeback.

The drawer he needed was to the right of Lacey's legs, and when Sam opened it, the back of his hand brushed the side of her knee. She crossed her legs to move out of his way with more grace than he'd ever exhibited in his entire life, and his brain handed the keys to the castle over to his cock. It throbbed, growing and thickening with each rapid beat of his heart, and Sam hated himself for his self-imposed summer of celibacy because someone crossing their *legs* shouldn't make him hard.

Instead of grabbing whatever it was he was supposed to be looking for, Sam's hand closed around the can opener. And because his brain had well and truly given up, he handed it to Lacey.

She twirled it around her finger and slid it into a pretend holster at her side like she was the gunslinging star of a Western film.

Sam couldn't believe anyone had believed they were dating. Lacey was a million times funnier and cooler than he was. What did he have going for him?

Sure, there was the money, the awards, the fame, and the homes, but what did he actually bring to the table?

What did it matter? They weren't dating. They weren't going to date, even if he did want her legs wrapped around various parts of his body. The only reason Lacey was at his house, sitting on his counter, was because he was terrible with names.

Tongs. He'd meant to grab tongs.

"So, why me?" Lacey asked when he was removing the tough foot muscle from the sides of the scallops.

"What?"

They'd fallen into a companionable silence over the last few minutes. Or at least Sam thought it was companionable because he'd almost forgotten she was there while he heated the cast iron skillet, minced garlic, and juiced a lemon.

"Why did you tell everyone that we're dating?"

"I didn't," Sam insisted, trying to focus on the scallop prep instead of looking at Lacey. "I told Edith I was seeing someone named Lacey. I didn't mean to implicate you."

"So this wasn't your incredibly weird way of trying to lure me back to your house so you could make me dinner?"

Sam shook his head. "Not even a little."

"I bet you won't forget my name this time," she teased.

"Never again," he vowed.

"Why did you tell Edith you were dating someone named Lacey?"

Sam sighed. "Because as much as I love being here and living the small-town life, it can get a bit...claustrophobic. I don't know if that's the right word. But the retired element of this town is very, *very* interested in my dating life. And setting me up."

"The small-town fishbowl effect," Lacey clarified. "I felt very 'on display' my first month here. I bet it's even worse for you being...you."

"Being famous?"

"Well, famously...aloof."

Sam knew a diplomatic phrase when he heard it. "You mean asshole."

Lacey held her hands up. "You said it, not me. I was trying to be nice."

"You think I'm an asshole?" The cold grip of impending anxiety twisted behind his sternum, seeping through his chest and down to his stomach with alarming speed.

"Not really," she said, readjusting her hair into a messy bun on top of her head. "But you've got a big reputation, buddy."

"I know about that." Lord, did Sam know about it.

"I'm very happy to know you can read."

He rolled his eyes, but turned so she couldn't see the smile he was fighting. She wasn't necessarily sugarcoating it, but there was a sweet edge to Lacey's honesty.

"You're guarded," Lacey explained. "I don't blame you. It can't be easy having everyone constantly want shit from you. There's nothing wrong with having boundaries."

Sam shrugged. Plenty of people disagreed with her. The hundreds of people who'd called him an asshole to his face—or to his back as he walked away—because he was tired and didn't have the energy or capacity to stop, talk, sign autographs, or take pictures. All the times he wished he had Peter's boundless energy for the general public hadn't given him the same ease with strangers.

There were nights when he couldn't sleep where he wondered if he would choose this life again if he knew at sixteen what he knew at thirty.

"I'm used to nobody giving a shit about my boundaries," he said, rinsing the scallops in cold water. "It's more"—Sam searched for the word—"*heightened* here. And fucking frustrating because no one is trying to be mean or take anything from me, they want to help, except I don't want their help. But how can you tell someone who looks like your grandparents to fuck off and leave you alone?"

"Have you tried 'fuck off and leave me alone'?" Lacey suggested cheekily, and then she squealed when he flicked the water off his fingers at her. "Is that why you told everyone I was your girlfriend?"

"Yes—no!" He patted the scallops dry with a paper towel. "I didn't tell anyone *you* were my girlfriend. But...yeah. Seemed like a good idea at the time."

"What about your friends? What did they think about your plan?"

The echoing silence answered for him.

"Oh shit." Lacey whistled. "You were going to lie to your friends too. How was that supposed to play out?"

Discomfort sat like a stone in his stomach. Lying to his friends was the hardest pill to swallow, but he'd choked it down. He didn't trust his friends to lie convincingly for him. Graham would've tried to talk him out of it.

"You—" Sam winced at the slip. "*She* was going to be conveniently busy a lot, and I was going to be my famously aloof self when it came to details. And then I was going to gradually drop hints about how things were hard and break up with her before Christmas."

Lacey shook her head. "You should've had her breaking up with you. More sympathy that way."

"Where were you for the planning stages? I could have used you."

"1467 Sycamore Street," she said. "Or at the studio."

"Well, the next time I have a stupid idea, can you magically appear and fix it for me?" Sam asked, moving his prepped ingredients next to the stove.

"How often are you having stupid ideas? Because if this is a full-time gig, it's going to cost you more than dinner and ice cream."

"What if I threw in lunch? How many dumb ideas a week does that get me?" Sam dropped a tablespoon of butter into his hot skillet, then seasoned the scallops with salt and pepper while the butter hissed in the pan.

"Maybe three. It depends on the level of stupid."

Scallops cooked quickly. In Sam's opinion, they were the best way to get a dinner that looked and felt fancy in under five minutes. As soon as they were placed into the pan to sear, Sam grabbed two plates from a cupboard and the lemon dijon dressing he'd made over the weekend for the salad. He flipped the scallops a minute later, humming satisfaction at the golden-brown color on the bottom. Salads were plated during the second sear, given a drizzle of dressing, and then it was time to pull the scallops from the pan. Immediately he melted two more tablespoons of butter in the pan, added the garlic and stirred until it became fragrant, then poured in the lemon juice, and a little salt and pepper. Another stir, and then he spooned the sauce over the scallops, completing the dish.

"Wow." Lacey sounded impressed. "That looks professional."

"It's not hard," Sam said modestly, though inside pride was bursting like fireworks.

"That's not what I said." Lacey hopped off the counter and came over. She waved the can opener under his nose. "I didn't get to use this."

"Are you sad about it?"

"No. Not really." She picked up a plate and turned to go to the dining room. "Sam...you don't have a table."

"Um, no."

"Why don't you have a table?"

"Because I don't really need one. It's just me."

"Where do you eat?"

"In the kitchen, usually. At the counter." Sam shrugged. "Sometimes outside on the deck."

Lacey set her plate back down on the counter. "Okay, here it is."

A hot, shameful blush spread across Sam's body. "Sorry. I wasn't expecting company...ever."

"No, it's fine," Lacey said, but Sam would swear the unsaid part of that sentence was "not like I haven't been on my feet all day."

"We could eat on the couch," he suggested.

"This reminds me of when I lived in New York," Lacey said

after they'd settled onto Sam's large sectional. "My apartment didn't have space for a table, so I ate either on my couch or in my bed."

"You lived in New York?"

Lacey nodded, cutting into one of her scallops with the side of her fork. "I did. From when I was eighteen until I was twenty. And again when I was twenty-five." She put half the scallop in her mouth, then her eyes drifted shut and she moaned. The sound went straight to his cock, which teamed up with his brain to remind him he could make her moan in other ways. "Oh my god. What the actual fuck, Sam. This is incredible."

He basked in the warmth of her compliment, even though outwardly he shrugged it off.

"If music doesn't work out, you could open a restaurant."

"Restaurants are terrible businesses."

"Take the fucking compliment, Sam."

He shouldn't like the forceful, snappish tone of her voice. Cranky kindness. But he did.

"Thank you," he mumbled, stuffing a forkful of salad into his mouth.

The modest meal didn't take long to eat. Lacey took enjoying his food seriously and made small sounds of approval with almost every bite. Sam was ready to squirm.

When they'd finished, she yanked the plate out of his hand and went to the sink to do the dishes, like she knew he would have argued if she'd offered. She seemed to understand him without him having to explain.

"I've got a stupid idea," he said, trailing after her into the kitchen.

"It's going to cost you lunch," Lacey warned him, rinsing off their plates.

Sam's heart was beating so hard he could feel the throb of his pulse in his neck. "What if," he began, resting his back against the counter and folding his arms, trying to appear cool and collected, "we didn't correct anyone and you pretended to be my girlfriend?"

The *whoosh-whoosh* of blood in his ears was deafening and made possible by the crystal silence in his house. Lacey didn't say anything for thirty seconds—he counted them. Then she laughed.

"No...oh no..." she struggled to breathe, but her laughter tapered off. "Oh, you're serious."

"Not that serious," Sam grumbled, his face on fire.

"You don't need a fake girlfriend," she insisted, "and even if you did, no one is going to believe it's *me*. You can do better than me."

"People already believe it," he reminded her.

"Congratulations, you tricked an old lady and some teenagers in my jazz class." Lacey dried her hands on her leggings.

"Then why did you get so mad at me at the grocery store if it's so unbelievable? If the fire is going to put itself out, you don't need to pour water on it."

Lacey opened her mouth to disagree, then shut it. While she took a moment to think, Sam wrote down what he'd just said about fire. It wasn't a bad line.

"I can't, Sam," Lacey said. "I don't see this ending well for me."

"What do you have to lose?" he asked, trying to nudge her in the direction he wanted without pushing her the other way.

Her mirthless laughter bounced around the high ceiling. "Because dating in this town once was enough for me. People talk. A lot. And when things end between us—like they're supposed to—I will take the blame for it, no matter how it goes down. I will get the judgmental, invasive questions disguised as concern."

"How do you know that?"

"Because they've got to ask someone, and it won't be the rock star."

Sam wanted to argue, but it was like trying to change Graham's mind. He'd have better luck fitting the Grand Canyon inside Rhode Island.

Lacey sighed. "Look, if someone asks, I won't confirm or deny for the next twenty-four hours so you can get your story straight, okay?"

"You don't have to do that."

"You're going to owe me lunch, remember?"

CHAPTER FOUR

THERE WAS something incredibly sad about drinking in a bar on a Wednesday night.

Lacey swirled the ice in her glass until it made a small cyclone in her whiskey and ginger ale. Normally she wouldn't have blown six bucks on a drink she could've made at home, but she was in the mood to drink alone without being alone. A midweek Moonie's was the perfect spot to achieve her goals.

After leaving Sam's house, she'd driven home, but when she saw the blue light of the TV through the living room curtains, she didn't go inside. Gavin and Leo were wonderful and she genuinely loved and adored them, but they were nosier than Crane Cove's entire population.

There were regulars dotted around the bar, some in the same state of self-imposed exile as Lacey, and others in small groups. One of those groups were some teachers, having what she knew they called "professional development." Her ex Mitch was in the group, and so was Marianne Warner, who'd cozied up to her and hired her as the assistant cheer coach at the high school, right up until Lacey had started dating Mitch. Then it was goodbye Marianne, and goodbye extra income from coaching.

Not that she would have made a lot, but every extra few hundred dollars counted when it came to her mountain of debt.

She should've said yes to Sam and asked for money.

Lacey gulped some of her drink to muffle the awful feeling in her stomach from even thinking that. She wasn't mercenary enough to ask for money. She wasn't desperate enough to ask for money. Not yet.

"I'm going to ask her." Marianne's voice cut through the country classic playing on the jukebox and scraped across Lacey's nerves like sandpaper.

She hadn't had enough to drink to deal with Marianne.

Her former friend dropped onto the empty stool next to her, with Mitch hovering behind.

"Lacey," she began, the edges of her voice fuzzy with alcohol, "are you really dating Sam Shoop?"

"Marianne, why are you doing this?" Mitch asked, and it was on the tip of Lacey's tongue to thank him, but he didn't stop there. "There's no way it's true."

Lacey's body tensed. No, it wasn't true, but she hated Mitch's tone. The patronizing sneer she could hear because she'd known too many men like him.

"How do you know it's not true?" Lacey challenged, forcing herself to relax and remain non-combative. They were school-yard bullies in full-grown clothing; allowing them to see a rise in her only encouraged them.

"Because he's Sam Shoop, and you're nobody," Mitch reminded her. "It's not like you're *that* good in bed."

A container of neon-colored swizzle sticks wasn't that far from her hands. Could she stab him through the heart? No, probably not. But his eyeballs were another story.

"I thought he was dating Jenna Fox," Marianne pitched in,

draining her Dirty Shirley. She got them because they came with a cherry, and she was convinced it was sexy to tie the stem in a knot with her tongue.

Less than two minutes in, and Lacey was already exhausted by them. "So why did you ask me?"

"Because Edith Nelson heard it straight from the horse's mouth," Marianne said, sliding her glass in Moonie's direction to try and get a refill.

"You know how else I know it's not true," Mitch continued like no one else had spoken, "because she's here, drinking by herself. Why aren't you snuggled up with your new boyfriend, Lace? Missing someone?"

"I wanted a drink, and Sam doesn't drink." Both things were true. Maybe she could skirt around the truth for twenty-four hours even in the face of direct questioning.

Mitch leaned in, pitching his voice low while Marianne complained loudly to Moonie that she wanted another drink after he'd ignored her hint. "You know you don't need to go to all this trouble to make me jealous, right? Kind of shooting for the stars there with Sam Shoop. If you want me back—"

"I don't," Lacey cut him. "I have moved on to bigger and better things."

"Oh my god, so it's *true!*" Marianne squealed.

Lacey should've known she'd hear that part. The accidental double entendre was absolutely true, though.

"If Sam said it was..." Lacey muttered into the last remnants of her drink.

"I want to know everything," Marianne gushed, linking her arm with Lacey's in the kind of grip that could only be loosened with a crowbar.

"There isn't a lot to tell. I wasn't expecting Sam to say anything."

Lacey shouldn't be encouraging this. Every word took her

down a slippery slope she had no good way back up without looking like a desperate, lying loser. But fuck if it didn't feel nice to have Marianne clawing to be her friend again and to have the upper hand this time.

"He's a really good cook," Lacey said, motioning for Moonie to close out her small tab. That was unnecessary fuel to the fire, but it paid immediate dividends.

"Guess you're really out of the picture, Mitch," Marianne teased, almost falling off her stool as she leaned across Lacey.

"You're drunk," he sneered.

"And yet she's not wrong." Lacey signed the receipt and pocketed her debit card. "It's been great catching up, you two. I'll see you around."

Extracting herself from Marianne mostly took speed rather than strength or skill. Drunks weren't known for their reflex time. Which also made dodging Mitch's grab for her arm as easy as dancing.

The puddles in the parking lot glowed with the reflection of neon and streetlights. It was between downpours, but a fine mist hung in the air and rested delicately on her skin and in her hair. She took a deep breath, filling her lungs with the cold, damp air, then unlocked her car.

The song on the radio after she started the engine was "Barcelona."

HARD RAIN DRUMMED against her window. Lacey's eyes were closed, but she couldn't sleep. She kept replaying the scene at the bar over and over in her head.

She'd told Sam she would neither confirm nor deny the rumor they were dating, but she'd done a lot more confirming than denying with Marianne and Mitch.

Maybe she shouldn't have told Sam no. What was wrong

with pretending to be his girlfriend for a little bit? Sure, she'd take the brunt of the gossip in the planned breakup, but being known as Sam Shoop's ex-girlfriend was a hell of a lot more appealing than being Mitch Appleton's ex-girlfriend.

Fuck, she'd done stupider shit for dumber reasons.

But Sam was...

Lacey sighed, stretched, and squirmed to find a position that might work better.

Sam was as elusive as sleep.

And he was supposed to be. Sam Shoop was supposed to have stayed forever in her memory as a single, fantastic night. He wasn't supposed to come back and be around to witness her lowest moments.

Maybe that was why she hadn't told him yet. That his forgetfulness was a blessing allowing her to be perfectly preserved in his mind.

If he even thought about her.

Lacey had spent the years since "Barcelona" first came on her radio wondering if the sexy yet sweet song was about her. The location was correct. But there was the strong possibility that she wasn't the first or last person he'd fucked in Barcelona.

Then he'd shown up in the last place she ever expected to see him. They'd lived in the same cities during various points in their lives, but had never run into each other. Not that there was anywhere to hide in Crane Cove. As quickly as her romantic brain could spin up a Cinderella fantasy, Sam brought it crashing down by asking if they knew each other. Though it had taken until tonight for her to be convinced he really didn't remember and wasn't just snubbing her.

Could she fake a relationship? Probably. She'd pretended to still be in love with guys she'd given up on while she figured out her next move before. But she could read them like flashing neon billboards. Sam was the bottom line of the eye test. Improv relied on being able to tell what the other person's next move was.

It would be nice to put the whole Mitch thing to bed once and forever. Plus, Sam was a great cook, and she'd absolutely hold him to the food part of the proposed bargain.

What else could she get out of this? Could she get out of Crane Cove? Sam had connections. A lot of them. The entertainment industry ran on word of mouth, and a few well-placed words could open a lot of doors for her.

Why couldn't she have thought of all the pros when Sam had asked her?

Fuck. Fuck. Fuck.

THE NEXT TIME someone asked her to be their small-town fake girlfriend, Lacey was going to make sure she got their number.

On Thursdays the studio didn't open until mid-morning, and Lacey tried to get there a half-hour before opening to get set up for the day. But since Tuesdays and Thursdays Gavin drove to Eugene and Corvallis to teach ballroom classes at the universities there, she had a tendency to lose track of time. So ten minutes before her day was supposed to start, Lacey stood in front of the studio door, fumbling with the keys that refused to stay in her hand.

"Mornin'."

Lacey jumped, dropping her keys again. "Fuck."

"I'll get them," Sam said, bending at the same time she did. Their heads collided with a brain-rattling smack.

"That's cuter in the movies," Lacey said, rubbing her head before accepting her keys from Sam. "What are you doing here?"

"I brought lunch," he said, and innocently held up a paper bag he'd repurposed from the yarn store.

"What's in there?" she asked, finally successfully opening the door and ushering Sam inside with a dramatic wave of her hand.

"Kind of a fall harvest salad," Sam said, stepping past her into the studio lobby. Lacey flipped on the lights and headed back towards the office. "Roasted butternut squash, chicken, apples, cranberries, candied walnuts, goat cheese, and a maple dijon dressing."

Lacey turned on the light in the office and dumped her stuff in Gavin's chair. "You brought me food?"

"I did say I'd bring you lunch," Sam reminded her. "For my stupid idea."

"About that." Lacey took the bag from him because she wasn't about to pass up what sounded like a fantastic salad. "Maybe it's not as stupid as I initially thought."

"No, it's pretty dumb."

"Okay, I won't argue about that, but I'm in."

"You're...in?" Sam frowned, like she'd spoken in Latin instead of English.

"I'll pretend to be your girlfriend for a while." Lacey sat down to change her shoes.

"Why?" he asked suspiciously.

"Because I'm a wonderful, selfless person," she answered sarcastically, lacing up her tap shoes. "Can we talk about this later? I have a class soon. Just...don't tell anyone I'm *not* your girlfriend, okay?"

"I think I can avoid talking to most people. When did you want to talk?"

"Um..." Lacey looked at the class schedule taped to the wall. "How about two? That's when I was going to eat lunch."

"I will be back around two." Sam took a step toward the

door, then stopped with his hand on the frame. "Why did you change your mind?"

"Because I need you too. You're not the only one with a big reputation."

LACEY WAS HALFWAY DONE with her salad when Sam showed up that afternoon. If he wasn't such a good cook, she'd be madder at him. But as it stood, it was hard to be mad at someone who made a salad taste like life was worth living.

"You're late," she said around a mouth of greens.

"Sorry," Sam mumbled, looking around the office for a place to sit. He settled for a corner of Gavin's desk. "How's lunch?"

"Good enough that I'd let you bring me another one." Lacey washed down her bite with her can of sparkling water. "Where's your lunch?"

"I ate at home. To avoid talking to people."

"Do you usually go home to eat and then come back to town?" she asked, half to make small talk and half out of genuine curiosity.

"No. Usually if I had something else going on in town, I'd eat at the hotel or Cranberry Brothers. But since I'm ignoring everyone I know at those places until we could talk, I went home."

"Smart." Lacey fished around for a candied walnut. "Do you still want to do this thing?"

"Yes," Sam said without missing a beat, "but I don't understand why you do."

"I told you, I've got a big reputation." When he stared at her, she sighed and filled in the blanks. "I briefly dated a guy in town who has made it his mission to make everyone think I'm the psycho ex-girlfriend of their nightmares. Or at least prove he's something special and convince everyone I'm not over him. I don't think it gets more 'onward and upward' than dating a rock star."

"I mean, I could be a rocket scientist."

"I think if you were a rocket scientist you'd be over the moon that I was even talking to you."

"So you're using me?" Sam crossed his arms.

"I think the usage is mutual, buddy." Lacey set down her salad on the desk. She had a tendency to talk with her hands, and flinging salad around the room wasn't going to make a good impression. "I thought about it, okay? I don't think my reputation can necessarily get any worse. Like...I've hit rock bottom, but I don't think you're a jackhammer. At least I'm in control of the whispering if I'm with you. The pros outweigh the cons. "

Sam was quiet for a moment, his hand hovering over his pocket.

"Can I write that down? That jackhammer thing?"

Lacey raised an eyebrow. "Why? Are you going to put it in a song?"

"Maybe. I liked the way it sounded."

"Sure. But I want credit or money." She thought for a moment. "More the money than the credit."

"If this ends up on an album, I'll write you a check," Sam promised, tapping his phone screen quickly with his thumbs, writing down her words. It wasn't Lacey's first time being a muse, but normally she didn't know she'd contributed to songs until after they were written, and they were usually written about her body. An ember of pride burned in her belly. A known lyricist like Sam had liked her words.

"So how do we do this?" he asked, putting his phone face down on the desk.

"I don't know. This wasn't my idea. Didn't you have a plan?"

"Yes, but it didn't involve playing off a live person." Sam linked his fingers behind his head and looked up at the ceiling.

"Maybe some ground rules," Lacey suggested, fixating on her salad so she wouldn't fixate on the flex of lean muscles in his arms. Sam wasn't a bulky guy; in a different life, he could've been a dancer. "How long will this last? What kind of PDA are we comfortable with? That sort of stuff."

"What are you comfortable with?"

"Well, we've already slept together, so..."

Sam slipped off the corner of the desk, catching himself before he fell on the floor. "We what?"

Lacey's cheeks heated. "We had sex."

"I didn't think we were starting with backstory, but we should have one, I guess..."

"Sam, we actually had sex." Lacey mimed penetrative sex with her hands. "You've seen me naked."

He regarded her suspiciously, eyes narrowed in disbelief. "No, I think I'd remember that."

Her traitorous body flushed with something other than intense embarrassment. Too bad he didn't actually remember her body.

"It was...umm...seven-ish years ago. You were on tour, and it was after your show in Barcelona..."

"No..." Sam shook his head slowly, like his brain was on an extreme delay. "She had really dark hair and—"

"I was going through a phase. My hair was super dark brown, and I did my makeup a lot heavier. I think I believed that she who died wearing the most eyeliner won." A nervous laugh bubbled up to break the tension.

"When were you planning on telling me?"

The accusatory tone activated Lacey's fight *and* flight response. The surge of adrenaline sent conflicting signals through her body to straighten her backbone to an iron will and to curl into a defensive ball.

"About half past never."

"I didn't deserve to know?"

"Your shitty memory isn't my responsibility." Her fight response had won.

Sam lowered himself back down onto the corner of the desk, his ego deflated like a forgotten party balloon.

"At least I can stop thinking I'm losing my mind." He combed his fingers through his hair, leaving it sticking up at a few odd angles that Lacey had no desire to smooth down. Disheveled was adorable on him. "I kept thinking I knew you."

"We definitely *know* each other."

He had the decency to blush profusely, and Lacey wondered if he remembered everything the way she did.

"So I guess that's a good first rule," Lacey continued when Sam didn't say anything. "No sex. We limit our affection to public spaces."

"Do we remember that night differently? Because I remember the sex being really good," Sam said.

"It was good," Lacey agreed, struggling to keep the smug smirk off her face, "but this is fake, remember? Fucking confuses things." Another thought popped into her head. "You can't real cheat on me while I'm your fake girlfriend, either. So I guess we're celibate until this is over."

"What do you mean I can't real cheat on you?"

"If you sneeze, the media reports on the size of the booger that flew out of your nose, Sam. And we both know the rumor mill around here could give them a run for their money, so if you're sleeping around, it's going to get out. Your dick causing drama defeats the purpose of our arrangement."

A half groan, half frustrated growl rumbled in Sam's throat.

"This was your idea," Lacey reminded him.

"Not the sex part," he muttered under his breath like a petulant teenager.

Lacey wanted to move forward, but the alarm on her phone blared like a tornado warning siren. Lunch time was over.

"Can we talk about this later?" she asked, putting the lid back on the salad container and holding it out to Sam. He took it like it was a bomb.

"Uh, sure." He drummed his fingers on the container. "When?"

"Tonight? Dinner?" Lacey suggested, her mouth already watering at the prospect of more Sam food. She found her lip gloss and reapplied so she wouldn't actually start salivating.

"It's Thursday." When she didn't respond to his blunt statement, he added, "It's barbecue night at Cranberry Brothers."

"Are you inviting me?"

"No." Sam's cheeks turned rosy at his quick refusal. "I mean, we're not ready. My friends will be there."

Lacey stood, and so did Sam. The office was small, and the tips of their shoes butted against each other. She didn't even have enough room to take a deep breath.

"What are you going to tell them? This is going to come up."

"I don't know. I'll try to be aloof." Sam casually shrugged one shoulder. A cheeky grin was hiding in the corner of his mouth. "Do you want to come over for dessert?"

Logically Lacey knew that the way he said dessert wasn't meant to be an *invitation,* but someone needed to explain that to the damp spot that was rapidly forming on her panties. Even if her brain forgot, her body would remember how he'd once tasted her like she was a delicate sorbet or the finest French chantilly cream.

"What's for dessert?" she asked, failing to not sound breathless.

"Strawberry ice cream."

Lacey managed to scrape together enough pieces of her brain to get his phone number and a promise to pick her up after he was done hanging out with his friends.

"Don't you need to know where I live?" she teased, her hand resting on the handle to the door.

"I know where you live. 1467 Sycamore."

"Okay, stalker."

"You told me last night, remember?" Sam clicked his tongue disapprovingly. "Look who has a shitty memory now."

Impulse control was a skill Lacey still struggled with, and that was how she justified what she did. She wiped off some of her freshly reapplied lip gloss onto her thumb, then smeared it on his lower lip. She batted away his hand when he tried to clean it off.

"Don't. It makes it look like we were doing something interesting in here."

Sam considered her for a moment. "Clever."

"You didn't bring me lunch for my good looks," Lacey joked, opening the door before her impulse control got any worse.

"They didn't hurt," Sam said casually, more to himself than to her. "I'll see you later."

CHAPTER FIVE

"SAM...SAM...SAM!"

Sam jumped. He'd heard Graham in his periphery, but his brain shelved the noise under general background noise. Cranberry Brothers was busy, but it was almost entirely locals and only a few tourists. The table their little group had secured was shoved into a back corner, which was how Sam liked it anyway.

"What?" Sam asked, reaching for the crumbs in the bottom of the popcorn bowl in the middle of the table.

"You were on a different planet there." Graham unbuttoned the cuffs of his dress shirt and rolled his sleeves up to his elbows.

It was remarkable how relaxed his friend looked two years after moving to Crane Cove. In his previous life, Graham had been the founder and CEO of a thriving tech company until he inherited the hotel in town and left California to run it. That was how he'd met his wife Eloise, and Sam had never seen him genuinely happier. There was a looseness to his shoulders that had never been there before, and any new lines on his face were from smiling instead of stress.

"I got about as far as Jupiter." Sam showed the bottom of the empty popcorn bowl to Sybil, a notorious popcorn stealer. In response, she calmly sipped her beer. "Did you need something?"

"Some explanations would be nice," Graham said, loosening his tie and unbuttoning the top button of his shirt. He and Eloise had come straight from the hotel to make it to barbeque night.

Sam played dumb. "About what?"

"I heard—" Graham began, but paused when his wife sat down next to him with two beers in her hands and a bowl of fresh popcorn balanced on top of them. He helped Eloise sort out her load, then kissed her temple before continuing. "We heard that you're dating someone in town?"

"Oh, that." Sam shrugged, ignoring the staccato beat of his heart as he geared up to tell his first big lie to one of the best friends he had in the entire world.

"Some details would be nice," Graham pressed. "Starting with why I had to find out from Kiki, who found out from Amara, who found out from Lenny the lunchtime line cook."

"He's been working on that all day," Eloise confided in Sam, giving his forearm a companionable squeeze. "We don't have anyone named Lenny working for us."

"But Amara still found out from someone who works in the kitchen."

"Well, Lenny the lunchtime line cook sounds like a very reliable source." Sam snagged the bowl of popcorn before Sybil could.

"I heard it from Edith, who said she heard it from you," Sybil said.

"Do you think Edith is a reliable source?" Sam asked, pushing the bowl back toward her as a peace offering.

"Normally I take her with a glacier-sized grain of salt, but since you're the one who told her..."

"We're figuring things out." Not a lie, mostly the truth.

"What does that mean?" Graham pressed.

Eloise massaged the back of her husband's neck. "Why don't we give Sam some breathing room? Hm? It's not like you haven't met Lacey before." She gave Sam a soft smile. "We're happy for you. Don't let Graham rain on your parade."

Graham looked ready to launch a rebuttal, but he was cut off by the arrival of their food. Cole and Chase McMahon usually spent the entirety of a Thursday night running around their establishment, but they always took a few minutes out of their busiest night to visit. Or maybe it was to needle their oldest brother, Connor, who had been sitting silently in the deepest corner of their table, nursing his beer.

"Make room. These plates are heavy," Chase said, and Sam wanted to laugh because Chase could probably have lifted Sam over his head. A plate of brisket was not doing anything.

"You're so bossy." Sybil stacked the full popcorn bowl inside of the empty one. "You'd think you owned the place or something."

Cole placed aluminum tins of sides down. Family style worked better for the group than individual orders.

"Did you ask him yet?" Cole asked his twin brother. Chase shot him a silencing glare.

"Not yet. I was getting to it."

"I tried to warn you," Sybil reminded Sam, scooping some mac 'n' cheese onto her plate before handing it to Eloise to be served brisket.

"Is this about the Boo-wery thing?" Sam asked, taking the tongs from Eloise when she was done and serving himself a hearty portion of brisket. Cole was a genius with meat.

"It's a fundraiser. For charity," Chase said with barely restrained eagerness. "You'd be a huge draw for the auction."

Sam frowned. "I don't really want to be auctioned off."

"It's a silent auction," Cole added, like that was supposed to help.

"I don't know..."

"Please," Chase begged. "It's going to be a really fun night. There's a costume contest. And you can bring Lacey."

Sam's fork paused halfway to his mouth. "What?"

"It's an easy date night," Chase pitched.

"Are date nights supposed to be hard?" Sam asked Graham.

"We donated a romantic weekend package. Two-night stay, spa gift certificate, and dinner for two," Eloise volunteered. "It's for a good cause."

"I don't even know what I would donate," Sam said, impending defeat on the horizon.

"A guitar lesson?" Graham suggested.

"No one is learning anything from a single guitar lesson," Sam pointed out.

"Yeah, but it's a guitar lesson from *Sam Shoop*," Sybil cooed, saccharine sarcasm dripping off her words.

"You could do a couple lessons?" Cole suggested cautiously.

"I don't think I'm much of a teacher," Sam said.

"You know more than someone just starting." Chase was grasping at straws. "Experiences tend to go for more than a guitar pick."

"So you're saying a football-throwing lesson with Jordy would go for more than a signed football that could be sold?"

The twins exchanged an excited look. "Do you think we could get Jordy to donate a throwing clinic?" Chase asked Cole.

"I'm guessing not, since he's currently got his arm in a sling," Graham reminded them. "He can't even shower without Annie's help."

"Which I'm sure has been *so* difficult for him." Sybil rolled her eyes.

"Why haven't you asked me to donate anything?" Connor asked from his corner.

"Because your only auctionable skill is being an overbearing pain in the ass?" Sybil said. She thought for a moment. "And pie."

"There. I'll make a pie a month for someone," Connor offered.

"Not as exciting as a spiral clinic with a future Hall of Fame quarterback, but we'll add it to the list," Chase said. "Sam, can you at least promise me you'll *think* about donating something? It's for the puppies and kitties."

"I will think of something," Sam promised, even if internally he was crossing his fingers behind his back.

1467 SYCAMORE STREET was a charming yellow and white bungalow with bright pink plastic lawn flamingos guarding the bushes. Sam parked at the curb, unsure of what to do. He couldn't call Lacey because the street had horrific cell service.

Did he ring the doorbell? Honk? Throw rocks at her window?

No. Honking was rude. Plus, it garnered a lot of unwanted attention.

Since he didn't know which window was hers, the doorbell it was.

Sam had his foot on the first porch step when the front door swung open and Lacey stepped out.

"Don't wait up," she called over her shoulder, and Sam thought he saw Gavin and Leo trying to sneak a peek before she shut the door. She didn't look much different from normal: black leggings, a cruise ship sweatshirt that had the neck cut out of it so it hung off one shoulder, and her blonde hair twisted into a bun.

So why did he have heart palpitations and dry mouth?

"Hey, stranger." Lacey's smile was bright and a little breathless, like she'd sprinted from her room to reach the door before her roommates.

Then it hit him like a ball bouncing off his head. This was so high school. Showing up after dark, walking up to the porch, hoping he didn't have to talk to the parents. Except Sam had never had this experience in high school. He hadn't experienced high school. Before the end of his freshman year he had a recording contract and a tutor to homeschool him while he went on tour.

All that was missing from this scene was a jock in a letterman's jacket threatening to beat him up because he dared to look at the prom queen.

"I didn't know what to do," Sam admitted as Lacey practically skipped down the steps.

"I mean, I was hoping for a trench coat and a radio over your head, but I'm impressed you got out of the car. Most guys just honk."

"So honking is acceptable?"

"No, but the bar is so low it's buried in hell." Lacey hopped off the last step. "I believe I was promised ice cream?"

LACEY FOLLOWED him in her car so he wouldn't have to drive back into town again. Sam was grateful. He'd spent over an hour driving back and forth that day. Even if he didn't have a lot to do, that was a lot of wasted time.

Maybe not wasted. He'd spent a lot of that time remembering what happened in Barcelona.

When they got to his house, Lacey boosted herself onto her spot on the kitchen counter.

"How was dinner?"

"There were a lot of people there." Sam opened the freezer and took out the coveted Tillamook strawberry ice cream.

"Do you ever get overwhelmed by a lot of people?" Lacey asked. "Like it never bothered me when I was on stage, but sometimes I'm in a crowded room and it's great and I'm in my element, but sometimes it's too fucking much and I'd rather take off my skin with a potato peeler than be there for another minute."

Sam stopped mid reach for the bowls. "Take off your skin with a potato peeler? Should I be worried that I'm alone in the woods with you?"

"I said *my* skin, not your skin."

"Still. That is...graphic." Sam shuddered. "I mostly just want to scream."

"That is a valid and much less violent way of coping."

"Tell that to my vocal chords."

Sam put two scoops of strawberry ice cream into each bowl, put the container back in the freezer, then handed Lacey her bowl.

It made sense to him now, how spies got away with it. A change of hair color and makeup had been enough to throw him off. Stick her somewhere he wasn't expecting to see her, and Sam had never stood a chance.

But where would he have thought he'd see her again? Barcelona?

Details about that night bobbed back to the surface throughout the day like messages in bottles finding the shore of a distant country.

The thumping, throbbing bass in the club he didn't want to go to in the first place, but he'd gone because it was his drummer's birthday.

"I was thinking about the night we met," Sam blurted. "I never actually heard your name. It was too loud."

"We did all that, and you didn't know my name?" A laugh laced her voice. "Damn."

"I felt like saying 'Hey, what was your name again?' would've killed the mood."

"You're right. I don't lick the assholes of guys who can't remember my name."

Not for the first time that day, blood rushed to his cock. Because those memories had popped up a lot too, except he kept substituting Now Lacey for Then Lacey.

"Did you ever get that tattoo?" he asked.

Lacey's spoon stopped part way to her mouth. "You remember that?"

"It randomly pops into my head," Sam admitted. Once he'd gotten her naked, she'd made a comment about how different her unmarked skin looked next to his ink, and he'd asked if she'd ever get one while scraping his teeth along her hip bone.

"Yeah. Vampire fangs right there," she'd responded breathlessly, lifting her hips to try and guide him. He'd bitten her instead.

"No, I never did." Lacey's cheeks were as pink as her ice cream. "If you'd told me then I'd be sitting on your counter one day eating ice cream and getting ready to pretend to be your girlfriend, I would've laughed."

"At which part?"

"All of it. You were supposed to be just one wild night."

"I was on your bucket list?"

"Not you, necessarily." Lacey pretended to write in the air. "'Fuck someone successful.' Check."

Sam laughed. It was hard to act like his ego was wounded with that kind of delivery. Besides, he'd had enough people jump into his bed because he was Sam Shoop that it was almost a relief that, at least for one person, he could've been *anyone*.

Lacey smiled. "Didn't we have an agenda?"

"Right." Sam dropped his spoon into his bowl. "Let me find some paper."

"Are you afraid you'll forget?" Lacey called after him as he went down the hall to his bedroom to grab his journal.

When he came back, Lacey's bowl was on the counter, empty, and he caught her red-handed taking a sneaky bite of his ice cream.

"Were you not done?" she asked around a mouthful of his ice cream.

"No, I wasn't." Sam dropped his notebook on the counter and slid his bowl away from her. "Aren't you afraid I might have cooties?"

Lacey grinned. "Remember that time I stuck my tongue in your butthole?"

"Is that going to be your comeback to everything?"

"Probably for at least the next week."

"Maybe don't say that in public." Sam tore a blank page from the back of his journal and wrote down

1. Do Not Bring Up Buttholes In Public.

"So we're not being honest about how we met?" Lacey asked.

"Not *that* honest."

Sam considered the meet-cute dilemma. Graham, Peter, and Jordy were all aware that "Barcelona" was about a one-night stand he'd had. Was Lacey aware that the song was about her and their experience? If she wasn't, Sam didn't know if he wanted to tell her. Would she think it was weird? Or would she make the same mistake the majority of listeners made and think it was a love song and he'd been pining after her for years?

"What if we tell a version of the truth and say we met

during dance lessons for Graham and Eloise's wedding?" he suggested.

"I do find the best way to lie is to tell the truth," Lacey agreed. "So we met at Graham and Eloise's dance lesson. Then what?"

"A little more honesty. We kept running into each other around town, fought over some strawberry ice cream, and I made you dinner."

"We sound sickeningly adorable. Can I have your ice cream, by the way? It's just sitting over there, melting, begging to be eaten."

Sam sighed and pushed his bowl back in her direction.

"Don't sigh at me. You have custody of the ice cream." She tossed his spoon into the sink. "Rule number two: affection remains public."

2. Affection remains public

"How public are we going to be?" Sam asked, looking up at her from his paper.

"I mean, I don't think we should attend any orgies," Lacey said, and he was embarrassed at how long it took him to realize she was joking. "But if this is going to be believable, we need to be seen in public together at some point acting like we're together."

It was a cheese grater to his nerves, but she was right. They needed to be seen together.

"I don't really want this to go beyond Crane Cove," he said. "So please don't post about me on any social media."

"My twelve followers will be very disappointed, but I think that's smart. I don't want your legions of groupies hunting me down." Lacey tapped her spoon against her bottom lip. "We need a launch event. Something that shouts 'We're a couple!' and proves this isn't just a rumor."

"What about the Boo-wery?" Sam suggested.

"The what now?"

"Cranberry Brothers is doing a fundraiser. There's supposed to be a costume thing, a silent auction. I'm assuming since Chase and Cole are in charge, there's going to be a decent turnout."

"Oh yeah. Gavin and Leo donated to that." Lacey tilted her head at him. "You want to do a costume contest?"

Sam shook his head. "No. I wanted to skip the event entirely, but it's the only thing I can think of that fits your parameters."

"We could rent a parade float and ride down Main Street."

"The costume thing will be fine."

CHAPTER SIX

LACEY ADJUSTED her bedazzled and be-shelled purple push-up bra in the bathroom mirror. There wasn't a lot to push up. But she was proud of what she'd accomplished on a shoe-string budget.

The purple push-up bra she'd had since her early twenties and it had somehow survived every move, escaping the donation bag because it was just too cute to throw away, even if she never wore it. Lacey had sewn and glued on shells, fake pearls, and plastic jewels. Her tits looked like a treasure chest. For her tail, Lacey had thrifted a skintight green wrap skirt for a few dollars, then had added some iridescent organza leftover from the dance studio to the hem, leaving it longer in the back. Then she'd spent the last week hand-stitching sequins in a scale pattern while she watched *Bob's Burgers* on repeat.

Less than twenty dollars, and she looked like a mermaid.

Sam was supposed to dress like a sailor, but she'd left his costume up to him. If he showed up looking like he belonged in *An Officer and a Gentleman* she didn't know if she'd go weak in the knees or be pissed because she'd look like dollar-store Ariel, minus the red hair, next to him.

"Lacey, darling, are you coming?" Gavin shouted through the bathroom door.

"Almost done!" she called back, fluffing her beach wave curls one more time. She pulled open the door. "How do I look?"

"You're going to give that boy a heart attack," Gavin said, looking her up and down. "Should we not wait up tonight?"

"Can you guys even stay up that late?" Lacey teased.

"No, we cannot," Leo said, putting on his cowboy hat.

After so many years together, they complained that they were scraping the bottom of the barrel for costumes. This year they'd stumbled upon the *Night At The Museum* movies and decided to go as the cowboy and the Roman soldier.

"Leo, I can't find my sword," Gavin complained.

"Is it in our bedroom? Because you were playing with it earlier."

Lacey stuck her fingers in her ears. "La la la."

"Oh, stop," Gavin laughed, giving her a gentle backhanded smack to her arm.

"We're supposed to be there already," Leo reminded them, tapping his watch.

Gavin looked at Lacey with fake exasperation. "He should know he needs to lie to us about what time to be ready."

"Half-hour buffer, minimum," Lacey agreed.

Leo rolled his eyes and went to find Gavin's sword.

LACEY DIDN'T HAVE butterflies walking into Cranberry Brothers. She had a flock of seagulls angrily fighting over a french fry.

What if Sam's friends took one look at them and knew they were lying? She knew she'd been doing her best on her end of things to be coy whenever anyone asked her about them, trying to build the suspense, but was Sam doing the same? Did they have enough chemistry to be convincing?

Gavin and Leo peeled off to register for the silent auction, leaving Lacey alone in the crowd. She was tall, even taller in her heels, but she stood on her tiptoes anyway to try and find Sam.

They should have come together. The brewery was crowded with adults in costumes, and she felt stupid wandering around like a kid who'd lost their mom at the grocery store.

Where was he?

Her first lap of the lower level yielded no results. She passed Sam's group of friends but he wasn't with them, and she was too nervous to approach them alone. For their part, they either hadn't seen her or were ignoring her because they didn't say hi or invite her to join them.

Lacey did a second lap, in case Sam had been in the bathroom. Not a sailor in sight. She fished her phone out of her small shell-shaped bag, easily her greatest thrifting find last week. Service sucked, but what else was new in Crane Cove.

LACEY

Where are you? I can't find you.

There wasn't an open seat anywhere, so she wiggled her way up to the bar to order a beer while she waited.

"Can I get a pumpkin ale?" Lacey shouted over the din when she got the attention of a short blonde bartender dressed like Tinkerbell.

"Do you want to add it to Sam's tab?" Tinkerbell asked when she handed Lacey her beer.

"Um, sure?" She frowned. "Do you know where he went? I lost him in the crowd."

"He's probably with Sherlock—Connor. You know Connor, right? Tall, blond, should actually be dressed like a lumberjack?"

Lacey knew exactly who she was talking about, but Sam hadn't been near that landmark of a man.

"I'll, um, find him. Thanks for the beer."

"I'm Mallory, by the way. You're Lacey, right? Because if you're not, I'm going to get in trouble for putting random tall blondes on Sam's tab."

"My reputation precedes me." Lacey toasted Mallory with her beer. "Nice to finally meet you. Wait, do you work at Moonies too?"

"I do!" Mallory smiled brightly at her, a lot more pleasant than the classic Disney fairy. "And occasionally the Crane Hotel. I get around."

"Mal, I need a little less chatty, a little more serve-y," Chase McMahon chided as he slipped behind her with a full dish bin for the kitchen.

"Or what? You're going to hit me with your whip?" Mallory shot back, pointing to the coiled whip at his hip. It was truly the necessary finishing touch on any Indiana Jones costume. And while Chase looked nothing like Harrison Ford, it worked on him.

"Do not tempt me, Mallory."

"It was nice to finally officially meet you, Lacey." With a final smile, Mallory moved down the bar to the next patron.

Lacey checked her phone. No reply.

Crane Cove had terrible service. That was a fact. Still, it stung that Sam hadn't even tried to get in touch yet. Was he not worried about where she was?

Someone bumped her from behind, and beer sloshed out of her glass.

"Oops. Sorry."

Lacey bit down on a sigh. She knew that voice. Marianne.

She shook spilled beer off her hand and pasted a smile to her face before turning around. "It's okay. Accidents happen."

"Lacey. Wow. You look....wow." Not a sincere syllable in the lot. It made Lacey nostalgic for drunk, slurring Marianne. At least that person was nice. Ish. "Where's your boyfriend?"

"Oh, he's around somewhere. I wanted a beer." She held up her glass, which was missing the top inch. "Nice costume."

Marianne was wearing one of the high school cheerleading uniforms. Lacey wondered if she'd borrowed it from a student or if she'd ordered herself one to relive her glory days.

Over Marianne's left shoulder, Lacey spotted Sam. She'd never been so relieved to see another person in her entire life.

"I've got to catch Sam before he disappears again. Have fun!"

Lacey squeezed past Marianne without waiting for her reply, moving through the crowd like a torpedo. She intercepted Sam, planting herself directly in his path so he couldn't miss her.

"Where have you been?" she hissed through a fake smile.

"Around."

She wanted to throttle him, but then she caught the movement of his eyes. Up. Down. Up. Down. Up. Slowly down. His Adam's apple bobbed as he swallowed hard.

Sam's voice was tight. "Where'd you find that?"

"This?" Lacey ran her finger over a strand of pearls. "I made it." She took in his outfit. A t-shirt with horizontal navy stripes and navy pants. "I thought you were going to be a sailor."

"I am a sailor."

She sighed. This was a fake relationship so she shouldn't be so disappointed that he'd put in zero effort.

"Aye aye, cap'n," Lacey said with a mock salute. "Why do you have a tab open at the bar? You don't drink."

"I enjoy the occasional root beer." Sam stuck his hands in his pockets. "So, now what?"

"I don't know. We mingle, I guess?" Lacey took a sip of her

beer. It was subtle, with hints of pumpkin and nutmeg. A small moan of satisfaction escaped. "This is good."

"I will take your word for it." Sam looked over his shoulder.

Open mouth, insert foot. Sam was sober, and the constricting guilt physically hurt.

"I'm sorry, does it bother you if I drink? I don't want to make you feel uncomfortable."

"Huh?" Sam turned back to her. "Does it bother me if...No, not at all. As long as you don't expect me to drink, we don't have a problem."

The guilt dissipated like smoke in the wind and was replaced by burgeoning annoyance. All that avalanche of anxiety, and he didn't even care. Hell, it seemed like he didn't even care that she was there at all.

"When did you get here?" she asked.

"Um, like twenty minutes ago?" He looked over his shoulder again.

Twenty minutes. She'd been there for probably ten. Sure, they were both late, but Sam didn't seem the least bit concerned about where she'd been.

Lacey looked over her shoulder at the area where she'd last seen his friends, but when she looked back, Sam was gone.

Normally when Lacey felt like everyone was looking at her, she could convince herself that nobody was and that everyone was too involved with themselves to even notice her. But she knew Marianne would be watching and waiting, so she stood in her place like Sam hadn't abandoned her and he'd be back soon.

People moved around her like a rock in a river. And like the river, no one paid her any mind. Lacey avoided these kinds of small-town functions because they reminded her of how alone she was in a place where it was hard to hide.

Where was Sam?

Lacey was done waiting. If Sam wanted to run off, she'd be

the Coyote to his Roadrunner. The Tom to his Jerry. She couldn't think of any more examples, but she was going to focus on that while she weaved through the crowd so she wouldn't lose her temper.

"Excuse me," she said, trying to squeeze around a small group of men.

"Shiver me timbers, it's a ho ho ho." Mitch wrapped a hand around her bicep. He was dressed like a pirate, complete with a stuffed parrot perched on his shoulder. "If you're nice, I'll plunder your booty."

"You're disgusting," Lacey snarled as his friends laughed.

"Oooh, little mermaid has her voice. What did you have to do to get that back?"

"Let go of me," she demanded. Mitch complied.

"Where's your boyfriend, Lacey?" Mitch looked around the room casually. "Nowhere to be found?"

Her cheeks were so hot someone could have friend an egg on them.

"He's around."

"Look." Mitch leaned in close and dropped his voice. "Whenever you're ready to drop this stupid act that you're dating Sam Shoop, I'll take you back. No questions asked. You really don't have to go to these lengths—"

Lacey turned and left. One of the great things she'd learned recently was that she didn't have to stand and have a conversation she didn't want to have. She could leave.

She really wanted to leave.

But she didn't know where Gavin and Leo were, she didn't know where Sam was, and she didn't want to walk home in her heels. Plus, she didn't have a coat. By the time she got home, she'd look like a mermaid that had just washed up on shore.

Stripes.

It was a flash in the corner of her eye, and Lacey's hand

darted out and grabbed the side of the shirt. The wearer turned, startled, and she saw white face paint. A mime. Not a sailor.

"Sorry. I thought you were someone else."

If this was how fake-dating Sam was going to be, she was going to have no problem making the breakup seem believable.

CHAPTER SEVEN

THE BID WAS up to a thousand dollars.

Who the hell was bidding a thousand dollars on a guitar lesson in Crane Cove?

Sam had been to charity auctions in Los Angeles and New York where his lesson would have gone for tens of thousands of dollars. Hell, he'd once donated tickets to a show that went for fifteen grand. But Crane Cove? He thought he was safe when he wrote down $250 when he'd arrived.

He could end this right now. Write down a big sum, and no one could outbid him. But Graham would lecture him about it. Or Eloise would be sweet but disapproving. She liked community involvement. Graham wasn't allowed to write big checks so no one had to attend an Under The Sea-themed benefit to buy the middle school new computers.

"Fifteen hundred," Sam muttered under his breath, writing down his new bid and auction number. If he ever found out who number thirty-two was...

"What are you doing?"

Sam jumped, the pencil in his hand cartwheeling through the air and bouncing off the wall. Graham stood behind him, dressed like Bert from *Mary Poppins*, with fake soot rubbed around his face and a pageboy cap on his head. He put his hands on his hips.

"Were you bidding up your own item?"

"Umm...maybe?"

Graham sighed. "Well, shit. I've been babysitting your paper all night, trying to make sure no one outbid *me*." He shook his head and crouched under the table to retrieve the dropped pencil. "I should've known something was up when it got above five hundred."

Sam's eyebrows shot up. "You're number thirty-two?"

"Yes, I am. Well, Eloise and I are. I don't know what all she's bid on, and I'm kind of scared to find out."

Graham wrote down a bid beneath Sam's and set the pencil down, then glared, threatening him to pick it back up.

"You really want a guitar lesson?" Sam asked, sticking his hands in his pockets.

"No. But I know you don't want to give one, so here we are." Graham mimicked Sam's stance and put his hands in his pockets. "You're going to give Eloise a cooking lesson, though."

"Why?"

"Because she wants one and she's never going to ask you directly. I think she's still a little scared of you."

"Me? Really? She's friends with Sybil." Sam frowned, his stomach sinking a little. "I *like* Eloise. I don't want her to be scared of me."

"You should come over for dinner soon. Bring Lacey too." Graham looked around. "Speaking of...where's your new girlfriend?"

"She's—" Sam turned to point to where he'd left Lacey, but she wasn't there anymore. "Shit."

"Isn't it a little soon for her to be sick of you?" Graham teased.

"This place is too crowded," Sam grumbled, rising up on his tiptoes to try and spot Lacey. She was tall. This shouldn't be so hard.

"Let me know what works for you two," Graham said. "We're a little busy with the *Claymore Abbey* ball, but after the first weekend in November our schedule opens up a bit. Oh, and I need to know if you'll be around for Thanksgiving or not. Jordy and Annie were talking about coming to visit, so I need a headcount, and if you're *not* going to be around, I need to find someone else to cook."

"I don't know yet." Sam clenched his teeth, biting down on a frustrated growl. Where had she gone?

Then, like spotting Waldo in a picture full of mimes, he saw her, ironically, grab a mime. Relief flooded his body, dousing the fires of anxiety.

"Try not to let anyone else win me," he begged Graham, before squeezing through the crowd toward his mermaid.

No, not his mermaid. His fake mermaid. His temporary, convenient, accidental, fake mermaid.

Sam put a gentle hand between her shoulder blades, and was rewarded with a stiff punch to his shoulder.

"Ow!" he protested, dropping his hand to grab his throbbing arm. "What did I do?"

Lacey's eyes widened. "I—I thought you were someone else."

Who else was touching her, and why was her first instinct to throw a punch?

"Are you training for the featherweight championship of the world?" he asked, but instead of laughing, Lacey's eyes welled with tears, and her jaw tightened with the effort of holding them in.

Adrenaline shot through his system like he'd touched an electric fence.

Sam bent his head close to hers so he didn't need to shout to be heard. "What's wrong?"

Lacey shook her head, taking a shaky sip of her beer.

"Do you want to go outside?"

The look she gave him clearly said that this was all his fault and she didn't want to go anywhere with him, but faced with a lack of options, he would have to do because she did want to escape. A small nod confirmed his suspicion.

Sam cautiously put a hand on Lacey's lower back to help guide her through the crowded brewery. Had her skin always been so soft? It was like touching flower petals.

The back patio was unlocked and, mercifully, empty. Lights reflected off small puddles, and every surface seemed to faintly glow from recent rain. It smelled like rain too. Petrichor. One of his favorite words.

Once they were clear of the door, Lacey moved away from him and his hand. His calloused fingertips missed her softness instantly, like they'd been granted one brief brush with heaven and—dear god, no wonder he'd written a song about her when he didn't even know her name.

"Why did you disappear in there?" he asked.

"Why...why did I..." Lacey laughed mirthlessly, then chugged the rest of her beer. "I didn't disappear. You did."

Sam frowned. "I was checking on my auction item."

"Do you even care that I'm here?" Lacey's voice cracked on the last word. She pressed her fingertips to the inner corner of her eyes. "Of course you don't."

"I never said that," Sam protested, stepping toward her. Lacey stepped away, maintaining their distance.

"You didn't have to. You didn't notice that I was twenty minutes late, you left without a word as soon as I found you—*I* found *you*—and after you abandoned me, I think I ran into every person in this town that wants this"—she gestured between them with her empty glass—"to be fake. And with the way this night has gone so far, I know exactly what they'll be saying about me tomorrow."

"What's that?"

"'Did you see her chasing him around all night? He's not that interested in her. She's desperate.'" Lacey's chin wobbled. "We're supposed to be pretending, Sam. Can't you act like you like me?"

Sam's stomach clenched and twisted, like it was trying to wring itself out like a used dish rag.

"I'm sorry," he said, unsure of what to do with his hands. Did he put them in his pockets? Behind his back? Cross his arms under his chest? Try to give Lacey a reassuring hug? "I guess I don't really know how to do this anymore. It's been a while since I've dated, real or otherwise. How do I fix this?"

"Maybe try to act like you like me."

"I do like you. You're fun to be around."

"You have to *act* like it, Sam. Pretend like you can't keep your hands off me, like I'm the funniest person in the room—"

"You probably are the funniest person in that room. I mean that." Sam crossed his heart for good measure.

Lacey sniffled, but a small smile danced across her lips.

"We didn't cover this is in our meetings," Sam pointed out.

"I didn't think we had to." Lacey swiped errant tears as they fell off her lower lashes. "Can I have a hug?"

Sam opened his arms and she stepped into them, wrapping her arms gently around his waist, her empty beer glass bumping against his vertebrae. He encircled her to the best of his ability, trying to cover as much of her exposed skin as he could. It was almost Halloween and the air was bone-chilling. Lacey was tall enough that she could rest her cheek on his shoulder, and floral-scented hairspray tickled his nose. His heartbeat noticeably slowed.

"Better?"

She nodded.

"I'm sorry I made you cry."

Lacey let out a shaky sigh. "It wasn't just you. I ran into Marianne and Mitch before you found me. They're the fucking worst." The tip of her cold nose brushed against his hot pulse and Sam swallowed hard. "I shouldn't let them get to me, but I really wanted to rub this in their shitty faces."

"We could still rub it in their faces," Sam reminded her, internally screaming at his thickening cock that this was fake and any kissing was for show. That she wasn't going to be touching him later, no matter how much he begged.

He was willing to beg, if it would make a difference.

"Just pretend to be a doting boyfriend for forty-five minutes, then we can leave." Lacey released him, wiping under her eyes one more time. "And maybe get me a snack."

The interior of Cranberry Brothers was stifling. Sam kept a hand on Lacey's hip, letting her guide them through the crowd back to the bar where she flagged down Mallory.

"Can I get another pumpkin beer?" she half shouted, leaning forward over the bar top. Her ass pressed against his groin, and Sam looked up, counting lights to try and distract his lecherous brain.

"Coming right up," Mallory promised, taking Lacey's old pint glass and returning after a moment with a fresh, full beer. "You found your wayward sailor."

"I did." Lacey straightened, then leaned back against Sam, giving him a quick, familiar kiss on the cheek, like she did it all the time and would keep doing it for a long while. Warmth spread from Sam's face to his chest.

"Can she get a snack too? Before all this beer goes to her head," Sam asked, placing his hand on her bare midriff.

"Sure, but it's probably at least half an hour. The kitchen is slammed," Mallory warned them, filling a clean pint glass with a clear bubbly liquid from the soda gun, and garnished it with a lime wedge. She put it on the counter, and Sam grabbed it.

"I mean, if we're going to be waiting anyway, can I get a brisket quesadilla and cajun tots?" Lacey asked, half addressing Mallory and half addressing Sam.

"Anything you want, baby," Sam said, nudging aside her hair with his nose to kiss her neck.

"Brisket quesadilla and Cajun tots. Coming up...eventually," Mallory said, tapping the order into the computer before moving back down the bar to help someone else.

"Baby? Really?" Lacey scoffed once Mallory was out of earshot. "I need a different nickname."

"What do you want? Schmoopy?"

Lacey laughed so hard she snorted. Pride and lust shot through Sam in equal measures.

"No, not that. It'll come to you." She patted his cheek. "Are you doing okay?"

"Having a grand time."

"You said that like you're in the middle of a root canal."

"I think I would've had a better time at my root canal if my dentist looked like you," Sam said.

Lacey rolled her eyes discreetly. "I don't think anyone can hear you. You don't need to lay it on so thick."

Sam wasn't laying it on thick, though. He'd barely brushed the surface.

CHAPTER EIGHT

ALL WEEK the rain had come down in sheets.

Halloween and trick-or-treating had been a very soggy affair. Kids dashed up walkways while parents stood on the sidewalks with umbrellas. Lacey loved Halloween and the costumes. She didn't want kids of her own, but she enjoyed other people's in short bursts. Handing out fistfuls of candy because Leo and Gavin were at a party was one of those times.

She'd been publicly "dating" Sam for a week. It was hard to tell, though. Either her expectations were too high or Sam couldn't remember that he was supposed to be obsessed with her because she'd seen him once on Thursday when he'd brought her lunch and dinner when she had a late class. Lacey had a text sitting unsent that demanded he take her out on a date for the spectacle of it. She didn't know if she'd send it. Because "dating" Sam was confusing for her body. When he'd touched her at the Boo-wery, or kissed her neck, shoulders, or cheek, her body had lit up like one of those strongman games at the fair. In a way, it was almost better he'd kept his distance all week.

The sun finally came out Saturday afternoon as Lacey was leaving the Crane Hotel. After three hours teaching Victorian era dances with Gavin, she was ready for a shower, baggy sweatpants, and to edit her text to Sam. She needed a date with him *for* the PDA. Maybe something where he'd need to touch her a lot. Did Crane Cove have pottery classes? Could she convince him to reenact *Ghost* with her?

Lacey took out her phone and deleted the original message she'd written for Sam and replaced it with a shorter one.

LACEY

You. Me. Date. Soon. In public.

Very eloquent and persuasive.

Her service was spotty, but she hit send anyway. Sam would get it eventually.

Could she give him the three dollars in her bank account to kiss her neck again? The phantom brush of his lips haunted her. Her nipples tightened and her skin flushed whenever she thought of it.

Leo was at the restaurant. Gavin claimed he was going grocery shopping, so if she hurried, she had at least half an hour of alone time at the house to break out her vibrator.

Maybe she'd think more clearly after an orgasm or three.

Lacey dropped her bag and phone into her passenger seat, resisting the temptation to check and see if Sam had texted her back yet.

It was a short drive back into town, which was good because she was getting close to the point where her gas light would turn on. She'd stretched her budget to the limit this paycheck. Eventually she'd claw her way out of the debt hole she'd dug for herself, but it felt like it would never end. And right on cue, feeling sorry for herself when it came to money made her miss and curse her mom in equal measures.

Lacey squinted. The sun reflecting off the water on the road made it hard to see, and she groped in her bag for her sunglasses. Did she even have her sunglasses?

They were in the drop-down glasses holder in her car, where they were supposed to be. It never failed that the one time she was responsible, she forgot where she put something. The relief when she put them on was instant. They didn't totally solve the problem, but her eyes relaxed.

Down the road, an animal was trotting on the shoulder, headed towards town. From a distance, it looked like a coyote. But as Lacey got closer, she realized it wasn't a coyote, but a muddy dog. And in her rearview mirror, it looked like a tired dog. She pulled over and parked her car on the shoulder.

Crane Cove didn't get a lot of traffic, but it was a busy weekend with the ball and people driving down the coast. People took the road too fast, and she'd feel awful if someone hit the dog because she hadn't stopped to check if it had a person nearby.

Lacey didn't see anyone walking down on the beach, or in the tall grass.

"Hello!" she shouted. There was no response but the dull roar of the ocean tide.

The dog hadn't changed its pace. It kept walking down the side of the road until it reached her car, then it stood by her back passenger side door like it expected to be let in.

"I don't pick up hitchhikers," Lacey told it, cautiously reaching down to check for a collar. There wasn't one. Just wet, sandy, bur-covered golden fur. The dog sat at her feet and leaned against her legs, looking up at her with soulful brown eyes. "Even really cute hitchhikers."

A soft whine broke her resolve.

"Okay, fine. I can give you a ride into town."

The dog hopped up into her backseat as soon as she opened

the door, and circled twice before making itself a bed out of her discarded clothes. Everything was going to smell like wet dog.

"You're lucky you're cute," she told the dog as she reentered the road.

What was she supposed to do with a lost dog? Lacey didn't remember exactly where the nearest animal shelter was, but she knew it wasn't in Crane Cove. She sure as shit wasn't going to start knocking on doors asking, "Is this your dog?" on repeat.

Maybe a veterinarian? Were they even open on Saturdays?

THE PARKING LOT of Crane Cove Veterinary Hospital was empty except for a single dark green truck near the entrance.

"Please be open," Lacey prayed, parking next to the truck.

The door was locked. But if there was a vehicle, there had to be someone inside, right?

She pounded on the door until her hands hurt. Finally, she saw a tall blond man in a red sweatshirt and black scrub pants emerge from the back.

"We're closed," he said through the glass door, pointing to the vinyl hours.

"It's an emergency," Lacey pleaded.

He sighed and unlocked the door. "What kind of an emergency?"

"I found a dog on the side of the road. It doesn't have a collar. Do you have any way to see if it belongs to anyone?"

"Bring the dog inside. I could check for a microchip," he offered. "But no one has called in the last few days to check for a missing dog."

"Thank you," Lacey said, rushing back to her car and opening the back door.

The dog cowered, trying to make itself as small as possible while whining.

"It's okay," Lacey soothed, patting her thighs enthusiastically. "We're going to find your family."

The dog wiggled, torn between its melancholy act and wanting to match Lacey's faux excitement.

"Come on," Lacey encouraged, patting her thighs again, which only got her more excited cowering wiggles.

The door on the opposite side opened, and the tall man from behind the door scooped the dog out like it was nothing. To be fair, it couldn't have weighed more than thirty pounds, but Lacey felt like she would've struggled a little.

"Come on, precious," the man cooed, and the dog licked his chin. "Nice to meet you too."

The man's name was Chris McMahon, and once she heard his last name, all of his tall, broad, blondness made a lot of sense. He was the second oldest boy in the McMahon brood and a veterinarian. Educated, employed, and gorgeous. Where had he been when Lacey had moved into town? Maybe she could've avoided Mitch if Dr. Chris, DVM, had been presented as an option.

But then Sam wouldn't be kissing your neck, the wicked, devious, excessively horny part of her brain reminded her.

Chris had put a temporary lead on the dog, but it didn't seem to matter since the dog was glued to Lacey's side. She picked burs out of the dog's fur while they waited for the vet to come back with the microchip scanner.

"This won't hurt," Chris promised the dog, like he was talking to a child who was concerned about getting a shot.

Lacey didn't know what she'd been expecting—bright lights and an alarm bell like winning a Vegas jackpot?—but the entire process was over in seconds. Chris held the scanner over the back of the dog's neck, then took the scanner over to one of the computers. He typed for a few seconds, waited, then frowned.

"So good news and bad news," he began. "Good news, this

dog has been a patient of ours before. Bad news, her owner died about a month ago."

Lacey's stomach and heart dropped like synchronized divers. "What?"

"Her name is Daisy. She's five. Her previous owner was a woman named Gertie Black who passed last month. My mom helped serve food after the funeral." Chris blushed a little at the overshare. "Gertie wasn't great at getting her to regular vet appointments, so she's due for some shots, flea and tick medicine, dewormer."

All Lacey heard was the sound of a cash register with every item Chris listed off. Was she financially responsible for a dog she'd found on the side of the road? Even if she could afford to keep Daisy, Leo was allergic to dogs.

"What's going to happen to her? I can't keep her. One of my roommates is allergic." Lacey scratched Daisy behind the ear. "Do you think Gertie's family is looking for her?"

Chris frowned. "I don't think so. Gertie's kids live in California. And no one's reported her missing to our office." He picked up the black office phone. "I'll call the shelter and see if they can take her."

"You can't take her?" Lacey's heart squeezed at the thought of sweet Daisy alone in a kennel cage, strange dogs around her barking all hours of the day and night.

"I already have four dogs," Chris said with the phone pressed against his ear. "If I bring home another one, my mom will kill me—Yeah, hi. This is Dr. Chris McMahon from Crane Cove Veterinary Hospital. I've got a dog that was just brought in..."

Lacey stopped listening. She sat cross-legged on the floor in front of Daisy, and the dog immediately laid down in her lap. Poor girl had been abandoned. She'd lost her mom and then had been let outside to fend for herself. Tears pricked Lacey's eyes. She knew exactly how Daisy felt.

"I'll talk to her and call you back. Thanks, Tricia." Chris hung up the phone. "So, more bad news. The nearest shelter is at capacity. Their director said they might have space for her on Monday after any weekend adoptions, but they said we could either find a foster in town or start calling some of the other shelters. What do you want to do?"

"Can I call someone?"

Calling Sam from the vet's office felt like calling from jail for bail money. What if he didn't have service? What if he did have service but didn't pick up? What if he said no?

She went straight to voicemail after two rings. Of course he hadn't picked up. It was an unknown number.

"Um, Sam, it's Lacey. Can you call me back at this number, please?"

Less than a minute later the phone rang. Chris answered, even though Lacey was almost positive it was Sam.

"Crane Cove Veterinary Hos—yeah, she's right here." He handed her the phone.

"Hi, Sam," Lacey said, stroking the soft fur between Daisy's eyes. The dog had her head on Lacey's lap.

"Are you okay?" he half asked, half demanded. "You sound like you've been crying. Are you hurt?"

"I'm fine," she promised, though her resolve not to cry in front of the vet almost waivered. "I need a really, really big favor."

"What kind of really big favor?" he asked, his voice calmer now.

"I found a dog on the side of the road. She was abandoned. I can't take her because Leo's allergic." The lump in her throat returned with a vengeance. "No one can take her, Sam."

There was a long pause on the other end of the call.

"You want me to take a dog?"

"Just for the weekend," Lacey promised, "until the shelter potentially has space on Monday. Or until I can put gas in my car to take her to a"—she swallowed hard—"shelter further away."

Another long pause, followed by a sigh. "I'll be there soon."

CHAPTER NINE

THE LIST of people Sam did favors for was short. The list of people Sam would drop whatever he was doing to help them was even shorter. He wasn't sure how Lacey had ended up on both of those lists, but as he pulled into the parking lot of the vet clinic, he couldn't deny that she was on them.

Her voicemail had nearly stopped his heart. He'd denied the call because he didn't know the number. When the voicemail had popped up moments later, he almost ignored it because he assumed it would be an IRS bot scammer. But the shaky sound of her almost in tears scared him half to death. The next time he talked to his therapist he was going to have to bring up how his mind immediately jumped to things like kidnapping or car wrecks. A dog was, in comparison, a minor problem.

The vet clinic smelled like antiseptic and wet dog. Sam's nose wrinkled. But he carefully smoothed out his expression because Lacey was sitting on the floor with a filthy dog in her lap, carefully picking debris out of its coat, talking to it in a soft, soothing coo.

Sam cleared his throat, and the dog's ears perked up. Lacey looked up and gave him a relieved, grateful smile. He might as well have slayed a dragon or rescued her from a tower, or whatever it was knights were supposed to do.

"Is this the dog?" he asked, noting the muddy pawprints in the lobby and on Lacey's gray sweatshirt.

"This is Daisy," Lacey said, scratching the dog behind her ears.

"Not Pig-Pen?" he joked.

"Chris said there's a dog wash in the back of the pet store."

Sam frowned. Who was Chris?

A tall, broad-shouldered blond man came out from the back room. Jealousy and attraction wrestled for dominance in his brain, because if Sam thought the guy was hot, Lacey probably did, too.

"You must be Sam," the man said with a friendly smile. "I'm Chris McMahon. I think you know my brothers."

A McMahon. Of course he was a McMahon. Now that he'd introduced himself, Sam vaguely remembered one or all three of the brothers he knew talking about one of them moving back after school. That must've been Chris they were talking about.

"I do know your brothers," Sam said with a complete lack of charisma.

"I feel like I need to apologize for two of them." Chris's friendly smile continued, and Sam needed to forcefully guide his brain back to the matter at hand.

"The twins are great. Cole's meat is great."

From the floor, Lacey covered a laugh with a cough.

Chris folded his arms, and Sam could see a vague outline of biceps through his Washington State University College of Veterinary Medicine sweatshirt. "So, Lacey and I gave Daisy a quick exam, got her updated on her shots and meds. She's a very good girl, just needs a bath, some food, and some snuggles."

"I've been working on the snuggles," Lacey said.

"I can send you home with some dog food," Chris offered. "Enough to get you through until Monday."

"I would appreciate that," Sam said, crouching in front of Lacey and Daisy. "Hey, Daisy. Do you want to come home with me?"

Daisy's tail thumped against the tile floor as it wagged. Sam cautiously extended his hand for her to sniff, which she did with great enthusiasm. The first tentative lick kicked him straight in the heart.

"Is that how you usually ask girls to go home with you?" Lacey teased.

"You know how I ask girls to go home with me."

THEY DECIDED that Daisy would ride in Lacey's car to the pet supply store. Daisy seemed very comfortable with her, and Lacey's car was already dirty. Sam put a note in his phone calendar to get her car detailed. As cute as Daisy was, the dog reeked.

The pet supply store had a lumberjack's hideaway vibe. Sam didn't know how else to describe it. There was a lot of wood and flannel. There was a full-service groomer on the premises in addition to the self-wash stations, but the kid working the cash register assured him that the groomer was fully booked up for the next few days, so Sam took a card. He didn't have a lot of confidence in his and Lacey's abilities to get Daisy fully clean.

"When I said I wanted a date, this wasn't what I had in mind," Lacey said as they lifted Daisy into the metal tub.

Right. Her text. He'd seen it after she called him.

"What did you have in mind?"

"Something that didn't involve me smelling like dirty dog."

She held out the hem of her sweatshirt to assess the damage to her sweatshirt.

"Do you want to come over and help her settle in after this?" Sam offered.

Lacey's cheeks turned pink. "I don't think I have enough gas to get to your house and back."

"We can stop at a gas station so you can fill up."

"I also don't have enough money in my bank account to fill up my gas tank." Lacey turned on the water to avoid looking at him.

"I can fill up your tank."

Lacey shook her head as she sprayed Daisy down. "I know I've made some jokes about you paying for everything, but I don't want things to get weird between us."

Sam frowned. "What do you mean weird between us?"

"Money makes things weird. You're already doing me a huge favor by taking Daisy in for a few days. I can't ask you for anything else. At least not today."

"It's a tank of gas, Lacey," Sam insisted.

"Yeah, and it all adds up. Trust me. A little here, a little there, and one day you're annoyed that you're buying me coffee instead of the other way around." Lacey got the nozzle close to Daisy's fur. It was amazing how much dirt was pouring off the dog.

"Look, I need your help, so I'm going to put gas in your car so you can help me. It's all a wash. We're even." He put a hand on her shoulder and gently massaged the tense muscle there until she relaxed a little. "So, are you going to do this whole thing while I stand here and watch?"

"Well, I'm already dirty—"

Dirty water splattered their clothes and faces as Daisy shook herself.

"Oh god. I think some of that got in my mouth," Lacey said, trying to talk without closing her mouth.

IN THE END, they did their best. Daisy needed a better brushing and a haircut, but she looked and smelled better. Her fur was a sunshine gold, with white paws and a white spot on her chest. Daisy was the perfect name for her.

While Lacey played beauty salon drying Daisy—her words, not his—Sam wandered around the store. Even if she was only staying for two days, the dog should have a bed to sleep in and bowls to eat and drink out of. And a collar. And a leash.

When Lacey and Daisy found him, Sam was pushing a shopping cart.

"Um, are you sure you want to buy all of that? Daisy is only staying for the weekend," Lacey reminded him, guilt woven into every word she said.

"I can donate it when I drop her off," Sam reasoned. "It's a bed and some toys. I don't want her getting bored and chewing on my shoes."

Lacey's eyes widened, and her face paled. "Oh god. You probably have expensive shoes. I forgot about that."

Sam resisted the urge to pinch the bridge of his nose. "Lacey. It'll be fine. I can replace them if anything happens."

Most of them. He wasn't going to mention some of the limited editions he'd brought with him from Los Angeles.

"I really appreciate this, Sam," she said, putting a hand on his forearm and giving it a gentle squeeze. Then she surprised him by leaning in and kissing his cheek. "Thank you. You're my hero."

His heart fluttered, and his cheeks burned. Casual appreciative affection wasn't common in his life, and neither was being someone's hero. At least not anyone who had spent any time with him.

"It's nothing," he mumbled, pushing the cart toward the register.

AFTER STOPPING at the gas station and glaring at Lacey until she let him put gas in her car, Sam led the way back to his house in the woods.

"I think I can almost find my way here by myself," Lacey declared when she stepped out of her car. "It's the turn right after I think we've missed the turn."

"I'm going to call the cartographers' society and nominate you for membership." Sam opened his trunk and took out all of the stuff he'd bought for Daisy, balancing it all precariously on the dog bed.

"Ah, so you're one of those people."

"What's that supposed to mean?" Sam asked, awkwardly shutting his trunk and nearly dropping his load.

"Part of the 'I'd rather die than make two trips' crowd." Lacey let Daisy out of her backseat. The dog immediately had her nose to the ground, investigating all the new smells of Sam's property.

"It's inefficient," Sam said defensively, taking careful steps to his front door. "Can you put in the code?"

"Oooh, you're trusting me with the door code?" Lacey teased, tugging Daisy along behind her.

"As you so charmingly put it, you've had your tongue in my ass, so what's a door code between friends?"

Lacey tipped her head back and laughed. The sound echoed through the trees and scared the birds. It warmed his heart and he turned toward the door to hide his satisfied smirk.

"So, we're friends?" Lacey asked when she'd calmed down, sidling up next to him.

"I dropped what I was doing and came to pick up a dog for you. I hope we're friends."

"We're friends," she confirmed with a soft smile.

"Six nine, six nine."

Lacey blinked at him. "What?"

"The door code. Six nine, six nine. Star."

Lacey tapped it in, but stopped before she hit the star button. "Sixty-nine, sixty-nine. Really, Sam?"

"I'm allowed to have a juvenile sense of humor like any other man," Sam said with all the faux dignity he could muster.

"But you're so smart."

"My best friend is Jordy Taylor. I've laughed at a lot of fart jokes."

"At least I can stop being so intimidated by your intellectual prowess," Lacey said, re-entering the door code and opening the door for them.

"I'm so glad our PR campaign is working and people think I'm an intellectual." Sam looked around his foyer, feeling lost. "I have no idea what to do with any of this stuff."

"Have you ever had a dog before?" she asked, closing the door behind them.

"No. Have you?"

"No."

"So we got a dog with no idea what to do with her?"

"Yup."

"Feels on brand for us." Sam sighed and put the dog bed down near his couch.

"Impulsivity and poor planning for the win."

Lacey unclipped Daisy's leash while Sam unloaded the dog bed. She sniffed around, nose glued to the ground like she was a bloodhound tracking an escaped criminal until she made it back to where Sam and Lacey were. Daisy sniffed her bed, then sniffed the couch. She jumped up on the couch.

"No," Sam chided. "You have a bed. Come lay in your bed."

Daisy circled twice, laid down, then yawned wide and rested her chin on her paws. She looked up at him with big, pleading brown eyes. His resolve dissolved like ice tossed into a volcano.

"Just for now," he amended.

"Is that all you wanted from me?" Lacey asked.

What he wanted from her was not something he should say to someone he'd just declared his friend less than ten minutes ago.

"Are you hungry?"

SAM LOVED FEEDING LACEY. There. He'd acknowledged the thought.

Cooking was an expression of care—and a way to show off, if he was being totally honest. It brought him joy, and his friends seemed to really like his cooking.

But Lacey appreciated his cooking. She *really* appreciated it. She made soft, contented noises while she ate, and did a little seated happy dance every so often. It was more rewarding than any professional cook telling him that he knew what he was doing in a kitchen.

And because he wanted her to come back and eat again, he let her finish his strawberry ice cream.

Sam sent Lacey home with leftovers and clamped down on the urge to ask her to video call him when she ate them.

It was just him and the dog now.

"You hungry, Daisy?" he asked. She'd slept through their dinner.

Daisy put her head on the back of his couch to look at him, and he heard the *swish swish* of her tail wagging.

Sam filled up her water dish and poured some of the dog food Dr. Chris gave him into her other bowl. Daisy trotted over and sniffed her bowls, taking a few drinks of her water, then sniffing her food again. She looked up at him with the most befuddled expression he'd ever seen on a dog's face.

"It's food," he said like she could understand him.

Daisy looked at the bowl, then back up at him.

"Go on. Eat your dinner," Sam encouraged.

Daisy sat down.

Sam sighed and sat down next to her, picking the bowl up. "This is your dinner," he explained, holding it under her nose. She looked away like the smell disgusted her. "You've got to eat."

After ten minutes trying to coax her to eat, Sam gave up and pulled his phone out of his pocket. What was he supposed to do?

The internet was full of solutions and suggestions. If they hadn't just been at the vet's office that afternoon, he probably would've panicked that something was seriously wrong with Daisy. As it was, he had to ignore the insidious voice in his head that urged him to jump to the worst conclusion possible.

"Boiled chicken," he read out loud from a website that seemed somewhat reputable. They recommended putting some cooled boiled chicken in with her food to make it more exciting and encourage her to eat.

Sam boiled up his last chicken breast, shredded it, then mixed it in with Daisy's kibble. She danced excitedly as he put the bowl down, and it reminded him of Lacey. Except, unlike Lacey who seemed like she would eat anything, Daisy nosed around her food, carefully only eating the chicken pieces and leaving the kibble behind.

"So much for that idea," Sam sighed, raking a hand through his hair.

She'd liked the chicken, and he had more of that. Back to the internet.

"What about"—Sam scrolled down the page—"I make you some food? Would you like that?"

Daisy wagged her tail.

Sam dug through his fridge and pantry for ingredients. The internet made making dog food look easy. So why was he so nervous he was going to fuck this up and hurt Daisy? Should he call the vet?

No. He didn't need to call the vet. Daisy had been outside for weeks eating whatever she could find—probably dead animals and garbage. Boiled chicken, rice, sweet potato, carrots, spinach, and peas weren't going to hurt her.

Daisy laid by the sink, watching him wash, prep, and cook the ingredients for her dinner. If she could've gotten on the counter, it would have been just like Lacey being there, except Daisy was quiet. Sam found himself filling in the silence, chatting to her because she couldn't talk back. Every so often, though, Daisy would sigh or groan in response to something he said, and Sam wondered how much she understood or if she had incredible timing.

"Bon appetit," he said, filling one of his bowls with her homemade dinner and placing it on the floor in front of her. Daisy jumped up and shoved her face into the bowl, eating with the same gusto that Jordy had for brunch food. Or any food, really.

Sam took Daisy for two walks before bedtime. He'd never been more grateful to live in the woods than after she took her first shit, because at least he didn't have to pick it up and carry it home with him.

Sam came into his room after finishing his nighttime skincare routine to find Daisy lying in his bed. He remembered having her lie in her bed before going into his room. He sighed and pulled back the covers.

"Just for tonight," he told her, and turned off his bedside light.

Then he turned it back on because Daisy had crawled from the foot of his bed to be level with his shoulder.

"Seriously?"

Daisy put her chin on his shoulder.

Women were nothing but trouble.

SAM

There's a girl in my bed

LACEY

She better be furry and have four legs.

Sam took a picture of himself and Daisy and sent it to her.

SAM

Does this count as cheating?

CHAPTER TEN

SUNDAYS WERE Lacey's only guaranteed day off. If she'd wanted to, she probably could have picked up a few private lessons, but she wanted a day to rest and recharge. She wanted that time more than she wanted to be out of debt faster.

She'd just finished applying a mud mask when the doorbell rang. Leo was at the restaurant and Gavin was on a walk, enjoying the sun before the rain was supposed to move back in that afternoon. Lacey decided to ignore the bell.

Then came the knocking.

"Move to a small town, they said. It's quiet, they said," she muttered while she stomped to the door. Whoever it was had better have a good reason for being so damn persistent. If this was about Christmas lights or a Turkey Trot, she was going to scream.

Lacey yanked the front door open. Sam took a step back, his eyes wide.

"Daisy and I were looking for Lacey. Have you seen her, Ms. Swamp Monster?"

Lacey narrowed her eyes and felt the drying mud crack. "Ha, ha."

Daisy barked once, torn between hiding behind Sam and investigating the strange-looking woman.

"We were out for a walk and saw your car," Sam explained, "and we thought we'd stop by and see if you wanted to hang out."

Lacey raised her eyebrows, further cracking her mud mask. "You drove twenty minutes into town to walk around my neighborhood?"

Sam blushed. "That does sound about correct."

Lacey resisted the urge to preen, though warmth spread through her body. "Let me go wash this off."

"We will be waiting with bated breath."

Lacey hurried more than she would admit to get ready. On her way out the door, she grabbed her raincoat, just in case.

"So, how's Daisy doing?" she asked when they reached the sidewalk.

"She's great...I think," Sam said, and frowned. "I don't know a lot about dogs."

Daisy walked ahead of them on her leash, her stride half graceful prance and half short-legged waddle. It made Lacey smile.

"I don't either, honestly. I always wanted one as a kid, but I couldn't have one."

They walked in silence to the stop sign at the end of the street. Even with the sun out, there was a distinct chill in the air. Lacey pulled her hands inside her jacket.

Sam looked left and right for cars before walking across the street. "Can I ask you a question?"

"I don't think that's a bad idea, since we're supposed to be dating," Lacey answered.

"Why was it so important to you to save Daisy?"

Lacey stopped in the middle of the crosswalk. All the feelings she'd had when she thought Daisy might be going to the animal shelter bubbled up again. "Because she reminded me of me."

Sam looked over his shoulder, realized she'd stopped, and stopped too, just short of the curb. "What's that supposed to mean?"

Lacey caught up to him. "I guess since we're supposed to be dating, this is something you'd know about me. My mom passed when I was seventeen. She was sick. It wasn't unexpected, but still, you know, hard at that age. Or any age, I guess." She stuffed her jacket-covered hands under her armpits. "My parents got divorced when I was six. They shared custody kind of sixty-forty until I turned eleven. Then my dad met my stepmom. She didn't like it when I was around. She didn't say that to me, but I could tell. I think she was jealous of the attention my dad gave me, which wasn't a lot to start with. He tried, but being a parent didn't come naturally to him."

"I'm sorry," Sam said. It was what people always said when they found out about her mom, but he said it softly, like he meant it, instead of it being the thing he was supposed to say.

"I stopped going to my dad's house when he married my stepmom. It made it easier for everyone. When my mom passed, I went to live with them. My stepmom made a big fuss about not kicking her daughters out of their rooms because I was only going to be there until the end of the school year. I slept on a pullout couch for most of my senior year."

"Fuck," Sam cursed under his breath.

"It motivated me to get the hell out of there," Lacey said. "When I graduated from high school, I got half of the money my mom left for me and I went to New York City to try and make it as a professional dancer."

"Did you?" Sam asked, pausing to let Daisy sniff a flower bush.

"Did I what?"

"Make it as a professional dancer?"

Lacey looked around the neighborhood. "Well, I'm here, so I'll let you figure that one out."

"So you needed to rescue Daisy because she reminded you of you."

Lacey nodded. "She lost her mom and the people who were supposed to take care of her abandoned her."

It sounded like Sam cursed again, but a passing car drowned out the sound. Daisy grew bored with the bush, peed on it, and their walk resumed.

"What about you? What are your parents like?"

"They're nice people, but we don't talk anymore."

Lacey frowned. "Why not?"

"It's easier for them," he said, stopping again because Daisy needed to investigate a tree that probably got peed on by every dog in the neighborhood. "My early career almost wrecked their marriage, so when I turned eighteen, I decided to stay away so they could preserve some sense of normalcy and privacy."

"That must be hard."

"It's better this way."

"Where are you from?" Lacey asked, searching for things they should know about each other.

"The Detroit area. What about you?"

"Around Pittsburgh."

"How did you end up here?"

They started walking after Daisy added her scent to the tree trunk.

"Well, the boyfriend I had been supporting financially while he tried to make his music career happen made his music career happen, and he dumped me. Then I twisted my knee, and the medical bills pushed me further into debt. And right when I thought I was going to have to live out of my car, Gavin reached out and asked if I was interested in a job. So I moved here because it's cheap rent and there's nothing to do."

Sam chuckled. "How did you meet Gavin?"

"I took a few workshops from him. We casually kept in touch. Then I ran into him and Leo when they were on a cruise —I worked on a cruise ship as a dancer."

"That explains the sweatshirt."

Lacey cocked her head at him. "You noticed what was on my sweatshirt?"

Sam's cheeks reddened. "I notice things."

"Except that we knew each other because we'd fucked before."

His face grew redder. "Okay, I notice *some* things." They reached the end of the block and Sam looked both ways again before crossing, even though there were rarely cars. "If you got the chance, would you go back to professional dancing or would you keep teaching?"

"If I got the chance to be a professional dancer again, I'd leave in the middle of a class," Lacey said. "But I think that ship has sailed. Or rather, it won't come back into port until after I get my finances figured out. You need money to survive not getting jobs."

"This is a good point. What else should I know about you?"

Lacey looked up at the sky and got a raindrop in her eye. "Fuck...um...Despite what everyone assumes about me because I'm a teacher, I don't want kids."

"That's good, because neither do I," Sam said. "If we were actually dating, I definitely would have made that clear already."

"Look at us. A match made in heaven."

They walked in semi-comfortable silence for half a block

before Lacey asked, "Would you have told me why your engagement broke up?"

Sam sighed. "I don't know. Maybe?" He stopped so Daisy could pee on another tree. "Do you want to know?"

Of course she wanted to know. She'd wanted to know why for years. The tabloid versions of the story were salacious, and she'd wondered if any of the "close sources" were telling the truth.

"If you want to tell me."

"We were young. It was incredibly intense, both emotionally and publicly. Maybe it was incredibly intense emotionally *because* it was intense publicly. People were invested in us like we were characters on their favorite TV show."

Daisy concluded her business and they started to walk.

"I'd been a working professional for years by the time I proposed, so I thought I was ready. And, fuck, I just wanted to be loved and wanted by someone who knew me."

The rain began to pepper their heads but Lacey didn't dare mention it. Sam might stop if she interrupted to point out something as trivial as the weather.

"I found out we weren't together anymore at the same time the world did. Adrienne was photographed without her ring on a sexy vacation with someone else who could further her career. It was her declaration of independence from me."

"Did you ever find out why?" Lacey asked.

"I got some intel from mutual friends before we did our postmortem," Sam said. "What I heard from our friends was that she'd wanted to break up for a while but the advantages outweighed the disadvantages. When we got together to talk, she said she felt a lot of pressure to be in a relationship with me, that she didn't want to get married but didn't feel like she could say no. Then the paparazzi swarmed the place, and when the articles came out about us possibly reconciling, I realized it was all a bunch of bullshit and a fucking set up. It really fucked me up."

"Has she ever apologized for all of that? I mean, you were young. We all did stupid shit before our prefrontal cortexes were developed. Some of us," Lacey pointed to herself, "have continued to do stupid shit. But is she sorry at all?"

"Well, I think the album I wrote to process our breakup and all of the stuff after kind of put the last nail in the communication coffin," Sam said with a grim smile.

"Do you regret it?"

"Which part?"

"All of it."

"Nah." He turned his face skyward, letting a few drops land before wiping them away. "I got to learn my lesson young. Relationships, marriage, that stuff isn't for me."

"God, I wish that was me," Lacey said. "I can't learn my lesson to save my life. One loser after an another."

"Present company excepted?"

"The jury is still out," she teased. "I mean, I gave you a rim job and—"

"What part of not bringing up my butthole in public wasn't clear?" Sam tried to sound stern, but there was a hint of laughter in his voice.

Daisy sat down unexpectedly, and Sam stumbled before he realized the weight at the end of the leash was no longer in motion.

"Come on, Daisy," he encouraged, and the dog lay down on the sidewalk instead. He tugged on the leash, but she would not budge.

"I think she's done," Lacey said. "Maybe she doesn't like the rain?"

Sam sighed heavily and walked the few feet back to the dog

and scooped her up in his arms, cradling her like a baby. "What kind of Pacific Northwest dog are you?"

"Maybe she needs a raincoat," Lacey suggested as they started to walk back to the house.

"She lived outside for weeks."

"Doesn't mean she isn't a delicate flower."

"Delicate Daisy." Sam shook his head. "What am I going to do with you?"

CHAPTER ELEVEN

ONE NIGHT WAS A LIE.

Sam woke up Monday morning relegated to a small sliver of his bed, while Daisy snored softly next to him, her body spread across the majority of his bed. For a twenty-five-pound dog, she knew how to take up a lot of space.

"Your morning breath is horrible," he grumbled, scratching her chest. Daisy sighed, unbothered.

On his nightstand, his phone lit up and buzzed. Sam groaned and rolled on to his side, checking the number. The area code matched the one Crane Cove and the surrounding areas used, so he decided to answer it.

"Hello?"

A chipper woman responded, "Hi, is this Sam?"

"That depends on who's asking."

"My name is Kiana, and I'm calling from the animal shelter. I understand you're fostering a..." There was a pause. "A mixed-breed female named Daisy. Is that correct?"

"It is."

Daisy gave him a dirty look that seemed to say that she was

unhappy he'd woken her up, and she hopped off the bed, the sound of her nails clicking on the wood floors echoing through the room.

"Well, I'm happy to tell you we had some adoptions over the weekend so we can take Daisy this afternoon if you're ready to bring her in."

Sam's heart plummeted like an elevator with a broken pulley mechanism. His chest shrank until there wasn't enough room for his lungs and he couldn't take a full breath.

You are not going to spiral, he chastised himself, clawing for calm. *Breathe in. Hold, two, three, four. Breathe out, two, three, four.*

The counting soothed him almost more than making sure he got adequate air. It felt like counting music.

"Sam? Are you still there?"

"Um, yeah. I am." Sam sat up in bed and drew his knees to his chest. "Do I, um, have to bring her in?"

"No, you don't need to bring her in," Kiana said. "Does that mean you want to keep her?"

Was he ready for the responsibility of a dog? Was it responsible of him to keep a dog with his schedule commitments? Loving something immediately didn't mean it was a good fit.

"Can I think about it?"

"How about this? You think about it and call me back at the end of the day. I'll be around until five."

"Okay. Thank you."

"Fostering is an option too, Sam. You could hang on to her while we work to find her a home."

The wave of anxiety rose like an approaching tsunami. Sam closed his eyes and focused on visualization, a technique he'd worked on with his therapist. If his anxiety was a wave, it would break before it hit him and he'd only be sprayed with mist.

"I'll consider that too. Thank you for the call."

"You're welcome, Sam. Have a good day."

Sam hung up and flopped back onto his pillow. No matter which way he turned, he was boxed in by an anxious thought. Was it selfish to keep Daisy? Was it cruel to give her away, not knowing what kind of home she would be going to?

Maybe Jordy wanted a dog.

Sam picked his phone up and found Jordy's number in his favorite contacts. It rang three times before Jordy picked up.

"Oh, hello, stranger. Finally decided to call home?"

Sam rolled his eyes, but some tension leaked out of his shoulders at the sound of his best friend's voice.

"If you weren't so fucking obnoxious, maybe I'd call more."

"You're such a charming bastard." Jordy chuckled. "What's up?"

Sam rubbed an eye with the heel of his palm. "Any chance you want a dog?"

"Eventually, but not yet. Why?"

"Because I have one right now and I don't know if it's a good idea." Sam blew out a tense breath. "She's really cute."

"Why'd you get a dog if you're not sure you want one?" Jordy asked, the sound of a sink turning on and then off in the background.

Sam stared at the ceiling. He hadn't told Jordy about Lacey —not officially. Odds were that he knew. Graham had probably called Jordy first when the rumor started floating around to see if he knew anything. Did he call her his girlfriend? Did he call her Lacey?

"My Lacey found her." Smooth.

"Oooh. *Your* Lacey," Jordy teased. "Why didn't Lacey keep her?—Hmm?" Annie's indistinct voice filtered through. "I don't know, I'll ask. Is this Lacey a tall blonde with great legs and no filter?"

"That is a very accurate description." Especially the legs part.

Jordy confirmed Lacey's identity, and this time Sam had no problem understanding the "Oh! I love her!" that followed.

"Annie says she loves Lacey," Jordy relayed.

"Yeah, I heard." It would be a more ringing endorsement if Annie didn't have a big, generous heart. Then again, if Annie had said she didn't like Lacey, that would've been a damning indictment. "So that's a no to the dog?"

"That's a no to the dog— Are you leaving?" The last part wasn't directed at Sam. Jordy's voice got slightly farther away. There was a pause, then, "Have a good day at work, sweetheart. I love you. No, Darnell volunteered to take me to PT. Yeah, no, we're good. I love you."

"Is Annie headed into work?"

"She is. Dr. Price going to shape young minds." Jordy's voice was borderline dreamy, and when he sighed he sounded like Daisy getting her belly rubbed.

"How's that all going? Still happy you moved her in so quick?"

"I am over the moon, bud. It's the best thing." He could hear Jordy's smile. "She's amazing. I wake up every morning and wonder how I tricked her into this."

"It's not weird living with someone?"

Jordy had entered his late thirties without having ever been in a serious relationship. For a long time, not wanting serious romantic relationships was something they'd bonded over, and Sam hated that the adjustment had been harder for him than for Jordy.

"Not at all. But you've also got to remember that we lived together for a few weeks in the spring."

"Yeah, but sharing space on vacation is a lot different from sharing your house."

Jordy chuckled. "You're right. My house has a lot more space than the lighthouse did." There was the faint clink of silverware on ceramic. "So when were you going to tell me you got a girlfriend?"

"Why didn't you ask when Graham told you?"

"Because I know you. You'll tell me when you're ready." Jordy paused. "Did I just sell Graham out for telling me?"

"Tossed him directly under the bus." Sam rubbed his forehead. "I don't know. It's all still new and we're figuring it out. Telling you and Peter and Graham about someone feels like bringing them home when you've got kids. Remember when Graham brought Eloise home? It felt like a huge deal."

"It was a huge deal. Speaking of bringing people home, are you going to Thanksgiving at Graham and Eloise's? And are you bringing Lacey?"

Sam heard the faint sound of Daisy's paw scratching the front door. Saved by the dog.

"Well, this has been fun, but I have to go let my dog out."

"Chicken," Jordy teased.

"I am absolutely running away from this conversation," Sam confirmed with a soft smile. "Love you, man."

"Love you too, bro. Stop being a stranger."

"Yeah, yeah, yeah."

NOBODY COULD SAY no to lunch and Daisy's big brown eyes. At least that was what Sam hoped as he walked into the dance studio. Disco music blared, and he peeked inside the studio. Gavin was teaching a step aerobics class. The class was a mix of men and women, all from the retired regiment of Crane Cove.

"Pick up those knees!" he yelled into his microphone headset. "If you want that cute tush, you've got to push."

Sam smiled and shook his head. Daisy pulled at her lead, and he turned to see where she wanted to go. Lacey emerged from the back office with a bagged salad in one hand and a fork in the other. Her eyes immediately went to the small cooler in his hand.

"Is that for me?" She mouthed and mimed because the music was so loud.

Sam nodded. Lacey dropped her salad in the trash and pointed to the office.

The disco music was muffled after Lacey closed the door behind them. Daisy's tail wagged her entire body and her delicate paws pranced in place until Lacey crouched down to say hello. Then she unceremoniously flopped to the floor, playing dead from excitement and simultaneously requesting belly rubs.

"Silly girl," Lacey cooed, acquiescing to the dog's demands for affection. "What did your daddy bring me for lunch, hmm? Who's a good girl? You're a good girl."

"Daddy brought chicken udon with a garlic peanut sauce, and Thai summer rolls, also with peanut sauce."

It wasn't until he saw Lacey's devilish grin that his words filtered back to him. Heat radiated from his cheeks so hot he worried he'd cook his bones. He'd called himself daddy.

"Thank you, Daddy," Lacey said. The combination of her on her knees and the silky sweet tone of her voice, like chocolate mousse, sent his circulatory system into panic mode. The blood couldn't decide if it was supposed to be in his face or his cock.

"You're not even curious about why I brought you food?" Sam asked, clearing his throat to try and loosen up his vocal chords because his voice had come out strained.

"You saved me from a clearance bagged salad. I wasn't going

to ruin this by being suspicious." Lacey gave Daisy a few more pats on her side, then pushed herself up from the floor and into her chair. "Was I supposed to be suspicious?"

Sam handed her the small cooler. "I need a favor."

"And you gave me the bribe first? Amateur." Lacey unloaded her lunch and did a happy wiggle.

"You haven't even tasted it yet," Sam teased.

Lacey looked at him with a blank expression. "What?"

"You do that when you eat," he said, and imitated her wiggle.

"I do n—" Lacey pursed her lips. "Okay. Maybe I do. But it's good food and should be celebrated." She swirled some noodles around her fork, then stabbed a piece of chicken. The first bite made her eyes roll back in her head. "Fuuuuck."

"Shhh. People are going to think we're having sex in here."

"This is better than sex," she said around a full mouth. Her eyes widened a fraction. "Oh, and it's a little spicy. You're fucking amazing."

Since they'd had sex—great sex, too—Sam couldn't decide if that was a compliment or a dig.

"So this favor," Lacey prompted, loading up her second bite.

"I'm supposed to travel to New York on Thursday to record, and I was wondering if you could watch Daisy."

Lacey raised her eyebrows. "You decided to keep her?"

"The shelter called this morning, and I couldn't bring myself to give her up. I told them I'd think about it until the end of the day but...yeah, I'm keeping her." Sam rubbed the back of his neck sheepishly. "So can you watch her for me?"

She frowned. "I can't keep her at my house, remember?"

"You could stay at my house with her," Sam suggested. "I'll leave food and pay you."

"How much?" she asked, taking another big bite.

"Five hundred?"

Lacey choked on her food, coughing for over a minute until she finally wheezed, "Five hundred *dollars*?"

"Is that not enough? I've never had a pet before so I don't really know what the rate is..."

"Nope. Five hundred would be great. Amazing. Are you sure, though? You don't want to take her with you?"

Sam had considered that. He'd chartered a private plane to take him from the Florence Municipal Airport to New York City, so he *could* take Daisy with him. But he worried she'd be overwhelmed and stressed by air travel and the city. New York was a lot to take in as a human, so he couldn't imagine how it would be for a dog who'd only lived in a small town. Besides, he was going to be incredibly busy during his trip, and he didn't want to trust her to a dog walker.

"I thought about it, and I think we'd all be happier if she stayed at home with someone she knows."

Daisy had her head on Lacey's leg, wagging her tail every time Lacey even glanced at her, and licking her lips with her best starving puppy dog act.

"I'm not sharing," Lacey told the dog. "Take up the people-food requests with your dad."

"She might be a little confused because she, um, does get people food," Sam admitted, a little embarrassed.

"Are you feeding her from the table? Because your food is really well seasoned and some of those seasonings might be bad for dogs."

"No, I'm not feeding her from the table. I've been, um, making her food from scratch because she didn't want the kibble Dr. McMahon gave us."

Lacey looked down at Daisy with a serious expression. "Girl, you have hit the daddy jackpot. Do not screw this up. All your poops and pees go outside, and keep your mouth off his shoes, understand?"

Daisy pricked up her ears and tilted her head to the side.

"Can you be at my house at five on Thursday so we can do the hand off?"

Lacey gave him a sidelong look. "AM or PM?"

"PM. Obviously."

She relaxed. "Oh, thank god." She looked at the calendar posted on the wall. "Thursday...Yes, I can make that work."

Outside the small office, the disco music stopped. Voices filtered through the door, and then the studio was quiet. The door burst open dramatically and Daisy jumped, scrambling to hide under the desk.

"Oh!" Gavin's hand flew to his chest. "I am so sorry. I didn't know you were here, Sam. Lacey didn't say she was going to have a gentleman caller for lunch."

"He surprised me," Lacey said, holding up her container of noodles.

"Nice to see romance isn't completely dead with this generation." Gavin took a step inside, then stopped. "I'm sorry, did y'all want some privacy?"

Sam stood awkwardly. "I was, um, just leaving. Come on, Daisy."

Daisy slunk out from under the desk, and Gavin gasped.

"Oh, what a pretty baby!" He crouched down. "Come here, sugar." Daisy took timid steps toward him, sniffed his outstretched hand, then melted into Gavin's touch as soon as he started scratching behind her ears. "I think I love you. I can't have a dog because my hubby is allergic, but you can come visit Uncle Gavin anytime, okay?"

Sam exchanged a look with Lacey, who rolled her eyes and smiled.

"She's kind of a snuggle slut, isn't she?" Lacey joked.

"Never met a hand she didn't want to have petting her," Sam agreed, and gave a low, short whistle. "Come on, Daisy."

Daisy's ears pricked up again, and she abandoned Gavin for Sam, taking a few short steps to sit in front of him at attention.

"Good girl." He picked up her lead, then gave an awkward little wave goodbye. As he reached the front door of the studio, he swore he heard Gavin say, "Next time, lock the door so you can lock that down."

CHAPTER TWELVE

"OKAY, I know you're here somewhere," Lacey said as she slowed down her car and leaned close to the steering wheel, peering through her supersonic windshield wipers to try and find the turn to Sam's house.

He'd offered to come pick her up, but Lacey had insisted that she needed to be able to get there herself or she and Daisy were going to be camping in the woods instead of staying at his house.

Did she miss it?

Her headlights hit a reflective strip, and she shouted with excitement. As always, the turn was right around the point where she thought she was lost.

Lacey drove slowly up the long driveway. The woods were almost pitch black, and the rain was coming down like a second Biblical flood was headed their way. Since she'd almost hit a deer leaving his house Saturday night, she wasn't taking any chances since her car wasn't insured as of a few weeks ago. The five hundred dollars Sam was giving her to hang out at his big house with their—his—sweet dog was going to pay for her to get it reinsured.

She parked, careful not to block his car, grabbed her duffle bag, then sprinted for the front door. It looked like she'd stood directly in front of a sprinkler when Sam opened the door.

"You found it," he said, a bit surprised. Daisy sat next to him, wiggling so hard that she looked like a hula girl dash ornament.

"There was a minute there I thought I was going to have to send up a flare for you to find me, but it really is the turn right after I think I'm lost." Lacey stepped inside, took off her shoes, put down her bag, then turned her attention to Daisy. "Hi, Daisy girl," she cooed in a sing-song voice, and scratched the dog behind both ears.

"I told her to sit and stay before I opened the door. I'm kind of shocked she did it," Sam said, walking backwards out of the foyer.

"She's a good girl." Lacey followed him into the house. "Do I actually get a grand tour this time?"

"You do." Sam pointed to the kitchen. "That's the kitchen."

Lacey rolled her eyes, even though she did want to laugh. She wasn't going to give him the satisfaction, though. Sam had brought her lunch every day that week and she'd noticed something: he enjoyed her approval. He would pretend like he wasn't watching her when she took her first bites of his food, but exuded satisfaction after her first sigh. She'd done a little experiment on him earlier that day and showed no reaction to her meal. No happy dance, no sighs, no moans. Sam's body language had become more tense with every passing minute. It took him three minutes to crack and ask her how she liked her focaccia sandwich. When she'd told him it was fantastic, he glowed.

She wasn't proud to admit that she liked him salivating after her approval.

Sam's confidence faltered for a second, but he quickly

smoothed his face back over and continued. He opened the refrigerator.

"I made Daisy's food for the next few days and separated them into the correct serving sizes. So in the morning and evening give her one of the bags. Easy enough. She *will* let you know if you forget to feed her."

"She has her priorities straight." Lacey boosted herself up on the counter, her body on autopilot.

Sam continued his inventory. "I made you a frittata for breakfast, so you can heat that up whenever. There's some ginger chicken and rice soup. There's also a ziti that just needs to bake. I wrote the instructions on foil, so take it out when you start preheating the oven."

"Why did you write the instructions on the foil?"

"So you don't lose the instructions," Sam explained, like that should have been obvious. Lacey felt uncomfortably seen, because she probably would have misplaced the instructions if he'd put them somewhere logical, like the fridge or the counter. Apparently she hadn't been the only person in this fake relationship paying attention.

"Did you write the instructions on Daisy too?"

"I tried, but she kept wiggling when I got near her with the sharpie."

This time Lacey did laugh, and a small smile played at the corners of Sam's mouth. She might have imagined it, but she swore his eyes swept down her body, then back up to meet her gaze. The small staring contest she did not imagine. They watched each other, like there was an unspoken question between them neither of them knew how to ask. The longer they kept their gazes locked, the harder it became for her to breathe correctly. Her skin tingled, like he was placing phantom kisses all over her. The body remembered. Lacey fought the urge to rock or wiggle, anything to provide a little friction to her neglected pussy. She was in charge, not her body.

Her body could be in charge later, after Sam had left the state.

Daisy's nails clicked on the floor as she came into the kitchen and sat in front of Sam. She pawed his leg to get his attention, and it broke the thread of tension between them.

"See. She will let you know when she wants dinner." Sam chuckled but there was no humor in it.

Daisy did a little happy dance when he fed her too.

Sam led Lacey down the hallway, past the half bath she'd used when she'd been here before.

"I finally get to see what's in the west wing?"

"As long as you promise not to touch the rose," Sam said, stopping at a closed door. "This is my room."

"And I'm not allowed in there?" Lacey guessed. Sam's cheeks grew pink.

"Actually, this is where you'll be sleeping. I, um, don't have a guest room set up."

So her plan to let her body take charge later was going to happen in his room. In his bed. In his sheets. Her pussy throbbed in anticipation.

"I made my bed, and I didn't want Daisy to mess it up," Sam explained, opening the door.

His room was a dream. The ceiling was tall, and a window that took up the expanse of the far wall made it feel like she could step out into the trees. The room was bigger than her first apartment in New York, and she hadn't even seen the bathroom yet.

"Aren't you worried someone is going to fly a drone up here and see you walking around naked?" she asked.

"Well, you're one of the few people that know where my

house is," he said, "and before you get any ideas about the drone, the window is tinted on the outside so no one can see inside."

"So I can walk around naked?"

If she hadn't been watching his reaction closely, Lacey might've missed the hard swallow.

"Mm-hmm."

"Good luck getting me to move out." She pointed to a doorway. "Is that the bathroom?"

"It's actually the portal to my dungeon."

"Demonic or sexual?"

"If you ask some people, the answer is both." Then he winked at her, and Lacey's legs threatened to give out.

Sam opened the door.

"Your demonic sex dungeon looks suspiciously like a bathroom," Lacey said, stepping inside and looking around.

Yup. She could live in this bathroom and be really happy about it. The shower had enough nozzles to qualify as a car wash.

"You know what, you're right. This *is* the bathroom. I get my houses mixed up sometimes."

Lacey caught him looking at her ass in the mirror. Nice to know she wasn't the only person attracted. Or she'd sat in something.

"Wait, do you actually have a dungeon in one of your houses— Wow, I cannot believe I just said that sentence."

Sam was almost directly behind her, and she watched him in the mirror take those last few steps and lean in to whisper in her ear, "Wouldn't you like to know?"

Lacey felt dizzy. Her mouth was dry and watering at the same time, because the body *remembered*, and her mouth remembered how he felt. So many parts of him. It wanted to know again, to make sure it hadn't forgotten anything.

Sam's phone chimed in his pocket.

"Goddammit," he muttered, stepping away from Lacey and digging for it. She took several deep breaths, trying to restore oxygen to her brain and find her equilibrium again. She checked in with her body, and her panties were embarrassingly wet.

Saved by the bell.

"I need to leave to get to the airport," he said, silencing his alarm. "Are you fine if you check out the rest of the house by yourself?"

"I won't get lost, right?" Lacey asked.

"No, I don't think so." Sam left the bathroom, his pace quicker than it had been when they'd entered. "Just don't go into my studio, don't touch my instruments, and don't answer the landline."

Lacey nodded until he hit his last point. "You don't want me to answer the phone? What if it's you calling?"

"I won't call the landline," he said. "If I need to talk to you, I'll call your cell phone."

Lacey frowned. "But how are you going to do that?"

Sam walked into his walk-in closet. "Have you never used your phone up here?"

Lacey shook her head. "I didn't see the point. You live in the middle of the woods."

"Check your service," he told her, taking a cozy gray sweater off a hanger. He slipped it on, breaking up his black-on-black ensemble.

Lacey did as she was told. Full bars. The best service she'd had in over six months.

"You have service!" she shouted, shocked and incredulous.

"I'm surprised you haven't noticed," he said, picking up a black suitcase.

"No one texts me," Lacey admitted before she could stop herself. It was pathetic, but true.

"That can't be right," Sam said with a small frown and an adorable, concerned forehead wrinkle.

"I don't really have any friends." In for a pathetic penny, in for a pathetic pound. "Gavin and Leo aren't big texters. And neither are you. So...that pretty much sums up my social circle." Daisy wandered into Sam's bedroom. "And Daisy, but she doesn't have opposable thumbs."

"But you're....you really don't have any friends?"

"Don't you have a plane to catch?"

Sam snapped back into action. "Right. Plane. New York."

Lacey followed him to the front door. "Have a nice trip. You'll be home Saturday?"

"I should be," Sam said, patting down his pockets. Satisfied with the results, he crouched down in front of Daisy, who licked his face. "You be good, okay? I'll miss you." He stood. "Thanks again. I'll feel better knowing she's with someone who loves her."

"You're going to miss your plane," Lacey reminded him.

Sam nodded and left through the garage. Daisy followed him and sat in front of the closed door, watching it like Sam was going to come back in at any second. It broke Lacey's heart.

"Daisy girl, do you want to play?"

LACEY WOKE a little before midnight to the buzzing of her phone. She'd fallen asleep on the couch in the basement watching a movie with Daisy.

SAM

I made it to my apartment in NYC. How's my baby girl?

Lacey smiled drowsily at her phone. It was precious that he

cared so much about a dog he'd known for less than a week. Everyone—including the media— that didn't know him thought that Sam was standoffish and borderline rude. And he should be because that man would be a raw, exposed nerve if he cared for everyone the way he cared for those he was close to. He'd taken better care of her in a few weeks of fake dating than any of her real boyfriends ever had. None of them had ever made her lunch and brought it to her at work. Hell, most of them couldn't even cook.

LACEY:

She's good. Misses her daddy

The three dancing dots in Sam's message bubble started and stopped several times.

SAM

And how's Daisy?

Lacey didn't know if he was being serious or messing with her. Maybe it was in her head, but she thought they'd been playing some version of chicken earlier, toeing the line between friendly and flirty. They'd said—well, she'd said—no non-public displays of affection. But, fuck, she wanted him.

LACEY

She's good.

SAM

What have you been doing?

LACEY

A little play time.

SAM

What kind of play time?

LACEY

Wouldn't you like to know?

Again, his dots appeared and disappeared, like he was writing and deleting. Lacey was close enough to the fire to feel the flames.

SAM

> Are you in my bed yet?

Lacey's pulse kicked into a different galaxy. Carefully, she extracted herself from the couch where Daisy was snoring and tiptoed upstairs. As she reached the top, she heard Daisy running up behind her. Lacey sighed.

"Sweetie, I appreciate that you want to hang out with me, but I'm trying to sext your daddy. I need this."

Daisy trotted past her, headed straight for the bedroom.

"I love you, but you're ruining my non-existent sex life," she shouted after her.

Lacey followed the dog down the hall, and wasn't at all surprised to find her already in Sam's bed, curled up on the left side of the bed. Did Sam sleep on the right side? The full body tingles started again as she imagined what he looked like spread across his sheets. Dark hair rumpled, the ink all over his body moving with his skin every time he shifted. Did he sleep naked? He did in her imagination. It would be so easy to reach over and stroke him.

"Fuck," she muttered, tossing her phone on the bed and stripping off her shirt and her bra. This was torture. And she didn't want to be the only one suffering.

Lacey found a white V-neck T-shirt in Sam's closet. She found a lot of them, actually, but she took the first one her hand touched and pulled it on over her head. The fabric was cool against her overheated skin, and her nipples got harder.

The shirt wasn't particularly big on her. One of the bigger downsides to being tall was that she would never look adorably tiny in men's clothes. It was a little baggy because of how men's clothes were cut, but the hem only went an inch past the waist-band of her panties once she'd taken off her pants.

She examined her appearance in the big mirror in the closet. Was it cute? Sexy? Lacey turned this way and that. Her ass was great, but her tits weren't exactly showstoppers. A boyfriend had once suggested she get implants.

Fuck it.

Lacey marched through Sam's room, scooped her phone off his bed, and went into his bathroom. The lighting was great. There was no way she normally looked this good. She rose up onto the balls of her feet so the curve of her ass would be visible over the counter, casually rested one arm on top of her head so the shirt rode up and exposed her hip, and took a mirror selfie.

LACEY

Not yet. I needed to borrow one of your shirts.

She sent the message, and then sent the picture. The wait for feedback was agonizing. Snakes mixed with the butterflies in her stomach until Sam's three little dots appeared. Then disappeared. Then appeared again.

SAM

Is that what you're wearing to sleep in my bed?

LACEY

Yes

Unless you have a problem with it

You could wear less

If you want

I've got great sheets

What am I supposed to take off?

She lifted the hem of his shirt up until her hand brushed the bottom of her boob, then she snapped a picture and sent it with the caption:

LACEY

This?

Quickly, she hooked her thumb into the waistband of her panties and tugged them down until they became dangerously close to exposing her and took another picture.

LACEY

Or this?

She paced while his dots did their appearing and disappearing act, her hands trembling. The last time she'd had this much adrenaline pumping through her body she'd just stepped off an amusement park drop tower.

Lacey almost dropped her phone when the screen changed from their text messages to the incoming call screen, and a second later, to Sam's face.

Sam was calling. Sam was *video* calling.

Her trembling thumb hit the accept button.

Sam was lying in bed, the light from his phone illuminating his face.

"Both is an option." His voice was deeper than normal, rumbly and a bit slower. Sleep heavy.

Lacey leaned against the bathroom counter, angling the camera so he could barely see her ass in the mirror. "You sound tired."

Sam smiled softly. "I am, but then you started sending me sexy pics, and now I'm not going to be able to sleep until I take care of the problem you caused."

"Mmm...what kind of problem did I cause? Is it a big problem?"

"You know exactly what kind of problem you caused."

God, she did. It was an *excellent* problem. And judging by the way Sam's bicep flexed in time with the beat of her heart, he was not ignoring the problem.

"Is there anything I can do to help?" she asked innocently, tracing the neckline of his shirt with the tip of her fingernail.

Sam moaned. "I thought you didn't want to do non-public displays of affection."

It was true. She'd said that. But lust had tangled her wants and needs into a knot that couldn't be untied, and the logical part of her brain had given up trying to keep her safe.

"I don't think it counts if we're not touching each other," she reasoned, sliding her free hand into the front of her panties. Her middle finger brushed her clit, and she shivered.

"It's your loophole," he told her, his breath catching.

"What are you doing with that hand?" Lacey asked.

"Wouldn't you like to know."

"I would, actually," she said, her own breath catching as she brought some of her own wetness up to lubricate her clit so she could play with it. "Let me see it, Daddy."

She saw any resolve Sam had evaporated like water in a desert.

"Hold on," he said, rolling onto his side. A low, warm light replaced the harsh blue of his phone screen. Sam resettled, and then the direction of his camera changed.

Lacey's mouth watered. Sam's cock was gorgeous. He wrapped his hand around the shaft and stroked it slowly, teasing both of them. A glistening drop of precum oozed from the head and Lacey licked her lips. She wanted it.

Sam groaned. "Fuck. You can't do that or I'm going to bust."

She'd forgotten her own camera was pointed at her face. Her cheeks were flushed, and her pupils had dilated.

"It just looks so good," she whined, changing her stance to give her a better angle to stroke her pussy.

"Oh yeah?" Sam's strokes got faster. "What's your hand doing? And don't deny it because I can see your arm."

And she'd forgotten about the mirror behind her.

"I think you know what I'm doing," she said.

"Show me."

She slowly took her hand out of her panties, wiggling her fingers in a mock hello in the mirror, and then brought her middle and index finger in front of her face. They were obviously wet. Lacey opened her mouth, stuck them inside, and sucked. The salt from her finger mixed with her own sweet, musky taste, and she moaned.

Sam did too.

"You like how you taste?" he asked breathlessly, his fist rapidly pumping his shaft.

"Mm-hmm," Lacey hummed. "Come on, Daddy. You're doing such a good job. Come for me."

Sam groaned, the movement of his hand supersonic. Then his abs contracted and several spurts of cum shot onto his stomach. His hand slowed and his grip loosened until he was idly stroking himself again. Then the camera flipped, and his face filled her screen.

"Fuck," he panted. "What am I going to do with you?"

"I don't know," Lacey said with a smug grin, "but you're going to clean yourself up and go to bed. And I'm going to get my vibrator, go somewhere Daisy can't follow me, and come until I can't walk right thinking about what you just did."

"You brought your vibrator to my house?"

"The walls are very thin at home. I'm pent-up, Sam."

He grinned devilishly. "You're going to have to stay pent-up a few more days. You're not allowed to come until I get home and can watch."

"What?"

"I want to watch you like you watched me. Fair is fair."

"Why do I have to wait until you get home? We have phones."

"Because I want to be there. I want to see everything, hear everything, smell everything. I want to watch you make yourself come in my bed, on my sheets, in my shirt."

"But—"

"You said it didn't count if we weren't touching each other."

She had said that. Horny Lacey should not be given the keys and allowed to steer the car. And Horny Lacey must have still been in control because she said, "Okay. But no touching. Because touching leads to fucking."

Sam chuckled. "Whatever you say. Goodnight, Lacey."

"Goodnight, Sam."

Sam hung up, and Lacey's screen returned to their texts. That had gotten wildly out of hand with no effort at all. Zero to one hundred and sixty in a few messages.

And she was going to let him watch her masturbate soon.

Anticipation sizzled in her belly. She could take the edge off, ignore his instructions, and do what she'd been planning to do all along...but she wouldn't. Lacey liked this little game.

CHAPTER THIRTEEN

SAM TUGGED on the brim of his baseball hat, pulling it lower over his face while he waited at an intersection for traffic to pass.

Good ol' Detroit Tigers shielding him from any roaming paparazzi.

His sunglasses helped. And so did his jacket, hiding his signature tattoos.

It was a beautiful, brisk, sunny day in New York City. A horn blared down the street, and the angry answering honk came a moment later.

Sam sipped his coffee and sighed. He loved New York.

Traffic thinned, and he walked across the street, arriving at the opposite corner as the walk sign turned from red to white.

Treacherous Studios was a fifteen-minute walk from his apartment. He could have hired a car to drive him from his apartment to the studio, but he loved walking in the city. Most of the time New Yorkers were too busy getting from Point A to Point B to glance twice at him.

But the sights, sounds, and smells were only fun for about two weeks. Then all of the extra-sensory input became grating and he needed a break. When he came back, it was fresh and fun again.

He preferred the pace of Crane Cove. The quiet streets. The fresh air that always seemed to smell faintly of rain. How people treated him like a person. The coffee—the cup in his hand was not Stardust, that was for sure. Sybil had ruined him forever. He tossed the half-full cup in a trash can before he entered Treacherous.

"Oh my god, he's on time!" Jenna Fox shouted gleefully from the black leather couch in Studio B.

"Only for you, J," Sam said, dropping onto the couch next to her and accepting her enthusiastic hug.

There was something to be said for friends who'd been around for a long time. Sam had met Jenna when they were both teenagers fumbling around in the music business, two tiny fish in a pond full of sharks. Jenna had been there for the spectacular rise and epic crash of his one significant romantic relationship. She'd never abandoned him, even in his most awful moments when he could barely stand to be around himself.

"I can't believe you agreed to do this," she said, resting her head on the back of the couch. "I would've thought a movie soundtrack would be beneath you, oh great artiste."

Sam chuckled. "I'm trying to beat Peter to the EGOT. I think he'll keel over if I get an Oscar before he does."

"Are you really?"

"No, but it would be fun."

Jenna studied his face for a second, a small frown almost appearing in her forehead.

"You look tired. When did you get in?"

"Um, I got to my apartment at about three this morning," Sam said, taking off his hat to run his hand through his hair, then he put it back on. "Had a hard time getting to sleep."

That wasn't exactly true. After he'd cleaned the cum off his belly, he'd slept like a rock. Better than a rock, if that was possible. It wasn't until he'd woken up an hour ago that he'd had the time and presence of mind to start overthinking what had happened between him and Lacey on the phone. Back in Crane Cove, he'd been distancing himself a little from her because spending time with her blurred the lines between fiction and reality. He'd tempted fate too much by bringing her lunch all week. If his alarm to leave for his flight hadn't gone off when it did, he wasn't sure what he would've done next.

Jenna wrinkled her nose. "Ew. Why did you get in at three?"

"I got a dog," Sam said.

Jenna gasped and backhanded his chest. "Shut up! No, you didn't."

"I really did." Sam dug his phone out of his pocket and opened up his photo gallery. The last dozen pictures he'd taken had been all Daisy. "Her name is Daisy. She's a rescue."

"Oh my fucking god, she's adorable." Jenna snatched his phone from his hand. "Why didn't you bring her? I want to kiss that face."

"Because I just got her and thought this might be overwhelming," Sam said, reaching for his phone, which Jenna held out of his easy reach.

"What made you want to get a dog? I didn't even know you were thinking about it." Jenna swiped through his photos, making happy noises with each new photo.

"I wasn't. I kind of adopted her as a favor to a, um, friend."

Jenna's head snapped up. "You hesitated on 'friend.' What's going on?"

And that was the problem with long-term friends. They knew him too well. Jenna would probably know if he coughed wrong.

"Nothing is going on," Sam said, trying to grab his phone

again but Jenna was more determined to keep it from him. "Give me back my phone, Jenna."

"Not until you tell me what's going on. You're hiding something. What is it? Are you seeing someone? Oh my god, you're seeing someone!"

How the fuck did she do that? How could she look at him and *know*?

"It's new," he deflected.

"It had better be new if this is the first I'm hearing about it. Tell me everything, or I'll keep going through your photos."

Sometimes it was like they were still seventeen hanging out on a tour bus.

"There isn't much to tell—Jenna!"

Jenna's eyes widened. "Is this her?" She turned his phone around to show him a sneaky picture he'd taken of Lacey and Daisy the day they'd brought her home. Lacey was sitting cross-legged on the floor, holding Daisy like a toddler that didn't realize they were too big to still be rocked to sleep. "Because if this isn't her, you have some explaining to do. One, why do you have a sweet photo like this of someone who isn't your partner, and two, what are you doing not dating her because yowza."

"Her name is Lacey," Sam said, taking advantage of Jenna holding his phone out to snatch it back.

"That answered none of my questions."

"Yes, it's her." Sam shoved his phone back in his pocket. He liked to think it was safe there, but he never knew with Jenna.

"Has she met the boys?"

Sam frowned. "Sort of? She's definitely met Graham, I think she's met Jordy once and—wait, aren't we supposed to be working? Doesn't this place charge by the minute?"

"You're not paying for it."

"Your work ethic is astounding."

"I haven't seen Grim yet, so this isn't even my fault," Jenna said with a wave of her hand.

Julius Grimbe was their producer for the song. Sam and Jenna had both worked with him before, and it wasn't like him to be late. On the rare occasions Sam was early, Grim had always been there waiting for him.

"Yeah, but we could still get ready. Some of us have dogs waiting on us."

"And girlfriends," Jenna teased.

"How's Houston?" Sam asked pointedly. Houston Walker was an oil heir who fancied himself a DJ. He was also Jenna's latest attempt at finding The One.

Jenna shrugged. "I think he's going to propose. Or dump me. The two things are shockingly similar."

"You don't sound excited."

"I will be. It's just hard right now. We're both traveling for work. I haven't actually seen him in like a month, and sometimes he still tells me I'm being clingy."

"You know that's not normal, right?"

"Sam, when you get serious about Lacey, you can lecture me on relationships, okay?" Jenna fished her phone out of the couch cushions. "I'm going to text Grim and see where he is."

The studio door opened, and Grim came in, shadowed by his recording engineer.

"I know, I'm sorry. I was here early and got pulled into a session next door by Big Bruce, and then he wouldn't let me leave." Grim dropped into his chair. For someone everyone called Grim, he dressed like a psychedelic grandpa. Burnt orange shirt under a green and yellow daisy square sweater vest. His style was borderline atrocious, but he was a musical genius.

"Big Bruce Montgomery?" Jenna asked, looking at Sam for confirmation, like he knew.

"Is there another Big Bruce?" Grim asked, polishing his glasses.

There wasn't another Big Bruce. Not that Sam knew of. Big Bruce managed some big names and had a lot of pull in the industry.

"He's got a new guy he's pushing pretty hard. Jace Kieffer. Big Bruce shoehorned him onto this project." Grim put his glasses on. "He's a little full of himself for someone who has one radio hit."

"I miss having that kind of confidence," Sam said, taking out his phone to silence it fully. There was a text message from Lacey. He casually shifted his position on the couch so his phone was facing away from Jenna before opening the message.

It was a picture of Lacey and Daisy in his bed, Lacey's face mostly hidden by Daisy's head.

LACEY

You didn't warn me that someone is a bed hog.

Sam smiled.

SAM

I'm considering moving out to her dog bed. I'd have more space.

LACEY

It's her world. We're just living in it.

SAM GOT BACK to his apartment at nine that night. It had been a long, productive day, but no one felt quite finished with the song, so they were going to work on it on Saturday too.

Exhaustion hung over him like a fog. Jenna had teased him about being an old man because he wanted to eat dinner right after they wrapped up at seven, when a lot of the people they knew wouldn't even entertain the idea of dinner before nine. New York might be the city that never sleeps, but Sam wanted to be in his bed before the next calendar day.

He dropped his Tigers hat on the console by the door, then his wallet. He ran his hands through his hair, trying to undo a day's worth of hat hair with his fingers. The apartment was dark, or as dark as it could be with the city lights coming in through the large, arched windows, as Sam went to the kitchen to make himself a cup of tea.

He filled the kettle and put it on the stove to boil, then boosted himself up on the counter to wait.

What did Lacey find so appealing about sitting on his counters?

While he waited, Sam sorted through his unread texts. One from Graham asking about Thanksgiving again. An entire series from Peter about absolutely nothing important, but it felt nice to be included in the train of thought. Jordy had sent him a few funny videos.

Lacey should be back at his house by now, feeding Daisy and cooking her own dinner.

Did she really come home after a long day of work to no missed messages? No one curious about her day? It broke his heart when she'd said she didn't have any friends to text. How could a rain cloud like him have friends and that ball of sunshine have none? It wasn't right.

Sam opened Jordy's text thread.

SAM

Not weird, but could I have Annie's number?

Jordy's face lit up his screen thirty seconds later.

"Hey," Sam said, hopping off the counter then putting his phone on speaker.

"Why do you want my girlfriend's number?" Jordy asked with a hefty dose of wary skepticism.

"It's not for me. It's for Lacey," Sam explained, grabbing a lemon from the bowl on the counter. "I figured since Annie screamed 'I love her,' maybe they might want to be friends."

There was no way that if Annie already had her phone number Lacey would be saying no one ever texted her.

"That's not a bad idea, actually. I think Annie needs a friend outside of me and the people she works with— Yes, I am talking about you. Sam wants to give Lacey your number."

Sam listened to their muffled side conversation while he sliced lemon for his tea.

"Chicken parm sounds great. Takeout sounds great, too... No, whatever you want is fine, sweetheart..."

"Jordan." Sam snapped his fingers. "What's the verdict?"

"Sorry. It's dinner time, and no one wants to cook."

"You can't cook," Sam reminded him.

"I signed myself up for a class once I get out of my sling," Jordy told him. "I'm finally going to learn now that I have some free time."

"No way." Sam smiled. "You got a girlfriend, *and* you're going to learn how to cook. Will the wonders never cease?"

"Ha ha ha," Jordy deadpanned. "Be nice or I won't give you Annie's number."

"I have alternate avenues," Sam reminded him. "Graham could get it from Eloise."

"Damn."

"Speaking of Graham, did you and Annie decide if you're coming to Crane Cove for Thanksgiving? I think Graham is getting antsy."

Jordy chuckled. "Graham passed antsy two weeks ago. I think he's in mild panic. Yeah, we're going. We were looking at flights before you called."

The kettle on the stove screamed, and Sam turned off the burner.

"Should I bring Lacey? Or ask her? She might have plans already..." He took a mug out of the cupboard, then got out his glass jar of rooibos tea and his metal basket infuser.

"Do you want to bring her?" Jordy asked.

Sam spooned tea leaves into his infuser, put it in his mug, then poured the steaming water into the cup. His friends were his safe place, and he guarded that safety fiercely. Even wonderful people like Eloise and Annie had felt like intruders at first. If this were a real relationship, would he be ready to let Lacey into that sacred space?

"I wanted you to tell me, not make me think about it."

"Mr. Control Freak doesn't want to make his own decisions? Is this one of those situations where you say something weird so I know you've been kidnapped?"

Sam rolled his eyes. "No. I think I'm overthinking it."

"That definitely sounds like you. Does Lacey *want* to come join our chaos?"

"She is chaos." Sam smiled softly. "I haven't asked her yet. I didn't want to bring it up if it was a terrible idea."

"Well, start there," Jordy said. "Maybe she has plans."

"When did you get so smart?"

"When I had a PhD move in with me." Jordy chuckled. "I love you, but I need to help Annie decide what we're getting for dinner because she has four different menus out and she's started scrolling her phone."

"Send me her number."

"Will do. Love you."

"Love you too."

Annie's phone number appeared a moment later, and Sam copy and pasted it into his text thread with Lacey.

SAM

This is Annie's phone number if you want someone to text.

He removed the basket from his mug and set it in the sink, then squeezed a lemon wedge into his tea. His phone buzzed on the counter.

LACEY

Sorry if I was bothering you today.

"Oh fuck," Sam groaned. Stupid fucking texts.

He hit the phone icon next to Lacey's name and listened to it ring.

"What?" Lacey said flatly.

"I didn't mean it like that," he said, pacing his kitchen in a short circuit.

"Sam, you're not my boyfriend, you don't have to spare my feelings, okay?"

"I'm not—" He growled in frustration. "It made me sad when you said you don't have anyone to talk to. You like Annie. Annie likes you. I would've given Annie *your* number, but I didn't know how comfortable you felt lying to her about us. Or if you even actually wanted to be her friend."

"Oh." Lacey's voice was small and contrite. "Um, thank you."

"You're welcome," Sam said.

"It made you sad that I'm a lonely loser?"

"Yes, it did." Sam picked up his mug and carried it to his bedroom. "And you're not a loser."

"The evidence would suggest otherwise," she joked hollowly. She sighed. "Do you ever have days where you're sad for no reason?"

"I find it easier to count the days when I'm not sad. You're having a rough day?"

"Kind of," Lacey admitted. "I think the best way to describe it is that I feel the way the sky looks."

"Doom, gloom, and probably going to rain?"

"Exactly."

"Do you want to talk about it?" Sam asked, setting his mug on his nightstand.

"There isn't much to talk about," Lacey said, "and I'm actually a little worried I'm going to cry because it's starting to settle in that you did a really sweet thing by getting me Annie's number."

"Please don't cry, sunshine."

"Are you workshopping nicknames for me?" she teased with a watery laugh.

"It just kind of came out," he admitted. "Is sunshine worse than baby?"

"Oh, hell no. Baby is bottom-of-the-barrel lazy. Sunshine is acceptable."

"Oooh, acceptable. What a high level of merit I have reached." Sam undid his belt with one hand, then his pants. "Did you feed Daisy yet?"

"Right after we went potty when I got home from work—er, to your house."

"Did you eat yet?"

"The ziti is in the oven," Lacey said. "I followed the directions and...oh shit, I forgot to turn on the oven."

Sam laughed. "How do you forget to turn on the oven?"

"I came home, took the ziti out of the fridge, took Daisy's food out of the fridge, thought I started the oven, took her for a walk, put the ziti in the oven, fed her, and then you called."

"You didn't think it was weird that the oven wasn't hot?"

"That really should have been a clue." Sam could hear the

smile in her voice. "Did you have a good day at work—wait, shouldn't you be resting your vocal cords?"

"If I need to rest my voice after one day of recording one song that I'm not even the lead vocal on, my voice is in serious trouble." He held the phone between his shoulder and his ear so he could take off his pants. "And I have tea."

"Well, if you have *tea*." The oven beeped on her end of the call. "So did you have a good day at work?"

"It's always nice working with friends," Sam answered honestly, kicking his pants off. "Jenna, Grim, and I got dinner when we were done, but they both gave me shit about eating during New York early bird time."

"You know someone named Grim? They sound like a Batman villain."

"Grim might take that as a compliment," Sam chuckled, sitting on his bed to take off his socks. "I wish I'd taken a picture of his outfit today. I think you'd enjoy it."

"So who exactly are Jenna and Grim to this whole song process?"

"Grim is our producer, and Jenna is Jenna Fox."

The silence lasted so long he thought he'd lost her.

"Lacey? Are you still there?"

"I'm sorry. I sometimes forget you're fucking famous. *Jenna Fox.*" Lacey's voice rose an octave. "You spent the entire day with Jenna *fucking* Fox. Do you know how much I love her?"

"Taking into consideration the pitch of your voice, I'm going to guess a lot." Sam put his phone on the mattress long enough to pull his shirt off over his head. "We're friends. Didn't you know that?"

"I mean, I guess I knew that. Vaguely. Believe it or not, I don't have posters of you on my walls anymore."

Sam flopped back against his pillows, laying on top of his

comforter in just his boxer briefs. "Anymore? You had posters of me?"

"I was once a reasonably straight teenage girl living in America. Yes, Sam, I had a poster of you on my wall. I think I got it out of a magazine."

Sam wondered what a teenage Lacey had been like. When had she gotten tall? Did she ever have braces? When did she start experimenting with dyeing her hair? Was she one of those awkward ducklings that had blossomed into a swan, or had she always been a head-turner?

Her voice called him back to the present. "Is Grim Julius Grimbe, by any chance?"

"Yeah, why?"

"Oh, nothing. I had an ex who would have committed actual murder to work with him. Now that I can put a face to the name, yes, Grim would make a great hipster Batman villain."

"Did you look Grim up?"

"No. My ex had a vision board, and Grim was on there."

It chafed that Lacey spared even a single thought for an ex of hers. In the next moment, he knew he was being ridiculous, because he'd spent years exorcizing the ghost of his ex. Hell, he'd done more than mention her in passing; he'd written an album trying to sort out what had happened.

"What's Daisy up to?" Sam asked, needing to change the subject even if he'd decided to be a sensible adult that didn't get jealous.

"She's in her dog bed. I put one of your shirts in there. She really does miss her daddy."

"She's a good girl," Sam said. A devilish thought popped into his head. "Have you been a good girl?"

"What happens if I haven't been a good girl?" Lacey purred. Sam's cock throbbed in response.

"You're not going to come until I get home, so it doesn't matter. Right?"

She hummed. "Mmm...might be worth it, though."

"How about this," Sam said, stroking his hardening cock through his underwear with the tips of his fingers. "If you're good, I'll bring you a treat. If you're bad, I'm going to punish you."

Lacey made a small noise, almost like a moan.

"Are you touching yourself?" Sam asked, squeezing his shaft through the thin material.

"You only said that I couldn't come." Lacey's voice was breathy. "You never said anything about touching."

"What are you thinking about?"

"Mmm...how you slapped my ass and choked me in Barcelona."

Sam slid his hand into his underwear and pulled out his cock. "Is that a punishment or a reward?"

"Both?" Lacey's voice caught on the end of the word.

"Are you touching your pussy in my kitchen?"

"N-no," she said, and another tiny moan slipped out. "I'm in your bed now."

It was Sam's turn to moan. This was torture. "Let me see you."

"Nuh-uh. Not unless you let me...come."

"That's not up for negotiation," he said as sternly as he could manage with a fist around his cock.

Lacey whined.

"I will make it worth your while, sunshine. I promise."

Her face filled his screen, and he hit accept on the video call.

"This had better be good," she told him.

Sam had no plan. He hadn't expected that to work. He just

wanted to see her with her hair on his pillow and her skin touching his sheets. It surpassed expectations.

"Did you like watching me come last night?" he asked, and Lacey bit her lip and nodded. "I'm going to like watching you come when I get home. I think it's going to be in my bed. Where do you want me to sit while you make yourself come?"

Her wet fingers came into the frame, and Sam noted the way her chest was moving faster.

"I was getting too close," she confessed, cheeks flushed. "I think I want you on the bed."

"I like that."

Lacey looked thoughtful. "I know what I want if I'm a good girl."

"And what's that?"

"I want you on the bed, but I want your hands to be bound so you can't touch yourself while I get off."

It was devious and cruel, and Sam was so fucking hard imagining it that he could have drilled concrete with his cock.

"And if you're a bad girl?"

"You get to slap my ass until I come."

It was the kind of win-win situation Sam craved and dreaded. He didn't know how he wanted this to play out anymore.

"Now turn your camera around so I can watch you come," Lacey commanded.

CHAPTER FOURTEEN

LACEY WOKE Saturday morning with her nerves simmering and a dog butt in her face.

Both were Sam's fault.

She rolled out of bed, careful not to wake Daisy, who lifted her head anyway.

"I just need a shower," she told the dog. Daisy rested her chin on her paws, watching Lacey head to the bathroom like she didn't believe her.

She talked to a dog now. She really did need a friend. Sam had sent her Annie's contact info, but Lacey couldn't work up the guts to send that first text. She was better in person. In person, Lacey didn't think, she just did. Like how she'd struck up a conversation with Annie at Queens because Annie had looked as miserable as she felt. The words had tumbled out with ease, but writing them down meant she had to think about them, and that was the death of her personality.

Sam's shower was glorious. The water got hot quickly, the pressure actually cleaned her hair, and Sam had fantastic products. Her hair, which she'd stopped coloring over the summer because a) she couldn't responsibly fit dye into her budget, and

b) her hair needed a damn break, hadn't felt this silky smooth in years. Lacey would've done unspeakable things for good hair products.

She wanted to do unspeakable things to Sam. Or have him do unspeakable things to her. Either way was fine. She wasn't picky. The indifference was what made their arrangement so delicious. Even if she lost, she won. But Lacey wasn't going to lose. Sam would never know if she'd made herself come or not, but she would wait for him to get home, even if she lied when he got there.

When Lacey got out of the shower, Daisy was waiting for her. As she dried herself off, the dog circled her, like she was urging Lacey to go faster. It had to be breakfast time. There was no greater clock than a dog's stomach.

Lacey took Sam's soft gray robe off the hook and bundled herself up. She would miss the robe. It had a white mono-grammed S on the right breast, and she wondered if he'd done that himself or if he'd gotten it as a gift.

Daisy led the way into the kitchen, and once her majesty had been fed, Lacey reheated some of the fantastic frittata Sam had left for her. Yup, she'd miss the food too. Leo was a phenom-enal cook, but Sam's food didn't come with a side of self-imposed guilt that she wasn't doing enough to pull her weight.

Lacey looked around the house. What was she going to do until Sam got home? He hadn't specified when, just that he would be headed back sometime that day.

She had no classes to teach. No errands to run—at least not anything that felt mission critical enough to justify driving into town and back. She would take Daisy on her morning walk, but then what?

She didn't have a book to read, and neither did Sam. His only hobbies seemed to be knitting and cooking. She'd found his yarn stash when she was looking for a book or a puzzle. That room had produced a lot of naked sheep.

Daisy walked to the front door, which was Lacey's cue to get dressed.

"I'm coming, I'm coming."

THE AIR WAS crisp and cold, and the ground was damp from overnight rain. A fine mist hung in the air as Lacey and Daisy picked their way through the woods around Sam's house.

Well, Lacey picked her steps. Daisy charged forward, then ran back, then charged forward, then ran back, over and over again. If she didn't have such good recall, Lacey never would have let her off leash, but the dog loved to run outside, even if it meant she'd be picking pine needles and twigs out of her coat later.

Lacey zipped Sam's sweatshirt up to her chin to fight the chill in the air. Overhead, birds chirped in the trees, and she craned her neck to see them. Little brown balls of feathers jumped and fluttered between branches.

The distinctive tapping of a woodpecker turned her head. She took out her phone, zoomed in, and took a picture of the black, white, and red bird. Then, she sent the photo to Annie. It was the best segue she was ever going to get.

LACEY

> Which bird looks like Woody the Woodpecker?
> I want to sound smart.

> This is Lacey, by the way. I don't know if you
> remember me.

ANNIE

> Of course I remember you! Hi!

> That is a white-headed woodpecker. Woody is
> a pileated woodpecker.

Now what did she say? She only knew the really popular birds: swans, bald eagles, hummingbirds, peacocks, Canadian geese, seagulls, flamingos....those kinds of birds.

ANNIE

> More fun cartoon facts: the Road Runner is a
> member of the cuckoo family. Like the clock.
> There's a Wile E. Coyote joke in there
> somewhere, but I don't know what it is.

Lacey grinned, looked up to check on Daisy, then typed,

LACEY

> So how have you been? How's LA? How's your
> member of the Holy Trinity of Fuckboys?

ANNIE

> I'm great. LA is finally cooling off to an
> acceptable temperature. Jordy is wonderful.

> I thought you weren't dating musicians
> anymore. How'd you and Sam end up
> together?

Lacey groaned. She'd forgotten that she'd told Annie that she'd sworn off musicians and Sam was definitely a Musician, capital M.

LACEY

> He's not pre-successful and hasn't picked up a
> guitar and sung at me yet. Note the distinction.
> Not To, but At. Plus he cooks

ANNIE

> Very good cook. I'm excited for Thanksgiving.
> Are you coming?

Thanksgiving? Was she supposed to be doing something on Thanksgiving? Her current plans were to watch the Macy's parade in her sweatpants and mourn what could've been with the Rockettes, all while holding a gallon of Tillamook strawberry ice cream.

LACEY

I haven't made any plans yet.

ANNIE

I hope you can come. Eloise's friends are so nice, but I sometimes feel like the 13th donut in a dozen.

But everyone loves an extra donut

That's us. The extra donuts.

Lacey stared at her phone. Annie thought she was an extra donut. An unexpected, happy addition.

LACEY

We should get T-shirts.

ANNIE

Ask Sam where he got the guys' jackets from

What jackets?

You haven't seen the jackets?!

SAM PARKED in his garage shortly after sunset. The nice part about traveling from east to west was that a good chunk of the long travel day was eaten up by the time zone changes. It was nothing short of miraculous.

Lacey's car was still in the driveway. Even after the last two nights, he wasn't sure if she'd be there when he got home. He'd half expected her to bolt again.

Sam had been reliving bits and pieces of their night in Barcelona over the last few days. It was impossible to do that without also remembering that he'd come back from his post-sex shower to an empty bed. Lacey had left without a word or a note. So he'd been sitting with an anxious pit in his stomach all day, unsure if he'd pushed too far with their calls.

Hell, he'd sent her one text all day and that was to say he was headed to the airport because he was scared he'd run her off by being eager.

When had he become this person? Sam had had plenty of casual sex. Loads of it. It didn't affect him. There was always someone else, so no need to stress. But he'd pushed through the rest of the recording that morning, then got in a car and went directly to the airport. Why? Because he was dying to know if Lacey had been a good girl or a bad girl.

Sam grabbed his suitcase from the trunk and went inside. The house was quiet for a second, then the scrabble of nails on wood echoed down the hall. Daisy sprinted toward him, barreling into his legs, her entire body quivering with excitement.

"Oh, hello," Sam cooed, sitting down on the floor to accept all of her love. Daisy climbed into his lap and licked his face and hands with enthusiasm. "Okay, okay. That's enough, thank you."

He listened for the sound of footsteps, but didn't hear any. It wasn't that late, so Lacey shouldn't be asleep. And her car was still there so she hadn't left. Where was she?

"Lacey?" he called, dragging his suitcase down the hall toward his room.

No answer. Maybe she was downstairs watching a movie?

The door to his room was open a crack.

"Lacey? You in here?" he called, and pushed the door the rest of the way open.

Lacey was laying on his bed on her side, wearing nothing but his silk Brunch Bros jacket. One of her long legs was drawn up in a figure-four, the other one extended, like a flamingo, and her upper body was propped up by her arm.

"I can't believe you never told me you had custom friend-ship jackets." She tsked her tongue in mock disapproval while she ran a fingertip down the teeth of the zipper. His eyes followed that finger all the way down to her hip.

Sam swallowed, his mouth dry and his brain void of any coherent thought.

Lacey rolled onto her stomach, stretching like a cat with her ass in the air. She wasn't actually naked. A delicate black thong barely covered anything. He wanted to break it like a string.

She drew herself up on her knees, and balanced near the edge of his bed. In the soft glow of the dimmed lights, her cheeks looked rosy. The jacket hung open, but still covered her breasts, which was disappointing yet tantalizing. She smiled invitingly at him.

"I was texting with Annie today," she said, playing with the zipper, "and she told me about the jackets. So I got a little nosey, checked your closet, and what did I find? Hmm?" Lacey's smile widened, but it was cracking at the edges.

Sam found enough brain power to move himself across the floor, dragging his suitcase behind him.

"You're wearing my clothes now?" he asked, parking his suitcase next to the bed. He reached out to touch her, but she swatted his hand away.

"Fake girlfriend perks," Lacey said. "And you're not supposed to touch, remember?"

He glared, but she knew it wasn't serious because she smiled at him again.

"Were you a good girl, sunshine?"

"I was a very, very"—she paused, and his heart found another gear he didn't know it had—"good girl."

His cock was so hard it threatened to pop the buttons on his fly. Not a great day to wear a button-fly instead of a zipper.

"I guess it's a good thing I brought home a present from New York then." Sam laid his suitcase on the ground and opened it. If there was one advantage to his desperately horny brain, it was the planning ability. When he'd been packing his bag, he'd thought to grab the leather handcuffs from the locked dresser in his apartment for this exact scenario.

Okay, not exact. Never in a million years would he have guessed that Lacey would go through his closet and pull out his Brunch Bros jacket. The only reason it was in Crane Cove was because he'd brought it for Graham's wedding and never took it back to Los Angeles.

Sam held up the cuffs, and Lacey gasped. They were custom black Italian leather with silver buckles for the wrists, and an adjustable chain to bind them together.

"Oh my god. You were serious." She grabbed them, turning them over in her hands, admiring the craftsmanship. "I don't think I've ever owned anything this nice."

"You like them?" She nodded, and internally Sam did a victory dance. He took them back and laid them on the bed next to her. "Maybe if you ask nicely, I'll use them on you."

There was a flash of interested hunger on her face.

"Not tonight, though," she said, and Sam wondered if there were going to be other nights. She looked him up and down in a slow, appraising, almost judgmental fashion. "Is that what you're going to wear?"

Sam looked down at his outfit. Dark jeans and a black cashmere sweater. Comfortable, yet stylish. "Is there something wrong with what I'm wearing?"

"You're a bit overdressed." Lacey put her hand on the cuffs, fingering the chain idly. "Strip."

Sam's knee-jerk reaction was to argue, put up some kind of fight, draw this out. But then Lacey spread her legs a little bit further apart, and he all but flung his sweater across the room.

"Going for speed over style?" she teased.

"I didn't see any dollar bills come out, so yes." He undid his belt with one hand and let it hang open. Lacey's fingers tightened around the chain. She liked that move. Sam tucked the knowledge away, in case he ever got to use it again.

He unbuttoned the top button of his jeans.

"Can you do that one-handed too?" Lacey asked, a little breathless.

"What? This?" Sam undid the next button with only his right hand.

Lacey bit her bottom lip and moaned. "I don't know why that's so fucking hot, but it is."

"If me unbuttoning my pants gets you going," Sam began, then nearly jumped out of his skin when something small but firm pressed against his ass. He looked over his shoulder, and there was Daisy, looking at him with soulful, how-dare-you-leave-me-waiting eyes.

Lacey laughed so hard she fell over on the bed.

"Daisy, girl, Daddy's busy," he told her. Daisy sat.

Sam sighed and pinched the bridge of his nose. There wasn't enough blood left in his brain to think. If he put her in the hall, she would scratch and whine at the door. That wasn't sexy. He couldn't put her outside because there wasn't a fence. If she wandered off because he was getting his rocks off, Sam would never forgive himself.

The sluggish synapses finally cobbled together a memory.

"Do you want to watch your show?"

Daisy's ears perked up.

"Come on, let's go watch your show," Sam said, hurrying to the door. Luckily, Daisy was directly on his heels.

By accident he'd discovered that Daisy liked to watch reruns of older shows. He'd been trying to work in his studio, and she hadn't been a fan of the door. Frustrated, Sam had taken her to the TV room to see if a snuggle would help. He'd scrolled through a lot of channels with nothing to watch and finally settled on a rerun of *Murder, She Wrote*. Daisy was enthralled. When he got up to use the bathroom, she didn't budge. So he went back into his studio. When he came out two hours later, she was watching an episode of *Matlock*.

Sam assumed that Daisy used to watch TV with her previous owner. If he could get her to stay downstairs for even one episode of something, he'd be happy.

"Do you want to watch *The Golden Girls*?" Sam asked and selected the channel.

Daisy made herself comfortable on the couch and didn't seem to notice when Sam crept out of the TV room.

Sam hurried back up the stairs, his pants sliding down his hips a little. If that little intermission had cooled Lacey's jets and she'd changed her mind, he was going to...still love that damn dog. But maybe he wouldn't try to make the dog biscuit recipe he'd found online.

Lacey was still on his bed, thankfully. But some of her femme fatale glow had dimmed. She smiled at him shyly, then watched the doorway after he'd entered.

"What did you do with her?"

Sam yanked open the rest of the buttons on his jeans, sexiness be damned. "I put the TV on for her."

That got Lacey's attention back on him. "You did what?"

"She likes rerun shows. So I put on *The Golden Girls*. Hopefully we'll be golden for about half an hour. Do you still want to do this?"

"Yes, I do."

Sam pushed his jeans down, then kicked them off his feet. "How did you see this going?"

Lacey lounged against the headboard, stroking the sheets by her hips. "I thought you could be up here," she began, "and you could have your wrists in front of you or above your head, whichever is more comfortable. The important part to me is that you can't touch your cock once I get started."

Sam played with the elastic waistband of his underwear. "Are these on or off?"

"Off, if you're comfortable with that. I want to see it." Lacey crawled down to the end of the bed. "Then I thought I could be somewhere down here, to remove the temptation for you to try and touch."

"It doesn't matter where you are, I'm going to be tempted to touch you," he pointed out, pushing his boxer briefs off his hips. The head of his cock got caught in the waistband, and when it popped free it smacked him in the stomach. Lacey licked her lips. "You're allowed to touch me, if you want."

She shook her head.

"If I start, I won't be able to stop."

"You say that like it's a bad thing."

Lacey stood firm. "We're not touching tonight." She unbuckled the handcuffs. "Do you want me to stop if you say stop, or do you want me to ignore you when you beg?"

"Ignore me," Sam said, settling into his spot at the head of the bed. "I'll say red if I need to end things quickly."

Lacey grinned, inching her way up the bed on her hands and knees. His jacket hung open, and he could see her boobs. Her dusky rose-colored nipples were hard and pointed. He wanted them in his mouth.

"We're playing Red Light Green Light?" she asked, sitting

back on her heels when she was level with his knees. "Put your hands where you want them."

Sam put his hands above his head. "I like Red Light Green Light. It's simple and direct."

"Do you have any red lights for this scene before we get into it?" Lacey asked, holding the handcuffs.

"Not that I can think of if we're not touching."

"Good. Now don't move."

Sam held still and held his breath as Lacey straddled his thighs, then rose up on her knees and leaned forward. His nose was level with her sternum, and if he moved his head forward even a little, he could kiss and lick her skin.

"Let me know when they're tight enough," she said, sliding the strap into the buckle on his left wrist, tightening the cuff.

"I like notch number four," he told her, and Lacey counted four of the holes, then slid the prong into the hole. She did the same on the other side.

"Are you sure this is the spot that you want?" Lacey asked, taking his wrists and holding them against the wall. Sam nodded. "Okay, then. You can't move your arms until I'm done."

Sam wasn't attached to anything. If he wanted to, he could have moved. But this was a game of willpower, though he wasn't sure what the prize was, he didn't want to lose.

Lacey smiled at him. "You look so pretty like this," she said.

Did someone hand her his manual? Or give her his password? Because she knew how to press all his buttons.

Deja vu swept over him, and a memory aligned perfectly with the present. He'd had this feeling that he'd known Lacey through the echoes of time back in Barcelona, and it surfaced again.

"You're always pretty."

She blushed, and rolled her eyes. "I'm still not touching you."

Lacey moved off his body, careful not to touch him, and grabbed a pillow before making herself comfortable closer to the end of his bed. She let her knees fall open, and Sam drank in the sight of her nearly naked body.

"That jacket looks better on you than it ever has on me," he told her, partly because it was true and partly because he wanted to see her blush again.

She didn't disappoint.

"Do you want me to keep it on?" Lacey rolled her shoulders and the silk dropped halfway down her biceps.

"That works," Sam said, then cleared his throat because that had come out in a pitch he hadn't spoken in since middle school.

"What about this?" Lacey's middle finger stroked the crotch of her panties.

"Off. Definitely off," he responded quickly.

"Close your eyes," she instructed.

Sam frowned. "What? No. Why?"

She sighed heavily. "Because I want to do something. Close your damn eyes, Sam."

That snappish tone shouldn't do such filthy things to his libido, but it did. Sam complied, closing his eyes even though he didn't want to miss a second of the show. The mattress shifted under his legs.

"Can I open my eyes?"

"Not yet." Lacey's voice was close.

"You're killing me, sunshine."

"Do you want me to stop?"

"No."

There was a smug chuckle, then Lacey instructed him to spread his legs, which he did. The mattress moved again, and he got the sense that she was between his legs. A cool, concentrated stream of air tickled his hard shaft, and Sam arched, his hips leaving the mattress.

"You're not supposed to move," Lacey reminded him sternly.

"That strictly had to do with my hands," he retorted. "Can I open my eyes now?"

"I suppose."

Lacey was laying on her stomach between his legs, her face about two inches from his cock and balls. She pursed her lips and blew again, making his cock throb. Precum leaked from the tip.

"It's a blow job," she explained, grinning.

Sam's head fell back, and he groaned. "You're a menace."

"I am." Lacey hung her thong on his cock like it was an ornament on a Christmas tree. "And you fucking love it."

He did.

Lacey pushed herself up onto her knees, still sitting between his legs, and cupped her breasts.

"You're being a much better boy than I thought you'd be," she said, and whimpered softly as she pinched her nipples.

"Did you think I was going to be a bad boy?"

Lacey nodded, biting her lip as she continued to fondle herself, pinching and rolling her nipples between her fingers, squeezing her perfect little breasts, doing almost all of the things he wanted to be doing to them.

"Mmm...I've been so fucking horny the last few days," Lacey confessed, one hand sliding down her belly toward her pussy. She stopped a few inches from the target. Sam waited for her to start again, and was about to ask what was wrong, when she leaned forward, putting her index and middle finger under his lips. "Spit."

He obliged. Careful not to lose his contribution to her little show, Lacey lay down, propping herself up on an elbow to keep an eye on him. She planted her feet on the bed on either side of his thighs, opening herself up to him. Her pussy was bare— either clean shaven or waxed—and Sam wanted to bury his face in there and drown.

"You like?"

"I want it," Sam admitted, on the verge of begging. Being handcuffed, unable to touch himself or her, had become one of his top ten worst ideas. And Sam had had some pretty fucking terrible ideas over the years.

"You can't have it," she reminded him. "You have to sit there and watch. Maybe—*maybe*—if you're a really good boy, I'll give you a treat when I'm satisfied."

Sam half groaned, half whimpered. The worst part about not being tethered to anything was that he couldn't struggle without compromising everything. There was no relief for the tension that was building in his body like a volcano. He had to remain still and take it.

Lacey was diabolical.

He should've tied her to the bed back in Spain so she couldn't disappear.

She started running her fingers in slow circles over her clit, using his spit as lube. Sam was torn between watching her hand to learn how she liked to be touched, and watching the pleasure build on her face. Her small sighs, moans, and whimpers were a symphony.

"What are you thinking about?" he asked softly.

"Mmm. A lot of things...like how fucking hot it was watching you stroke that gorgeous cock over the phone...mmm... and...you know..."

Barcelona.

Lacey's fingers picked up speed. Her eyes fell shut and her breathing changed, becoming rougher, and her chest flushed.

"There you go," he encouraged. "Come for me, sunshine."

Her muscles tensed, and her toes curled around his sheets. Lacey gasped, then groaned out a plaintive "Fuck." Tremors rolled across her body in waves, and she kept rubbing her clit, but slowly and gently, instead of desperate.

By degrees, the tension in Lacey's body ebbed like the tide leaving the shore, and then she relaxed, a dreamy grin on her glowing face.

"Holy shit. I need to edge myself for a few days more often," she sighed, her head falling to her shoulder like it was too heavy to hold up. "And you didn't move at all. Such a good boy."

With a small grunt of effort, Lacey pushed herself up onto her knees, once again straddling his hips without actually touching him. She put one hand on the wall just above his bound wrists, and the other disappeared between her spread thighs.

"Open your mouth," she instructed, and Sam did. Lacey placed the same two fingers she'd used to make herself come on his tongue, coated in her sweet, salty wetness. "Suck."

Sam obediently closed his mouth around her fingers and sucked them clean, swirling his tongue around her fingertips to be sure he didn't miss anything.

"Good boy," she purred and pulled her fingers out of his mouth with a *pop*.

Lacey undid the buckles on his handcuffs, and Sam's arms dropped to his sides. He rolled his shoulders to loosen them up and get the blood moving correctly again.

"How do you feel?" she asked, moving to sit next to him instead of nearly on him. Sam would've preferred fully on him, with his cock nestled snugly inside of her.

"Pent-up," he admitted, his cock throbbing. Precum had leaked from the tip and ran down the shaft like a candle that had been left burning too long. "And messy."

"You should take a shower," Lacey suggested.

"Are you going to join me?"

She grinned at him. "Not a chance."

SAM STEPPED out of his steamy shower, languid contentment marred by a nagging anxiety, and wrapped a towel around his waist.

History had a horrible habit of repeating itself. The last time he'd left Lacey alone in his bed to go shower, she'd left without a word before he was done. No note, no number.

Her thong was still on his bathroom sink where he'd left it, but that didn't mean anything. She could've left them as a souvenir. Lacey easily could've gotten dressed, grabbed her bag, and been most of the way back to her house by now.

This strange, twisting vulnerability surrounding sex was something Sam hadn't felt in more than a decade. Not since he was young and inexperienced. Normally he'd be strategizing how to get a bed partner out of his house as soon as possible, not avoiding going into his room to see if they were still there, *hoping* they were still there.

Sam towel-dried his hair. Then did his skincare routine. Then brushed his teeth. Procrastination and avoidance were a fine art he'd mastered years ago. But he couldn't stay in the bathroom indefinitely.

His bed was empty.

His bedroom was empty.

Lacey had hung his Brunch Bros silk bomber jacket back in his closet where it belonged.

Disappointment hollowed him out.

Sam found a pair of sweatpants and a T-shirt to go downstairs and collect Daisy. At least she would be happy to see him. That was his favorite part about having a dog so far.

Murder, She Wrote had to be over because Sam heard the telltale whistle of the intro music to *The Andy Griffith Show* before he even entered the TV room. Maybe he'd watch an episode with Daisy before bed. Let Sheriff Andy, Aunt Bee, Opie, and Barney Fife make him laugh.

Sam entered the darkened room, illuminated only by the black and white TV show, and went to the couch. Lacey was there, wearing one of his T-shirts and a pair of his sweatpants, spooning Daisy, one arm wrapped around the dog, her fingers buried in her fur. She gave him a sleepy smile.

"There you are. I was"—she yawned—"starting to think you'd had a slip and fall."

"You're still here?" Sam was shocked.

Lacey frowned, pushing herself up on her elbow. "Was I supposed to leave?"

He shook his head. "No, it's fine. I, um, just thought you had."

"I can go," she offered, fully sitting up and making Daisy cranky in the process. The dog grumbled, looking back at Lacey incredulously.

"No." He hoped he didn't sound desperate. "You can stay. If you want."

"I'm tired," Lacey admitted, relaxing back into the couch. "Thanks for not making me drive home."

Sam sat on the arm of the couch. "Are we watching Andy?"

"I was going to go to sleep..."

"Then let's go to bed," he said, grabbing the remote and turning off the TV. "You're tired. I'm tired. Daisy is tired."

The room was dark and silent.

"Sam? Are you still here?"

"Um, yeah. I'm waiting for you to come back upstairs with me."

"Oh. Okay."

Daisy's tags on her collar jingled as she got off the couch and trotted past Sam. Sam stood, and was about to ask Lacey if she was coming when her hand found his wrist.

"There you are." He could hear the nervous smile in her voice. "Is this a good idea?"

"We only have bad ideas, sunshine."

"True." Lacey wrapped her hand around his and led him to the door. "Good thing we've got Daisy to chaperone us."

"Better than a nun with a toothache," Sam agreed.

Daisy did chaperone them. She settled into the expanse of mattress between them, and when Sam woke up in the middle of the night, she was still there, even though he and Lacey gravitated toward each other in their sleep, squishing her between them like a shared stuffed animal.

For once, the return to sleep was swift and easy.

CHAPTER FIFTEEN

SOMETHING WAS WRONG WITH DAISY.

Sam sat in the fluorescent lit exam room that somehow smelled like antiseptic and wet dog with Daisy at his feet, her head resting on his foot, waiting for Dr. Chris McMahon to come back with the test results.

Daisy hadn't fought them for the blood draw and had laid perfectly still for the X-ray. Sam wasn't sure if that was a good sign or a bad sign. Now that he'd had some time to calm down—and had been thoroughly reassured by Dr. McMahon that Daisy's vitals were fine—he could see that he'd come flying in, guns blazing, and probably owed the staff a catered lunch.

Sunday Daisy had acted pretty normal. They'd taken several more walks than normal because she kept sitting by the front door, but he didn't think anything of it. On Monday, she kept compulsively searching the house like she'd lost something. Her appetite was off too. By Tuesday evening, Sam was very concerned. Daisy would lay by the door, but she didn't want to go out. Or, if she did go out, she came right back inside as soon as she'd done her business. She picked at her food, eating less than half of what she normally did, and had no interest in any of her toys.

And that morning, Wednesday, when she didn't eat her breakfast, Sam had lost his mind a little.

There was a soft knock at the door, and Dr. McMahon entered. Sam's face became hot because, one, Dr. Chris McMahon looked a little too good in his white coat and blue scrubs, and two, because he was very aware of the scene he'd caused and embarrassment had firmly settled in.

"Daisy's bloodwork and X-ray are back," the vet began, sitting on his stool, "and medically, there's nothing wrong with her."

Sam had been bracing himself for the worst, and hearing "nothing wrong" was like missing a step on a staircase.

"Nothing wrong? She's not eating, she's not playing, she doesn't want to go on walks. There has to be something wrong. What did you miss?"

"I don't think we missed anything," Dr. McMahon assured him. "Since her test results are clear, it sounds like she's maybe reacting to a change in her routine or surroundings. Dogs can experience depression and anxiety like people do, and Daisy is a very smart, sensitive girl. Do you think that could be what's happening?"

Sam opened his mouth to argue that that couldn't be right, but then shut it as he reviewed her symptoms again. He could have overlaid them with his own when he had a depressive episode and they would have matched exactly.

"Is she going to be okay?"

"I believe so," Dr. McMahon said in that avoidant way doctors had. "You mentioned you had a work trip. Given Daisy's history, it's possible she's reacting to that absence and will be fine again in a few days."

Sam nodded, only feeling marginally better that Daisy wasn't dying.

"Thank you," he said.

"Any time," the vet answered, "but maybe next time call the office before you come in."

LACEY DIDN'T FEEL WELL.

That wasn't true.

She felt like she'd been frozen, thawed in the pits of hell, and then run over by a steamroller. Simply not feeling well would have been a relief.

The flu had to be making its rounds already. Half the toddlers she taught were coughing or had snot faucets for noses. Who knew what germs the teens were bringing with them from school.

It had to be almost the end of the day, right?

Lacey looked at the clock.

Nowhere near the end of the day. It made her want to sit on the floor and cry, except the floor was hard and cold, and that made her want to cry too.

Maybe she should've stayed home. Gavin had offered, but the winter recital was sneaking up on them, and they needed time to prepare. The toddlers needed to look like they'd learned *something* since September, even if they were going to forget every bit of choreography once they hit the stage.

At least it was lunch time. Lacey was going to curl up in the office and take a nap.

The front door of the studio opened, and the oppressive dread of interacting with anyone sat in her chest like a concrete block.

Then she heard the familiar jingle of Daisy's collar as she shook the rain out of her coat.

The dog nearly ripped Sam's arm out of its socket when she saw her.

"Daisy!" Lacey cried, sitting on the floor and opening her arms wide. Since when did it take so much energy to smile?

Sam let go of the leash, and Daisy scrambled across the floor and into Lacey's lap, wiggling with glee. Lacey hugged her the best she could, squeezing her eyes shut as Daisy bathed her face in kisses.

"Yes, yes, yes, I missed you too," she laughed.

Sam cleared his throat, and Lacey looked at him. He stood in the doorway, seemingly conscious of the "no street shoes" rule in the studio, hands in the pockets of his black raincoat, looking a little sad, and Lacey's heart skipped.

She'd snuck out Sunday morning. She wasn't proud of it. But she'd woken up with only Daisy between them, Sam's hand over top of hers, and had been overwhelmed by the flutters. It was too much, too perfect, too hard to remember that this was all fake. So she'd slipped out of bed, grabbed her bag that was already by the front door from the night before, and bolted. Sam's clothes were buried in the bottom of a dresser drawer like contraband.

"Hey, stranger," she said, like she hadn't left without saying goodbye and then participated in a mutual radio silence.

"The vet thinks Daisy's depressed," Sam blurted.

Lacey blinked, confused. She pointed at the happy, panting dog in her lap. "This Daisy?"

Sam nodded grimly.

"I'm not a doctor of any kind, but she seems fine."

"This is the happiest she's been in days." He folded his arms and frowned.

Lacey rubbed Daisy's ears. "I think you scared Daddy, sweet girl."

"I think she missed you. Thought you'd abandoned her."

She looked at Sam again, and it made her stomach sour. This didn't feel like it was just about Daisy.

"Sam, I..."

The underside of her jaw went numb, and her mouth flooded with spit.

Nope. It wasn't Sam that had made her feel sick.

Lacey jumped up, dumping Daisy off her lap unceremoniously, and sprinted for the toilet. The first wave hit her as she entered the bathroom, and she heaved her breakfast into the porcelain bowl. Bile burned her throat, and tears filled her eyes as she continued to retch until there was nothing left, and even then she dry heaved several more times.

She flushed the toilet with a groan, slumped against the wall, and whimpered.

A sharp bark made her turn her head. She had an audience.

In the doorway, Sam held Daisy by her collar while the dog struggled to get loose.

"Well, this is embarrassing," she joked weakly, wiping her eyes with the heel of her hand.

"How long have you been sick?" Sam asked, though it sounded like the start of an exhausting interrogation.

"I didn't feel great last night, and I woke up feeling like hot, gooey garbage," Lacey admitted.

"Why didn't you stay home?"

"Because some of us have to work," she said, pushing herself to her feet unsteadily. "I need a paycheck. It's not that bad."

"You just threw up."

"Whoop-dee-doo."

Lacey turned on the sink and dipped her face under the

faucet, catching water in her mouth, swishing it around and spitting it out until the awful taste was dulled.

The front door opened, and Gavin's voice rang out. "I'm back and I brought lunch!"

In the mirror, Lacey saw Sam's eyes narrow and she didn't have the energy to catch him before he stormed out to intercept Gavin.

She groaned and trailed after him.

"Lacey's sick." It was more of an accusation than a statement.

"I know," Gavin said, placing the takeout bag on the front desk to take off his coat. "I told her to stay home this morning, and she wouldn't listen. You know how she is."

Sam opened his mouth, clearly ready to lay into her boss, but stopped, confusion replacing anger. "You told her to stay home?"

"Of course I did. I'm not a monster." Gavin reached down and scratched Daisy behind her ears. "Are you here to take her home?"

"No."

"Yes," Sam contradicted her loudly and firmly.

"I have classes," Lacey complained.

"That we can cancel," Gavin told her, shaking his head.

"But we've got so much work—"

"Today is not the day they're all going to magically understand, sugar. One missed class isn't the make or break right now." Gavin dug around in the bag and produced a wrapped sandwich. "Here. This is from Leo. Now go home."

Lacey's stomach churned as she accepted the sandwich. She couldn't even consider eating it. The idea of putting anything in her mouth made her want to vomit again.

"Where's your coat?" Sam asked.

"In the office," Lacey told him. She wrapped her arms

around herself. She wanted her coat. Not because she wanted to leave but because the chills were back.

Sam let himself into the back office and came back with her coat and her bag. Lacey didn't have the strength to argue with him *and* Gavin, so when he held up her coat, she slipped it on. And when Sam zipped her up like a little kid, she didn't argue because it felt nice to be taken care of for thirty seconds.

"Come on," he grumbled, shouldering her bag.

The warm, fuzzy feeling evaporated.

A frigid wind cut through Lacey's clothes when they stepped outside, an awful reminder that even though she felt cold, her skin was hot.

"Fuck," she cursed, trying to make herself as small as possible while still walking to her car.

"Almost there," Sam assured her, putting a hand on the small of her back to guide her to the parking lot.

"I need my keys," she told him, holding out her hand for her bag.

Sam ignored her and unlocked his car. He opened the back door for Daisy, and then the passenger door.

"I don't think you can drive from over there," she said.

"Get in."

"Why?"

"Because you look like shit and I'm not letting you drive." Sam pointed to the passenger seat. "Get in."

Lacey was too tired to argue. It was an unfortunate recurring theme. She dropped into Sam's front seat, relieved when he shut the door because it blocked out the wind. Daisy put her front paws on the center console and rested her chin on Lacey's shoulder.

"Sweet girl," she cooed.

Sam got in and started the car. Before she could think about it, he turned her seat warmer on high and turned up the heat.

Lacey's eyes were dry and her eyelids were heavy. It couldn't hurt to close her eyes for the short drive home, right?

THE SOUND of a garage door closing woke Lacey up.

That couldn't be right. Sam didn't have the garage door opener for her house. And even if he did, there was no way to park in the garage. It was full of Leo and Gavin's stuff.

"Hey, sleepy sunshine," Sam said softly, unbuckling his seatbelt. "We're here."

"Where are we?" Lacey mumbled, rubbing her eyes.

"Home—my house."

Lacey frowned. "Why didn't you take me to my house?"

"Because I can't take care of you there," he said like it was the most obvious thing in the world. "Come on. Let's get you tucked into bed."

"I think this counts as kidnapping," she told him, unbuckling and stepping out of the car. She felt like she'd been beaten with baseball bats.

"I don't think I need to tie you up until you're feeling better." Sam let Daisy out of the backseat and grabbed Lacey's bag. "You didn't even make it out of the parking spot before you fell asleep."

"Be nice to me. I'm sick."

"Ah, so you admit it." Sam let Daisy into the house first, waited for Lacey to shuffle past him, and then shut the door. "Do you want to steal some more clothes?"

Lacey mustered up as much innocence as she could. "Steal?"

"I'm missing some items." Sam put her bag on the kitchen counter and dug out her water bottle. "Go make yourself comfortable. I'll be in in five."

She wanted to argue. She wanted to tell him that she could

take care of herself. That she wanted to go home. But she didn't have the energy. And she didn't actually want to go home. Sam's bed was better, and her house didn't have Daisy. So Lacey trudged down the hall to his room and started taking off her clothes. How had she even gotten dressed this morning? It was so much effort.

Lacey had just slithered under the covers, having exchanged her tight clothing for Sam's comfy, baggier clothes, when he came in with her water bottle and a laptop.

"What's that for?" Lacey asked, melting into the pillows. Daisy jumped up on the bed and circled a few times before crumpling into a useless pile of bones on top of Lacey.

Sam held up her water bottle. "Hydration." He held up the laptop. "Entertainment."

"I don't think I have the energy to watch anything."

"It's for me," he said, sitting on the other side of the bed. "You're supposed to be sleeping."

Lacey smiled at him, then yawned. "Are you my nurse now?"

"Since you can't be trusted to make good choices, yes. Go to sleep."

"You're so grouchy," she teased, but closed her eyes obediently.

"That's because you and Daisy are having a contest to see who can stress me out more."

"Am I winning?"

"Go to sleep, sunshine."

IT WAS dark when Lacey woke up. Had she slept all night? Or had it only been a few hours?

She stretched, slowly becoming reacquainted with her

surroundings. Sam's house. Sam's room. Sam's bed. Sam's sheets. Sam's clothes. Surrounded by Sam. Lacey smiled. He should start a home goods line.

Where was he?

The bed was empty. No Sam, no Daisy. Lacey pushed herself into a sitting position. The door was closed, so maybe they'd left her to sleep. She still felt like hot garbage, but at least less gooey.

"Sam?" she called out, but her voice stuck in her throat and she sounded more like a frog.

No answer.

Maybe they'd gone on a walk.

Gingerly, Lacey peeled back the covers and got out of bed. She shivered. Was Sam's house always this cold? It had seemed perfectly comfy over the weekend. She went into his closet and grabbed a sweatshirt and a pair of socks. Then she went into his bathroom and put on his robe, too.

The house smelled good, like ginger, citrus, onion, and garlic. Despite the background nausea, her stomach growled. Even the flu wasn't a match for Sam's cooking.

Sam was seated at the kitchen island, headphones on, laptop open, and he was writing in a notebook. Daisy was laying by his stool, chewing on a toy like it had wronged her family. A pot of what she guessed was soup simmered on the stove. The same overwhelming contentment she'd felt Sunday morning welled back up inside her at the quaint domesticity of it all.

Lacey sat on the stool next to Sam's, hugging his robe tightly around her.

"Hey," she said softly, and laid her cheek on the cool granite counter.

Sam put down his pen and rubbed the back of her neck, working out a knot that had been there for months, and after a minute, took his headphones off with his free hand, hanging them around his neck.

"Still feel like crap?"

Lacey gave a tiny nod, then moaned as Sam's fantastic fingers dug into the knot in her neck. If she hadn't felt like death reheated in a gas station microwave, she probably could've been persuaded to show some gratitude.

"I'm making soup," he told her.

"It smells really good." Her eyes drifted shut.

"Are you hungry?"

"Yes and no. I'm scared I'm going to throw it up."

"From what I saw earlier, you're a champion puker."

"The compliment every girl wants to hear." Lacey smiled, and opened one eye. "Why are you doing this?"

Sam's cheeks flushed. "Massaging your neck?"

"Kidnapping me to make me sleep in your big comfy bed, wear your clothes, and feed me. You could've just dropped me off. Left me to rot in my own misery."

"You sound so very put upon," Sam said dryly, but she saw the twitch at the corners of his mouth.

"This is torture. I think it goes against the Geneva Convention." Lacey sighed, closing her eyes again. "Do you really think Daisy's depressed because I haven't been around for a few days?"

"It's the best explanation I can think of. She's been fine since we saw you."

"Mmm...were you sad I didn't come around for a few days? Is that why you kidnapped me?"

"You keep saying that word. I do not think it means what you think it means."

"Adorable, but avoidant. Did you miss me, Sam?"

The rain drummed against the windows and the wind whistled through the trees every fifteen seconds. Lacey knew because she counted three gusts before Sam responded.

"Of course I missed you, sunshine."

"Didn't feel like it when you didn't come see me for four days."

"You snuck out without saying goodbye," Sam reminded her, still massaging her neck. "How was I supposed to interpret that?"

"That I'm working on my audition for Cinderella?" Lacey joked half-heartedly. She put her hand over Sam's on the back of her neck. "I missed you too, Sam."

"Sometimes," Sam began quietly, "I get in my own head about people and how they might feel about me. And instead of doing something about it, like asking or reaching out, I hide. I thought maybe—"

Lacey didn't want to know what he'd thought, because there was every chance he was right and she'd have to admit it. Especially if that thought was that Saturday night meant more than some sexy fun.

"I get it," she interjected. With a monumental summoning of strength, she straightened her spine. "Can I try the soup?"

Sam nodded and closed his laptop before standing up and going to the cupboard for bowls.

"So, Graham's been up my ass, and not in a fun way, about Thanksgiving." He ladled soup into the bowls. "Did you want to go?"

"You know how I feel about free food." Lacey began to sweat, and shrugged off the robe. "The studio is closed that week because Gavin and Leo are visiting Gavin's mom in Atlanta, so I don't have any plans."

Sam handed her a bowl across the island with a frown on his face. "What were you going to do for Thanksgiving?"

Lacey shrugged and blew on a steaming spoonful. "Eat Kraft macaroni and cheese directly from the pot while watching *Planes, Trains, and Automobiles*."

That hadn't even been on her potential list of things to do, but it was worth saying to see Sam shudder.

CHAPTER SIXTEEN

SAM COULDN'T CONVINCE Lacey to skip work.

He'd tried, and failed, to tell her that she needed another day of rest. She was so stubborn, she reminded him of himself. Or Graham. Graham could really dig his heels in. But compared to Lacey, they were both wishy-washy flip-floppers.

She didn't look one hundred percent like herself, but she didn't have the same "please put me out of my misery" look she'd had on her face when she'd finished throwing up at the dance studio. So, Sam agreed to drive her into town because she threatened to walk if he didn't and he believed her.

Sam dropped her off at her house, fully prepared to sit in the car and wait for her to come back out, but Gavin's car was still in the driveway, so he let Lacey convince him that Gavin could give her a ride to work.

He worried, though.

So, Sam drove to Stardust, determined to kill an hour or two, then conveniently pop over to the dance studio with an iced coffee to see how Lacey was doing. If she'd overdone it and needed to go home, he could take her back into the woods, tuck her into his bed, and make her leftover soup while she watched

Derry Girls on his laptop. Apparently Annie had suggested it. It was funny, and Sam loved The Cranberries.

Stardust was humming with activity. The birdwatching group had settled themselves at the long table in the backroom for their post-hike debrief, and a mix of residents and tourists filled in the other seats. Why couldn't he be the only person that wanted to hang out on a Thursday morning?

Sam stood in line, tattooed hands in his pockets, thinking about refractory rhymes and how there wasn't a rhyme for poem, which seemed ironic, and he wondered if he could work that factoid into a song. While his brain tried to work that out in the background, he saw that Sybil had new flowers. This bouquet looked like fire; yellow to orange to red to burgundy flowers filled the vase. He didn't know the exact frequency, but Sam suspected Sybil was getting new flowers every few days. Who could be sending her flowers that often?

A not entirely polite tap on his shoulder toppled the house of cards that was his train of thought.

When he didn't turn around right away, the tapper said, "Where's your girlfriend?"

That got Sam's attention. He turned around. "Excuse you?"

"Lacey. Your girlfriend." "Girlfriend" was said with invisible air quotes that Sam did not appreciate. "Where is she?"

Sam stared at the guy. He couldn't place him, but he looked familiar. About Sam's height but with a stockier build, brown hair, brown eyes, and was wearing gym clothes. Overall, unremarkable. Maybe Sam could get a pass for forgetting who this guy was.

"Is that any of your business?" Sam asked coolly.

"Asking as a friend."

Sam wanted to say that Lacey didn't have any friends in town. Her words, not his. But he wanted to see where this was going more.

"I'm sorry, I don't think we've met."

"Mitch." He stuck out his hand. "Appleton."

The name clicked into place. Mitch Appleton. Lacey's ex-boyfriend. Even if he hadn't dated Lacey, Sam would've known him as "that asshole," which is how Sybil and Connor usually referred to him when they saw him in public.

Sam looked at Mitch's hand, but didn't take it.

"I don't shake hands," he lied. Sometimes playing into the aloof persona worked to his advantage. He didn't want to shake Mitch Appleton's hand.

Mitch put his hand down. "So where's Lacey?"

"Again, why is that any of your business?"

"Just, you know, people hear things. Like you and Lacey are dating. But no one ever sees you out together. Might seem a little...fishy." Mitch let the last word hang in the air for a moment. "If it's just sex, I get it. She's a good fuck. So what if she ran around and told everyone you're her boyfriend? Kind of worth it for the head, right?"

In his pockets, Sam's hands clenched into fists. He'd never hit anyone before. Never been in a fight. His hands had simply become too valuable for him to even consider throwing a punch. But he'd make an exception for Mitch Appleton. He could afford the bail, the fine, the lawyer, whatever it took to wipe the smug look off the bastard's face and soothe the boiling rage under his skin.

"Mitch!" Sybil barked from behind the espresso machine. "Get. Out."

"What did I do?" Mitch asked, but it was more like a whine.

"You're being a dick," she said. "If you're going to act like yourself, go somewhere else."

"I wasn't being a dick," he insisted. "I didn't do anything."

"One, I can hear you," Sybil said, putting a coffee on the bar next to the flowers. "Two, I've known you for almost twenty years. I can tell when you're being a dick. It starts with you opening your mouth. Now get out, or I'll take you out."

Mitch pursed his lips and his face grew red. For a second Sam thought he was going to blow his top, but he turned on his heel and marched out the door. He tried to slam it behind him, but the soft close Sybil had installed so the door wouldn't close too quickly on any of Crane Cove's more elderly population made it impossible.

Sybil caught Sam's eye and inclined her head. "Come here."

Sam did as he was told and got out of line, looking at her over top of the espresso machine.

"You good?" she asked, pouring steamed milk into espresso.

"Yeah, I'm good," Sam lied. The anger had drained but had left behind a burning guilt. Maybe Mitch had a point. Maybe he wasn't treating Lacey enough like a girlfriend for anyone to notice. Maybe he was making more problems for her while his problem got solved. He didn't like that.

"Don't listen to Mitch. He's got his dick permanently caught in his zipper."

"So you don't agree with him?"

Sybil hesitated, then shrugged. "I honestly wasn't sure if you two were still together. It's not like you've been out with Lacey since the Boo-wery. Not that you need to perform your relationship for people, but it has been mostly sneaking around."

"Sneaking around?"

"You've been seen coming in and out of the office at the dance studio. That's the only thing I've heard, and I hear a lot back here."

Sam frowned then mumbled, "We've done things."

Sybil pretended to gag as she put another coffee on the end of the bar. "Did you want a coffee or a tea?"

"Coffee, please." He needed the caffeine because apparently his brain wasn't working.

"Just one?" Sybil prompted.

"For now. I'm going to hang out for a little while and then take Lacey one at work."

Sybil gagged again, but started working on the next order.

"Any more advice?" Sam asked.

"Ignore Mitch. Everyone else does." She cleaned the steam wand. "If you're both happy, who cares what people are saying?"

Sam nodded and got back in line. Was Lacey happy? She'd asked him for a date the day they'd gotten Daisy, and that date hadn't exactly happened yet. What counted as a sufficient date? What would satisfy the rumor mill? What would make Lacey happy?

A table opened up as Sybil put his coffee on the end of the bar. It was next to the window, which wouldn't have been his first choice, but beggars couldn't be choosers. Sam sat with his back to the wall, tucked back as far as he could be and blew on his coffee before taking a sip.

Where could he take Lacey on a date?

If he wanted to make them both happy, he would cook her a nice dinner at his house and they could watch a movie with Daisy and then go to bed early. But their relationship was performance art so they needed an audience. Hiding in his house wasn't helping either of them.

What counted as nice, fun, and public?

It was Thursday. Barbecue night at Cranberry Brothers was nice and public. It was also crowded, which significantly cut down on the fun aspect.

Should he ask Lacey what she wanted to do? Or was that wrong?

Maybe Jordy would know.

SAM

Are you supposed to ask your girlfriend what she wants to do for a date or do you plan something on your own?

Fifteen agonizing minutes later, he got a reply.

JORDY

Nobody knows. It's a test. You're probably going to choose wrong.

I'm kidding. Kind of. In my experience, it's the thought that counts. So if you're going to ask for her opinion, have options so it shows that you put effort in.

SAM

This is confusing and hard

You're so cute when you care about something

Are you coming to Thanksgiving? Annie wants me to ask you because she said asking Lacey was awkward

We're coming to Thanksgiving. Lacey loves free food.

So you're the perfect match

Why don't you cook for her. Do the candles and shit.

I already cook for her. I need something different.

This is your problem. You set the bar too high.

Ask Graham. He might have some spots. Like wherever he takes Eloise.

The Tidewater. Sam had been there. It was a phenomenal restaurant, but Graham took Eloise there specifically because it was outside of Crane Cove. Sam also knew that Graham prebooked reservations for the entire year in advance and pretended like it was spontaneous.

SAM

You've been no help. Thank you.

JORDY

Love you too!

A string of heart emojis filled Sam's screen, and he rolled his eyes.

Peter would've been a great choice, but according to the calendar Peter's assistant Dempsey had created to help everyone keep track of Peter's schedule, Peter was in Australia on a press tour. It was the middle of the night in Australia. So that ruled Peter out.

"Is this seat taken?"

Sam looked up from his phone as Graham sat down across from him.

"What if that seat was taken?" Sam asked, putting his phone face down on the table.

Graham raised an eyebrow.

"Good point." Sam picked up his coffee cup. "Shouldn't you be at work?"

"I'm getting coffee for a management meeting," Graham explained. "What are you doing here this early?"

"I dropped Lacey off, and I'm trying to wait an appropriate amount of time before I surprise her at work with coffee."

Graham's posture perked up and he leaned forward. "Oh, so you *are* still together."

"Was that in question?"

"A little." Graham shrugged. "If you dropped her off, does that mean you're having sleepovers?"

Sam rolled his eyes. "I think you've been spending too much time with the twins."

"Maybe. *They* like to spend time with me." That was possibly a pointed dig. "Is Lacey coming to Thanksgiving?"

Sam nodded. "She is."

"Eloise is working on a seating chart," Graham told him. "She's making little place cards and everything."

"So not a sweatpants dinner?"

Graham ignored him. "Should be about thirteen people. Can you handle that, or should I start assigning dishes?"

"Is Connor coming?" Sam asked, menu calculations firing off in his brain.

"Yes. We're having a later dinner because the McMahons have their family meal in the afternoon."

Sam nodded. "If Connor can handle rolls and dessert, I can do everything else."

"You're a saint and a martyr," Graham said gratefully.

"No, I'm a glutton for punishment," Sam corrected and took a drink of his coffee. "I want to take Lacey on a date, but I don't know what to do around here."

"Why don't you cook for her?" Sam shook his head. "Okay... um...You could probably bribe the maître d' at the Tidewater for a reservation..." Sam shook his head again, and Graham frowned, pursing his lips while he thought. "I don't know. You could do dinner at the hotel? Amara will give you shit, but the food is great."

Amara, the chef at the hotel, would absolutely give him shit if he went on a date there. She'd probably plate his food in the shape of a dick, too. The meaner Amara was to you, the more she liked you, Sam had learned. She and Graham had deep respect for each other and had weekly screaming matches in the walk-in.

"I think I might suck at this," Sam admitted. Defeat loomed

on the horizon. He was never going to figure this out. He did nothing but let Lacey down. She deserved better.

"You're out of practice. I sucked at it too," Graham reassured him. "I probably still suck at it, but ninety percent of being in a relationship is showing up to do the work, even if it's imperfectly."

"But planning a date shouldn't be this hard," Sam complained.

"That's because you're putting too much pressure on it. You're going to have lots of dates, Sam. This one doesn't have to be the end all, be all, most perfect date in the history of dating."

"You're so wise now that you're a married man," Sam said dryly.

Graham shrugged and pushed back his chair as Sybil shouted for him to come get his drinks. "It's a marathon, not a sprint."

TWO HOURS LATER, Sam watched Lacey dance with toddlers through the picture window of the dance studio. She wore a big, fluffy pink tutu, fairy wings, a tiara, and what appeared to be his sweatpants, directing the chaos with a star-topped wand. The under-five set twirled around her like tiny tutu-ed tornadoes.

The song ended, and Lacey led her students in their stage bows, then they all lined up by the door for stickers. One by one, Lacey put a sticker on the back of one of their tiny hands, then sent them to their adult in the lobby. As soon as they'd all exited the studio, her posture deflated, like someone had pulled her plug.

Sam took that as his cue to go inside.

He held the door open for the exiting students, giving small smiles to the kids who said thank you, and ignoring any stares from their adults. He didn't want to take pictures or sign auto-graphs; he wanted to give Lacey the iced coffee in his hand. His unfriendly aura paid off.

Sam stood in the doorway of the studio while Lacey picked up the supplies from class, still dressed like a fairy princess on her day off, waiting for her to notice him in the mirror. When impatience got the best of him, he cleared his throat. Lacey jumped, nearly dropping her armload of tutus.

"I brought coffee," he said, and held up the iced drink like a holy relic to ward off the evil glare she gave him. It worked. Lacey sighed, and dropped the tutus into a pile on the floor.

"Thank you," she said, exhaustion radiating off her in waves. Either the miniature humans had drained her, or her sparkling personality had been an act. Probably both.

Sam handed her the coffee, and Lacey drank it in gulps.

"I want to take you on a date," Sam blurted.

The ice at the bottom of Lacey's drink rattled as she finished it.

"You asked me to take you on a date," Sam barreled ahead, a freight train with slipshod brakes, "and with everything going on, we haven't gotten around to it. So it's time. For a date." He waved a hand between them. "You and me."

Lacey stared at him, and the second hand on the clock got louder with every passing second.

"You want to take me on a date? I puked in front of you yesterday. I'm pretty sure you saw me sleep with my mouth open. What part of the last twenty-four hours of unhinged sexi-ness brought this on?"

"You asked," he reminded her.

Lacey patted his shoulder. "So happy I finally made your to-do list."

Sam sighed. This was going about as well as an unmed-icated root canal. "I didn't mean it like that."

"I know." She tapped the tip of his nose and smiled. "I'm teasing you." She used her straw to fish around for any drops of coffee left in the bottom of her cup. "Can we sit down to talk about how you're going to razzle-dazzle me? I'm fucking beat."

Sam frowned and pressed the back of his hand to her forehead. Warm, but not the furnace she'd been the day before.

"You should've stayed home," he scolded her. "You're still sick, sunshine."

"I have to work, Sam. Money doesn't grow on trees."

Lacey moved past him into the lobby, and then back to the office. She dropped into the desk chair unceremoniously and held the icy cup to her head.

"This is stupid," Sam protested, shutting the door behind him.

"This is America."

He wanted to grumble and growl, but Lacey looked exhausted and he didn't want to add to that. All of the energy she'd had to argue with him that morning was long gone.

Sam pushed the keyboard to the side and sat on the desk.

"Come here," he said gently, and patted his thigh. With a sigh, Lacey laid her head on his lap and closed her eyes.

"Is this our date?" she asked, moving the cold cup to her cheek.

"No. It's supposed to be public, remember?" Sam smoothed back some of the wispy hairs that had escaped her bun, and kept stroking her hair because Lacey melted under his touch. "Do you want to go to Cranberry Brothers tonight?"

"Absolutely not. Unless you want to take a corpse." Lacey turned her head to peer up at him. "You're not into necrophilia, are you?"

"Not on my list of kinks," he assured her, and Lacey closed her eyes and turned her head back. Sam resumed stroking her hair. "Are you sure? Everyone will be there tonight."

"I can't meet your friends like this."

"You've met my friends," he reminded her.

"Yeah, but not as your girlfriend," Lacey said, then added, "Fake girlfriend."

"You don't think your *Weekend At Bernie's* impression will win them over?"

Lacey chuckled. "No, I don't think it will. Was Cranberry Brothers your date idea?"

"Yes, but not my only one." Sam hadn't spent all that time at Stardust agonizing for nothing. "They're playing *Dirty Dancing* at the movie theater Saturday night. We could get dinner and see the movie. Sorry it's not super creative—"

"That's one of my favorite movies," Lacey interrupted. "If you buy me popcorn and licorice, it sounds like the perfect date."

"You're making this too easy on me."

"You can fly me to Paris a different week." Lacey sat up straight with a small groan, and tossed her empty cup into the trash can. "I need to get set up for my next class."

Sam stood, then helped Lacey out of her chair. "Will you call me if you feel any worse? I'll come get you."

"I'll be fine," she promised, but he didn't believe her.

Sam didn't believe her so much that as soon as he left the dance studio, he sent a message to his Crane Cove group chat.

SAM

> Lacey doesn't feel good so I'm not going to BBQ night tonight.

CHASE

> So you ARE still a thing! Connor owes me $20

ELOISE

> Is she okay? Is there anything we can do?

Seems to be a bug. I made soup.

That soup is magic. Let us know if you need anything.

WHEN LACEY LEFT the dance studio at five, Sam was leaning against her car, and the look of utter exhaustion and sheer relief on her face in the fading sunlight broke his heart. There wasn't anyone around to see, but he opened his arms and Lacey stepped into them, laying her head on his shoulder.

"Oh, thank god." She sighed as he wrapped his arms around her. "Are you taking me home?"

Sam pressed a kiss to her feverish forehead. "Of course I am, sunshine."

Lacey fell asleep in his car again, and when she woke up in his garage, he swore he heard her murmur "Kidnapper" under her breath, but that didn't stop her from going straight to his bed and face-planting onto the mattress. Daisy jumped up next to her.

The tension that had built all day eased out of Sam's body. Lacey was back where he could take care of her and know she was safe. No more worrying. No more dark cloud thoughts.

"Sam?" Lacey said into the mattress.

"Yeah?"

"I need to borrow some clothes."

CHAPTER SEVENTEEN

LACEY WAS PUTTING in her earrings when the doorbell rang.

Sam was ten minutes late, and she still wasn't ready. Where did the time go? When she'd started getting ready, she thought she'd be early, sitting around, twiddling her thumbs. When did she get off track?

The pants she tripped over going to her bedroom door answered the question. The outfit. Most of her closet was strewn around her room. Nothing had looked right. Nothing had felt right. A baggy cream-colored sweater partially tucked into a long navy blue skirt with a daisy pattern was what she'd settled on. Lacey was worried that she looked like if Meg Ryan had taught kindergarten in a '90s rom-com, but it was her vanity versus the clock, and the clock had won.

Sam rang the doorbell again.

"I'm coming!" Lacey shouted, not sure if he could hear her.

She combed her fingers through her curls again, trying to soften them, then half walked, half ran to the front door. She opened it right as Sam rang the bell for the third time.

"You're so impatien—are those for me?"

Sam looked at the brown paper-wrapped bouquet in his hands like he'd forgotten it was there. "These? Oh, um, yeah. They are." He held them straight out to her.

Lacey took the bouquet and admired it. Dahlias, roses, and daisies, in pink, white, and burgundy, and a few other flowers she didn't recognize offhand. It was beautiful. None of her boyfriends had ever gotten her flowers for no reason before. She'd gotten the odd bouquet after a performance, but never just because.

"What are these for?" she asked, stepping back to let him inside.

"Supporting local small business," Sam said, not moving from the doorway. "We're going to be late for our reservation."

Lacey smelled her flowers. Soft and sweet. "I need to put these in water."

"We're going to be late," he reminded her.

"And whose fault is that?" Lacey went to the kitchen to find a vase.

Both of theirs, technically, but she wasn't going to point that out if he didn't notice.

"They'll be fine if you leave them on the counter."

"I don't want them to die."

Lacey couldn't find a vase so she put the flowers in a sturdy glass in the sink with some water. Sam was still on the front porch.

"Did you need to be invited in? Are you a vampire?" She put on her raincoat. The temperature had dropped fifteen degrees overnight and the sky was spitting icy rain.

"We need to go," he insisted.

"Sam. We live in Crane Cove. It takes two minutes to drive anywhere. We're fine."

. . .

THEY WERE NOT FINE.

Sam had picked a new tapas restaurant downtown called La Taberna. Because it was still new and novel to the residents of Crane Cove, the place was packed. Lacey heard the hostess tell the couple in front of them it was an hour wait for a table if they didn't have a reservation.

"Reservation for Finch," Sam said when they got to the host stand.

The hostess stared at him. Sam stared back.

"Has anyone ever told you that you look like Sam Shoop?" she asked.

Lacey put a hand on his chest. "He's a Sam Shoop impersonator. Getting the tattoos was a commitment, but it's really paid off."

The hostess blinked like her brain was recalibrating. "Huh... Finch?" She tapped her tablet a few times. "So, our policy is to only hold reservations for ten minutes on busy nights. It's twenty minutes past your reservation, so we gave away your table."

"Okay, I was joking. He is Sam Shoop. Can we have our table?"

"I, um...let me talk to my manager."

The hostess all but ran from her post toward the back of the restaurant. Lacey looked at Sam. A deep frown creased his forehead.

"Why did you give them my last name instead of yours?"

"Because you never know who's going to be weird," Sam grumbled. "This is a fucking disaster."

Lacey slid a hand into one of his back pockets. "No, it's not. It's tapas. What's our worst-case scenario here? We go somewhere else? Not a big deal." She kissed his cheek, and Sam's eyebrows snapped upward in surprise. "Stop trying so hard. It's just me."

The hostess came back, trailed by a man who had to be the manager. Given the way his facial expression changed when he saw them, Lacey guessed that the hostess had said "Sam Shoop is out front" and the manager had said "No, he's not," and panic was setting in because Sam Shoop didn't have a table at their restaurant. Lacey felt bad for him. He looked ready to crap his pants.

"I understand that you had a reservation," the manager began, and Sam interrupted him.

"I know we were late and you can't hold a table indefinitely, but we've got a movie in an hour. Is there anything you can do?" Sam's tone was very gentle, especially considering he was stiffer than a brand new pointe shoe.

"I'm sorry." The manager looked ready to offer up his first-born child as an apology. "If you want, you can wait for seats to open at the bar."

Lacey squeezed Sam's butt in an attempt to distract him from whatever doom spiral he might be headed towards. When he didn't immediately answer, she did it for them.

"We'll come back another night."

"Are you sure?" Sam asked her, and she nodded.

"Yeah. It's not a big deal."

The manager scrambled to give Sam one of his cards, telling Sam to call the next time he made a reservation and he would personally make sure the table stayed available.

"I think he just wants you to call him," Lacey joked once they were outside. Sam was still brooding like a distant storm cloud, so she took his hand and squeezed it. "You good?"

"No," he grumbled. "Where are we supposed to eat?"

There it was. The bottom line of the eye chart expression she couldn't make out. Sam was upset, but Lacey couldn't tell if it was her, the situation, himself, or some unrelated fourth thing that had crawled up his ass. She worked hard to keep her expression and tone light.

"We could go to Cranberry Brothers," she suggested, "or we could try and make it to Queens and back before the movie. Here's a fun alternative: we have popcorn and candy for dinner. Mmm...Skittles and Sour Patch Kids."

She smiled brightly, ready to do or say anything to get Sam to crack a smile. He rolled his eyes and her heart shriveled, then it nearly exploded when he grabbed the back of her neck. For an eternal second she thought he was going to kiss her, and the world slowed to a halt; raindrops hung suspended mid-fall, the biting wind ceased to move, and her pulse paused, waiting.

"You're ridiculous," he told her, "in the best possible way."

"Ta-da," Lacey said weakly, the world returning to normal in fast forward. Sam released her neck, and she tried not to let the crushing weight of disappointment change her posture.

"Isn't that pizza place close to the movie theater?"

"Pete's?" Lacey tried to recreate a map of downtown Crane Cove in her head. "Yeah, I think it is. You want to get pizza?"

"I wanted to take you to tapas."

"Pizza is fine. It'll be quieter too."

"We're supposed to be seen."

Lacey frowned. "Why is this so important all of a sudden? We've been believably private for—" The door opened, and Lacey took Sam's hand and walked them further down the sidewalk to a closed storefront. "We've been believably private for weeks. What's the big deal?"

Sam clenched his jaw, not holding eye contact with her. "Your ex is an asshole," he finally said.

"You're going to have to be more specific. That could apply to all of them."

"Mitch."

Sam's entire demeanor clicked into place, and Lacey understood why her notoriously private fake boyfriend had tried to parade her around a busy restaurant like a show pony.

"Oh yes. He is an asshole. What asshole thing did he do to get into your head?"

Sam crossed his arms and looked down at his feet. "He said some shit..."

"What kind of shit?" Lacey prompted.

"That I'm letting you tell everyone I'm your boyfriend so I can fuck you. And that the head is worth the headache."

"If he only knew." Lacey laughed.

"Knew what?" Sam asked, taking her hand and intertwining their fingers as they started the walk to Pete's Za.

"That we're not fucking, so you're not even getting head for the headaches."

Sam's face contorted as he struggled to keep it straight. Pride swelled in Lacey's chest. Making him laugh was like being able to command the clouds to part to reveal the sun.

Maybe a little head wasn't out of the question. Sam had gone above and beyond taking care of her when she was sick. What could it hurt to wrap her lips around that gorgeous cock and slide as much of it as she could down her throat? Give them both a little treat?

Why had she even said they shouldn't have sex? To protect herself? From what? Orgasms? What was wrong with the languid contentment that followed a particularly good fuck? Nothing. Nothing at all. It had been so damn long since she'd had *good* sex. And it wasn't like Sam was an unknown quantity; she knew he could deliver exactly what she was craving.

Pete's Za was essentially a hole in the wall. Lacey wondered what the space had been in a previous life. The white subway tiled walls reminded her so much of being in a New York City pie shop that it made her nostalgic for being nineteen and grabbing a slice for her walk home after an audition. Pizza over subway fare had been her motto back then.

They weren't the only ones who'd decided they wanted pizza, so they got in line. Lacey leaned back against Sam, and he curled an arm around her waist. Casual. Like they did this kind of thing every day. Then his lips brushed her neck and he nuzzled the sensitive spot behind her ear, and her pussy felt anything but casual.

Sam released her when the line moved and it was their turn to order. Lacey didn't want to move. She wanted to stay in her spot and get more kisses.

"Veggie slice, please," Sam said to the teenage boy behind the counter. He reminded Lacey of a lemur, all long, awkward limbs.

"Make that two," Lacey added, then looked at Sam. "I used to tell myself pizza didn't count if it had vegetables on it."

"It's a complete meal if it has vegetables," Sam agreed, digging his wallet out of his pocket to pay. "Carbs, protein, vegetables. And you can eat it and walk at the same time."

"See, you get it."

The pizza was delicious. Every time she had Pete's, Lacey couldn't believe she didn't eat it for every meal. Who needed other food when there was pizza?

"There's a pizza place by my apartment in New York that's open until three in the morning," Sam said, shaking more red pepper flakes onto his slice. "I always stop there when I record late. I need to take you."

Lacey paused mid-chew. Did Sam know what he'd said? The way he kept eating, she didn't think so. A slip of the tongue, or forgetting who he was talking to. He probably said stuff like this all the time to his friends.

"You know how I feel about free food," Lacey reminded him.

"Would you ever live in New York again?"

Lacey chewed slowly, using the time to compose her answer. "I don't know if I'm cut out for it anymore. My skin is too thin for that hustle culture, and it's too expensive. I love the city and I'd visit again in a heartbeat, but I'm not mentally cut out to have my entire living space be roughly the size of your bedroom, minus the closet and bathroom. Maybe if I win the lottery."

"What would you do if you won the lottery?"

"Pay off my debt." It was a simple answer, but it was the one she had. Paying off her debt dominated all of her choices. Once she solved that problem, she'd move on to what she *wanted* to do with her life—whatever that was.

Sam frowned a little. "How much debt are you in?"

Heat flooded her cheeks. "Enough that I'm going to shove my mouth full of pizza and change the subject. How 'bout them Yankees?"

"I'm a Tigers fan, actually."

"No wonder your songs are full of heartbreak and disappointment."

Sam narrowed his eyes. "Who do you root for? Not the Astros, right?"

"Whoever has the cutest uniforms," Lacey answered with a cheeky smile. Sam rolled his eyes.

"We're fixing this. You're going to be a Tigers fan so you can be miserable with the rest of us."

"Misery loves company."

Sam smiled softly. "You're good company, sunshine."

Lacey's insides turned to goo. If she'd been standing, she would've needed to sit down. It was settled. She needed this man's penis in or around her mouth before midnight so she could properly express her gratitude.

CHAPTER EIGHTEEN

"HUH. It's kind of empty in here," Lacey said as they settled into their seats.

The theater was mostly empty. The Lightbox Theater had three-hundred and forty seats. Sam knew because he'd bought three-hundred and twenty of them. He hadn't been quick enough to beat the Crane Cove Cinema Club, but from what the theater manager had said, the dozen or so members had pre-purchased tickets for the entire Saturday Cinema Series for the year, so he never would've won that race. At least they had the decency to sit together in a cluster closer to the screen. The other few couples and single patrons were dotted around the theater.

"Maybe people are busy," Sam suggested, offering Lacey their bucket of popcorn.

Lacey picked out a few pieces. "It's Crane Cove in November. There's not a lot to do on a Saturday night. And it was busy downtown, so I thought more people would be here."

Sam set the bucket down to take off his jacket. "Isn't it nice to have an empty theater?"

"I guess so," she said, and as the lights dimmed, Sam swore he saw a hint of a mischievous grin that got his blood pumping.

The iconic drum phrase that kicked off "Be My Baby" by the Ronettes and *Dirty Dancing* thumped through the speakers. Lacey's elbow rammed into his chest as she struggled out of her coat.

"Sorry," she whispered, her face awash in gray light from the screen.

"It's okay," he whispered back, trying to focus on the opening credits. Unfortunately, the dancers reminded him of Lacey dancing—or at least how she'd danced when he'd met her. And that reminded him of their one night together in Barcelona, and then he needed to adjust where he was holding the popcorn bucket.

As the credits faded into the opening monologue backed by Frankie Valli and the Four Seasons, Lacey leaned over.

"I really appreciate everything you've done for me this week," she whispered in his ear, and kissed his cheek. His cock throbbed almost painfully at the innocent contact.

"Don't worry about it," he whispered back, then almost jumped when her hand squeezed his thigh right below where he'd set the popcorn bucket.

"I want to show you how grateful I am," she continued, the warmth of her breath sending goosebumps down his body. "You were so good to me." Her teeth scraped his neck. "Let me be good to you."

Blood rushed to Sam's cock so quickly he saw spots. He was...what was the word? Surprised? Shocked? Stupefied?

Lacey's grip on his thigh loosened. "I mean, I know it's not exactly what we agreed on, but it *is* technically in public. If you're not into it..."

He'd been thinking about synonyms too long. "What did you have in mind?"

She took one of his hands off the popcorn bucket and brought it to her mouth, then wrapped her lips around his index finger and sucked. When she swirled her tongue around the tip of his finger, Sam had to disguise a moan as a cough. Lacey released his finger with a quiet *pop*.

Fucking hell. He wasn't going to survive to "Hungry Eyes" at this rate. He might not even make it to the watermelon line.

Sam nodded his consent, then looked back to the screen. Okay, maybe he'd make it to the watermelon part. It wasn't that far off—

Lacey tugged at his belt. Popcorn spilled out of the bucket as Sam jolted, surprised.

"Here?" he asked, his voice a high-pitched whisper.

She nodded, working his belt open with one hand.

"Relax," Lacey mouthed.

Relax? How was he supposed to relax? They were in public. A movie theater. The Crane Cove Cinema Club was less than a hundred feet away. Sam thought Lacey meant she wanted to blow his cock and his mind later, maybe at home.

What if someone saw? His reputation could handle it. Hell, he'd probably get high fives and fist bumps. *Rock star caught receiving blow job in movie theater* played really well in the tabloids. Could Lacey's reputation survive? It wasn't like she had a lot of support if shit hit the fan.

Then again, she was the one trying to unbutton his pants. He wasn't going to stop her.

Dread and desire made him almost queasy. Still, he helped her unbutton his pants. Then he repositioned the popcorn bucket to his other leg to shield his rigid cock from view if anyone walked down the side aisle.

"Mmm," Lacey hummed as she stroked his shaft. Pleasure rippled through his body. She casually rested her head on his shoulder and murmured, "Don't worry about being quick."

Lacey continued to work him with her hand, and it took everything in Sam not to squirm or moan. He was watching the crowd more than the movie, but no one had even glanced their way.

The screen grew darker as Baby Housemen went for a walk on the Kellerman grounds and found the staff quarters. As Baby offered to help carry a watermelon, Lacey slid out of her seat and knelt on the floor in front of him. She licked his cock from the base to the tip, and as the doors opened to the staff dance, she took him into her mouth.

Lacey wasn't fucking around. She sucked his cock, sliding her mouth up and down his shaft, like she meant business. Sam gripped the armrest with his free hand, torn between watching the movie to act natural in case anyone looked over, or watching the scene between his legs. He ended up doing a rapid up down, up down, up down with his eyes, switching between the screen and Lacey.

A hand on his hand made him look down again, and Lacey was looking up at him. She took his hand off the armrest and put it on the back of her head, then winked at him.

Fucking menace.

She was fucking perfect.

Sam gripped her hair, guiding her head up and down, pushing her gently to see how far she could take him. No one wanted a lap full of puke.

Lacey wrapped her fingers around the base as a stop guard, and then put her hand on his again, pushing down harder. He could take a hint when someone had their mouth full.

He forced her head down, using her mouth the way he wanted, increasing the speed and intensity. Pressure built in his groin, and want warred with need. He wanted this to last forever, but he needed to come. It was so close, like hearing the horn of a freight train while being stuck on the tracks. Sam tapped the back of Lacey's head twice to warn her, but she kept going. He looked down at her again for confirmation, and she was watching him. That same wink, and a gentle buzz around his sensitive cock as she hummed an affirmative "Mm-hmm."

It was all too much, and Sam lost the tentative grip he had on his body. He came hard, his body spasming with each wave. He bit the side of his cheek to keep from shouting, and tried to just breathe through the intensity.

Languid contentment spread through his veins like a warm summer afternoon. If there had been a fire in the theater right then, Sam would've been useless to get up and save himself. It would've been too much effort.

Sam stroked Lacey's hair and mouthed, "Good girl." She grinned, then opened her mouth to show him just how much he'd come. The room spun as she swallowed it all down.

He should've tied her to the bed in Barcelona and never let her leave.

Lacey popped back into her seat like nothing had happened, like she'd been searching for her phone or her purse instead of sucking his cock like it was a popsicle she needed to finish in sixty seconds or less. She casually rested her head on his shoulder as Sam tucked his flagging cock back into his pants and redid them.

"I'm going to get you back," he whispered.

"Pass the popcorn."

CHAPTER NINETEEN

LACEY PULLED at the hem of her plaid skirt, unable to stop fidgeting with it.

Thanksgiving with Sam and his friends had seemed like a decent idea when he'd proposed it. An easy way to prove to everyone that they were Definitely A Couple. Except her stomach was doing its best impression of the rock tumbler she'd had in elementary school.

Was she underdressed? Eloise never looked anything other than immaculate, like she was headed to a photoshoot high-lighting quiet luxury, and Lacey worried that her plaid skirt and black sweater wouldn't be up to par. She'd never been to a fancy Thanksgiving before. On the other side of the same coin was the fear that she was overdressed and today was the day she'd see Eloise Thatcher in an extra-stretchy tracksuit.

She could've asked Sam, but his brain was full of turkey. He'd been preparing all week, making homemade vegetable stock for the brine and chicken broth to roast the turkey. Lacey wasn't sure what any of that had to do with turkey, but Sam was very adamant it was necessary. He'd bought the biggest turkey she'd ever seen from a nearby farm, and on the drive to pick it up, Sam explained the special way those particular turkeys were raised in great detail. It was the most she'd ever heard him talk without someone else adding to the conversation. The way home was all about brining and roasting methods. She'd contributed approximately three words that weren't "Oh, wow" or "Really?"

They'd been spending a lot of time together since she'd recovered from her twenty-four-hour flu bug. Sam either came into town to have lunch with Lacey, or she drove to his house after work to have dinner. For Daisy's sake. No one wanted a repeat of the sad dog episode. So they'd watch TV or a movie, and then sometimes Lacey would be too tired to drive home, so she'd spend the night in Sam's bed, with Daisy tucked between them like the world's snuggliest barrier.

They hadn't talked about what had happened on their date. Sam had vaguely warned her he was "going to get her back," but nothing had come to fruition. It had wrecked her peace for the rest of the movie. Every time Sam so much as shifted in his seat, she thought something was going to happen, that he'd sink to his knees in front of her, hide under her skirt, and bury his face in her pussy. Or when his hand ended up in her lap she initially thought he was going to finger her, but he just wanted to hold her hand. Which was sweet, but not an orgasm.

She'd thought about pressing the issue, thought about walking into his room naked sometime to see what he'd do about it. But she wanted it to go both ways. It was like they were locked in a horny chess game—it was Sam's turn to move, but he kept picking up pieces only to put them down again, and she was about ready to flip the board.

There were cars lined up along the sidewalk in front of Graham and Eloise's storybook Victorian home. Sam pulled into the last remaining spot in the driveway.

"I thought everyone wasn't coming until later?" Lacey said,

recognizing Chris McMahon's truck as one of the vehicles on the street. The rocks tumbling in her stomach picked up speed.

Sam shifted into park. "Slight change in plans. Bitsy McMahon had an appendectomy on Tuesday and didn't feel like cooking anymore, so everyone is hanging out."

Lacey frowned. "They're not cooking for her?"

"The McMahon boys were told to get the hell out of the house because they were smothering her." Sam shrugged. "Bitsy said she wanted peace, quiet, and soup."

"She doesn't feel abandoned?"

Sam laughed. "I think Bitsy's Christmas wish is to feel more abandoned by her sons."

This fit with what Lacey knew about the McMahon matriarch. Three of her five adult sons lived at home, and she wasn't subtle about trying to set them up with potential partners in a bid to get them to move out or at least move on.

"Are you nervous?" Sam asked. Lacey nodded. "Don't be. Annie loves you, so Jordy will love you because he agrees with everything Annie says. Peter is going to talk your ear off. I'm sorry I can't stop that from happening. Graham is the most like me, so don't take it personally if he says three words to you. Eloise will likely be in anxious hostess mode. You've met Sybil, and Mallory, and the McMahons. You're going to be fine." He leaned across the car and kissed her forehead. "You can always come hide in the kitchen with me."

Lacey wanted to stay in the car forever, getting little forehead kisses and pep talks.

"I know it's all fake, but I really do want them to like me," she confessed.

"They're going to like you, and it's going to make my life hell when you leave me."

When she left. Not if. *When.*

That four-letter word hurt like she'd slammed her finger in the car door.

Daisy pushed her muzzle between them, and then her entire head, one of her panting smiles stretched across her adorable face. If everyone wanted to meet the girl who had stolen Sam's heart, they would. She had four legs and was freshly groomed.

"You ready to meet your aunts and uncles?" Lacey asked, adjusting the autumn leaf sailor bow she'd made for Daisy's collar. It was festive without being turkey legs or pumpkin pie.

"Can you walk Daisy in, and I'll bring the turkey?" Sam asked.

It was a testament to Sam's control issues that he hadn't brined and stored the turkey at the Thatchers' house. No, the entire process had happened at his house, and he had lugged everything into town from the woods like a tightly wound pioneer. The only person he even allowed to contribute was Connor, and he was only in charge of pie and rolls. Lacey had dubbed him "The Carb King."

"You don't need help with the rest of your bounty?"

"Lugging things is why God gave the McMahons such broad shoulders."

Lacey laughed and got out of the car. She opened the back door and used her body to block Daisy from jumping out. At home, they let her roam off lead within reason, but in an unfamiliar neighborhood, Lacey was worried their dog might take off.

And there she went again, thinking of Sam's house as *her* house and his dog as *their* dog. She'd confused Annie a few times recently because she used "home" interchangeably between Gavin and Leo's house and Sam's house. It was her childhood all over again, shuttling between houses, calling each home, but everything feeling temporary. At least she knew this was temporary. Would Sam let her walk away as easily as her dad had when she'd decided at thirteen she didn't want to stay at his house anymore?

Lacey clipped Daisy's lead to her collar, mentally shaking off the Holiday Melancholies the same way Daisy shook rain out of her coat.

"Let's go, Daisy," she said cheerfully, walking the dog up to the front door. Was she supposed to knock? Ring the bell? Walk right on in like she'd been invited and not Sam's tacked-on plus one?

The decision was made for her as the door flung open. Lacey jumped backward as Annie lunged forward to hug her. It took some creative footwork to keep them both upright.

From the corner of her eye, Lacey saw a few spying heads disappear from a front window.

"You're here!" Annie exclaimed, finally succeeding in wrapping her arms around Lacey.

"Of course I am," Lacey said, hugging her back. "I was loosely invited."

"You're also late!" Graham called from inside the foyer, then appeared in the doorway. "Oh. I'm sorry. I thought Sam was out here too."

"He's getting the turkey," Lacey explained. "I don't think we're that late."

Annie squatted down to greet Daisy, giving her all the head scratches and ear rubs the dog thought she deserved and pretended she'd been deprived of. Daisy was a con artist for love, and Lacey respected that.

"Graham and Eloise have a timetable," Annie said. "You've thrown off their groove, so to speak."

Sam came up the steps carrying the turkey in its roasting pan and cut Graham off before he could speak.

"We're not that late, and you should've accounted for this in whatever spreadsheet you made for foreplay."

Graham blushed. Lacey was going to have to interrogate Sam about that little jab later.

"Did you preheat the oven?" Sam asked as he stepped inside.

"Yes. It's been warming for at least half an hour, as instructed, chef."

Graham said "chef" with such dry sarcasm that Lacey had to bite her cheek to keep from laughing. But when Daisy noticed Sam carrying a lot of meat and abandoned pets for food she was never going to get from her overprotective daddy, Lacey did laugh.

"She's an optimistic opportunist," Lacey explained to Annie, who looked a little miffed as to why the dog had left. "When did you get in?"

"Late last night. I slept until nine, which felt like noon." Annie linked her arm with Lacey's and they walked inside. "Jordy has fully embraced his retired old man era, so he got up at seven, read the paper, did his PT exercises, drank a cup of coffee, took a shower, made me a cup of coffee, and then woke me up by calling me sleepyhead."

"Give that man some babies so he can be a grandpa already."

Annie smiled fondly. "Someday. Soon. Maybe after we've been together for a year."

Lacey raised her eyebrows. "You've actually thought about having his babies?"

"I've been thinking about having his babies since I met him. Jordy awakens some very primal, populate-the-Earth instinctive urges in me." Annie squeezed Lacey's arm. "Have I ever told you how nice it is that I can overshare with you?"

"The feeling is mutual. 'We overshare because we care' should be the Extra Donut slogan."

A squadron of McMahons filed out the door to Sam's car.

"Does Jordy actually read the paper?" Lacey asked, a bit dubious based on what she knew about Jordy Taylor from the media and from some anecdotal stories from Annie.

Annie grinned. "He skims it, but he's really looking for the sports section and the cartoons."

"That sounds more like it."

"It's cute, though," Annie clarified, and Lacey knew she was in the presence of a woman deeply in love. She glowed when she talked about Jordy. Positively beamed. The warmth that radiated off of her made Lacey want to sweat. It made her long for that kind of security.

Had Lacey ever felt that secure in a relationship?

No, she didn't think she had.

"Coming through!" a McMahon announced from behind them, and Annie and Lacey quickly moved to the side. It was Chase, carrying one of the boxes of food Sam had organized in the trunk. Cole and Connor followed with more boxes, and Chris brought up the rear, carrying Daisy's bowls and the special Thanksgiving meal Sam had prepared for her. Lacey had been outwardly laughing but inwardly swooning. The way Sam cared for Daisy gave her the closest thing she'd ever had to baby fever, except instead of children, she wanted to have twenty more dogs with him.

"What's going on?"

Lacey and Annie both jumped. Sybil Morgan stood behind them in the entryway to the dining room.

Annie put her hand on her chest. "Graham was right. You need a bell."

Sybil looked at them blankly, so Lacey answered the question. "We were watching the Thanksgiving parade."

The corner of Sybil's mouth twitched, almost spreading into a smile, and Lacey chalked that up as a win. It was the closest she'd ever come to making her smile.

"If we wait, maybe we'll see Snoopy," Lacey said, really pushing for even a smirk. No such luck. Sybil quickly walked away, heading deeper into the house.

Lacey looked at Annie. "Was it something I said?"

A hand touched Lacey's shoulder, and she turned to see who it was. She was face-to-face with Peter Green.

"Jesus Christ, you're prettier in person," she blurted.

Peter Green—how was it humanly possible that Peter Green was touching her?—smiled warmly. Lacey was pretty sure she'd seen everything he'd ever been in. She'd even seen him on Broadway when they were both a lot younger. It was surreal to be this close to him.

"You must be Lacey," he said. "It's so nice to finally meet you. I've heard so much about you."

Liar, Lacey thought. She doubted Sam had said more than three words about her. Those three words were probably "She's named Lacey." But she wasn't going to call him out over it. He was being nice and she couldn't afford to alienate anyone who was being nice to her.

"I am. It's weird to finally meet you." She heard Annie choke on a laugh and her words filtered back to her. "Not weird. Nice. It's nice to finally meet you."

"And a little weird," Peter said with a conspiratorial wink.

"It's just that I've watched you forever—in movies!" If her foot got any further in her mouth it was going to choke her. She looked at Annie and mouthed, "Help me."

"Peter, this is Daisy." Annie flourished a hand downward to where Daisy was sitting patiently at Lacey's feet waiting to be adored. "Daisy, this is your uncle Peter."

Peter didn't crouch or kneel. He sat cross-legged on the floor to shower Daisy with the affection the spoiled dog had come to expect. It was a good thing Peter was single, because any partner would've been incredibly jealous listening to him talk.

"Thank you," Lacey whispered to Annie. "I was on a road to ruin."

"Oh, honey." Annie patted her arm sympathetically. "You were already downtown after getting a speeding ticket."

"So," Peter said from the floor, Daisy laying across his lap, "are things serious? I mean, you got a dog together."

Heat rushed to Lacey's face.

"Um...well, I found her and she's more Sam's dog and...it hasn't really been that long..."

"How did you meet?"

Lacey was glad for an easy question. "The first time was in Barcelona when he was on tour. The second time was during a dance lesson."

Peter's petting hands still. "You met him in Barcelona? Spain? On tour?"

"Yes?" Lacey didn't know why she'd answered like she wasn't certain.

Peter frowned a little. "I thought you had dark hair."

"What do you mean?"

"You're the girl he wrote the song about, right? It's just when he was explaining it, he said you had dark hair."

"It was dark at one point. I like to dye it," Lacey explained, still confused. "What song are you talking about?"

"'Barcelona,'" Peter said like she'd known for years. "It's such a beautiful song. I wonder if Sam will finally understand it now that you've reconnected."

The room didn't spin or tilt, but it was dangerously close. It reminded Lacey of jumping on one of those playground merry-go-rounds after pushing it as fast as her legs could carry her. Off kilter. That was it.

It really was about her. There was every chance Peter was mistaken, but the odds were in his favor. The first time Lacey had heard the song, she'd spent the rest of the day convincing herself it wasn't about her. It could be about anyone; it was probably about his ex-fiancée. That's what she'd told herself. And she'd believed herself readily.

Ironically, Lacey had auditioned for the music video. She'd made it far too, before the director decided she was too tall and not Sam's type anyway.

"What do you think it's about?" Lacey asked, forcing herself to keep her body relaxed.

A soft smile crinkled the corners of Peter's eyes. "It's about instant connection. About that moment when you meet someone and reality pauses and only you two exist. How you then feel like you've known that person your whole life, like they're able to look through the keyhole to your soul." He scratched Daisy under her chin. "He's always so miffed about it being used as a wedding song, but it makes perfect sense to me. It's the most romantic thing he's ever written."

Lacey wanted to disagree, to say the song was about how she'd tongued Sam's asshole, not about an instant romance, but Peter made sense. It was his voice. The shadow of a British accent made him sound like an expert.

Peter rubbed Daisy's chest. "Have you thought about making her a therapy dog?"

And just like that he'd moved on. Lacey understood and appreciated the jump his brain had made.

"Currently her caseload is full with me and Sam," Lacey half joked. "I think she's relieved when we leave the house so she can get a break."

"She's a very good girl," Peter cooed.

Eloise Thatcher breezed down the hallway like a woman on

a mission, her heels clicking on the hardwood floors. In her hands were a thick stack of rust-colored napkins.

"Peter." She sighed, exasperated. In her green dress and pearls, Eloise looked and sounded like a frazzled '50s housewife. "Do you have to sit in the middle of the floor?"

Peter pointed to Daisy. "There's a dog in my lap. Have you met Daisy?"

"Yes. Please move out of the walkway before someone trips on you. I don't think we have enough insurance to pay for you if anything gets broken." Eloise shook her head. "If a McMahon fell on you..."

"Okay, okay." Peter gently removed Daisy from his lap and stood up, brushing any dog hair off his trousers. He eyed the napkins Eloise was holding. "Would you like me to take care of those?"

"I can do it," she said, holding them closer to her body.

"Eloise," Peter said gently, like he was talking to a skittish horse, "they're napkins. I think I can handle napkins. I can't even break them if I drop them."

Eloise hesitated for a moment, then passed him the stack. "Let me show you what I want."

The pair went into the dining room. There was a commotion deeper in the house that ended with a resounding bellow from Sam for everyone to get out of the kitchen. The group exited like clowns from a Volkswagen Beetle, splintering off in different directions.

Jordy beelined for Annie like he was attached to her by a retractable string.

"Does he ever let you help in the kitchen?" he asked, putting an arm around Annie's waist.

"I was allowed to hold the can opener once," Lacey said with an upbeat smile, even though everything was still moving too fast for her to make sense of it. "Mostly I sit on the counter and talk to him."

"I don't think it would have the same effect if I did that." Jordy grinned at Annie, and Lacey would've sworn an unsaid joke passed between them. They were sickeningly cute. She should be taking notes.

"You never know unless you try," Lacey said. "I'll let you borrow my skirt so you can show a little leg."

Jordy laughed.

"She's funny," he said to Annie.

"She's fucking hysterical," Annie confirmed. "Wait until she actually gets going. This is a warmup." She put a hand on his chest. "Did you know you're part of the Holy Trinity of Fuck Boys?"

"The holy what-now?"

"Actors, musicians, professional athletes," Annie and Lacey said in unison, making the sign of the cross as they did so.

Jordy laughed again. "You should do standup."

"No way." Lacey shook her head. "That shit is hard."

"What are your life goals?" Jordy asked.

"Um..."

Lacey was saved by Eloise.

"Jordy, leave her alone," she chastised, joining the group. "At least wait to interrogate her until dinner so she doesn't have to repeat herself." Eloise smiled at Lacey. "We're so happy you could make it. Can I get you anything to drink? Wine? Water? Hard liquor directly from the bottle?"

"Water would be good."

As a group they began to migrate away from the dining room. Lacey spared a glance over her shoulder at Peter. He was supposed to be folding napkins, but she saw him pick up a place card, walk around the table, and swap it with another place card. Hopefully Eloise wouldn't have a conniption that he had tampered with her carefully arranged seating plan.

Eloise poured Lacey a glass of water from a pitcher on a sideboard in the hall, making pleasant small talk the entire time. She asked the usual questions, and Lacey gave the nice, polite, filtered answers. Nothing that would get a response of "I'm so sorry" or "That must have been hard." Where did she grow up? Pittsburgh. When did she start dancing? When she was three.

Over Eloise's shoulder, Lacey saw Peter leave the dining room. A minute later, Sybil entered for thirty seconds, then left. No sooner was Sybil out of sight then Peter re-entered the dining room for roughly thirty seconds, then left. While Lacey spoke briefly about her time working on cruise ships, Sybil scurried back into the dining room. Lacey wanted to know what was going on, but there was no way in hell she was going to ask Sybil.

"What's going on over here?"

Lacey jumped, water sloshing over the rim of her glass and onto her sweater. She'd been so engrossed in watching Sybil and Peter run in and out of the dining room that she hadn't noticed Chase McMahon join their little group.

"Getting to know Lacey," Eloise said. "Did you know she used to work on cruise ships?"

"So you're a pirate." Chase grinned. "You know, if I'd known you were still talking to men at all after dating Mitch, I might've tossed my hat in the ring."

Sybil appeared at his elbow and, like an avenging angel, smacked Chase upside the back of his head.

"She's dating your friend. Keep it to yourself."

"Ow." Chase rubbed the back of his head but seemed unfazed. "I was just saying..."

"Stop saying," Sybil looked at Lacey, and Lacey fought the urge to duck behind Jordy for cover. "Ignore him. I do."

"It's why I'm so attention-seeking." Chase grinned. "So is there a reason we're all standing in the hall when there's a perfectly good football game about to start?"

"Because not everyone gives a shit about football?" Sybil suggested.

"That's because you've never had the game explained to you by a professional," Chase said, patting Jordy's shoulder. "It will completely change the way you watch the game."

Sybil's expression didn't shift a centimeter. "And yet I remain uninterested."

"I could be persuaded to be interested in football," Lacey offered with a please-love-me smile. Jordy was Sam's best friend, so she was a bit desperate to win him over and absolutely refused to examine *why* she was so desperate to win him over.

"You don't have to be," Jordy said diplomatically, "but I would like to watch the game..." The tentative request was directed at Annie, who seemed entirely oblivious he might need her permission.

"Why are you looking at me like we don't watch football all the time? Of course we can watch the game. It's Thanksgiving. I think there's a law about it, at least in the south."

The small group moved toward the living room, and Annie hung back with Lacey on the outer edge.

"The Phantoms aren't playing, so Jordy should be moderately well behaved." There was a twinkle in Annie's eyes as she said it.

"Is he having a hard time moving on?" Lacey asked. Jordy Taylor's retirement had happened abruptly after a motorcycle crash early in the season, and she knew she wasn't the only person curious if the legendary quarterback's cheerful press appearances matched his demeanor at home.

Annie shook her head. "Not really. I was worried he'd regret it pretty quickly, but he tells me all the time that this is the happiest he's ever been."

If Lacey had said that same sentence, she would have been smug as hell. This was why Annie was a better person. She was humble and a tiny bit clueless that *she* was why her boyfriend was happy to give up his career to wait for her at home.

The missing McMahons—Connor, Chris, and Cole—were in the living room, along with Mallory Morgan. Daisy, who'd wandered off the second Lacey let go of her leash, had her head resting in Cole's lap, looking at him lovingly as he pretended he wasn't feeding her small bites of cheese every time Chris looked away. It was something she and Daisy had in common; the quickest way to their hearts was through their stomachs.

Guilt needled her. Sam was all alone in the kitchen, cooking away, and they were all watching football. Sure, he'd yelled at everyone else to get out, but it didn't seem fair. These were his friends. He should be out here, and she should be in the kitchen stressing about side dishes and turkey temperatures. But given his dedication to the selection of the bird, she'd probably need a crowbar to pry him out of the kitchen.

She'd watch a little of the game, then go check on Sam. That seemed fair.

Except Sam's friends, his little makeshift family, were entertaining to the point of distraction. The McMahon boys and the Morgan sisters bet on everything and anything with cutthroat intensity. The football game alone wasn't enough; they bet on which commercials would come on next and what the announcers were going to say. It was a good thing they hadn't turned it into a drinking game, because Mallory was cleaning up on the word "penetration."

Jordy talked to the TV like the players could hear him.

"If you'd run your fucking routes, you'd get more targets,

Barlowe. For fuck's sake." Jordy shook his head. "He does shit like this and wonders why the Phantoms traded him."

Lacey leaned over to Annie. "What is he talking about?" she whispered.

"A route is the path a receiver is supposed to run to get open," Annie explained. "From what I've gathered, Barlowe used to be on the Phantoms, and Jordy stopped throwing to him because he was never where he was supposed to be."

Mallory was making piles of money on the coffee table. "Fast food." She touched one stack. "Laundry. Dishes. Car. Pharmaceuticals." She touched every additional pile as she named the category. "Does anyone want to get more specific?"

Connor put a five-dollar bill on fast food and then another five above it. "Taco Bell commercial."

Mallory stacked her money on top of his. "Wendy's."

Money went onto the table. Cole and Chris each had money on it being a car commercial, but Cole said Subaru and Chris said Ford. Chase picked pharmaceuticals, and no one was shocked when he said it would be for erectile dysfunction.

"The way you keep picking that is making me suspicious," Sybil said, putting a five down on dishes, but refused to get more in depth.

"It has to work eventually," Chase reasoned.

"Does Bitsy let you all gamble like this?" Graham asked, nursing an old fashioned on the couch with one arm casually around his wife.

"Hell no," Mallory said, making notes of the different bets. "But this is how we run things when she isn't looking."

"And Greg is okay with that?"

"He pretends he doesn't see a damn thing." Mallory put her notes down on the table to signify betting had ended.

"I feel like we're aiding and abetting a pack of teens,"

Graham said to Eloise, who smiled softly at him and stroked his cheek.

"That's because you're eighty-five on the inside," she told him, then kissed his cheek.

Mallory cheered when the Wendy's commercial started and scooped up the money on the table.

"I feel like you're cheating," Connor said with a stormy frown.

"It's a live feed, and they do not publish the order of commercials beforehand." Mallory counted her winnings.

"Did you check?" Sybil asked.

"It's called using your resources. You have access to Google too." Mallory handed Sybil one of her five-dollar bills. "For correctly guessing that Connor would accuse me of cheating at some point tonight."

"Should've bet twenty," Sybil said. "That was like betting on the sky being blue."

"Yeah, but it's not always blue. Remember that really bad wildfire when it was orange?" Cole reminded them. "Imagine betting on the sky being blue and waking up to that."

"That would be my luck," Chris groaned. From what Lacey had seen, Chris should never visit Las Vegas or Reno. In fact, he should avoid Atlantic City while he was at it. The casinos would bleed him dry in a matter of hours with his luck.

Time moved in strange ways. Because Lacey was more interested in the side bets happening than the game, the first half was over before she knew what had happened. And the halftime report started a strange lightning round of betting that she couldn't look away from. They were well into the third quarter before she could move herself off the couch.

"I'm going to check on Sam," Lacey told Annie.

"Be careful," Graham warned. "He bites."

"I know," she said, then blushed because she *did* know.

CHAPTER TWENTY

SAM HAD STARTED COOKING because a therapist told him he needed a hobby where the result wasn't subjective. Music was extremely subjective; any kind of art was. But cooking? Cooking was fairly obviously good or bad. The same applied to knitting.

The turkey resting on the counter was objectively stunning. Sam was proud of that damn turkey. Cooked to exactly one hundred and sixty-five degrees according to his wireless meat thermometer, it was a beautiful golden brown and smelled heavenly.

Sides that needed to be baked were in the oven. The potatoes for the mashed potatoes were bubbling on the stove, and the gravy he'd made from the turkey drippings was simmering and thickening.

He was the motherfucking king of the kitchen.

"Knock, knock."

Sam had been so zoned in on his triumphs that the voice caught him off guard and he jumped, startled. If it had been anyone other than Lacey, he would have bitten their heads off. But his girlfriend—his *fake* girlfriend—was the exception to the rule. Lacey was the exception to a lot of rules. One that sprang to mind was the No Sleepovers rule. Sam had invented an entire playbook of reasons and excuses to keep Lacey at his house late enough that she gave up on driving home and slept in his bed. Daisy might've been a furry barrier, but the last thing he saw before he fell asleep and the first thing he saw when he woke up were his girls.

His girls. He'd been wrestling with that particular revelation.

"It smells really good in here," Lacey said, having traversed the kitchen while he got his heart rate back under control. She wrapped her arms around his waist and wrecked his pulse all over. "I feel bad you've been in here all by yourself for hours."

"Don't feel bad," he assured her, locking his arms around her. "It's been heaven."

Lacey tilted her head to one side and slightly raised her eyebrows. "Heaven, huh? Should I vacate your paradise?"

Vacate his paradise. He needed to write that down before he forgot it.

"You can't. I've trapped you," Sam teased, squeezing her and making her laugh.

"This feels very Hades and Persephone coded. If you break out a pomegranate, I'm running."

There it was. Half a song appeared in his head like someone else was typing it. Sam groaned and released Lacey, taking out his phone to tap out the lyrics before they vanished like smoke. He'd need to do more research later, but the skeleton of the idea was there: paradise, hell, Hades and Persephone, longing, love, loss.

After months upon months of being starved for inspiration, Sam suddenly couldn't stop writing. His brain had woken up after a long hibernation, and he had more than an entire album's worth of songs in some stage of development. All thanks to Lacey, the greatest accidental muse he could've asked for.

Sam wrote as much as he could manage to distill into actual words, then tucked his phone into his back pocket. Lacey had gone to the stove and was eyeing the simmering gravy, so he opened a drawer and handed her a spoon.

"Try it," he urged, craving her approval.

Lacey dipped her spoon into the gravy, then blew on it gently before putting it in her mouth. Her eyelashes fluttered, and she moaned.

"Is it good?" Sam asked.

"Find out for yourself."

So he did. Lacey was close enough that he could wrap his hand around the back of her neck and pull her to him, though it wasn't much of a pull because at the slightest pressure she stepped into his space, her body fitting against his like all their grooves and curves had been designed for each other.

There was no hesitant brush of lips, no soft exploration. His tongue plunged into her mouth, and she answered with the same greedy desperation roaring through his body. Lacey gripped the hair on the back of his head tightly in her fist, and a sound rumbled in Sam's throat that was half moan, half growl. Faintly he remembered that he was supposed to be tasting the gravy on her tongue, but the only thing he could comprehend was Lacey.

"Fuck, you taste good," he said against her mouth, unwilling to separate enough to speak properly. Lacey smiled against his lips.

"That's not the first time you've said that," she reminded him.

The memory of his face being buried in her pussy on a hotel bed rocketed to the top of his mind.

"Fuck dinner. I want to eat you."

FRET ME NOT 225

That was the wrong thing to say because it made Lacey laugh. Sam loved making her laugh, but not when he was hoping to get her naked. His cock was so hard that it was testing the structural integrity of his pants.

"But you worked so hard," she said between kisses.

"Let me work hard on you." He sounded pathetic and he didn't care.

"We don't have time," Lacey pointed out, even as she slid her free hand under his shirt to caress his stomach.

"I can be fast," Sam promised, nipping at her bottom lip to make her whine. "It would be so good."

Her grip on his hair tightened. "What was that you told me when I wanted boxed mac 'n' cheese? Fast rarely means good?"

Sam groaned. "Do you have to use my own words against me at a time like this?"

"Should've lowered yourself to use the powdered cheese."

"I made you homemade mac 'n' cheese."

"And it was delicious." Lacey grinned at him. "I might be almost as spoiled as Daisy."

"No one is as spoiled as Daisy." Jordy's voice made Lacey jump away like she'd been caught with her hand in the cookie jar. Sam wanted her back. "Don't let me interrupt. I just wanted to know when dinner was going to be."

"You already interrupted," Sam huffed.

Lacey edged toward the door. "I'm going to see if Daisy needs to go potty."

"Jordy can—" Sam began, but she was gone before he could finish. He glowered at his best friend, who didn't seem one ounce ashamed of himself. "You're a fucking cockblock."

"Cockblock seems a little intense. Unless you were going to fuck your girlfriend on Graham's countertops." Jordy grinned and came to inspect the turkey. Sam smacked his hand when he tried to touch the golden, crispy skin. "Is talking about mac 'n' cheese how you get your engine revving these days?"

Sam rolled his eyes. "About as much as talking about birds gets yours going."

"Talking about birds *does* get me going these days," Jordy said. "Annie gets talking, and she's so fucking smart. It's hot."

"I'm glad ornithology lectures make you so happy." It sounded sarcastic, but Sam sincerely meant it.

There was a brief, awkward lull. Jordy was thinking, and that was a dangerous pastime.

"Are you happy?"

Sam turned off the heat under the boiling potatoes and picked up the pot, using the task to buy himself time to think for a few seconds. Finally he said, "Yeah, I am happy."

Jordy nodded, crossing his arms. "Good."

Sam poured the potatoes into the strainer he'd put in the sink earlier. "You're being weird, Jordan. What aren't you saying?"

"I'm not being weird. I'm...relieved."

"Relieved?" Sam put the potatoes back into the pot and moved it back to the stove. "Can you just tell me what's going on inside your head?"

Jordy looked up at the ceiling. "I think about you a lot. I wonder how you're doing, if you're okay, if you've gotten out of bed today. I've been afraid for a while that you'd do something...permanent."

"Besides the tattoos?" Sam gave Jordy a wry smile in a vain attempt to diffuse some of the tension building in the room.

"Whenever you'd go super quiet...I worried this would be the time I wouldn't be enough to make you stay. You're my best friend, Sam."

"Isn't Annie your best friend now?"

"It's different. I want to spend every day with her, but I

want to spend every day with you too." A soft smile replaced the melancholy frown on Jordy's face. "My stupid dream is we all buy a big plot of land and build a commune. Walk to each other's houses whenever we want. No more stupid planes and long car rides."

Sam raised an eyebrow. "Do you really want Peter popping in?"

"Yes. I miss having my people close."

Sam started to season the boiled potatoes so he could mash them. "You know I've never been actually suicidal, right?"

"Yeah, but how far is it from 'everyone would be better off if I wasn't around' to...well, 'everyone would be better off if I wasn't around ever again'?"

That was the gut punch Sam hadn't been expecting. Because there wasn't a very long way from garden-variety intrusive thoughts to the insidious sort. Sam couldn't pretend like he hadn't spent the entire summer wondering if Jordy would be better off if he never spoke to him again. That his life would be enriched by Sam's permanent absence.

Jordy shrugged. "I don't know. I just want to make sure that you're safe and you're happy."

"I'm safe. I'm happy." It was true, too. Not a little half lie. Not skirting close to the truth. He really was safe and happy. "I'd be happier if you and Annie moved closer, but baby steps."

Jordy chuckled. "Never say never. Maybe in a few years."

"If we can convince Peter to move here, we could recreate LA without all the traffic and pollution."

"I know where Graham hides his spare key," Sam said, mashing the potatoes.

"Speaking of hiding, where *is* your house?"

"I'll never tell."

"But Lacey knows?"

"She'll never tell."

"Are you sure?"

"I can do things for her that you can't."

"Yeah, but she and Annie are *really* chatty."

Sam stopped mashing. "Did you send your girlfriend to find out from my girlfriend where my hideout is?"

Jordy grinned. "No, but it was worth pretending to see the look on your face."

"See if I give you directions now."

"Is it serious? Between you and Lacey."

The question took Sam by surprise. It shouldn't have. Sam had been prepping answers to various relationship questions all week. What surprised him was his body's reaction to the question. His pulse jumped from a comfortable resting to a frantic racing. His stomach twisted into a knot. Things weren't serious. They were fake as fuck. But good luck telling his body that.

"We haven't been dating that long," Sam deflected.

"She knows where you live, and you have a dog together," Jordy pointed out. "I'd call cohabitation and joint custody serious."

"When the fuck did you learn the word cohabitation?" Sam asked, tasting the potatoes and adding more salt.

"I'm in love with a PhD. She's going to help me beat Peter in Scrabble."

"There's playing the long game, and then there's whatever you're doing." Sam was finally satisfied with the potatoes, and cracked the oven to check on the dishes cooking in there. Golden brown perfection.

"You're being avoidant."

"No, I'm just not ready to answer the question." Back into half-truth territory. Because he wasn't ready to answer the question, to Jordy or to himself. Kissing Lacey had only muddled things further. His brain, heart, and cock had teamed up to demand to know why he was wasting precious brain cells answering Jordy's questions when he could be thinking of ways to get Lacey alone so he could touch her again. "Not all of us know in three days."

"It's been longer than three days, and the dopey-ass look on your face when she's around says otherwise. But that's just my opinion." Jordy shrugged. "Do you need any help?"

"Yeah. Help me find the fucking oven mitts." Sam couldn't remember where he'd put them down. "I do not have a dopey-ass look on my face."

Jordy snorted, looking around the kitchen counters. "Yes. You do. It might not be full-blown heart eyes, but for you? It's pretty damn dopey— Ah-ha!" He held up the lost oven mitts. "They were behind the turkey."

Sam sighed. "Of course they were." He took them from Jordy. "I don't look any more dopey than you do looking at Annie."

This did not have the desired effect. Jordy smiled. "I know how fucking stupid I look when she's around, and I don't care. I love her, I'm going to ask her to marry me as soon as it's reasonable, and I'm going to enjoy looking dopey for the rest of my life."

The presentation of the meal was not the triumphant moment Sam had envisioned. There was chaos in the dining room. Eloise's carefully constructed seating chart was ruined. The place cards had been moved around the table. In fact, the only person who didn't seem at least a little bit confused was Peter, who looked like the cat that ate the canary. Sybil sat next to him, looking very much like the canary in question.

Lacey was seated across the table between Chase and Annie, and Sam glared at Chase until he got the hint and asked Sam if he wanted to switch places.

Sam did.

When he'd settled into his new seat, Lacey leaned over and kissed his cheek. "You did a really great job on everything."

The flush rushed over his body like a wildfire through bone dry prairie.

"You haven't even tried it yet."

"I'm very familiar with your cooking," she reminded him, squeezing his knee. "I have no doubt this is going to be the best Thanksgiving I've ever had."

Sam relaxed a little and kissed her softly, just because he could. It was supposed to be a quick peck, but Lacey lingered, so he did too.

WHEN IT WAS all said and done, it was the best Thanksgiving Sam had ever had. He was surrounded by people he loved, and those people loved him loudly enough in return that he barely ever questioned if they really liked him.

Daisy spent the entirety of dinner—after she'd wolfed down her meal like she was in a speed-eating contest—under the table, laying on Sam's feet. When it was his turn to say what he was thankful for, Sam said that he was grateful for Daisy, who gave him a reason to go outside every day.

Then Lacey said, "I'm grateful to be here," and Sam wondered what that meant all through dessert.

He waited until they were in the car to ask.

"What did you mean when you said you were grateful to be there?"

Lacey yawned, fighting off a food coma. "It was nice to feel like I belonged for a few hours." She stretched and didn't say anything when he drove past the street he'd need to turn on to drop her off at Gavin and Leo's. "I don't know how hard I should try to keep making friends with them, though, since you'll get them all in the breakup."

"What breakup?" Sam rolled through a stop sign.

"Ours. In the future. When you feel sufficiently safe from the old ladies, you break up with me and I go back to having no friends." Lacey paused thoughtfully. "Except for Annie. Giving me her number was the nicest thing any of my boyfriends has ever done for me."

Sam gripped the steering wheel. "That's fucking awful."

"No, I mean that it's the nicest significant thing. Anyone can do flowers and dinner. You went out of your way to get me Annie's phone number when you didn't need to. You've really raised the bar."

"Your bar was in hell," Sam grumbled. "You've got the worst taste in men." *Me included.*

Lacey laughed ruefully. "You're not wrong. They all start off nice and become complete shitheads."

"Except me. I started out a shithead. What you see is what you get."

Lacey scoffed. "You like to act like you're a shithead, but you're the biggest softie I've ever met." She reached across the car and tucked some hair behind his ear. He needed a cut. "Shitheads don't make their dog's food from scratch."

Sam's heart ballooned in his chest, growing so big it squashed his lungs and made it hard to breathe. He didn't want her to go, but he didn't know how to make her stay. The easy answer, the one he'd get if he told anyone what was actually going on between them, was to tell her how he felt, how having her around made him not simply happy but joyful, how she soothed hurts she hadn't caused. But Lacey never seemed to miss an opportunity to remind him they were in a fake relationship that was very temporary.

This was the universe's way of punishing him for telling Jordy he couldn't fall in love quickly. To have the thing he'd sworn he didn't want dangled in front of his face.

"I'm not soft. I'm hard. Like my mattress," Sam said, knowing it would make Lacey laugh. And it did.

"You own the most comfortable bed in the world. It's why I keep letting you trick me into sleeping over, even though Daisy farts and kicks, and you snore if you get even the tiniest bit blocked up."

"If you think I snore, I've got terrible news for you."

"I do not snore!" Lacey said indignantly.

"I'll record you sometime. And I'm not sure all those farts are Daisy's."

CHAPTER TWENTY-ONE

SAM STARED at the menu like he'd forgotten how to read. He'd gone to brunch at the Crane Hotel before, so it wasn't that he needed a lot of time to study the menu and make his choice. His brain refused to cooperate. The words on the page were simply letters arranged in non-alphabetical order.

Sleep had been elusive.

When they'd arrived home the night before, he and Lacey had gone into their nighttime routine. Lacey tidied up the kitchen and picked up Daisy's toys, and Sam took Daisy for her bedtime potty break. It was while he was politely looking away while Daisy did her business that it hit Sam that they *had* a nighttime routine.

Their routine was such that when they got inside, Daisy started going down the stairs to the TV room. She got halfway down before she turned to look at Sam, like she was saying, "Hello, dummy, it's time for television." So he trooped down the stairs after her, turned on *Midsomer Murders*, and set the sleep timer for the TV.

"Come to bed when you're done," he told his dog, scratching her behind her ears.

Sam couldn't believe this life now. One day he'd been an infinitely cool rock star without anything tying him down, and now he talked to his dog like she could understand him.

Upstairs, Lacey had been tucking herself into bed.

"Where's Daisy?" she'd asked, frowning.

Sam had gone to his closet to change. "She's watching her English murder mysteries," he'd told her.

"Does it make you nervous that our dog could probably get away with murder?" It had given Sam the warm fuzzies to hear her call Daisy "our dog."

That was probably what had triggered his insomnia. Trying to untangle the mess of feelings he was having, to sort them into perfectly understandable little boxes, then trying to shove them down and away. Next to him, Lacey breathed softly, sleeping on her side, oblivious to his turmoil. There was a space between them, reserved for Daisy, and Sam wondered what would happen if he invaded their No Man's Land.

He never got to find out. Daisy jumped onto the bed and took her spot with the kind of tired, put-upon sigh that only a truly spoiled dog could make. It was like she was saying that being everyone's favorite was such hard work.

When Sam finally did sleep, he dreamed that his feelings were different colors of paint on a palette, but they wouldn't stay in their designated spaces and ran together. In his dream he was frustrated, and angrily swiped his brush through the paint and smeared it onto the canvas. It made a beautiful picture.

Then he was awake again, trying to scribble notes in his nightstand notebook by the harsh light of his cell phone flashlight.

"Saaaam." Jordy's voice pulled him back like he was a fish on a line.

Sam handed his menu to their server. "Tell Amara to surprise me."

"Your food is going to be shaped like a dick," Graham warned as their server headed to ring in their orders.

"She'd have found a way no matter what I ordered," Sam said, picking up his coffee. The Crane Hotel was the only place outside of Stardust where someone could buy Sybil's house blend.

The self-titled—despite Graham's many protests—Brunch Bros hadn't been able to get together in a little over six months. Their last brunch had also been at the hotel restaurant. Sam wondered if now that Jordy had retired if they'd be able to make it a little less than six months before their next get together.

Peter sat across the table, picking the leaves off the celery stalk in his Bloody Mary like a lovelorn poet picking petals off a flower. Something was off with him. Normally he'd be talking their ears off or interrogating them for updates on their lives. Sitting in quiet contemplation wasn't a strength of Peter's. It wasn't a strength of Lacey's either.

There she was again. Straight to the front of his mind with the barest hint of provocation.

"Sam? Are you okay?" Graham asked, frowning.

Sam nodded, a little confused by the question.

Graham's frown deepened. "It's just that you've been holding your cup in the air for thirty seconds without taking a drink."

Sam took a gulp, draining half the cup. He set it back in its saucer, and his fingers were barely out of the handle before a roaming server filled it back up.

"I just had some lyrics I was bouncing around."

Graham's frown disappeared, instantly replaced by a curious and encouraging smile. "How's writing going?"

Sam poured the smallest amount of cream into his coffee to get it back to the perfect shade, focusing on the swirl instead of the prying eyes at the table.

"I've, um, written about fifteen songs. Fifteen that are basically ready to record, anyway. I've got more notes and shit floating around." He waved his hand dismissively. "It'll probably amount to nothing."

The resonant silence at the table made his ears ring. Sam glanced up. Unsurprisingly, they were all staring at him.

"What?"

They all exchanged silent looks in a language he wasn't privy to, and then Graham spoke.

"Sam, the last time I asked you how writing was going, you told me to fuck off. When Eloise asked, you said you had a few titles."

"Yeah. So?"

"That was right after the Cranberry Festival."

"I need to start having Annie ask him..." Jordy's voice tapered off as Sam's attention drifted away from the table again.

Fifteen songs since the Cranberry Festival in September. Except he knew he didn't have anything written in September. He hadn't really had the itch to write until October.

October.

When he'd spilled coffee on Lacey and gotten them tangled in his stupid lie.

It wasn't that she was his muse. He wouldn't call her that. The songs he was writing weren't *about* her. Not all of them. Maybe two. But having Lacey around was inspiring. She was the much-needed oil to the stuck cogs of his brain. The way she talked, how she moved, how she twisted her hair into a bun when she sat on his countertop while he cooked and then continually had to tuck little tendrils behind her ears—it all inspired him.

Did that make her his muse?

"He's gone again," Peter said as sound filtered back into his senses. "Absolutely besotted."

Sam frowned, unable to connect the dots of what he'd missed. "Hmm?"

"I said Lacey must be a good influence on you and you were off in la-la land again." The soft, knowing smile on Peter's face made Sam instantly suspicious.

"She's a horrible influence," Sam countered, leaving out that the horrible influence was that she encouraged his inner eighty-five-year-old homebody.

Was she still snuggled up in his bed with Daisy?

A young man in a suit that looked like he'd bought it hoping to gain several more inches in the shoulder department trekked across the dining room toward their table. Trekked was a generous word; it was the stiff-legged, "I'm-going-to-shit-my-pants" speed walk of someone who needed to deliver bad news.

He stopped by Graham's elbow and cleared his throat nervously. "Um, Mr. Thatcher?"

Graham took a healthy swig of his breakfast cocktail. "Yes, Trevor?"

Trevor looked ready to faint. Sam wanted to tell the poor kid to unlock his knees.

"I know that you're, um, busy, sir, but, um, you see there's a, uh, problem with the, um, computers at the front desk—"

"Did you try turning them off and then on again?"

Trevor wobbled.

Graham sighed and took a sobering drink of his coffee. "I'll come take a look."

Trevor nodded and practically fled the dining room at the same poop-pants speed walk pace he'd entered.

"He's new," Graham explained, "and would you believe he's Kiki's cousin? I think she's been trying to scare him."

"Kiki has a family?" Jordy sounded surprised. "I always assumed she beamed down from another planet."

"She does. They're nice." Graham took another bracing

drink of coffee. "I'd bet good money the computers will be fine by the time I get out there."

Jordy pushed back his chair in unison with Graham.

"Did you have a strong desire to watch me play tech support?"

"I have to pee."

"If you wouldn't suck down mimosas like this is your last chance to get them..." Graham started as they left the table.

"Can I ask you a weird personal question?" Peter said as soon as Graham and Jordy had exited the dining room. "It's okay if you don't want to answer."

In all the years he'd known him, Sam had never once known Peter to ask permission before asking a question. It was always "full speed, damn the torpedoes" with Peter. So, Sam was curious and nervous about what kind of question Peter could possibly have that invited any kind of caution.

"Um...sure?"

"What's sex with Lacey like?"

Sam froze. The clatter of emotions in his chest almost drowned out the reasonable sound of his brain. "What?"

Peter's face turned scarlet. "That came out wrong. What I meant was...Lacey is the girl from the song you wrote. The Barcelona song. So you'd slept together before and now you're back together and I was wondering how that's going? Is it better? Worse? Different? Were you nervous?"

"It was—" Sam stopped himself. He didn't need to lie about this. This was an opportunity for honesty. "We actually haven't had sex yet. Not since Barcelona. How did you know that, anyway?"

"I asked Lacey how you met, and she said it was in Barcelona when you were on tour. And when I took into account the timing, the love song, and the way you are with her now, it was obvious."

Heat crept up Sam's face. "What love song?"

Peter sighed like Sam had asked him how to spell orange. "'Barcelona.' It's a love song. I think you're the only one that hasn't caught on."

"But I'd known her for *one* night at that point," Sam pointed out. "How could it be a love song?"

"Do you not believe in love at first sight?"

Sam shook his head, even though the first time he'd ever seen Lacey immediately popped into his mind. "No. Do you?"

"Of course I do," Peter said with conviction. "I believe in love at first sight, soulmates, true love, all of it. Love is too important to not take it seriously. What you wrote about Lacey went so far beyond sex. It was about connection and safety."

Sam didn't like the ache blooming in his chest. He needed to steer the conversation back to safer ground. "What does this have to do with my current sex life with Lacey?"

Peter flushed. "When I was younger, I met the love of my life, but the timing wasn't right. We've reconnected, and I'm worried I'll..." He waved his hand like he'd be able to pluck the right word out of thin air. "Disappoint her, I guess."

"Did you used to disappoint her?" Sam asked, curious because this conversation was upending some long-held beliefs he had about Peter.

Peter shook his head, rubbing salt rim of his Bloody Mary off with his thumb. "No. It was transcendent. For her, too. I asked. A lot."

Sam was having a hard time reconciling his assumptions with reality. Whenever they'd talked about sex as a group, Peter had not participated, and by some unspoken agreement, no one pressed him about it. "So you're not a virgin?"

Peter laughed. "No. Just debilitatingly monogamous."

A thought tickled the back of Sam's mind.

"Peter...how long has it been?"

Peter turned as red as his Bloody Mary, but Sam never got his answer because Jordy picked that moment to drop unceremoniously back into his chair.

"That was an Austin Powers pee," he said. "I didn't think it was ever going to end."

"Why are you the way you are?" Sam asked, wadding up his napkin to throw at his best friend. "Does Annie know how gross you are?"

"She thinks I'm hysterical," Jordy said proudly.

"I thought PhDs were supposed to be smart."

"She is," Jordy insisted. "She picked me."

"They're going to take back her degree," Peter teased, but his heart wasn't in it. How concerned was he about his sexual performance if he couldn't give Jordy a hard time?

Should Sam be more concerned?

That nagged him for the rest of the meal. It never failed to amaze him that he could be engaged in a conversation with half of his brain, while the other half was off to the races worrying about something unrelated.

Was he afraid to take things to the next step with Lacey? Is that why he hadn't taken advantage of the *many* opportunities he'd had to engage in good old-fashioned hanky-panky with her? Why had he been telling himself he was waiting for *her* to bring it up when he was capable of expressing his desires like a grownup? He wanted her; that wasn't in question. He wanted Lacey's long, graceful, strong legs wrapped around his hips or his head. He wanted to reacquaint his mouth with every inch of her body, even her toes. He wanted to make her moan, and sigh, and gasp, and scream his name until she was hoarse.

When had he become a coward?

. . .

THAT QUESTION LOOMED large in the forefront of his mind when he drove home, parked in his garage, and then sat in his car, engine off.

He could just talk to Lacey. Tell her that he wanted to alter their deal. If she disagreed, they carried on the way that they were and, in due course, broke up.

There was a painful, sour twang in his chest, like he'd touched the wrong string on his guitar. Sam gathered his guts and went inside.

The house smelled like childhood nostalgia. Tomato soup and grilled cheese. Daisy was sprawled out in her usual spot on the kitchen floor, waiting for Lacey to pay the cheese tax. After the dog's rancid farts the night before, Sam doubted Lacey would be feeding her dairy anytime soon. Daisy's tail thumped against the floor when she saw Sam.

Lacey was peeking under her grilled cheese with the aid of the biggest spatula Sam owned, wearing nothing but a very over-sized hoodie he'd been sent as PR and some of his tall wool socks. The black sweatshirt grazed the tops of her thighs and made his mouth water. He stood behind her and wrapped his arms around her waist, and kissed the impossibly soft skin on her neck. Lacey sighed softly and leaned against him.

"How was boys' brunch?" she asked.

"Good," Sam said, his lips traveling up toward her ear. "I would've made you lunch if you'd waited."

"I didn't know when you were getting back, and you didn't feed me breakfast. A girl might get the impression you're sick of being her on-call chef."

"You were sound asleep," he told her, nipping at the shell of her ear, "and too cute to wake up."

Lacey laughed. "You dirty, filthy liar. You just told me yesterday that I snore."

"Doesn't mean it's not cute." Sam kissed the tender spot

behind her ear, and Lacey almost dropped her grilled cheese mid flip. "You and Daisy were harmonizing."

Lacey tossed the spatula on the counter then turned in his arms so they were face-to-face. Her gaze darted from his lips to his eyes, but she frowned.

"What are you thinking about?" Sam asked.

"All the rules I want to break," she admitted, her fingers playing with the hair at the base of his skull.

His heart jumped. So did his cock. "I'm willing to renegotiate if you are."

Lacey chewed on her bottom lip while she thought.

"This is still a fake relationship," she said right when Sam thought the suspense would kill him. "No getting cozy because we're kissing and fucking."

He raised a doubtful eyebrow and looked at her clothes. Exhibit A that they'd already crossed the cozy bridge. Lacey sighed dramatically.

"You know what I mean. We're breaking up next year."

Next year. Could be January first. Could be December thirty-first. Sam didn't know her timeline, but he knew that he wasn't in a hurry.

"Next year," he agreed with no conviction.

"When were you last tested?"

"June. It came back negative."

Lacey nodded. "Mine was in September. After Mitch and I broke up. It was negative, but I had a boyfriend give me chlamydia once and I've been Safety Sally ever since."

"When was that?"

"About four years ago. Penicillin is a wonder drug." She plastered a brave, cheerful smile on her face, then became somber. "I don't want kids. If we have an accident, I'm taking care of business."

"I was also serious when I said I didn't want kids, so I support that."

Lacey nodded again, but it wasn't an affirmative nod. She was buying time with the motion, the wheels in her head visibly spinning. Sam knew that look; he wore it often.

"What are you thinking about?" he asked as gently as he could.

"I'm nervous," she admitted in a whisper. "What if I'm not song-worthy anymore? I'm not the young twenty-three-year-old you fucked. I'm old. Things creak."

Sam unsuccessfully tried to bite down on a laugh. It was too ridiculous, though. Lacey believed she was over the hill with all the conviction of someone who had just crossed from their twenties into their thirties, and if Jordy's aches and pains reports were to be believed, they hadn't seen anything yet.

"We're the same age, so I'm going to creak too." Sam rested his forehead against hers. "When did you figure out the song was about you?"

"I didn't. Peter told me yesterday. Were you ever going to tell me?"

"Not if I could help it. I didn't want to scare you off." Peter's interpretation of the song replayed in his head. "It's not a love song."

"I know. It's about a good old-fashioned fuck."

Sam grinned. "There was nothing old-fashioned about that fuck."

"I don't know about that. The Greeks were kinky, and I'd call 700 BCE old-fashioned."

He pressed her against the counter. "You've got an answer for everything, don't you?"

"You'll have to keep asking questions to find out." Lacey trailed her thumb down his racing pulse. "This isn't going to ruin everything, is it?"

A shiver slid down his spine. "I don't think good sex has ever ruined anything."

Lacey looked unsure, so Sam decided to ease her worries in the best way he knew how. He cupped the back of her neck with one hand, the other hand sneaking under the hem of his sweatshirt to grasp her hip, and he kissed her.

It was supposed to be a slow, gentle exploration, but she moaned against his mouth and the very thin thread that held Sam's self-control together snapped. A low growl rumbled in the back of his throat, and their kiss quickly became frenzied. Her fingers dug into his shoulders while both of his hands went to her ass, squeezing and kneading the well-toned muscle.

Lacey sucked on his bottom lip and stars danced behind Sam's eyelids. His cock was already so hard he worried it would bust through the zipper of his jeans, and all the memories his brain associated with Lacey sucking made it throb painfully.

She pushed his jacket off his shoulders and down his arms, and Sam let it drop onto the floor with a muffled thump. Then she tugged at the collar of his shirt, then the arms, and then the hem, unsuccessfully trying to undress him.

"Off," she snarled against his mouth, and Sam obeyed. His shirt joined his jacket on the floor. "Good boy."

"What's my reward?"

The tips of Lacey's fingers traced the lines of ink all over his skin. "Hmm...I'll let you lick my pussy."

That was a better answer than he'd hoped for and his mouth watered. Sam had no issues ceding control of this encounter as long as it didn't stop. Before she could take back his prize, he boosted her up onto the counter and pushed her knees wide.

"Eager?" she asked, breathlessly.

"Practically starving," Sam replied, bending down so he was eye level with the crotch of her panties. He hooked two fingers into the fabric there, was pleased to find it damp, and pulled it to the side. He licked his lips. "Perfect."

There would be time for teasing a different day. He didn't have the patience or willpower for it at the moment. Sam knew what he wanted, and he made damn sure he got it. The first taste of her on his tongue was salty sweet heaven, and he moaned loudly.

"Oh fuck," they said in unison.

Lacey sank her fingers into his hair and tugged, pulling him closer. "More," she demanded, like stopping had ever been an option.

Heaven was a place on Earth, and it was located between Lacey Finch's thighs. Sam was just a gifted sinner who'd been granted access. For the price of her moans and her sighs, he'd worship the altar of her body for a lifetime.

"Clit," she gasped, and Sam flicked his tongue across it. Lacey's back arched.

"Fingers," she groaned, and he slid two fingers inside of her easily, his tongue still working at her clit. "Oh, fuck, yes, yes, *yes*."

Sam was so desperate for his own pleasure that he wanted to crawl out of his skin. Both of his hands were busy with Lacey, and the angle he needed to be at to lick her glorious pussy meant he couldn't even rub up against the cabinetry. The head of his cock was oozing precum, and his underwear was becoming increasingly wet and uncomfortable. He wouldn't stop, though. Not until—

"Oh, fuck," Lacey whined, and she squirmed. Sam maintained his course. If she needed something different, she'd tell him. He wasn't about to fuck this up by going rogue. "Please, please, please...oh, god, Sam..."

A breathless squeak announced her inner walls convulsing around his fingers and her thighs clamping around his ears. Sam continued until the tension in her body eased and the death grip she had on his hair slackened. Even then he allowed himself casual licks of her pussy until she pushed his head away.

"Stop before I die," she panted. Lacey took deep breaths, and frowned, her nose twitching. "Is something burn—oh fuck! My sandwich!"

The forgotten grilled cheese was charred to a blackened crisp.

"I'll make you another one," Sam promised after he'd turned off the stove, careful not to say anything about the tomato soup that had bubbled away to nothing but a red mess.

"Orgasms and sandwiches. What more could a girl want?"

"More orgasms?" Sam suggested, unbuttoning his pants and sliding down the zipper for some much-needed relief.

Lacey held out her arms. "Take me to bed."

CHAPTER TWENTY-TWO

LACEY BOUNCED when Sam dropped her on the bed. She laughed, still giddy from her kitchen counter orgasm. It had been a long time since anyone had taken the time or effort to go down on her properly, and Sam's obvious enthusiasm for the task made it even more delicious.

"Take off your pants," she commanded, propping herself up on her elbows to watch.

He'd undone his pants in the kitchen, and now she could see what a mess she'd made of him. The dark wet spot by the head of his jutting cock was incredibly satisfying. She'd done that. She'd made him so hard that his cock wept. When Sam pushed off his pants and underwear in one go, his erection bounced like a spring, head glistening. Lacey licked her lips.

A blur of white and creamy gold fur catapulted onto the bed next to her, and Lacey shrieked.

"Daisy! No!"

Daisy crouched, rump high in the air, tail wagging furiously, and tongue lolling out the side of her mouth, ready to play.

"Daisy, no," Sam chastised, hooking his fingers under her collar and guiding her off the bed. "It's not playtime for you."

He waddled like a penguin for several steps before pausing to kick off his pants that were still around his ankles. Lacey admired his ass, which was surprisingly free of any tattoos.

"Let's find you a nice, cozy, English murder in the countryside, hmm?" he said in a singsong voice, leading Daisy out of the room quickly. He looked over his shoulder as they exited and said firmly to Lacey, "Stay."

Lacey let her knees drop apart, and she winked. Sam looked up at the ceiling, like he was thanking whatever higher power was up there, and then disappeared down the hall.

Once the jingle of Daisy's tags had faded, Lacey sprang into action, scrambling to undress. If she'd known Sam was going to pick *today* to try and fuck her, she'd have prepared better. Cute underwear. Makeup. An expensive but visually satisfying Brazilian wax. The shower she'd taken yesterday hadn't been an everything shower, it had been a most things shower. Legs and pits got shaved. She'd assumed she was safe to leave her pussy for a bit longer. The hair was sparse, but she preferred it smooth. Too late now.

She ran to the bathroom to brush her teeth because she couldn't remember if she had and was startled by her appearance in the mirror. Her messy bun was more messy than bun, and there was smudged mascara she hadn't quite managed to wash off last night under each eye. Did Sam need glasses? Or was he so desperate to fuck something that his standards had slipped to whatever low level she was occupying?

Lacey wiped away the leftover mascara and attacked her hair with a brush. Presentable and fuckable was attainable before Sam got back from distracting their dog with her murder shows. She grabbed her toothbrush—a nice electric one she couldn't afford but had magically appeared next to Sam's one night—and squeezed toothpaste on it, then bounced from one foot to the other while she brushed her teeth. There were little beeps when she was supposed to switch to a new section of her mouth, but Lacey always got bored and moved on before the beep. She'd never made it to the automatic shutoff feature at the end.

Spit. Rinse. Rinse out the sink.

As she turned off the water, a hand closed around her throat and Sam drew her back against his body, his cock pressing insistently against her ass.

"I thought I told you to stay put," he growled in her ear, all bark and no bite. The play still sent pleasant shivers down her spine and made her pussy throb.

"I'm not very good at following directions," Lacey said innocently, grinding her ass against him. Sam's breath caught and his eyes fluttered before he could steel his expression again.

She liked how they looked together in the mirror. Sam's dark hair contrasting with her blonde, his inked skin compared to her blank. The letters on his knuckles—AWRY—looked almost sinister against her throat.

"Can I take over?" he asked, his mask of dominance betrayed by his thumb stroking her pulse tenderly.

"Yes, please," Lacey breathed, eager to relinquish the baton of control. "Red light, green light?"

Sam nodded. "Just red and green work too, sunshine."

If his hand hadn't been around her neck, she'd be a puddle on the floor. How the hell did he manage to make her feel so safe and cherished? It was a good thing she wasn't his real girlfriend. She probably wouldn't survive the experience.

"Since you can't follow directions"—he nipped her earlobe—"I'm going to have to teach you a lesson."

"Don't threaten me with a good time."

"You're such a brat."

Lacey grinned. "And you love it."

She thought Sam rolled his eyes right before he forced her to bend over the bathroom counter.

"Hands on the counter. That's a good girl." He rubbed the spot between her shoulder blades. "You're going to get your ass smacked, and you're going to count them. Understood?"

Lacey wiggled her ass. "Yes, Daddy—oh!"

The first two smacks were delivered consecutively, one right on top of the other. They stung so good her toes and fingers curled.

"You're supposed to count," Sam reminded her. "We're going to start over."

"I wasn't read—y," she protested, her voice catching on the last syllable because he'd delivered another smack to her other ass cheek.

"Stop making excuses. Start again."

Smack.

"One."

Smack.

"Two."

Sam bent over and kissed her shoulder. "That's better. Keep counting."

Lacey sank into the feeling of Sam's palm connecting with her flesh, embracing the sting and the warmth. She counted each hit, and every few smacks Sam would praise her with words and small kisses. The pleasant aura of her earlier orgasm seemed to return and she relished in the floating feeling.

Smack.

"Ten," she moaned, her eyes falling closed. They snapped back open when Sam's fingers began to rub her clit. She rocketed up onto her toes. It was like he'd touched her with a live wire. "Oh my god."

"You're so fucking wet," he commented, his fingers sliding easily from her clit into her pussy. It was true; she was drenched. A shower would be required after this. Or at least a damp washcloth.

A witty retort died on Lacey's tongue as Sam worked some kind of black magic with his fingers. Another intense orgasm built like an oncoming storm, and she braced for it.

Sam withdrew his fingers and she whimpered.

"What the fuck?" she complained, looking over her shoulder to glare at him.

Sam was unperturbed. "You need to clean up the mess you made first."

She frowned. "What mess?"

Sam pressed his erection into the cleft of her ass.

Right. That mess.

"Go wait by the bed," he instructed. "On your knees."

Lacey hurried to obey. She arranged herself on her knees by the bed, tender ass resting gently on her heels. In the bathroom, the sink turned on, ran for a little bit, then turned off. When Sam came out, his hairline was a little damp.

"Good girl," he said, and Lacey preened, sticking her chest out triumphantly.

Sam moved with the grace and authority of a jungle cat on the prowl. He made his way across the room to stand in front of her, one hand lazily stroking his cock.

"Open your mouth. Stick your tongue out."

She did, and Sam tapped the head of his cock against her outstretched tongue.

"Suck."

Lacey eagerly took him into her mouth. This was something she'd thought about a lot since their date to the movie theater, especially when she got a chance to touch herself. She sucked with enthusiasm, bobbing up and down his shaft. Sam gathered her hair into his hand and wrapped it around his fist. After she gave him a tiny consenting nod, he used his grip to guide her, forcing her to her limit with every push of her head and thrust of his hips.

Sam pulled out with a *pop*. "Fucking hell…I'm going to need a minute." He released her hair, then combed it with his fingers. "You did *too* good, sunshine."

Lacey smiled even though she needed to catch her breath. "What show did you put on for Daisy?"

"*Midsomer*," he said and sat down on the bed. "Wanted to make sure we had lots of time."

"Got plans for me?" she asked, rising from her knees to straddle him, careful not to impale herself on his cock, no matter how tempting.

"*Midsomer* might not be long enough." Sam kissed her, and when his tongue slipped into her mouth, Lacey could taste traces of herself. Their hands explored the less scandalous parts of each other's bodies, like their shoulders and backs, a tender respite in the middle of the intensity.

Sam eased Lacey onto her back, her legs locked tightly around his waist, like she was afraid if she gave him the chance he'd change his mind and run away.

"I can't decide what to do with you first," he admitted.

"Fuck me?" she suggested.

He patted her thigh. "Let go so I can get a condom."

Reluctantly Lacey released him, and Sam stretched across the bed to reach into the nightstand. There were a handful of condoms in there, and she wondered when he'd stocked them because they hadn't been there when he'd gone to New York. She'd snooped.

Sam put the condom on with practiced ease and speed.

"How do you want me?" she asked.

"On top. I don't want to miss a thing."

Sam settled on his back, and then Lacey straddled his hips. "Like this?"

"Perfect," he said, his eyes roaming her body. "You're fucking perfect."

A flush raced across her body, settling in her chest and face. She didn't feel perfect. But the way Sam was looking at her, she almost believed him.

The head of his cock nudged at the entrance to her pussy and Lacey slipped him inside easily. He filled her, touching places that made pleasure ricochet through her body, and they moaned in unison.

"That's my girl," Sam praised as she found a rhythm that felt so good she never wanted it to end. "Ride that cock like a good girl. Make us both come."

She was too close, too primed, because as soon as Sam's thumb found her clit, it took less than a minute for her walls to clamp tightly around his cock and her muscles to contract almost painfully. Her orgasm wasn't gentle. She screamed and shuddered, and when she thought she couldn't go on anymore, Sam fucked her from below so hard her brain rattled.

"Oh my god!" she shouted, and bit his shoulder to muffle the accompanying scream.

That sent Sam over the edge too. With a muffled curse and a grunt, he shuddered, his cock pulsing deep inside her.

They lay like that for a while, Lacey's face buried in his neck, and Sam's arms loosely wrapped around her, trying to catch their breath.

"Sorry it was kind of quick," Sam finally said. "It's been a while for me."

Lacey was too high on her own brain chemicals not to laugh. When she caught her breath again, she said, "Efficient. The word you were looking for was efficient."

· · ·

"THIS IS A REALLY GOOD GRILLED CHEESE," Lacey said, torn between taking small bites to savor the sandwich or inhaling it.

"I think you're still dazed from your afterglow," Sam responded, wiping out the pan he'd used.

After they'd cleaned themselves up, Sam had wrapped Lacey in his luxurious robe and steered her toward the kitchen to make her the promised grilled cheese.

"This is the best post-coital experience of my life. Five-star service."

"I aim to please," he said, opening the fridge to look for something.

"The uniform really puts it over the top," she continued, grinning. She'd gotten the robe, and Sam had pulled on a pair of black sweatpants that rode low on his hips. He hadn't bothered with a shirt, and Lacey was grateful. It was nice to be able to openly appreciate his body.

Sam brought two cold bottles of water to her spot at the counter and put one in front of her.

"You need to hydrate, sunshine," he told her, then clasped the back of her neck in one hand and kissed her. She loved how he did that. It was gentle, yet commanding, and the combination made her dizzy.

"You're bossy," Lacey said, a bit dazed, when he released her neck.

"Yes." Sam's hand slipped into the neckline of the robe and cupped her breast. "You like that almost as much as you like bossing me around."

She loved him.

The feeling crashed into her world like a meteor, wreaking havoc and destruction in its wake. There was no warning—or maybe there had been, but she'd ignored the wailing sirens by plugging her ears.

No, she didn't. That was post-orgasmic bliss and a damn good grilled cheese talking. She couldn't love him. She didn't have much of a plan where her life was concerned, but falling in love with Sam Shoop was *not* on the list.

Except that her chest ached when she looked at him, like her heart was only just learning how to beat properly. And when she was away from him, she was only killing time until she could see him again.

This was horrible. This was a disaster.

Sam kissed her again, one hand in her robe, one hand on her neck, and her worries blew away like dandelion fuzz.

This was wonderful.

"I had an idea," he said, withdrawing his hands to sit next to her. "More of a favor, actually."

That cooled her jets. Nothing good had ever started with a boyfriend asking her for a favor. Sam wasn't even her boyfriend, he was boyfriend adjacent, and it still made her wary.

"What kind of favor?"

"I'd like to take Daisy on the road with me eventually," he began, "but I'm not sure how well she'll travel. I've got some short trips coming up, and they could be good for a test drive."

"What does that have to do with me?" Lacey asked, taking another bite of her grilled cheese to remind herself of Sam's admirable qualities.

"I'd like for you to come with me so Daisy isn't alone or with a stranger."

That stung like floor burn. Sam didn't want her company, he wanted a babysitter for the dog.

"I don't think Daisy has ever met a stranger," she pointed out, adjusting the neckline of her robe so it covered more, "and I have work."

"You have a few weeks off for winter break. I saw it on the

calendar in the office. I've got a trip to Vegas during that time. You could come on that, no problem."

"Because sitting in a hotel room with a dog is everyone's idea of a fun time in Vegas."

Sam frowned. "Did I do something wrong?"

Lacey took another big bite of her grilled cheese. Chewing would give her time to cool down. This was why she shouldn't have fucked him. Because fucking him had fucked with her head. It made her heart want to believe that she was in love with him, and being in love with him made her irritated that he wasn't in love with her too. It was like standing on the subway platform in New York, watching the estimated arrival of her train say three minutes for ten minutes without a train in sight. She shouldn't be shocked because it happened all the time, but she was.

She swallowed. "No, you didn't. I'll think about Vegas."

"It seems like a win-win to me," he said. "Daisy gets both of us, I get both of you."

The frosty wall forming around her heart melted a little. "What do I get out of it?"

Sam smiled softly. "The hotel does have a world-class spa. So massages, facials, maybe a mani-pedi." He shrugged. "You don't have to spend the entire trip sitting with Daisy like you're her nanny."

"Do you think they'd let Daisy get a pedicure?" Lacey teased, starting to warm to the idea.

Sam's face became serious. "Lacey, I am a respected, serious musician with a reputation to uphold. Of course our dog can get a pedicure at the spa."

"So what's happening in Vegas?" She stuffed the last of her sandwich in her mouth.

Sam became very interested in an invisible spot of grime on the kitchen counter. He rubbed at it with his thumb.

"A, um—it's just an awards show. My team wants me to be more visible before we start working on the album."

Lacey narrowly avoided choking on her sandwich. "Album?" She coughed, crumbs tickling her throat. "When did you write an album?"

A hot blush spread over Sam's face. "Here and there. It's fine, I guess. Grim can hopefully go in and fix all my bullshit, half-baked ideas."

She grabbed his chin and forced him to look at her. "Nu-uh. No, sir. We are not shitting on our hard work before it's even done. If you're not going to be nicer to yourself, I'm not going to fuck you anymore."

His eyes widened. "So if I'm nice to myself, you'll have sex with me?"

She nodded. A roguish smile spread across his face.

"I am the greatest musician to have ever lived. I am a literal creative genius—"

Lacey began to laugh as Sam rose from his seat and loomed over her.

"Why are you laughing? You told me if I was nice to myself, you'd fuck me," he said, barely fighting back his own laughter. "Was this not what you wanted?" His nose brushed hers.

It was on the tip of Lacey's tongue to tell him that she loved him. The feeling had bubbled up again, intense as ever, but she bit it back. He didn't need to know, and she didn't want to spoil things.

"I could put on another episode of *Midsomer* for Daisy," she offered, "Though if we're going off your last performance, maybe something shorter? Like *Scooby-Doo*?"

"You're going to regret that," Sam promised, eyes sparkling.

"Don't threaten me with a good time."

CHAPTER TWENTY-THREE

IT WAS the longest two and a half minutes of Lacey's life.

But as her teen class hit their final marks, she could breathe again. This was going to work. They were going to crush their winter recital number. Maybe she wasn't a completely crap dance teacher after all.

The music ended, and she broke into a wide smile. Her hands shot into the air as she cheered.

"Yes! That's it!" she shouted.

It wasn't perfect, but that was fine. They still had time. And to be at the cleanup and fine-tuning stage several weeks before the performance was a huge weight off her shoulders.

Lacey glanced at the clock. "Look, I know we've still got time left, and you can stay if you want, but I also know tonight is the tree lighting, so if you want to go—"

Teenage girls scattered like pool balls. There were quick calls of "Bye, Lacey!" and "See you later!" as they all rushed to get out the door.

The Crane Cove Tree Lighting was a big deal. It was always December first, no matter the day of the week, and several town committees and organizations were involved in the planning. The tree was set up in the middle of the historic section of downtown, since the street was closed off anyway, and the tree lighting festivities were supposed to include warm beverages, live music, caroling, crafts, and Santa's arrival.

Lacey cleaned up the studio then went to the office, scaring the daylights out of Gavin when she opened the door.

"What are you doing?" he asked, one hand pressed dramatically to his chest. "Don't you have a class?"

"I let them go early," she said, sitting down to change her shoes. "I'm really proud of them. They're a week ahead of where I thought they'd be, and I wanted to end on a good note."

"Are you going somewhere?" Gavin pointed to the wool socks she was pulling on.

"The tree lighting like everyone else."

"With Sam?" he teased.

Lacey blushed. "He and Daisy are going to pick me up and we're going to walk over. Graham warned him that parking is nuts."

"Careful," Gavin warned, "or people are going to think you're in love with that boy."

"That ship has sailed," Lacey said without thinking.

"You should save yourself the rent and move in with him. If we didn't work together, I'd never see you."

It was true. Since they'd had sex, Lacey had given up any kind of facade that her sleepovers at Sam's house were accidental. She hadn't been to her home at Gavin and Leo's in a week.

"By the way, I put your mail in your bag," Gavin said. "I don't want to pry, but—"

He was cut off by the phone ringing. Lacey tucked her work shoes in their usual spot and grabbed her coat. Whatever Gavin didn't want to pry about could wait until later.

Sam and Daisy were just walking up to the door when she reached it. Her stomach fluttered, and her heart played hopscotch. After trying to tamp down those feelings for a few days after she'd realized she loved him, Lacey had given up and let them happen. Either she'd get over it or he'd catch up. It wasn't worth the mental gymnastics.

"You're early," they said at the same time when they met on the sidewalk.

"I was worried about parking," Sam said. "I'm about three blocks from here."

Lacey crouched down to pet Daisy, whose tail was wagging her entire back end, then stood and kissed Sam tenderly.

Or at least she tried to kiss Sam tenderly.

Kissing him was still too new, and she got drunk off them and lost her mind. Anything more than a brief peck and her tongue was liable to end up in his mouth, and vice versa. The way his tongue slid over hers reminded her of how his tongue slid over her skin—all of it—and her pussy clenched in anticipation.

Daisy pawed at her leg, jealous, and whined.

Sam grinned. "If I walk away and come back, will you say hello to me again?"

Lacey gave his chest a playful, one-handed shove.

"I have something for you," he said, and reached into his jacket pocket. He fished out something knitted and handed it to her. The soft wool was a blush pink, and as she turned it over in her hands, she saw that the headband had a cable knit heart pattern.

"I would've made you a hat, but your hair is always up," he explained, a blush so vivid it was noticeable in the fading sunlight spreading across his cheeks. "It's to keep your ears warm."

"I know how a headband works," Lacey teased, putting up a front to disguise the lump forming in her throat. "When did you make this?"

"Today. I had a lot of meetings, and I like to tell myself I think better when my hands are busy." He rocked back on his heels, then up on his toes. "Do you like it?"

Lacey slipped it over her head and fitted it over her ears. "I love it," she told him, and kissed him again. Daisy whined again, then barked once, when she felt the kiss had gone on too long.

"We could go home," Sam suggested, the hands on her waist lowering to trace the curve of her ass.

"No. This is an adorable, *public* opportunity to remind all your fans that you've got a girlfriend before any sneaky relatives come into town," Lacey said, adjusting the collar of his coat. Sam sighed heavily and took her hand.

There were a lot of things about small-town living that grated on Lacey's nerves, but Christmastime in Crane Cove was not one of them. It was the closest she would ever get to living in a Hallmark holiday movie. Downtown businesses had spent the last week decorating their storefronts and the city had hung lights on the trees and from the streetlights. It really did look like a movie set.

The closer they got to the historic section of downtown where the tree was, the more people they saw, all headed in the same direction. It seemed like the whole of Crane Cove had turned out for the event.

Booths, housed under tents, were set up along the street. From what she understood, there was a market every weekend until Christmas, rain or shine. Unless it was *really* rainy, and then it would be moved into the community center. Several booths had long lines, and Lacey guessed those were the booths with the hot drinks and food.

"Divide and conquer?" she suggested to Sam and he nodded.

"What do you want to eat?"

"Definitely carbs. Lots of sugar."

"I think I can make that happen." Sam kissed her forehead, right below her cozy headband. "Do you want to keep Daisy with you? I think she's pretty sick of me."

"Sure. I missed her."

Sam handed Lacey the leash. Daisy tried to follow him as he squeezed through the crowd, headed for a booth that sold fresh mini donuts.

"He'll be back," Lacey promised when the dog looked at her nervously. Or as nervously as a dog could look. Sometimes she thought she read too much into Daisy's facial expressions, but that was probably because she'd gone through a massive *101 Dalmatians* phase as a child.

"I'd get used to that view," said an unfortunately familiar voice behind her. *Mitch.* "I'd just keep walking if I was him."

Lacey took a deep, calming breath before turning to face her ex-boyfriend. She plastered a big, cheerful smile on her face. The look of malevolent boredom on his face made her stomach roll. "Enjoying the festivities, Mitch?"

"So, what are you going to do when he leaves you, hmm?" Mitch asked. "Because it's going to happen. I might not be available when he does."

It was far from the nastiest thing Mitch had ever said to her, but something in Lacey snapped. She wasn't going to take it anymore. She wasn't going to play nice.

"You could be the last man on Earth, and I still wouldn't get back together with you. I think a lot of women around here share that sentiment," she said. "And as much as you deserve to die alone, you won't, because the universe isn't fair and you're really good at sniffing out easy targets. I hope you end up with someone you deserve."

Like she'd been cued from on high, Marianne showed up at Mitch's side and wrapped her arms around one of his.

"I changed my mind. Can you get me a hot chocolate,

babe?" she purred, laying her head on his shoulder in an obvious sign of possession. It would have been more subtle if she'd peed on his leg to mark her territory.

"On a date?" Lacey guessed cheerfully.

Marianne practically preened. "We are." Her eyes scanned the empty space next to Lacey. "Did Sam Shoop finally dump you?"

Lacey took back any charitable thoughts she'd had about not even Marianne deserving to be stuck with Mitch for all eternity. They were perfect for each other.

"No. He's getting us snacks," she said, scanning the crowd for her fake boyfriend. She found him in the donut line talking to Delores, the owner of Knot and Purl. They must have been talking about the headband he'd made her because they both looked in her direction, and Sam's face broke into a big smile when they made eye contact across the crowded street. She gave him a little wave, and he winked at her. The triple somersault her heart did received tens across the board from the judges.

"I want snacks," said a voice on Lacey's right. She jumped. Kiki smiled at her. "Hi."

Marianne looked Kiki up and down, and her face contorted like she'd stepped in dog poop. "You know this is a *Christmas* celebration, right?"

Kiki, who looked chic as hell in her long black wool coat, pointed to her black Santa hat. "Duh."

"The goth thing was funny in high school, but now it's just sad," Mitch said, and Lacey wished Daisy knew a command for bite.

"At least I didn't peak in high school," Kiki responded, unfazed by their pathetic attempt at bullying.

Mitch's face grew red. In the chilly evening air, Lacey could almost see the steam billowing out of his ears. Right when it looked like he was about to blow his top, Marianne tugged on his arm.

"I think the other booth has a shorter line," she told him, and they marched off across the street.

"I can't believe I ever let him fuck me," Lacey said, shaking her head.

"I can't believe I ever had a crush on her," Kiki said, and when Lacey's eyebrows jumped up, she added, "I was young and overrun by puberty. The cheerleader uniform was too much for my little gay brain to handle. I sympathized a lot with my heterosexual male peers."

"Because girls are so pretty?"

"*So* pretty." Kiki grinned at her. "I did eventually get to see what was under one of those uniforms."

Lacey's eyes widened. "Marianne's?"

Kiki snorted. "God, no. Mercifully she was too old for me and extremely straight, so I never got off the starting line. But Astra O'Donnell?" She let out a low whistle. "What a babe. We used to make out in the baseball dugout during PE. You know, for fun." She winked at Lacey.

"Was that your first girlfriend?"

Kiki shook her head. "No. Not officially. Astra wasn't even out to herself at the time. I was her dirty little secret. Her family was super religious too, so she viewed me as a gray area. It doesn't count if the person making you come is a girl type thing."

"That doesn't make any sense."

"As long as I got to touch her boobs, I did not care."

Lacey laughed. "You're funny."

"Thank you," Kiki said sincerely. "Can I get that in writing so I can present it to Graham as evidence?"

"If you find me something to write on, I'll give you an affidavit."

The line moved forward, and Kiki took a giant step to follow it. She had a pensive look on her face. Lacey had known her just long enough to be concerned that she was lost in thought.

"You know," Kiki finally said, "I think it's nice that Mitch and Marianne finally got together. They can torture each other and save the general population."

"I was thinking the same thing. They deserve each other." Lacey surveyed the crowd. "Is it always this busy?"

"For the tree lighting? Oh yeah. Crane Cove loves an event." The line inched forward, and so did they. "I'd say it's a little busier this year because it isn't raining."

"Thank god for that." She looked over at the donut booth. Sam had picked the better line. He was being handed a white paper bag. Her stomach growled. "Why is this line moving so slowly?"

"Because Sybil is at the other end," Kiki explained, and pointed out the other beverage booths that all had shorter lines. "Oregonians will wait outside forever if something is good."

"But why isn't she *inside*," Lacey asked, "where it's warm?"

"Because our scariest friend is a big ol' nostalgic softie." Kiki smiled, and Lacey let herself bask in the warmth of being considered part of the group, even if it was going to end. "She got her start doing these kinds of markets."

"But her shop is right there." Lacey pointed to Stardust.

"She has a great view of the tree," Chase said, putting an arm around Kiki's shoulders. "All the tents block her view if she stays inside."

"Don't you have a business to run?" Kiki poked him in the stomach. "Leave us alone."

Chase pouted. "I need cocoa, and you're so close to the front."

Lacey frowned. There had to be at least fifteen people ahead of them still. "We are?"

"Don't look behind you," Chase cautioned. "You'd think Sybil was giving away a car."

The line moved forward as Sam joined the group. Daisy danced excitedly, her precious little paws getting tangled in the leash.

"Silly girl," Sam mumbled with a laugh as he knelt down to untangle her. Their opportunistic pup immediately made a play for the donuts, and he narrowly avoided having the bag snatched from his hand.

"Daisy!" Lacey scolded, and the dog cocked her head to one side, a picture of confusion and innocence. "Don't look at me like that. I'm not sharing with you now—Sam, don't reward her for that."

Sam's look of confusion and innocence matched Daisy's, like he didn't have his hand in the donut bag.

Even if Daisy hadn't been naughty, Lacey didn't know if she would have shared once she bit into the first cinnamon sugar-covered delight. Warm, soft, and sweet, they were the perfect treat at the end of the day. The bag was empty before they got to the front of the line. Kiki, Chase, and Lacey chatted animatedly while Sam stood quietly, occasionally contributing a quip. It wasn't like when they were alone, or even with his very close friends, and Lacey liked that, even though she had to ignore the aura of guilt that surrounded her smugness.

Graham and Eloise wandered up when they were three people away from the front of the line. They made it seem very casual, like they just wanted to talk, but when they reached the front of the line, they ordered first. But as penance, Eloise and Graham paid for the groups' drinks. Lacey noticed that Sybil didn't give Graham his change.

Chase went back to Cranberry Brothers, but Kiki hung on, an unbothered fifth wheel on an accidental double date. They browsed a few booths before the clock struck six, then they went back toward the Stardust booth to get a better view of the tree.

The lights around them dimmed as the mayor spoke about the magic of the season, about the importance of community, and the value of tradition. Sam positioned himself behind Lacey and wrapped his arms around her during the speech, while Daisy laid across her feet. The sense of rightness, of belonging, and of family hit her so hard it threatened to knock her over. She hadn't felt this safe and loved since her mom died, and as the tree lit up, a tear slid down her cheek.

What was she going to do if this ended? Would she ever be this happy again?

Sam kissed her cheek, then whispered, "Are you okay?"

Lacey nodded, fighting not to sniffle. "It's so beautiful," she choked out.

And it was beautiful. The crowd sang "Have Yourself A Merry Little Christmas," and it sounded like a hymn, a prayer for the season ahead. Lacey shut her eyes to listen and made a wish, believing for a moment in the so-called magic the mayor had mentioned.

Next year all her troubles would be out of sight.

CHAPTER TWENTY-FOUR

SAM WANTED TO GO HOME.

Which was ironic because he was technically at home. But Los Angeles didn't feel like home because Lacey and Daisy were hundreds of miles away. It was just a house that was in desperate need of a leggy blonde on the kitchen counter and a yellow dog underfoot.

There was a blonde in his house, but it was the wrong blonde.

"What's this soup called again?" Jenna asked, watching him suspiciously as he cracked eggs and added them to his measuring cup of lemon juice.

"Avgolemono," he said, separating two egg yolks from their whites. "It's Greek. You'll love it."

"But why are there eggs?"

"It makes the soup creamy and silky without using any cream," Sam explained, whisking together the eggs and lemon juice.

Jenna's face remained unsure. "It looks like you're going to make a cake."

"You need to learn to cook."

"That's what Houston said." Jenna twisted her new engagement ring. "And his mom. And his grandma. Basically everyone who showed up at the proposal had advice for me to be the perfect wife."

The edge of anxiety in her voice cut through Sam's concentration.

"Jen, are you okay?"

"Who? Me?" A weak, nervous laugh slipped past her lips. "I'm fine. I'm happy. I'm engaged." She held up her left hand, the large oval-cut diamond sparkling in the kitchen light. Her tight smile told him not to reserve any time in June for a wedding. "How's your relationship going?"

Sam removed the chicken thighs from the broth they'd been simmering in and added the rice, giving the soup a good stir before putting the lid on the pot.

How was his relationship going? If he didn't count the strange tension that had appeared between them after the tree lighting, everything was great. Lacey had basically moved in, which was perfect for him because he got to fall asleep with her every night and wake up to her every morning. In the evenings, he got to hear about her day while he made her dinner. Sam never felt like he had much to contribute. She was instilling work ethic and confidence in children, and he was sitting in the basement strumming his guitar or banging on his keyboard, pretending to make music.

When he'd landed in Los Angeles, he tried to call his therapist. When he'd gone to Crane Cove, he'd let his sessions lapse, partly because he felt in a better headspace, and partly because Vanessa's license didn't extend to Oregon. Her phone went to voicemail, and the message said that she would be out of the office for the month of December and anyone having a crisis needed to call emergency services. Sam didn't think his situation qualified as a crisis, even if it felt like a near disaster to him.

He needed to talk to someone, but his closest friends weren't an option. If he told Jordy, Jordy would inevitably tell Annie, who would tell Eloise, who would tell Graham. If he told Graham, the same thing would happen in reverse. Despite having a motor mouth, Peter was a vault for secrets, but the situation would either disgust him because Sam had violated the sanctity of love, or he'd treat it like a movie plot. Because Sam couldn't explain why being in love with Lacey was a problem without owning up to the fake dating scheme.

"I think I'm in love with her."

Jenna's jaw dropped. "Oh. My. God. Sam!" She hugged him tightly, compressing his rib cage until it became hard to breathe. "That's amazing!"

"It's not, actually," he grunted. Jenna released him, and he took a deep breath, re-expanding his chest. "Lacey isn't really my girlfriend."

Jenna frowned deeply. "Not your girlfriend? I don't understand."

Sam took two forks out of the utensil drawer and started to shred the chicken thighs.

"Lacey and I agreed to be in a fake relationship."

"Like a publicity stunt?"

"Umm, sort of?" A hot blush burned his cheeks. "Sometimes small-town life can be claustrophobic and I wanted some breathing room, so I made up a girlfriend."

"And you asked Lacey to play the part?"

"Umm..." His cheeks grew hotter. "On accident. Someone asked me my girlfriend's name and I said Lacey and..." He let his silence fill in the blank.

"Why the hell did she agree to this? Is she a fame hunter or something?" Jenna asked, her tone shifting from bewildered to aggressively protective.

"No, she's not," Sam assured her. "She dated a real fucking

loser when she first moved to town, and dating me squashes any lingering doubts about her feelings for him."

"I don't know." Jenna was skeptical. "I've gone out with some guys purely to get back at an ex. Are you sure she's not trying to make him jealous?"

Sam snorted, unable to imagine a single scenario where Lacey would even let Mitch lick the bottom of her shoe. "Absolutely not. If you met him, you'd understand."

"Okay, so you love her. Why is that a problem?"

"Because to her, our relationship is fake. It's transactional. She reminds me of that all the time." His stomach quivered at the carousel of memories. He hated that he found himself parroting her assertions in moments of anxiety, when it was easier to keep the status quo than risk pushing her away.

Jenna pointed to the chicken he'd shredded. "Do you cook for her?"

"Yeah."

"And you don't think there's *any* chance she feels the same way about you?" Jenna raised a doubtful eyebrow. "Have you considered maybe using your big boy words to tell her how you feel?"

"No, Jen, that never crossed my mind," he retorted dryly. "Of course I've considered it. But it feels like every time I'm about to say something, she brings up the fakeness of our relationship. It's like she can read my mind and is cutting me off at the pass."

"Do you want to vent, or do you want advice? Because I don't want to waste my brainpower trying to fix your life if you're going to be stubborn."

Sam lifted the lid of the pot and stirred the rice, checking the doneness of the grains. "What would you do?"

She was quiet as he refitted the lid, then said, "I'd probably be a coward too. But that doesn't mean you should be. If you're not in imminent danger of her skipping town, you can think about it some more, but don't wait forever."

"What do I even say?" he asked, and took the lid off the pot again. He needed to temper the eggs so they wouldn't scramble when he put them in the soup, so he began slowly adding hot broth to the egg-and-lemon mixture, whisking constantly.

"Have you tried 'I pretty much hate everyone, but I don't hate you. Will you be my real girlfriend?'"

"I don't know why I invite you over," Sam said. The gate bell rang in the front entry. "Can you go see if that's Grim?"

"It's because you value my musical contributions," Jenna called over her shoulder, already halfway to the monitor. She pressed the speaker button and said, "Sam Shoop's House of Whores and Horrors. What's the password?"

"Butt plug," Grim answered, his voice slightly distorted by the speaker. "I grabbed bread. Let me in."

Jenna opened the gate, and then the door after Grim rang the bell. He was wearing another crochet granny square sweater monstrosity.

"It smells good. What did you make?" he asked.

"Avian lemon soup," Jenna answered, completely butchering the pronunciation.

"Avgolemono," Sam corrected, moving the soup off the heat to add the egg-and-lemon mixture, then the shredded chicken and remaining herbs.

Jenna shrugged. "Close enough."

"So, what are your thoughts on the direction of the album?" Grim asked as they sat around the table. "Anything clear up since we last talked?"

AFTER FOUR DAYS of being away from home, Sam could've

kissed the pilot when he told them that they had a tailwind and would land a half hour ahead of their original estimate.

Lacey's car was in his driveway, and a layer of anxiety melted away. He'd get to see her immediately, no waiting. Since he was earlier than he'd told her, he didn't know if she'd be home when he arrived. Fuck, he'd missed her.

Daisy's nails scrabbling to find purchase on the hardwood floors was the first sound he heard when he opened the door. The dog zoomed to the garage door, but her brakes failed and she skidded into the wall when she tried to stop. Sam chuckled and crouched down to give her some long overdue love.

"Sam?" Lacey shouted from the bedroom.

"Let's go surprise Mommy," he whispered to Daisy, who recognized the word "Mommy" and went sprinting to the bedroom. Sam followed, leaving his suitcase by the door.

"Sam?" Lacey called again, uncertainty creeping into her voice.

He entered the bedroom right as she was exiting the bathroom, wearing his robe and her hair in curlers, with the blow dryer raised in self-defense. Her face lit up when she saw him, and she dropped the blow dryer, running across the room to him.

"Sam!" Lacey's brakes worked about as well as Daisy's did, and she slammed into him, making him stumble several steps backward. He didn't even get to say hi before her mouth was on his.

Oh yes. He'd missed her a lot.

"You're early," she scolded when she finally extracted her tongue from his mouth.

"We had a tailwind," he said, reaching for the belt of the robe. Lacey smacked his hand.

"Not yet. Go take a shower first."

Sam started to remove his clothes, hoping she'd change her mind if he got naked.

"Why is your hair in curlers?"

"That's for me to know and for you to find out," she said. "And my hair wouldn't be in curlers if you'd gotten home *when you said you'd be getting home*, Samuel."

Sam undid his belt. "My name isn't Samuel."

Lacey frowned. "It isn't?"

He shook his head. "Nope. Not a Samuel."

"Samson?"

"You can keep guessing, but I doubt you'll get it."

"Is it one of those things where everyone calls you Sam but that's your middle name?"

"Nope." He pushed down his pants and was satisfied when Lacey's eyes immediately went to his thickening cock.

"Was the answer ever revealed in a teen magazine?"

"No, it was not. Do you still want me to shower? I don't mind the curlers."

That made Lacey laugh. "Yes, but I do. They're not comfortable when I lay down. I'm convinced my grandma slept sitting up her entire adult life." She gingerly patted her hair. "Go take a nice, long, hot shower. I've got a surprise for you."

Sam's cock perked up at that. It was highly unlikely the surprise would be something mundane like a vacuum, and very likely it would lead to Lacey being naked.

A hot shower did feel good. He soaped up his body and stood in the steaming stream, trying to judge exactly how long he was supposed to stay there. Was five minutes enough? Ten?

Plus he had his own surprise for Lacey sitting by the door.

"Can I come out?" he shouted over the water. No response. "Sunshine?"

Still no answer.

Sam turned off the water and stepped out of the shower, quickly drying himself off and wrapping the towel around his hips. Lacey's rollers were in the sink, so he spent a few minutes putting those back into their case, then he crept out of the bathroom. There was no sign of Lacey or Daisy.

They weren't in the hallway or the kitchen when he went to gather his bags, which meant Lacey had probably taken Daisy downstairs for some TV time. His cock throbbed in time with the beat of his heart, rapidly growing hard again.

The hollow thundering of bare feet running up the stairs echoed in the silent house. Lacey reached the top of the stairs, and her eyes widened when they met his. She hastily closed his robe tighter around herself. Her hair, which he so often saw up in a bun or a ponytail, was done in loose, bouncy curls. She could've given any pageant queen a run for her money.

"Sam! You're supposed to be in the shower," she admonished.

"I needed my luggage," he said, pointing to his bags.

"You don't need clothes. Trust me."

Sam raised an eyebrow, a smirk quirking the corner of his mouth. "But what if I wasn't getting clothes?"

Lacey sighed defeatedly and pinched the bridge of her nose. "This is not going how I planned."

"Can I help?" he asked, still amused by the situation.

"Just...stay put for five minutes, okay?" She started walking quickly toward the bedroom. "Do. Not. Move."

He looked at the clock on the microwave. "Is this an actual five minutes, or the five minutes you use when you're almost ready to leave the house?"

"Sam." Her lips pursed together in flustered silence. "Don't be cute when I'm trying to be sexy. Stay. Put."

It took a lot of effort not to laugh, but he managed it. Barely.

Lacey was so cute when she was mildly peeved at him. It only made him want to annoy her on purpose. Sometimes it got him punished in the sexiest ways.

If a watched pot never boiled, then a watched clock did not move. Five minutes passed like five years. The anticipation was going to wreck his nerves. The mix of anxiety and excitement was almost too much to bear.

"Sam," Lacey beckoned from the bedroom, and he had to force himself to walk and not run.

Soft light spilled into the hallway, and Sam's pulse became supersonic. He took a few deep breaths in a vain attempt to calm himself as he reached the door. Lacey was standing next to the bed, still encased in his robe. Sam frowned.

"I couldn't see that you turned down the lights?"

Lacey's hands hovered over the knotted tie around her waist. "Look, this was going to be really sexy, but you got home early and threw off my groove, and I couldn't decide what I wanted to do, so..."

She undid the knot and unwrapped herself like the early Christmas present of his dreams. The robe fell to the floor, and Sam's jaw fell with it. Lacey was wearing a powder-blue lingerie set with the most delicate light pink bows. He would've counted them if he could remember any numbers. Sam's eyes scanned her body slowly from top to bottom, desperately trying to sear this moment in his memory for all eternity. His mouth went dry when he hit her long, perfect legs: she was wearing white thigh-high stockings, held in place by tiny clips attached to silly little suspenders held up by a garter belt around her waist.

Lacey giggled. "Okay, it was worth it for the look on your face."

Sam's brain found enough function to say, "Wow."

"So you like it?" she asked, her confidence rising like the sun.

"'Like' is not a strong enough word," he said, doing his best not to drool as he spoke. "When did you get that?"

"This morning. I ordered it online." Lacey grinned and crooked a finger at him. "Come here."

Sam rushed toward her like his survival depended on fucking her. His towel fell to the floor in his hurry, and in a feat of strength and acrobatics he would never be able to achieve again, he managed to pick Lacey up, her legs instantly wrapping around his waist. He supported her weight by securing his hands on her ass. Their mouths crashed together, and he walked the last few feet to the bed until he hit the mattress and they fell forward.

"Fuck," he moaned into her mouth. "Goddamn, I want to feel you around my cock."

"Soon," she promised, then sucked on his tongue. Pre-cum leaked from the head of his cock onto her stomach.

"Sunshine, I want to feel you, *all* of you, around my cock. Nothing between us." He rocked his hips for emphasis, the friction sending shivers over his body.

Lacey pulled back a fraction to study him, a few different emotions playing across her beautiful face. Consideration, but mostly caution.

"Sam, it's not that I don't trust you," she began, making her tone as gentle and appeasing as possible, "and this might sound kind of stupid since I've already had your cock in my mouth, but—"

"You want a test first?" Sam offered.

Lacey relaxed and nodded. "I know I'm being paranoid—"

"You're not being paranoid," he told her. "Whatever you want, whatever you need, I'm more than willing to do it. Anything for you, sunshine."

Sam would've told her he loved her then, except Lacey stole the words from his mouth by putting her tongue there, and then all higher function left his brain when she reached between them and began working his cock with her hand. She had no idea how much she had him in the palm of her hand, both literally and figuratively.

"I fucking love it when you're hard for me," she panted against his mouth. "You're going to fuck me so good, aren't you?"

"Mm-hmm," he hummed, and then pulled his cock free from her grasp. "But if you keep doing that, we're not going to make it to the good stuff."

Lacey pouted. "I don't get to play?"

"Not until after I've had my fun with you."

Sam kissed his way down her body, forging a trail from her mouth to her jaw, down her neck, across her collar bone, and over the small slope of her breast. He teased her nipple with his tongue through the sheer fabric, and Lacey arched her back with a whine. He repeated the process with her other nipple, and she whimpered plaintively.

"Sam..."

He took a small amount of pity on her and reached between them to stroke her pussy through her panties. Except instead of soaked fabric, he touched hot, silken, wet skin. His mouth popped off her breast to look down to see if his sense of touch was lying to him.

"Are these...crotchless?" he asked in wonderment.

Lacey had the audacity to giggle triumphantly, so Sam silenced her by swiping his thumb across her clit, which turned her merriment into a moan.

"Yes. I wanted to make things—oh fuck, Sam—easy for you."

Fuck teasing her. Fuck drawing this out. A primitive, animal instinct overtook him, and Sam grabbed Lacey behind her knees and roughly forced her legs open and back so she was bared to him, open and glistening in the soft light. He buried his face in her cunt, licking and sucking and probing her with his tongue, tasting her like he was a starving man.

Her fingers sank into his hair and held his head in place, like there was any chance he'd stop eating her out. His house could have been on fire and he wouldn't have stopped. He needed her high-pitched whines, her breathy sighs, and desperate moans. He needed the salty sweet musk of her on his tongue.

Her thighs trembled under his hands as he tasted her first orgasm. It wasn't enough. He needed more.

Sam sucked on her clit, and Lacey squeaked like a mouse. He pulled back to blow on her cunt and noticed something he hadn't before in his desperate dive for her pussy.

"Is that a butt plug?"

Lacey groaned. "I don't know anymore. My brain is mush. Fucking hell, Sam."

"You've made me fucking feral, sunshine." He pushed her knees further back, tilting her ass upward. The butt plug was one of the ones with the fake jewel on the end, making her ass look like the treasure that it was.

"You're so pretty like this," he praised her, releasing one leg so he could twist the plug, gently tugging so the widest part stretched her asshole, then pushing it back in. "Dripping wet with your ass full."

"I want to be stuffed," she gasped, her voice catching as he manipulated the plug. "Please, please, please fuck me—with your cock, you loophole-finding bastard."

"Such language," he teased, pushing the plug back in. "I don't know if you deserve to be fucked."

Her hand shot out and grasped his throat. Pleasure rolled through his body like a wave. "If you don't fuck me *right now*, you're never going to see my pussy ever again."

Goddamn, he loved a power play.

Sam grasped her dainty wrists and pinned them above her head. "You're not in charge right now, sunshine."

Lacey struggled against his grip. "Let go of me."

Sam paused, but didn't let go. "Red or green?"

Her struggling stopped. "Green."

"If you don't behave, I'm going to spank your ass so hard you'll remember your manners every time you sit down for a week."

Lacey's eyes widened and her breathing quickened. She liked that idea. He could work with this line of thinking.

"I'm going to let you pick your punishment. My hand or the paddle?"

Lacey's eyes grew wider. "You have a paddle?"

"Get on your hands and knees, ass up in the air," Sam instructed and let go of her wrists.

Lacey hurried to comply, rolling over and pushing her ass against his groin. The jeweled end of her plug rubbed against the sensitive head of his cock, and he clenched his teeth to keep from moaning.

"Don't move." He moved off the bed and hurried over to one of his suitcases. Inside he'd packed some of his favorite tools and toys, ones he thought Lacey would enjoy as much as he did. If he'd known she wanted to be stuffed full, he would have packed his strap-on harness to give her the full double penetration experience with a single partner.

The paddle he selected was made of silicon, like a spatula, and shaped like a ping-pong paddle. It proved a nice, sharp sting, with a low chance of accidental injury.

Sam walked back to the bed and showed Lacey the paddle.

"We're going to do this until I'm satisfied you've learned your lesson," he said. Lacey wiggled her ass.

Smack. Thwack.

Sam spanked her twice in quick succession, once with an upward follow-through, and the second time he pressed the paddle against her skin at the end to dull the resulting sting.

"Yes," Lacey moaned, her chest melting into the mattress, making her ass stick further into the air.

He shouldn't reward her for outwardly enjoying what was supposed to be a punishment, but Sam had a difficult time denying Lacey anything she liked for very long. He repeated the process on her other cheek, then kissed her between her shoulder blades.

"Have you learned your lesson?"

"Not even a little bit."

By the time Sam dropped the paddle on the floor, Lacey's ass was red and her pussy was clenching around thin air. He wasn't much better; his cock was so hard the slightest movement of air was agony.

Sam gingerly rolled a condom down his aching shaft.

"Are you finally going to fuck me?" Lacey asked, watching him over her shoulder with a languid, satisfied expression.

"For as long as I can," Sam promised, and kissed her shoulder. "On your back, sunshine. I want to see your face when I enter you."

With a soft sigh, Lacey rolled onto her back, then wrapped her arms around his neck and pulled him down for a long, lazy kiss. Sam didn't know what would burst first, his heart or his balls.

He rubbed the head of his cock against her clit, and Lacey jerked.

"Oh, yes, please," she moaned. "Give it to me."

The bliss on her face when he pushed inside her was worth every minute he'd waited. Lacey arched and gasped, and her cunt clenched around his cock like it was giving it a hug. And as much as he'd wanted to pound her into the mattress earlier, now he wanted to make love to her. To put into motion all the things he couldn't find the right time or words to say. Sam rocked into her, rolling his hips against hers, praising her or whispering sweet nothings with every thrust.

Despite his gentle pace, his orgasm hit him like a tidal wave. He'd ridden the edge too long and paid for it as his muscles tightened to a borderline painful point. Or maybe it was a reward. His oxytocin-flooded brain couldn't suss out the difference.

When his soul returned to his body, Lacey was rubbing his back in soft, soothing circles, pressing tender kisses to his shoulder.

"You good?" she asked, and all he could do was nod.

They stayed like that for a while, until Sam became dangerously soft. He held the base of the condom as he pulled out.

"I'm not going to lie," Lacey said, pushing herself up on her elbow to look, "I half expected that thing to be busted."

"Why?" Sam panted, easing the condom off and tying a knot in the end.

"You came *hard*," she told him.

He stood on shaky, noodle-like legs. "How's your ass?"

"Deliciously sore." Lacey grinned triumphantly. There was something about a well-fucked partner that made him want to crow with pride.

After they cleaned up in the bathroom, Lacey changed out of her lingerie and into one of his T-shirts. Her voluminous hair went back into its usual bun. It was well past midnight for his Cinderella.

"I missed you," Lacey said as they sat at the kitchen counter, sharing an open carton of Tillamook strawberry ice cream. Two spoons. No bowls.

"Are you talking to me or the ice cream?"

She rolled her eyes. "You. I've had the ice cream every night."

"I thought it looked a little low." He winked and she blushed, trying to hide her grin with a spoonful of ice cream. "I missed you too."

CHAPTER TWENTY-FIVE

THE TAIL END of the morning rush was filtering out of Stardust when Lacey walked up Friday morning. It had been a long week. All of her classes, which had been performing beautifully, seemed to fall apart, missing steps and cues like it was the first time they were running through their dances. It was frustrating and distressing, but at least they had one more week to try and pull it all back together.

Sam had only been home for two days before he returned to LA to work on his new album. She had assumed the plane flew back to California and then back to Oregon between trips, but she found out that Sam paid for his pilots to stay at The Crane Hotel because the trip was so quick. They'd run into Stacey and Wes when Sam took her out to lunch, and they were not the stodgy old white men she'd been expecting. They were in their early forties, married, and absolutely hilarious. It was comforting to know that he had nice people flying him around the country.

Two days hadn't been long enough, though. The ache of missing him had barely dulled, and he was gone again. It didn't matter that it was only for a few days, and then he'd have Stacey and Wes fly him back to Crane Cove so they could go to Las Vegas. If it hadn't been so close to the recital, she might've said "Fuck it" and gone with him to Los Angeles. But the recital was the next weekend, and Lacey didn't know if he needed space after what had happened the night he got back.

He'd told her he loved her. The problem was that he had said it during sex, so she didn't know if he'd meant it or if he was simply overwhelmed by the glory of her pussy. It wouldn't have been the first time a man had told her he loved her in the heat of the moment only to walk it back after he'd rolled off of her. But Sam didn't walk it back; he didn't even mention it again. Lacey couldn't tell if he even realized he'd said the words. He wasn't acting any different. If Sam had given her any indication that he wanted to tell her something, she might have brought it up, but he didn't, which left her wondering:

Did he love her? Or was the sex so good it scrambled his brain and he said things he didn't mean?

Stardust was almost empty when Lacey got to the counter.

"Can I get a large iced seafoam latte, please?" she said, digging her wallet out of her bag. Her hand brushed the unread mail Gavin had given her. She needed to make time to look that over, even though it was probably just statements.

The girl behind the counter nodded and rang in her order, shouting it to Sybil who was behind the espresso machine making drinks. Lacey ran her debit card. She shouldn't be treating herself, but the $5.95 wasn't going to erase her debt, and she'd had a long week. Plus, she'd saved so much money shacking up with Sam, she could cover the cost.

The credit card machine beeped.

Declined.

Lacey frowned. That couldn't be right. She didn't check her bank account often because it was depressing, but she hadn't had any unexpected expenses and she'd budgeted herself down to the penny.

"Try it again," the girl behind the register said. "Sometimes it's temperamental."

Lacey ran her card again. *Declined.*

"Do you have another form of payment? Cash? A different card?"

Lacey tried to swallow the lump that formed in her throat, but it wouldn't budge. Her face, neck, and ears felt impossibly hot, and her heart and mind raced.

There had to be an error. A mistake in the system. The reader was broken.

"I, uh—" She didn't have any cash. She'd given the last of her cash to one of her students in exchange for a wreath to hang on Sam's front door. It was for a school fundraiser, and just like the coffee, she figured she could swing it since she hadn't been buying things like food or gas. Her credit cards had been cut up a long time ago to remove the temptation to use them.

"Cassidy, switch me spots," Sybil said, moving behind the register. Cassidy dashed behind the espresso machine, clearly happy to be out of the awkward situation. "What's going on?"

"I don't know," Lacey whispered, her voice choked by tears that were forming in her eyes. "It keeps declining."

"Have you checked your bank account?" Sybil asked gently. Lacey shook her head. "This one's on me."

"You don't have to—"

"Stop." She cleared the transaction. "There's a box of tissues in the bathroom."

Grateful, Lacey hurried to the bathroom and locked herself inside. She blinked and the tears that had filled her eyes fell down her cheeks. She took a deep breath in, and let it out through pursed lips. Nothing was wrong. It was all going to be fine.

Lacey took her phone out of her pocket. It had automatically connected to Stardust's wi-fi, so she opened up her bank's app, still telling herself that everything was going to be fine.

It wasn't.

Her checking account was empty. Worse than empty. It was overdrawn.

Bile rose in her throat, and she leaned over the toilet and vomited.

Lacey sat on the floor of the bathroom, trying to pinpoint exactly when her debit card number had been stolen. She got paid on the fifteenth and the thirtieth of every month via direct deposit. All of her bills were set up for automatic payment so she wouldn't forget.

The mail.

She emptied her bag onto the floor and the letters fanned out. Some statements, but also notices of missed payment. Threats of action if payment was not made in a timely manner.

Lacey vomited again, but it was mostly bile. Her breakfast had jumped ship the last time she'd heaved.

Then she did the only thing she could think to do in her situation: she cried.

Her pity party was short-lived. Someone knocked on the door.

"Almost finished!" Lacey shouted, shoving her belongings and the cursed letters back into her bag. She flushed the toilet, then splashed water on her face, and rinsed out her mouth. She used the tissues Sybil had mentioned to blow her nose and clean up the bit of mascara that had run under her eyes. Her resulting appearance was pathetic.

Lacey put her head down when she left the bathroom, not making eye contact with the next occupant. She grabbed her drink from the end of the counter and left. The urge to go home, to hide under the covers with Daisy, was strong, but she couldn't miss work. Even if Gavin understood, she needed the money.

Maybe Gavin would know what to do. He was older and arguably wiser.

By the time Lacey got back to the studio, she was glad she'd walked. The cold air gave her an excuse for her splotchy complexion. Gavin was in the office doing some bookkeeping with the glasses he proclaimed he didn't need perched on the end of his nose.

"There you are. I thought you got lost," he teased, taking off his glasses and folding them.

"No. I decided to walk." Lacey set down her coffee and hung up her bag, then her coat on top, like all of her past due bills would shine through if she didn't cover them up.

She changed from her outdoor shoes to her studio shoes, searching for the words to explain what had happened to Gavin, wondering how she could make herself sound like less of an irresponsible failure, when he cleared his throat.

"Um, Lacey, we need to have a potentially...awkward conversation."

Nausea rolled through her stomach again. The day could get worse. She was going to get fired.

"Leo and I were talking—"

Okay, maybe not her job.

"And since you're always at Sam's instead of at home, we were thinking—I'm so bad at this. I should have had Leo do it." Gavin pinched the bridge of his nose and took a deep breath. "We need to either raise your rent or have you move out so we can rent it out for more money. My mom needs to move into a care facility, and they're not cheap...I'm so sorry. We've been crunching the numbers and—"

Lacey shook her head, forcing herself to paste a smile on her face. "No, no. It's fine, it's fine. I understand. Um, I, uh, need to look at my budget and talk to Sam..."

"I know things are tight. I'm so sorry. If we had any other option—"

"Gavin. Stop. Take care of your mom. I'm, um, going to go warm up before class."

Lacey retreated to the studio and cranked a Jenna Fox song to try and drown out her brain. If she couldn't hear herself think, maybe she could catch her breath.

Dance was the only consistent thing in her life. No matter what kind of shit storm she found herself in the middle of, there was dance. When her mom was sick, there was dance. When she passed, there was dance. When she wanted to be anywhere but at her dad's house, there was dance. Through all of her highs and lows, Lacey had always been able to sink into the music and movement.

So, she danced.

AT THE END of the day, Lacey wanted Sam. She wanted his borderline blunt way of solving problems. Her life didn't need finesse; it needed a battering ram. Or a bulldozer.

The most frustrating part was that she'd tried so hard to fix the mess she'd made of her life. If she'd half-assed it, maybe it wouldn't be so painful. But she'd moved to a small town she'd never heard of because she could cut her living expenses by more than half. No friends? No problem. No one to tempt her into going to the bars or clubs, or out to eat, or on trips. With a very strict budget she'd seen the light at the end of the tunnel, even if it was a very long way away.

Lacey fed Daisy her dinner, then went to the bedroom to pack instead of eating the human food meal Sam had left. She'd lost her appetite.

Her appetite didn't improve while she packed. Her wardrobe seemed even more pathetic when held up to the harsh light of going to an industry event with Sam Shoop. Not that she was going to the event. He hadn't asked her to do that. But they were going to be in Vegas together, and all of his industry friends owned eighty-dollar T-shirts and six-hundred-dollar jeans. Maybe she would stay in the room with Daisy for the entirety of the trip. Steal leftovers from room service trays left in the hallway to be collected like the troll she was. No one had to know she was there. Sam could introduce her as the dog nanny if someone caught a glimpse of her.

Tears filled her eyes again. How was there any moisture left in her body? Hadn't she cried enough for one day? But there was no holding back the sobs. For as long as she could remember, Lacey had been unable to stop crying once she started. After the initial tears, every little thing set her off.

Which meant when Sam walked into the bedroom unexpectedly, her sobs turned into wails.

"Why are you here?" she croaked.

"I own the place," Sam joked, which only brought on a fresh wave of tears. "Oh shit. Sunshine, what's wrong?" The mattress sank a little under his weight, and then his arms were wrapped around her, his familiar, comforting scent filling her snot-clogged nose. Lacey pressed her face into his neck and cried for several more minutes.

"Everything," she finally managed, sniffling and wiping her nose on the sleeve of her sweatshirt. "I've had the worst fucking day."

"What happened?" he asked, trying to help her dry her face with his own sleeve.

Lacey recounted the events of the week, including how her dancers were falling to pieces, and then told him about what happened at Stardust, followed by what Gavin had said when she got to the studio. Sam listened patiently, his thumb stroking the back of the hand he held.

"I feel like such a failure," she blubbered. "I'm so stupid."

"You're not stupid," Sam reassured her. "Have you called the bank yet?"

Lacey shook her head. "No. I meant to, but the day got away from me."

"You need to call the bank so they can start investigating and get your money back. It might take a few days. Do you have any money anywhere else you can use? Stocks? Bonds?"

"Do people still have bonds?"

"Lacey, focus."

She shook her head. "No. Everything I had was in my bank account."

"Did your mom leave you anything?"

"Yes, but the accessible portion is long gone."

Sam frowned. "What do you mean the accessible portion?"

Lacey let out a shaky sigh. "The money she left for me was divided in half. I got the first part when I turned eighteen. The other part—" she groaned— "the other part is held in trust until I get married. It was supposed to be a wedding present."

"What if you never got married?"

"I don't think she thought that was a possibility. I was a hopelessly romantic kid. Life beat it out of me." Lacey bit her bottom lip to stop it from quivering.

"I could give you money—"

"No!" she shouted, much more forcefully than she'd meant to. "No," she said again, softer. "I don't want that."

Sam stared at her in disbelief. "Why not? You need money, I have money."

"Because money makes things weird in relationships. It ruins them. I don't want that to fuck up anything between us. You're too important to me, Sam."

There. She'd said it. The first litmus test to see if any kind of emotion between them would send him running for the hills.

"But—"

"I mean it. I hate every boyfriend I ever gave money to. I don't ever want you to resent me like that." She wiped her nose on her sleeve again. "I'll figure it out. I can try and get a second job. Not that this is a great time of year to be looking, but I'm so fucking sick and tired of being in debt. I hate this."

Sam gathered her up in his arms and squeezed her tightly. He kissed her temple, letting his lips linger, then said, "Stay here. Live here. It'll save you a couple hundred dollars a month."

"I can't—"

"Oh, for fuck's sake, Lacey. Yes, you can. You'll take care of Daisy when I'm gone. Work in exchange for rent, if it'll make you feel any better."

It mollified her a little and she relaxed against him.

"I don't want to be a burden."

"You're not." He pressed another kiss to her temple.

"Maybe I shouldn't go to Vegas."

His body stiffened. "Why not?"

"Because." Lacey knew she was winding herself up again for another meltdown, but it was like watching an oncoming avalanche while stuck in a hole. "I have nothing to wear, I'm broke, I'm going to end up embarrassing you because of the first two things—"

"Fuck's sake, Lace," Sam groaned. "I don't care what you wear. I'd prefer you were naked all the time, but that's just my opinion. You have to come. Otherwise I'll have to explain to Stacey and Wes why I made them fly up here a day early for nothing."

"Why *did* you come home a day early? I thought I was meeting you at the airport tomorrow."

"Because I missed you. You're important to me too." He thumbed the end of her nose playfully. "And I was worried you'd get cold feet and not turn up."

Lacey laughed. It was watery, but it was a laugh. They cuddled for a while, Sam stroking her hair and rubbing her back, and Daisy joined them once she realized no one was going to go downstairs and turn on her TV.

Eventually, Sam helped her finish packing, and she talked him out of bringing everything of Daisy's with them for a weekend trip. Then they took Daisy out for her evening walk, sticking to the paved driveway because the recent rain had created a lot of mud, before getting into bed nice and early. They snuggled together, bodies fitted together like spoons in a drawer, and Daisy laid on their legs because she couldn't wiggle her way in between them.

Lacey fell asleep in the safety of Sam's arms and under Daisy's comforting weight, counting her blessings instead of her mistakes.

CHAPTER TWENTY-SIX

THE PLANE TOUCHED down in Las Vegas shortly before noon. Lacey spent most of the hour-and-a-half flight asleep. Sam spent most of the flight alternating between watching her and knitting Christmas presents. The repetitive motion of the knitting needles soothed his nerves and paying attention to the pattern and stitches took his mind off his anxiety about flying.

But nothing seemed to be able to soothe his nerves or take his mind off of the anxiety he felt about Lacey.

She'd been so distraught the night before that for a second he'd thought something had happened to Daisy. Then he remembered that he'd seen Daisy on his way in and she was fine. It had been a relief that she had merely lost all her money to a security breach.

It frustrated him that she wouldn't let him help. He wouldn't miss a few thousand dollars, especially if it provided the woman he loved with some peace. But he had to respect her reasons, even if he didn't agree with them. Those reasons had made her say he was important to her, that their relationship was important to her, and when he wasn't actively worrying, Sam was so giddy he was practically floating.

Maybe he could rig a card game or a slot machine. Would a casino care if he provided the funds? It was something to think about. A reverse heist of sorts. Or maybe fake a lottery ticket. Peter could help him set up something that elaborate and stupid.

The first thing Lacey said when she stepped off the plane was "Holy shit! It's cold."

"I told you!" Wes shouted from inside the flight deck. "Sunny and fifty-nine, oh so fine."

"It's not any colder than home," Sam pointed out, pulling her hat down a little lower on her face. A long lens camera could be anywhere, especially during an event weekend.

"Yeah, but it's *Vegas*. It's supposed to be hot."

"I'll bring you back in the summer so you can roast," he promised.

They approached the black SUV waiting near the plane. The airport ground crew were loading their bags into the back.

"Wow." Lacey let out a low whistle, which made Daisy's ears perk up. "We're fancy."

Sam recognized the bodyguard that opened the back door for them. John Paul—a name Sam actually remembered because he associated it with the former Pope—was not a physically imposing man. He was shorter than Sam, but had the kind of broad chest and shoulders that made him look like a pit bull. John Paul was no-nonsense but not controlling, and best of all, not chatty. If he spoke, it had a purpose.

John Paul gave a curt nod of hello. "Sam."

"John Paul," Sam said, and then put an arm on the small of Lacey's back. "This is Lacey Finch, my girlfriend, and this is Daisy, our dog."

John Paul gave Lacey the same curt nod, but when he saw Daisy, his professional tough guy demeanor fell away. A broad smile crinkled the corners of his eyes, and he spoke to her in a high-pitched, sing-song voice.

"Oh, hello, beautiful girl. Who's a good girl? Are you a good girl?"

Daisy wiggled and pranced, her tail wagging at the speed of sound. Lacey was going to have to fight John Paul for dog-walking duty. Maybe he needed another guard, because if it came down to it, Sam had a feeling John Paul would protect Daisy first.

Lacey put her lips close to his ear and whispered, "If you play your cards right, I might be a very good girl for you later."

Sam didn't care if she was a good girl or a bad girl, as long as she was a naked girl.

"I think the hotel has the Hallmark Murders and Mysteries channel. That should keep Daisy busy for a bit," he said as they climbed into the SUV.

"Maybe we can get her to branch out. *Columbo. Monk. Diagnosis: Murder*," Lacey joked and buckled in.

"I bet we could get John Paul to babysit."

"But would we get the dog back?" Lacey raised her eyebrows, then winked as John Paul got into the driver's seat.

"Straight to the hotel?" he asked, glancing into the rearview mirror.

"Yes, please," Sam said, relaxing into his pre-heated seat. There were a lot of downsides to celebrity, but this was not one of them.

John Paul pulled up the current routes and traffic conditions on the console screen, and selected a route that, while not direct, offered the least amount of traffic.

Lacey commented on the various billboards as they passed them. Las Vegas was clogged with advertisements for shows, strippers, and lawyers.

"How many wedding chapels do you think Vegas has?" she asked after reading a sign for a drive-thru wedding experience.

"I'd imagine a lot. I think a lot of the hotels on the strip have them. Plus, Vegas is known for it," Sam said, looking out her window at the sign.

A wild idea entered his mind. If she didn't want his money, would she take her own?

"Lacey," he said, "how much money did your mom leave you as a wedding present?"

She thought for a moment. "I think the total is at about $67,000 now. Why?"

"Would that take care of your debt?"

"Yes." Her eyes widened as it dawned on her what he was getting at. "Sam, you're not serious."

"I'm very, very serious." He took her hands and squeezed them, his heart racing. Nervous nausea tossed his stomach like a beach ball in a hurricane. "Let me help you. We're in Vegas, for fuck's sake. There's no better place in the world for an impulsive, quickie wedding. We could be in and out before the show starts tonight."

"Have you even thought this through? We'd be *married*."

Married to Lacey. He loved the sound of that. The advantages kept piling up, too. If they were married, he'd have more time to get her to love him back in the same way he loved her.

"Isn't doing borderline stupid, very impulsive things on brand for us?" he asked. "How hard would it be to get your money after you got married?"

"Not hard. I'd need to send a copy of the marriage license to the firm that handles the account and they'd cut me a check."

"So you could potentially be solvent before Christmas," Sam pointed out, and Lacey's eyebrows knitted together in consideration of this point. He was winning her over. "I'm not seeing any downsides here."

"We don't have a pre-nup."

"I don't need or want your money, sunshine."

Lacey rolled her eyes. "I know that."

"Do you want my money?" he asked, and she shook her head. "So why is a pre-nup important?"

"Because I don't want anyone to ever be able to say I married you for your money," she said quietly. "I don't want anyone to think I'm a gold digger."

"My lawyer can draw up a post-nup on Monday." *Dear god, Athena is going to get a kick out of this.* "Look, you don't have to marry me, and if you do, we don't have to stay married. But I think it's the easiest and quickest way to help you, and I'm offering to do it."

Lacey looked down at their joined hands and pursed her lips. Sam couldn't breathe while she thought. Finally, she gave a small nod.

"You're right. Let's do it. Let's get married."

"Congratulations," John Paul said from the front seat, and Sam startled. He'd forgotten the bodyguard was even in the car with them. "Do you want to go to the marriage license bureau or the hotel?"

"The what?" Sam asked.

"The Clark County Marriage License Bureau. You can't just show up at a chapel without your paperwork," John Paul explained. "My wife and I made that mistake. It's not like it is in the movies."

Sam was astounded. "You're married?"

"You can fill out the application online, actually," John Paul continued. "Then you can run in, show them your IDs, and we can find a chapel."

Lacey squeezed his hand to get his attention. "Not to sound ungrateful, but even if it's not a real marriage, I'd rather not get married in leggings and a sweatshirt I got for free."

Sam took a good, hard, objective look at Lacey. She looked like she'd just woken up from a nap. Probably because she had just woken up from a nap. And he could see how that might make her feel less than bridal.

"You start filling out the online application, I'll work on organizing the ceremony," he told her.

Sam: Do you want to go to a wedding?

Jenna: Whose wedding and when?

Sam: Mine. Today.

His phone rang immediately.

"SAM SHOOP, THAT ISN'T FUNNY!" Jenna shrieked.

"I'm not trying to be funny." Sam took Lacey's phone when she passed it to him to fill out his portion of the application. "I can explain more soon, but do you think you could play fairy godmother to the bride?"

Jenna squealed. "Yes! When will you be at the hotel?"

"Umm..." Sam looked at the directions on the console. "Forty-five minutes to an hour?"

"I will be ready and waiting," Jenna said, and squealed again as Sam hung up.

"Who was that?" Lacey asked.

Sam finished his portion of the application, reviewed the answers, and hit submit before passing Lacey back her phone. "Your fairy godmother."

CHAPTER TWENTY-SEVEN

THE RIDE in the service elevator was not what Lacey had expected when she signed up to join her fake rock star boyfriend in Las Vegas.

Scratch that. He was her fiancé. Soon to be her husband.

Butterflies filled her stomach. *Husband.* Her inner child, that little girl who had mainlined fairy tales like they were vital to her survival, was celebrating. The pragmatic, adult side of her brain reminded her that this marriage wasn't real and Sam was doing her a gigantic favor.

It wasn't the romantic proposal she'd dreamed of, but at least this time when a man offered to marry her for her money, he wasn't planning on using it for himself.

When her money problems had started, her ex-boyfriend Jace—the cause of all those money problems—had suggested they get married to access her inheritance. In the same breath as "this will solve your problem," he talked about how it could fund studio time and equipment and clothes for his music career.

At least Sam was being altruistic. As soon as she could, she would release him from their sham marriage. She loved him, and she wanted to be his wife, but not like this. Not out of pity.

The elevator doors opened, and their small entourage, which had grown to include two members of hotel security, a concierge, and two bellhops to manage their bags, exited into the corridor.

Sam's suite was at the end of the hallway. The last time Lacey had been in a hotel room that large and fancy was with Sam in Barcelona, but she hadn't gotten to properly appreciate the accommodations because she was too busy appreciating his body.

The suite had a living room, dedicated bedroom, and a luxurious bathroom with a tub so large Lacey wanted to weep because she would actually be able to fit in it. It was spacious enough she could probably wedge Sam in there too.

The team of people who'd brought them to their room filed out, and John Paul offered to take Daisy for a walk. Sam quickly agreed.

"Outsourcing my job already?" Lacey joked. Humor was her best defense against the rising tide of nerves.

"Trying to get you alone," Sam said as he curled a hand around the back of her neck.

There was a knock at the door.

Sam growled. "Fuck."

He stalked across the room and peered through the peephole. More obscenities graced his lips as he yanked open the door.

"Fairy godmother, present and reporting for duty."

"We literally just got here. How did you know?"

Jenna Fox breezed past Sam into the suite. Lacey's eyes widened. In her wildest dreams, she never would have allowed herself to even hope that Jenna Fox would say hello to her, let alone help her get ready for her wedding.

But Jenna didn't say hello. She wrapped Lacey in a tight, surprisingly strong hug.

"I'm so excited to meet you. I've heard *so* much about you."

Lacey laughed nervously, gingerly hugging Jenna in return. "So my name and the fact that I exist?"

Jenna looked over her shoulder at Sam. "It's like she knows you." She grasped Lacey by the shoulders and held her at arm's length, studying her closely. "Okay, I can make this work. How long do I have?"

"How long do you need?" Sam asked, plucking a few grapes from the fruit tray on the dining table.

"Ideally? All day. But I think I can have her vow-ready in two hours."

Sam coughed, choking on a grape. "Two hours? What takes two hours?"

Jenna ticked items off on her fingers. "Hair, makeup, picking a dress, nails..."

"I don't need all that," Lacey insisted, feeling more like a burden than ever. "I just don't want to get married in this." She gestured to her outfit.

"Look, I understand that Sam is rushing you down the aisle before you change your mind about him, but you should feel special. You should feel *bridal*." Jenna linked her arm with Lacey's and tugged her toward the door. "Sam, we'll meet you at the venue. Text me when you pick one."

"Wait, what? Why?" Sam followed them toward the door. "Why are we meeting at the venue?"

"Because you're not supposed to see the bride before the wedding." Jenna opened the door and pushed Lacey through. She smiled at Sam and wiggled her fingers at him. "Bye, love you, see you later." She pulled the door closed before he could object. "Come on. I'm just down the hall."

"You really don't have to go to all this trouble," Lacey said as Jenna hurried them to her room.

"This isn't that much trouble." Jenna touched the keycard to the door and pushed it open. "I've known Sam forever. He's basically my little brother, which makes you my sister-in-law, and that means you deserve the best." She dropped her keycard onto the first flat surface she saw. "Unfortunately, Sam gave me very little notice, so you're going to get the good enough treatment."

"Good enough is great."

Jenna's room looked like Sam's except it had clothes everywhere, including a rolling rack of dresses by the window, and a small team of people setting up for hair and makeup. Jenna dragged Lacey over to the rack of dresses and began pulling options.

"Do you have any kind of specific vibe you were thinking of?"

"You really didn't need to do all of this—"

"The dresses are all options I didn't go with for tonight and the glam squad was already booked." Jenna frowned at the rack of dresses. "I don't have anything super bridal. No white. Nothing long...Unless you want a suit. Do you want a suit? There's one here somewhere. I just felt it made me look too much like I was running for Congress."

Jenna Fox was a force of nature, and Lacey gave up trying to resist her efforts to make magic happen. When would she ever get this kind of opportunity again? To have one of her all-time favorite artists fussing and fawning over her? Likely never.

"Short and sparkly," she said, and Jenna got to work.

SAM PACED the lobby of the wedding chapel, checking the clock continuously because the minutes were passing in hours while he waited for Lacey to show up for their wedding.

John Paul had gone above and beyond the call of duty and found a chapel that had two consecutive time slots available so they could ensure some form of privacy for their wedding. Then he'd gone to the hotel florist and purchased a pre-made rose and baby's breath crown meant for a person, but he'd tied it around Daisy's neck so she could look pretty for the wedding, too.

That man was going to receive a hefty bonus at the end of the weekend.

Sam's clothes felt too tight. The black suit was custom, so it fit him perfectly, but even with the neck of his black shirt open to his sternum, he felt like he couldn't breathe correctly. He tugged on the cuff of the jacket, then rubbed his thumb over the black floral embroidery that started there and traveled up his arms.

Where was Lacey?

Were they lost? Stuck in traffic? Had she changed her mind and was hiding under Jenna's bed?

The chapel wouldn't let him check in for the ceremony until Lacey arrived, so he had nothing to do but pace and wait.

The door opened, and Jenna swept in, wearing a metallic gold two-piece ensemble that made her look like a goddess from ancient mythology. The slit on the skirt went dangerously high up her thigh, and Sam hoped the top was reinforced with tape underneath because if she sneezed too hard there could be a wardrobe malfunction.

"Sorry!" she said, holding up her hands. "My hair and makeup took longer than I expected."

"Is this the bride?" the receptionist asked, putting some paperwork on the counter.

Jenna burst out laughing. "Oh, god, no. Absolutely not. No, no, no."

Sam glared. "Okay, it's not *that* funny."

"The bride?" the receptionist prompted.

The door opened again, and Lacey entered. Time stopped for Sam. Her blonde hair was styled into a low bun with a few loose pieces framing her beautiful face. Then there was her dress. It was short, hitting roughly mid-thigh, putting Lacey's glorious legs on full display, and so sparkly that she shimmered like a diamond. The beading was silver, but when the sunlight from the windows hit it, a pattern on the side—it was either a butterfly or a flower, he couldn't quite tell—became an iridescent purple pink. The sweetheart neckline gave the optical illusion of cleavage, and Sam wanted to kiss her bare shoulders.

She couldn't be real. She was too perfect. It was like she was a fairy plucked from a magical forest. She should be cavorting with unicorns, not marrying him.

"I'm going to assume from the stunned look on your face that I did good," Jenna said, and Sam blinked a few times to restart his brain.

"Um, yeah. You did good. Real good."

Brilliant use of words, Sam.

"If I could have the bride and groom over here, we can go over the details for the ceremony," the receptionist said.

Sam met Lacey at the desk and put a hand on her lower back as the receptionist explained the ceremony to them. It was a maximum of fifteen minutes, if they wanted to use their own vows they needed to be two hundred words or less, and their officiant could do religious or non-religious.

"Non- religious," they said at the same time. The receptionist marked the choice on their form.

"Would you like to say your own vows?"

"We don't have anything prepared," Lacey said. "A simple ceremony is fine."

The receptionist ran her finger down her checklist. "Would you like to hold your rings, would you like your officiant to hold your rings, or would you like your witness to hold your rings?"

Sam's heart skipped a beat and a wave of cold washed over his body. Rings. He'd forgotten about rings.

"Fuck," Sam muttered.

"It's fine," Lacey reassured him, which only served to make him feel worse. He should've gotten her a ring. She deserved a ring.

"I've got this!" Jenna declared. "This will be fairy godmothering at its finest." She peered over the top of the counter, looking at the desk below. "Can I borrow some Post-it notes?"

The receptionist handed her the stack.

"I used to do this instead of paying attention in math. Let's make that D in Pre-Algebra worth it."

Sam and Lacey exchanged a look, and Sam shrugged.

"I need to check your marriage license and your identification," the receptionist said.

John Paul produced the manila envelope with their marriage license and handed it to Sam, who handed it to the receptionist along with his driver's license. Lacey handed over her driver's license, and the receptionist did some checks.

"Would you like to go by Samwise or something different for the ceremony?"

Sam shut his eyes and braced himself.

"Your name is *Samwise*?" Lacey gasped.

"My dad is a big Tolkien fan. He hoped I would be loyal, brave, and kind."

Lacey pressed a kiss to his cheek. "He got his wish."

Sam put on a stoic face, even though internally he was a pile of goo. "Sam is fine."

"After your ceremony, you'll sign your license, along with your witness and the officiant, and then we will mail it in for you for filing. After about ten days, you can order a certified marriage certificate as proof of marriage." She handed back their driver's licenses. "I will go inform your officiant you're about ready to start."

"Thank you," Sam said as she went into a back room.

"Wow. This is really real," Lacey murmured.

Sam kissed her forehead. "It is. Sorry about the rings. I didn't think about it."

She leaned into him and closed her eyes. "It's fine. I don't need one."

The receptionist came back with two people in tow, a short, squat woman wearing black, and a tall, skinny man with a camera.

"This is Janette, your officiant, and Kieran, your photographer."

Janette smiled, her apple cheeks rosy. "Sam, Lacey, it's wonderful to meet you. If the groom and guests follow me to the chapel, we can get started."

Sam, Jenna, and Daisy headed to the chapel with Janette and Kieran. John Paul would remain in the lobby to monitor the area for unwanted guests.

"Wait!" Lacey shouted, and hurried as fast as she could in her heels to catch up. "I don't need a processional. Let's just do this together."

"You're the boss—I mean bride," Janette said with a twinkle in her kind eyes.

Lacey took Sam's hand and squeezed it tightly. He squeezed hers in return.

Together. They'd do this together.

The chapel was small and starkly white. It held six rows of short pews, three on each side of an aisle with a red carpet, and then a fake flower arch at the end. Janette walked ahead of them down the aisle, and Jenna took a seat in the front pew. Daisy trotted alongside Sam, confused but happy by her family walk.

Sam and Lacey stopped in front of Janette and faced each other, hands clasped together, and Daisy obediently sat at their feet, her face raised to watch.

"Sam, Lacey," Janette began and a profound sense of calm fell over Sam like a warm blanket, "today you embark on one of life's greatest journeys. Today you've chosen to knit your lives together and become your own family. Marriage is not always easy, but when undertaken with the curious combination of seriousness and joy, it is wholly worth the effort. Are you ready to begin?"

"Yes," Sam said and Lacey nodded.

"Lacey, we'll begin with you. Say, 'Sam, today I join my life with yours, for better or for worse, in sickness and in health.'"

"Sam," Lacey began softly, and squeezed his hands, "today I join my life with yours, for better or for worse, in sickness and in health."

"I promise to be a thoughtful and considerate partner, to celebrate your accomplishments and to help shoulder your burdens."

"I promise to be a thoughtful and considerate partner, to celebrate your accomplishments and to help shoulder your burdens."

"Now, Sam—"

"I remember," Sam said. "Lacey, today I join my life with yours, for better or for worse, in sickness and in health. I promise to be a thoughtful and considerate partner, to celebrate your accomplishments and to help shoulder your burdens." He paused, and glanced at Janette. "Can I go off-script a little?"

"It's your wedding."

Sam looked deep into Lacey's eyes. "It is my joy to be your

husband. Asking you to marry me was the easiest decision I've ever made."

Tears welled up in Lacey's eyes and her bottom lip quivered. She swallowed hard and mouthed, "Thank you."

"Lacey, do you take Sam to be your lawfully wedded husband?" Janette asked.

"I do," Lacey whispered, a tear sliding down her cheek.

"Sam, do you take Lacey to be your lawfully wedded wife?"

Solemnly, Sam answered, "I do."

"Do we have the rings?" Janette asked, looking between the couple, who looked at Jenna.

Jenna proudly held up two paper rings crafted out of neon pink Post-it notes. "We do!"

Janette pursed her lips to keep from laughing, and nodded. She motioned for Jenna to bring them up to the front. Jenna practically skipped and presented them to the officiant with an unnecessary amount of flair before taking her seat again.

"These, um, rings are a symbol of your devotion. The circle is unending, like your love. Place them on each other's fingers— left hand, as a reminder."

Lacey took one of the paper rings and gingerly pushed it onto Sam's ring finger, and he did the same, his touch lingering as he savored the moment.

"Sam and Lacey, by the power vested in me by the state of Nevada, I now pronounce you husband and wife. You may kiss your bride."

An excited smile bloomed on Lacey's face and she wrapped her arms around his neck, kissing him soundly before he had the chance to make the first move. Sam curled his arms around her body, so happy he thought he'd explode like a firework, and dipped her. Faintly he heard Jenna cheer and Daisy bounced, unsure what the fuss was about but happy to be included.

A bridal fanfare erupted from the chapel speakers and they

walked out past Kieran, who was taking photos as fast as his shutter allowed. In the lobby, they signed their marriage license and Jenna signed as their witness, and then it was done, all neat and legal.

"What time is it?" Jenna asked, looking around for the clock. "Oh shit. We need to go or Inger is going to murder us."

Sam looked at the clock. 3:15. It was, without traffic, about a fifteen-minute drive back to the venue. The red carpet had started fifteen minutes ago. They'd make the red carpet, but there was a chance a chunk of the journalists would already be in the press room writing their stories. Sam was okay with that; less people to talk to. Inger, his publicist, would have a fit.

"I'll see you back at the hotel?" Lacey asked.

Jenna's head whirled around. "What? No. You're coming with us, aren't you? Aren't you Sam's date?"

Lacey blushed, and Sam did too because he knew what was coming next. "He never asked me."

"Sam!" Jenna shouted.

His defense was weak. "It was hard enough to get her to come."

Jenna rolled her eyes. "Lacey, love, you can be my date. It will be less depressing to have you sitting next to me than a seat filler or a Z-lister."

"What happened to Houston?" Sam asked as they headed for the cars. Maybe it was his fault for assuming, but he thought Jenna's fiancée would be there. He would've sworn he remembered her saying he would be.

Jenna shrugged. "His plans changed, and he couldn't make it."

If by some miracle they made it down the aisle, Sam was going to stand up and object.

"What about Daisy?" Lacey asked.

Sam and Jenna both stopped walking and stared at each other, the mutual panic palpable.

John Paul interjected, "Can I make a suggestion? Sam, you take Daisy on the red carpet. When you're ready to go inside, I can take her back to the hotel and get her settled for the night."

Sam liked the idea. Daisy would be a huge hit and a great distraction. He'd seem charming with a dog as his date.

"John Paul, I think you might be a genius," Sam said.

CHAPTER TWENTY-EIGHT

RED CARPETS MADE SAM ANXIOUS. They always had. The amount of people, the flashing lights from the cameras, all the photographers shouting for his attention. It was overwhelming. Then he had to answer the same questions over and over again with polished perfection, knowing any misstep would cause out of proportion headlines.

Daisy was, as predicted, a hit. The dog had an enviable natural poise and posed like an expert for the cameras.

Sam lost Lacey and Jenna pretty quickly in the organized chaos. One moment they were next to him talking to a journalist, Jenna chatting animatedly, Lacey playing the role of supportive, silent friend, and then they were gone.

He found them inside after he handed off Daisy to John Paul. Jenna was still talking with her hands, her drink threatening to slosh over the rim with every gesture, and Lacey stood next to her with an expression he recognized. The tight, almost pinched mask of pleasantness was the same one she wore whenever she had to talk to Mitch, except it was Jace Kieffer. Sam didn't know why he was there, except to maybe try and get in with Grim, who was part of the small group.

"Working on your disappearing act?" Sam teased when he reached them, curling an arm around Lacey's waist and kissing her cheek.

"Magic is my Plan B," she joked, though her smile didn't quite reach her eyes.

Was it the crowd? Was she worried people were looking at her? Sam wanted to tell her that everyone in the room was so self-absorbed they didn't know she existed, but Jace Kieffer spoke before he could.

"I'm Jace Kieffer. It's nice to finally meet you, Sam."

Sam looked at the offered hand, but chose to keep his arm around Lacey instead of shaking it.

"I know who you are. Your name has been shoved in front of my face a lot recently."

It was irritating how much the powers that be wanted them to work together. It made Sam dig his heels in and refuse at every turn. He'd been sent some samples of Jace's work, and it was...not good. Soulless. Market-driven crap designed in a boardroom. Jace was a good-looking guy. In the right context, Sam might have even tried to sleep with him, but there was something about him that grated on Sam's nerves.

"Well, I'd really like the opportunity to work with you—"

"Does anyone know where the bathroom is in this place?" Jenna interrupted, looking around. She reminded Sam of a gold flamingo.

"I'll help you find it," Lacey offered, and linked her arm with Jenna's. The two women walked away, leaving Sam with Grim and Jace.

"How do you know Lacey?" Jace asked once they were out of sight.

The back of Sam's neck prickled. "How do *you* know Lacey?"

"We dated," Jace said, "and I don't mean to, like, get in your business or anything, but you should know that Lacey kind of... gets around. She's a serial groupie."

A memory surfaced in Sam's mind, of the first walk he and Lacey had taken Daisy on. Was Jace the ex-boyfriend who'd recently broken into the music industry? The same one who'd bled her dry and left her hanging when he'd gotten his record deal? It would explain the look on Lacey's face.

Sam had been too late to save Lacey's reputation in Crane Cove from Mitch, but he could sure as shit save her from fucking Jace Kieffer.

Sam's eyes narrowed and he took a step toward Jace, pitching his voice low so no one around them could hear. "If I *ever* hear you say another nasty thing about my wife again, I will end your career like *that*." He snapped his fingers for emphasis. "If I get so much as a whiff of a rumor, you're finished. I can and will find out. Do you understand me?"

"It's not that serious—"

Sam's blood boiled, but his voice was ice cold. "Do. You. Understand. Me?"

Jace nodded rapidly. "Yes, yes. I understand. Very much understood."

"Go away."

Jace walked away quickly, vanishing in the crowd.

"I'm sorry, did you just say *wife*?" Grim asked in disbelief.

Sam stretched his neck from side to side, and took some calming breaths to bring down his blood pressure. "I did."

"*When?* And why wasn't I invited?"

Sam shrugged. "About forty-five minutes ago? It was kind of a last-second thing. We didn't send out invitations."

A big, surprised smile stretched across Grim's face. "Wow. I mean, this explains why this album is so fucking sappy by Sam Shoop standards, but damn. Congratulations. You weren't trying to beat Adrienne down the aisle, were you?"

Sam frowned, confused. It was rare for anyone to utter the name of his ex-fiancée in front of him.

"Honestly? I don't think about her anymore. What are you talking about?"

"She's getting married on New Year's Eve. You really didn't know?"

Sam shook his head. "I try to spend as little time as possible on the internet."

Grim chuckled. "You're smarter than I am. You really don't keep up with Adrienne?"

"I really don't."

"Good for you, man. But don't be surprised if she shrieks down the internet when you announce your marriage."

"Announce? I don't think we were planning on announcing."

Grim shrugged. "Suit yourself. I'd run it by Inger, though. Because she might want you to get in front of the story before it breaks."

"What do you mean 'before the story breaks'?"

"Journalists watch marriage filings like hawks, especially during these events when everyone is in town and making stupid choices—not that you made a stupid choice. I didn't say that. Other people make stupid choices. Lacey seems really nice."

Sam broke out in a cold sweat. It had never occurred to him that anyone with an internet connection and three working brain cells could look up his marriage. He wasn't ashamed of Lacey, he could never be ashamed of Lacey, but he hated having people poke around in his business. Especially something that was so delicate.

How long would it take the world to find out? How long until Lacey's life was dissected under a microscope? Could she handle that? Would he ever be able to convince her to stay if being with him meant having her life broadcast to the world?

CHAPTER TWENTY-NINE

BY THE END of her first fancy awards show, Lacey knew two things to be true:

1. Her feet were killing her.
2. She was starving.

Jenna begged her and Sam to go to an after-party, but Lacey had no interest. Not with Jace lurking.

Jace walking up to her and saying hello had been a shock. Lacey should've known that being with Sam meant that eventually she might run into her parasitic ex-boyfriend, but in the whirlwind of the day, it hadn't occurred to her to decline Jenna's invitation on the off chance that bottom feeder might be present.

The first thing she asked after Sam helped her into their waiting SUV was, "Can we order room service?"

Sam chuckled and slid in next to her. Once the door was shut, he cupped the back of her neck and gave her a long, thorough kiss that made her feel like a sparkler on the Fourth of July.

"Whatever my wife wants."

Wife. Those four little letters strung together shouldn't have sounded so nice coming from Sam's mouth, but they did. They made her feel warm and protected. If she could shove the circumstances of their wedding out of her mind, it felt wonderful to be married.

If Lacey had any regrets about the day, it was that she had been too anxious to enjoy most of it. She'd worried herself sick that Sam was going to instantly regret his decision. That he would back out at the last second and leave her alone and embarrassed at the altar.

But then he'd said it was his joy to be her husband and the cotton candy dam holding back her emotions broke. Dissolved. No matter how she put it, she'd been toast.

"Your wife wants to take off her fucking shoes," Lacey said, kissing him again. She slipped her tongue into his mouth and got a thrill because, legally, he was hers.

"You don't want to leave the shoes on?" Sam asked, caressing her upper thigh and getting dangerously close to the hem of her short dress with every pass.

To his credit, John Paul was doing a very good job of pretending he couldn't see or hear them in the backseat.

The ride to the hotel was mercifully short, and John Paul parked in the loading dock again. Sam leaned forward, resting his elbows on the two front seats.

"John Paul, you wouldn't want to keep Daisy in your room tonight, would you?"

"She's an excellent snuggler," Lacey added, leaving out that Daisy farted, snored, and hogged the bed too.

"Consider it my wedding present," John Paul said with a knowing smile.

While Sam gave John Paul overly complicated instructions for babysitting Daisy overnight, Lacey went to the bedroom and took off her shoes and rubbed her feet. Jenna was about half a shoe size smaller than she was, and while it worked in a pinch, her feet had paid the price. Someday she'd apologize to her feet for all she'd put them through over the years by only wearing cozy slippers and getting weekly pedicures.

The door to the hallway clicked shut, and Lacey's heart took off. They were alone—really, truly alone—for the first time since they'd met in Barcelona. Her pussy clenched at the memory and the opportunity for uninterrupted fun.

It was their wedding night, after all.

Sam walked into the bedroom, jacket gone, looking over the leatherbound room service menu. He stopped in front of her, still reading the menu and asked, "What are you in the mood for?"

Lacey grasped his belt and began to unbuckle it. "You, mostly."

Sam put his hand on hers to stall her and her heart dropped. "Hold on. I need to tell you something first."

"What?"

"When I was in LA last time, I got tested."

Lacey's heart sank further. "Sam, what are you trying to tell me?"

Sam frowned, confused, then laughed. "Fuck, I'm sorry. I didn't mean for this to be a wedding present, but I got the results back and they're all clear." He took his hand off hers. "I didn't want to tell you after things got hot and heavy."

She fell back on the bed. "When did you find out?"

"Yesterday." He cringed. "I'm going to be honest, it's part of the reason I came back early. I was going to tell you last night, but things have been...irregular."

Lacey pushed herself up on her elbows. "Mr. Shoop, are you saying that you hopped on a private jet and flew home because you wanted to see if you could fuck me bare?"

The guilty blush that spread from his neck up to his cheeks told her everything she needed to know.

"I'm flattered, by the way." She sat the rest of the way back up and unbuckled his belt, followed by his pants. "What are you ordering me for dinner?"

Sam looked back at the menu and Lacey pushed his pants and underwear down. His cock was at the stage where it was thicker than it was long, and as she looked at it, it pulsed. She waited until he moved his mouth to speak, then licked the tip. "W-what do you want to eat?"

"Hmmm..." Lacey wrapped her lips around the head of his cock and sucked. It pulsed and expanded in her mouth, and a salty bead of precum landed on her tongue. She pulled off him with a *pop,* and worked his shaft with her hand. "You know I'll eat anything."

He groaned and made a move to join her on the bed. Lacey put her free hand on his chest to stop him.

"No, no, no. Order us some food first."

Sam narrowed his eyes in a pathetic attempt at feigned annoyance, and picked up the room phone. He dialed room service, and as soon as he said hello, Lacey began to suck his cock with gusto. Watching him fight for his life to order appetizers, entrees, and dessert gave her endless satisfaction and made her pussy throb. She rocked her hips, trying to get some relief from the mattress, but it wasn't enough. Sam cupped the back of her head to hold her still, and slowly, gently, forced his cock down her throat. Lacey relaxed, letting him feed it to her until she choked, then he pulled back and she gasped, then grinned up at him.

Maybe she could find a 24-hour chapel and marry him all over again. Really enjoy the experience this time. They could rent a limo, put up the partition, and he could fuck her while they drove down the Strip.

Sam hung up the phone, replaced it on the receiver, and then grabbed her by the throat. Lacey's grin grew.

"You," he snarled, "are a very, *very* naughty girl."

"I thought I was being a very good girl," she responded innocently, "sucking my husband's cock."

There was a flash of intense emotion across his face and his grip tightened. Lacey's pussy was so wet it had spread to her inner thighs. Her hosiery was destined for the garbage, and if she didn't get her dress off soon, it would need some serious cleaning.

"Strip," he commanded, and released her throat. The small rush of blood made her body tingle.

Lacey stood, then turned around and bent over the bed. She looked over her shoulder at Sam. "I need help."

Carefully, like he seemed to understand that the dress wasn't hers and probably wasn't Jenna's either, Sam eased the hidden zipper down her back. When the bodice didn't immediately fall away, he peeled it off her body.

"Oh, sunshine," Sam ran his fingers over where the dress had dug into her skin, "you poor thing."

"It could've been worse. I could've had to wear a bra too," Lacey joked. If there was one upside to being less than gifted in the bust department, it was being able to forgo a bra whenever she wanted.

Sam finished taking off her dress and her underwear, then began to kiss the tender spots on her back. It was sweet, but not quite what she wanted. Right as she was about to complain, he cupped her breasts, pinching and twisting her nipples how she liked. Lacey moaned and arched, grinding her ass against his cock.

"Are you going to give it to me?" she whined.

Sam's cock slipped between her damp thighs and rubbed

against her clit. A shudder rolled down her body and she moaned again. "Do you want me just like this?"

Just like this. Bare. Nothing at all between them. After so many years of meticulous condom usage, it felt illicit and taboo to even consider.

She nodded. "Yes, please. I want your cock. I want your bare cock inside my pussy."

Sam bit her shoulder to stifle his own moan. A slight adjustment of his hips, and his thick, rigid cock pierced her entrance, spreading and stretching her open. His hand found her throat again, but he didn't grip, just used it to hold her against him. She was so wet that it took hardly any effort for him to fill her to the root, and once he was buried in her, he was still, like he was savoring the feeling.

Lacey savored the feeling. She would never admit it to anyone not wanting to wear a condom, but it did feel different. Better. But a lot of that heightened sensation was because it was Sam and she wanted to be close with him in this way.

"Fuck, you feel amazing," he groaned, and started to roll his hips. The angle, this quasi-standing position he'd put them in, felt incredible. Every movement sent bright sparks of pleasure through her body.

"Oh, god," she moaned, and craned her head to catch his mouth in a hungry, desperate kiss.

That spurred something in Sam, and his pace quickened. The hand that had still been fondling her breast slid down her belly and questing fingers found her clit. He rubbed and stroked, and even pinched, until Lacey clenched around him, screaming into his mouth as her orgasm tore through her.

When she'd relaxed, her body soft and pliable, he put the hand on her neck between her shoulder blades and pressed her chest into the mattress. Sam grasped her hips and fucked her hard, his balls slapping against her clit. He was using her for his own pleasure now, and she loved it.

"I'm getting close," he warned through gritted teeth. "Where do you want it?"

Lacey considered her options through the haze of post-orgasmic bliss. "If you come in me, will you clean up the mess you make with your mouth?"

It seemed like a long shot, but if she was going to ask anyone to fulfill one of her niche fantasies, it was going to be Sam.

"Yes. Fuck, you're bad."

His grip on her hips tightened and he slammed into her repeatedly until he pushed himself as deep as he could go and shuddered. Inside, she could feel his cock pulsing, emptying itself. Lacey clenched around him, and Sam gasped.

When he pulled out, Lacey tilted her hips to keep his load inside. He'd agreed, so he was going to get all of it. She watched him unbutton his shirt and take it off, dropping it to the floor. Then he stepped out of his pants and laid down on the bed.

"Come here," he beckoned, and Lacey crawled to the head of the bed and straddled his face. Sam always ate her pussy like he was starving and it was the best thing he'd ever tasted, and this time was no exception. He squeezed and kneaded her ass while he attacked her cunt, licking, sucking, and probing her with his tongue, moaning happily the entire time. Another small orgasm rolled through her body, and by the time Sam was lazily licking her like a cat with a bowl of cream, she was spent.

She dropped off his face and landed next to him on the bed. "Wow."

Sam licked his lips. "Wow indeed."

Lacey put a hand on her chest and felt her heart thundering under her palm. "You didn't mind that last bit?"

"Do you like tasting yourself off my cock?" he asked, and she nodded. "Same concept, as far as I'm concerned. Plus, I think I taste better coming out of you."

They lay there, kissing on the verge of sleep, until there was a knock at the door. "Room service!"

Sam rolled to his feet and went to the closet to retrieve a robe. It looked fluffy and warm, and as he left the bedroom, Lacey scrambled to the closet as fast as her cooked noodle legs would carry her and grabbed the second robe.

Lacey went into the bathroom to clean up. When she emerged, the room service attendant was gone but had left behind a vast assortment of silver-covered dishes.

"We are never going to be able to eat all of this," she said, and sat down at the table. "Why did you order so much food?"

"Someone"—he looked pointedly at Lacey— "distracted me while I was ordering."

"I have no regrets." She started to take off the lids and stacked them at the end of the table. Steak, chicken, charcuterie, lobster, crème brûlée. The options felt endless. "It's like a buffet."

They ate, sampling the different dishes, and then Lacey lured him to the bath. It was a tight squeeze, but they both fit. Lacey used Sam as a backrest and pillow, laying her head on his shoulder and placing tender kisses on his neck.

She sighed dreamily. "This is nice."

"Mm-hmm." Sam took a deep breath, sinking them deeper into the tub. "Not to ruin the moment, but we need to decide when we're going to tell people we got married."

Her chest tightened. Currently they were in their own, blissful bubble. The only people that knew they'd gotten married were the people at the chapel, John Paul, and Jenna. Would people in Crane Cove be as excited as Jenna? Would his friends be as supportive as John Paul? And if people knew they got married, they'd have to tell them when they got divorced.

"Do we have to tell people?"

"There's a high probability it's going to get out," Sam told her, swirling the water with his fingers. "Apparently the press watch those filings, and anyone can look up your name in the Clark County Clerk's database to see if you got married."

"Seriously?" Lacey looked at him in surprise. "Those things aren't private?"

"Nope. Public record. It might already be out there. We might have a week before it gets out. I don't know. Grim suggested telling Inger so she could craft something—a statement or whatever. Do you want to get ahead of the story or wait and see?"

Add Julius "Grim" Grimbe to the list of those in the know.

"Can we talk about this in the morning? There's a lot of factors to consider."

Sam nodded. "Yeah, um, sure. You're not embarrassed by me or anything, are you?"

Lacey was taken aback. "No. Where did you get that idea?"

"You don't want to tell anyone."

Open mouth, insert foot.

"No, of course I'm not embarrassed by you. It's just that we entered into this relationship to get people out of our business, and I'm realizing that by putting out one fire, I created another one behind me. People are going to be *very* in our business when they find out." She cupped his cheek and brought his face to hers for a small kiss. "It's only been a few hours, but you're proving to be a much better husband than boyfriend."

That made Sam snort and roll his eyes, but there was a smile playing in the corners of that perfect mouth.

CHAPTER THIRTY

THE NEWS of his marriage broke in the morning while they ate breakfast in bed, but it didn't break in the way Sam expected.

Pop Star and Former Member of Sweet Destiny Adrienne Dodson Marries in Surprise Vegas Ceremony Hours After Ex Sam Shoop Does the Same.

There were variations of the headline being sent to him by an irate Inger, who was also asking if he wanted to comment on any of the stories. The content of the articles was mostly focused on Adrienne, who had been very willing to comment on the reports in the middle of the night.

"We got swept up in the moment," Dodson gushed, *"and decided to go for it."* About her planned wedding ceremony in the coming weeks, Dodson says they still plan to go through with it to celebrate with friends and family. *"I just want to celebrate being in love!"*

Sam texted Inger back.

SAM

> I don't really have a comment. I did get
> married, but you don't have to confirm or deny.
> The record is public. I'd appreciate it if you
> squashed any stories about Lacey

INGER

> You're going to have to give them something
> else

> Dangle a vague carrot. We'll come up with
> something.

The amount of information the press had already gathered about his wife was disturbing. The devil worked hard, but the media worked harder. Underpaid interns couldn't have gotten much sleep last night.

Not even ten minutes after he'd settled things with Inger, his group chat went nuclear.

BRUNCH BROS

PETER:

> YOU GOT MARRIED

> IN VEGAS

> WITHOUT US!?!!

GRAHAM

> What the fuck? Where was the heads-up?

JORDY

> I COULD HAVE GOTTEN ON A PLANE AND
> BEEN THERE IN AN HOUR WHAT THE HELL

SAM

> None of this looks like "Congratulations!"

PETER

> I'm mad at you.

SAM

For getting married?

PETER

For not inviting us.

SAM

It was a quick decision. I didn't even have time to get a ring.

JORDY

We're going to need a FULL debrief soon.

"I don't think I want my phone anymore," Sam said, tossing it down to the foot of the bed.

Lacey blew on her coffee to cool it down. She had the satisfied glow of a well-fucked woman. And she should. They'd made the most of their dog-free night and fucked two more times before going to sleep. Sam was pretty sure he'd shot dust instead of cum the last time, though.

"I'm going to ignore mine as long as possible," she said. "What are we telling people?"

"It was a quick decision. Keep it simple."

"Smart." She sipped her coffee. "When are we going home?"

"Soon. I know it's recital week for you."

That earned him a kiss. Sam was confused but wasn't about to look that particular gift horse in the mouth. If remembering a major event that she'd been stressing over for weeks got him affection, he'd memorize her entire schedule down to the due dates of her bills.

That reminded him.

"Totally random," he began, "but now that we're married, if it comes down to the wire this month and you haven't gotten your money from the lawyers or whoever is sending it, you'll let me help you, right? It could be a loan, if that makes you feel better. You can pay me interest in blow jobs."

That made Lacey laugh, which had been his plan. If he softened the suggestion with a joke, maybe she'd take it.

"Okay. But only if it gets *really* close."

THEIR FIRST WEEK of marriage was spent largely apart. Lacey was so busy with recital prep that she left their house early in the morning and came home late at night. She was incredibly grateful for Sam; without him, she'd have survived off of protein shakes and granola bars. And because the universe was cruel and refused to let her have too many nice things at once, she started her period early and burst out crying when Sam brought her lunch at the studio. He'd been doing that for weeks, but he was her *husband* instead of her boyfriend. It felt different.

And Saturday night he was backstage for the recital, volunteering his sanity to help wrangle the dancers.

If she wasn't in love with him already, that would have sealed the deal.

But there was a horrible, insidious voice in the back of her head that said every sweet thing he did in public was to keep up appearances, to convince their town that they were truly married. There would have been more questions if he *didn't* show up to the recital.

Lacey hated those thoughts. She wanted to know how he felt. And if she could ever stop being a fucking coward who was afraid to rock the boat, she'd ask him.

After she got her money. At least then she could afford to hide in shame.

She'd planned on Sunday being a "slug day": she was going to lay around the house in her pajamas and stare at the ceiling.

She wasn't going to think a single thought. Her brain was fried from the last seventy-two hours. So she was surprised to see Jenna's name appear on her phone while she was mindlessly scrolling. The two had exchanged numbers in Vegas, but Lacey couldn't imagine why Jenna was calling.

"Hello?"

"Lacey!" Jenna cheered on the other end. "How are you? How was the recital?"

"I'm good. Exhausted." She rubbed her eyes. "The recital went really well. I had to go on stage with the littles, but they're so cute no one cares."

"I'm so glad. So, I remember Sam saying something about how you used to be a professional dancer? Or maybe you said that? I don't know, but I have you linked with professional dancer in my brain. Is that true?"

Lacey sat bolt upright on the couch. "Yes, that's right."

"Okay, obviously nothing is for sure because you'd need to audition—"

Her pulse blasted into outer space like a rocket.

"But I lost a dancer for my tour that starts in the spring. And I thought of you!" Jenna laughed nervously. "I thought it would be really fun to have you on tour. If you're interested, I'm totally willing to fly you down for the audition."

"Oh my god." Lacey was stunned. Her brain was simultaneously flying at a million miles per hour while also not moving at all.

Jenna was offering her the opportunity she wouldn't even allow herself to dream about. She could be a professional dancer again. She'd be on tour with a legit musician. Dancing with Jenna Fox could open all kinds of doors that had been shut in her face.

Her debt was about to be wiped out, *and* she had a job offer on the table. She wouldn't be in danger of being dependent on

Sam anymore. With her own career and her own money, Lacey could go to him as a confident woman with her shit together and something to offer besides great sex.

"Lacey? Are you still there? Did I lose you?"

"Yes! I mean, no." It was Lacey's turn to laugh nervously. "No, you didn't lose me, and yes, I'm still here." She stood and started pacing. "What if it doesn't work out? What if you're wasting your time with me?"

"Not to get your hopes up, but the headliner *really* likes your personality and I've heard she has a lot of creative say." Jenna hinted with all the subtlety of a herd of stampeding elephants wearing bells.

"Okay. Yes! When do I come down?"

"Can you come down tomorrow? I know that's super short notice but—"

"Yes!" Lacey interrupted, unable to stop smiling now. "The studio I work at is closed for winter break, so I have a little bit of free time."

Jenna squealed. "I'm so excited! I will get everything sorted and send you the information. I'll see you tomorrow, Lacey!"

"Bye—and thank you!" Jenna had already hung up. Lacey squealed, literally jumping for joy.

Sam emerged at the top of the stairs, looking a bit like a meerkat poking its head out of its den. "What's going on?"

"Jenna offered me a job! I'm going on tour!" Lacey blurted, and squealed again, spinning in an excited circle. When she stopped, Sam was staring at her with a blank expression on his face.

"What?"

Her joy fizzled. "Jenna just called. She's flying me to LA tomorrow to audition for her tour. But she also said it's basically a done deal."

"What does that mean?" Sam asked, his voice eerily calm.

She'd expected a bigger reaction from him. More excitement. Any excitement.

"It means that I'm going to be a professional dancer again. I'm going on tour for—shit, I have no idea how long her tour is. I guess it doesn't really matter." Lacey's wheels were spinning but not getting any traction. Sam wasn't having any kind of reaction to anything she was saying. "I'm sure we could be divorced before the tour starts. Oregon doesn't require a separation period. Since it's uncontested, it should only take a month or two."

"You looked it up already?"

She hadn't. She'd overheard one of her dance moms talking about her own divorce when they'd been setting up for the recital dress rehearsal. But she'd filed the information away in case she needed it.

"I thought it was good to know."

Sam put his hands in his pockets. "Okay then." He turned and went back downstairs.

Lacey stood rooted to her spot. Had that actually happened? Had Sam not put up a single ounce of emotion when she told him that she was leaving? No joy, no shock, no anger or indignation.

She really was a stupid, hopeless romantic who had a penchant for getting played by musicians.

Her phone buzzed in her hand.

JENNA FOX

What's your middle name? For the ticket.

CHAPTER THIRTY-ONE

THE HOUSE ECHOED when Lacey wasn't there.

Maybe it echoed when she was there, too, but it felt cavernous without her.

Sam signed for the dining room table he'd ordered back in November, and locked the doors behind the delivery drivers. He stared at the table, made from native Oregon trees he couldn't remember the names of, and wanted to throw every empty chair out the window.

It was one of many Christmas surprises he wouldn't be able to give to Lacey.

The most important one, the one he'd been most excited to give to her, was sitting on his nightstand mocking him.

It was her engagement ring—or her wedding ring, he didn't know what to call it since they were already married—but not the paper one that Jenna had made for them. Those had fallen off somewhere between the chapel and the hotel. This ring he'd called around Portland until he found a jeweler that could quickly bring the vague idea he had in his head to life. Then he'd paid for them to drive it down to Crane Cove so Lacey wouldn't be suspicious. It had been easy to sneak it into the house because she'd been so consumed with recital week.

He'd wanted a ring that looked like the sun. So he'd gotten one. A round center stone, surrounded by a halo of marquis cut diamonds in various sizes. It would have looked stunning on Lacey's finger.

The plan had been to give it to her on Christmas, but that wasn't likely to happen. He didn't know when—or if—she was coming home. Fuck, she'd brought up getting divorced. She would get her money from her mother's estate, her job with Jenna, and she'd be gone in the wind. Once she had her own money, what did he have to offer her that he hadn't already given? This was why he'd never wanted to be in a relationship again. He had tried so hard, and in the end, it meant nothing.

There was an invisible weight on his chest that made it hard to breathe. He'd have been better off if a semi-truck had been parked on his sternum.

He hadn't said goodbye to Lacey. He'd slept on the couch in the TV room and she'd left before he came upstairs. There wasn't a note or a text. She was just gone.

Daisy whined and pawed his leg.

"Right. Dinner." Sam wasn't hungry, but Daisy was. When would it occur to the dog that Lacey wasn't coming home?

He wanted to sleep. If he was asleep, he didn't have to deal with any of this.

As Sam portioned out Daisy's dinner, his phone started to buzz on the kitchen counter. He nearly dropped her bowl in his rush to get to it. Maybe it was Lacey.

It was Jenna.

"What do you want?" he snarled. This was her fault, wasn't it?

"What happened to hello?" Jenna asked, and didn't wait for

the answer before saying, "And why aren't you being supportive of your wife?"

"Who says I'm not being supportive?"

"When I asked Lacey what your reaction was to the news, she said you didn't have one. That you said 'Cool' and walked away."

"I didn't say 'Cool.'"

"Close enough," Jenna snapped. "What is wrong with you?"

"Nothing," Sam snapped back, "except that one of my best friends went behind my back, and now my wife is leaving me."

"Went behind your— Sam, I didn't go behind your fucking back."

Sam clenched his fist to try and stop his hand from shaking. His muscles were quivering with pent up emotion. "Why didn't you ask me first?"

"Ask you?" Jenna shouted. "I don't have to ask *you*, Sam! This is your wife's career, not yours. She is an autonomous person who can make her own damn decisions. I'm so fucking *sick* of men thinking they can control what women do. I'm fucking disappointed in you, Sam. There's a lot of guys I'd expect this backwards, reductionist, misogynistic, downright Neanderthal behavior from, but not you."

"She's my wife," Sam insisted, though he felt like he was running up an icy hill—getting absolutely nowhere and only hurting himself.

"And I will support her in not being your wife if you can't pull your head out of your ass."

Jenna hung up before he could issue a rebuttal.

Who the hell was she to tell him how to handle his marriage?

. . .

TWO LONG, lonely days later, Sam could see Jenna's point. Or points. He was pretty sure there'd been multiple, but it all boiled down to him being an unsupportive ass.

When she'd told him about the tour, Sam had been shocked, but when she mentioned divorce, he'd shut down. It had been easier than trying to voice his complex swirl of emotions.

He'd stewed in his wrongness. Sat in his own mental filth. If it hadn't been for Daisy, he would have stayed in bed and rotted. But she needed him. She required that he get out of bed, feed her, and take her to go potty.

His wife needed him too. Or, at least, he hoped she did. Because he needed her.

Sam flew to Los Angeles on Christmas Eve, when it was abundantly clear to him that she wasn't coming home. He was going to storm the castle, and then grovel at Lacey's feet like the deeply sorry asshole he was.

But when he pulled up in front of Jenna's house, which looked like Barbie's Christmas Dream House, he couldn't bring himself to use the gate code. Or even buzz to be let in. He didn't deserve Lacey. She was better off without him.

Sam was halfway to his house when the computer screen on his dash lit up with Peter's name and number. He pressed the phone icon on his steering wheel.

"Why are you calling?"

"And a bah humbug to you too," Peter responded. "I was calling because I just finished Jordy's family's annual reading of 'Twas The Night Before Christmas—"

"You do not do that," Sam interjected in disbelief.

"I do. It's for his nieces and nephews. *Anyway*"—the word was pointed enough to cut—"Jordy said that Graham said that you bailed on Crane Cove Christmas—"

"Try saying that five times fast."

"Stop interrupting. Graham said that you're in the City of

Angels, and I wanted to invite you and Lacey to my parents' house for Christmas, if you don't have any other plans. Don't worry about gifts, we keep things shockingly simple because nobody in my family has the patience to wait for Christmas."

Sam wondered how long Peter could hold his breath underwater because he didn't seem to need to breathe when he talked.

"Umm," he began awkwardly, "Lacey isn't with me. But Daisy is. Is it okay if I bring the dog?"

"Of course you can bring Daisy! She's such a good girl."

Daisy tried to crawl into the front seat at the sound of her name, and Sam had to turn his arm into a barrier to keep her in the back.

"What time should we be there tomorrow?"

"Whenever you want, but no earlier than ten. Grandma should be nice and socially lubricated by her morning cocktail by then."

For the first time in days, Sam felt like smiling. "Charlotte Parker and Estelle Whitman are going to be in the same room? You should charge admission to the show."

"Battle of the Hollywood Starlets," Peter boomed in a faux announcer voice. "Hopefully everyone leaves alive."

SAM ARRIVED AT PETER'S PARENTS' Los Angeles home at eleven in the morning. He'd truly held out as long as he could, but he couldn't be alone with his thoughts anymore. The overflowing wastepaper basket, filled to the brim with rejected apologies, was proof of that.

The Parker-Greens owned a mansion in Beverly Hills that, by current celebrity standards, was quite subdued. It felt like a home instead of a showpiece purchased to show off how much money they had in the bank.

Sam parked in the brick paved circular driveway, and he and Daisy walked up to the door. He hoped a holiday with the Parker-Greens would brighten her spirits, because Lacey's absence was starting to wear on her too.

Maybe he could use that as his opener to talk to her. "Hey, Daisy's depressed. Coincidentally, so am I. Please come home." No. That was too guilt-trippy.

The door burst open, even though his finger still hovered over the bell.

"Sam!" Peter shouted, and pulled him into a bone-crushing hug. Daisy danced around their feet, begging to be included. Peter noticed and crouched down to give her love too. "I couldn't forget about you, sweet girl." He stood and waved them inside. "Come in, come in. We've got *White Christmas* on, and Grandma is bitching about how much damn mileage Bing Crosby got out of that damn song. Her words, not mine."

Sam followed Peter through the foyer and towards the kitchen. The interior of the house looked like someone had pointed to a holiday issue of an interior design magazine and said, "Give me that." Knowing Charlotte Parker, that might be exactly what she'd done.

"Mom, look who's here," Peter said as they entered the kitchen, which was a disaster zone.

Charlotte Parker brushed one of her winter blonde curls out of her face with the back of her hand, leaving a smear of flour. At almost seventy, she was still a strikingly beautiful woman, and anyone could draw a line from her to Peter and understand where he got his looks from.

"Oh, Sam, thank god," she breathed, wiping her hands on the front of her apron that was probably being used for the first time ever. "I got a bit lost in this recipe—"

Peter's father, Arthur Green, was watching from the

boundary between the kitchen and living room with a mug, probably filled with tea, in his hands and a twinkle in his eye.

"I don't understand why you didn't call the caterers," he said with an affectionate smile. "It's worked fine for the last thirty-odd years."

"Because I wanted to do this right. We never get to spend holidays together," Charlotte huffed, and looked imploringly at Sam. "Help me. Please."

Sam gave Peter a suspicious glare, but pushed up his sleeves and headed to the sink to wash his hands.

"YOU CALLED ME IN AS A RINGER," Sam accused after Christmas dinner was in the oven. He and Peter were sitting by the pool with mugs of seasonally appropriate hot cocoa, even if they weren't weather appropriate.

"It's called insurance," Peter clarified, taking a sip of his cocoa and getting whipped cream on the end of his nose. He was lucky that Daisy was inside lounging with Grandma Estelle and soaking up seventy-three years of Hollywood gossip while she got her ears scratched, or he'd have gotten a tongue bath.

"You're lucky I was in town."

"There's always a Plan C," Peter said, and added, "Dad bought a frozen lasagna from Costco—did I tell you my dad finally discovered Costco? He's obsessed."

"He can buy tea by the pound."

"Never. He still imports it from jolly ol' England. None of our Yankee swill." Peter finally noticed the whipped cream on the end of his nose and brushed it off. "Where's Lacey?"

Sam closed his eyes and sank into his pool chair. "If I tell you some secret shit, can you promise to keep it to yourself *and* not to freak out?"

"She's not sick, is she?"

Sam cracked an eye to look at his friend. "No, she's not sick."

Then Sam launched into his story. How he'd met Lacey in Barcelona, how he hadn't recognized her years later, how he'd started that ridiculous rumor and how it had spectacularly back-fired but also succeeded at the same time. He told Peter about their fake dating ploy and how he'd slowly fallen in love with Lacey, because how could he not?

"Lacey's had some really shitty exes," Sam explained, "and they got her into financial trouble. She had some inheritance from her mom, but she couldn't access it until after she got married—"

Peter took a sharp intake of breath. To his credit, it was the first sound he'd made the entire story.

"So when we were in Vegas, I suggested we get married so she could get the money and clear her debt."

"How did you propose?"

Sam frowned. "I asked her if she wanted to get married?"

Peter sighed heavily, putting his mug on the pool deck and sitting up. "No, I mean what was the proposal like?"

"I...asked?" Sam searched his memory. "I laid out all the reasons why we should get married...which were pretty much all getting her money for her."

"Disappointing. Continue."

"When we got back from Vegas, Jenna offered Lacey a job as a dancer on her tour, and she's taking it. She's leaving me before the tour starts." The memory was an open wound, and recalling it was like rubbing salt and lemon juice in it. "I...didn't react well—actually, I didn't react at all."

"Mm-hmm." Peter steepled his fingers, deep in thought, then asked, "Do you want to stay married?"

"Of course I do. I love her. Why else do you think I jumped on the opportunity when it presented itself?" Sam looked up at the cloudless sky. It didn't look or feel much like Christmas. "What if she's done with me?"

"Well, if you don't do something about it, she will be." Peter stood, stretched, and started pacing. "Do you want my advice?"

"I don't think it can get me into any more trouble than I've already gotten myself into."

"Starting with optimism. Love it." Peter flashed a thumbs-up. "If I was Lacey, I'd be questioning if you really had feelings for me."

"This is getting weird..."

"Shut up." Peter turned on his heel and did an about-face. "Your proposal was pragmatic, not romantic. In fact, I don't remember hearing you once saying that you've even told Lacey that you're in love with her. Have you?"

The back of Sam's neck grew hot. "I think I might have... once...when we were having sex."

Peter groaned.

"I don't know! She never brought it up, and she was always bringing up how we were going to break up. What was I supposed to do?"

"Be bold! Be brave!" Peter's hands flew while he spoke. "Don't let her go and leave it all up to fate. Do something big and romantic. If you don't feel a little bit stupid doing it, you're probably doing it wrong."

Sam scooted back in his chair. "I'm a little scared of what you have in mind."

Peter opened his mouth, stopped walking, and then closed his mouth. "Nothing. I've got nothing. Graham had a ball. You could write her a song?"

The idea hit Sam so hard it was like turning on a light and getting shocked by the switch.

CHAPTER THIRTY-TWO

LACEY HAD BEEN STAYING with Jenna for over a week. She hadn't intended to stay that long. Just a few days so she could cool off and Sam could figure himself out. But in those few days, Sam never reached out. No calls, no texts, no random photos of Daisy. And then Jenna had called off her wedding with Houston, and they'd been clinging to each other like the only available pieces of driftwood in the middle of the ocean.

They were their own little Heartbreak Hotel. They lounged in their pajamas, watched too much TV, ate dessert for breakfast, and ordered take out for dinner. Jenna was a good distraction. She almost kept Lacey from wallowing about how Sam was spending Christmas in Crane Cove surrounded by people who loved him. He probably hadn't thought about her at all.

LACEY HAD to go home eventually. She missed Daisy, and all her stuff was at Sam's house. Plus, her car was in Crane Cove. She would need to drive that back to Los Angeles before tour rehearsals started in January.

She'd read somewhere that humans were just complicated

houseplants, so she was trying to soak up some sunshine by Jenna's pool in a futile attempt to perk herself up while she looked at flights.

Jenna joined her, two steaming cups of coffee in her hands. "Here," she said, giving one to Lacey before lowering herself into a lounge chair. "This is about all I can cook."

"The mountain of menus in no way tipped me off," Lacey said, blowing on her coffee. "Thank you for everything, by the way. I don't know what I would've done without you."

"Have you talked to Sam yet?" Jenna asked, adjusting her huge sun hat to protect her face.

Lacey shook her head.

Jenna sighed dramatically. "That boy. I swear...I love him like a brother, which means right now I want to throttle him like a brother." She squeezed Lacey's arm. "You're welcome to stay as long as you want."

"You keep saying that. I don't know if you like my company or you're afraid to be by yourself."

"Both."

"I'm sorry about Houston."

Jenna flicked her wrist dismissively.

"Over him so soon?" Lacey raised her eyebrows when Jenna shrugged. "Why'd you say yes?"

"Because he asked." Jenna stared into her coffee like it was a crystal ball. "They ask, and I can't think of a reason to say no. I don't know if my expectations change or if the ring rips off the rose-colored glasses, but as soon as it's on, all I can see are the problems. I want to be married. I want kids. But I can't seem to find someone I want to see at the end of the aisle. What made you marry Sam?"

It was on the tip of Lacey's tongue to give the obvious, flippant answer: money. But she'd said no to other proposals that would've gotten her to the same place.

"Because he's kind. And generous. And funny. He's a great cook and a good listener. Whenever I've needed him, he's been there." A lump formed in her throat as the past few months danced through her memory. "I could have said no, but I didn't want to. I love him."

"Would you take him back?"

"In a heartbeat. But I have to know he wants me half as much as I want him."

Jenna nodded. "How's looking at flights?"

"Awful. But I found one tomorrow afternoon."

"So soon?" Jenna pouted. "Can you push it back one more day?"

Lacey laughed. "Jenna, I've been here forever already."

"Just one more day. I'll put you in first class."

"Using my love of champagne against me. You're an evil genius. Sold."

"Perfect." Jenna brightened considerably. "I want to take you out tomorrow night. I've got a thing and you're going to be my date."

"A thing? What thing?"

"You'll see." Jenna sipped her coffee a little too nonchalantly.

"I don't have anything to wear unless it's an activewear event."

Jenna wasn't deterred. "You can shop my closet."

"I'm not really in the mood for people," Lacey protested the next night as they pulled up to the curb. She peered out of Jenna's tinted window and frowned. "The All-Nighter?"

"You know it?" Jenna handed her keys to a valet.

"Yeah. My ex-boyfriend used to play here."

Lacey had a lot of memories of sitting at the bar of this particular club, watching Jace play, dreaming about what their life would be like when he made it big. The All-Nighter was one of those venues in LA that musicians played when they were close to making it big, or had slipped off their pedestal. It had a classic dive bar atmosphere while also serving expensive drinks.

Jenna linked her arm with Lacey's and marched her inside.

"We're going to have fun," she insisted. "And I need your help. I'm scouting a second opener for my tour."

"Why didn't you just say that in the first place?"

"Oh, look, there's Grim. Grim!" Jenna shouted and waved at the man Lacey had met once. He waved back. His jacket reminded her of her grandmother's couch.

They squeezed through the crowd. Whoever was playing must be good, because it was standing room only. Lacey wished she'd checked the marquee before they entered, but Jenna had rushed her inside.

"I was getting worried you weren't going to make it," Grim said, rising off his seat to give Jenna a hug and a kiss on her cheek. He gave Lacey a one-armed "we don't know each other well yet" hug, and then sat back down. He pulled out his phone, typed something, and then slid it back into his pocket.

"Oh, you know, traffic," Jenna said with a flippant wave of her hand.

Lacey frowned. They weren't late. Not according to the time Jenna had told her. She opened her mouth to point that out, but the lights dimmed and the crowd erupted in excited screams. The energy was palpable and damaging to her hearing; Lacey covered her ears.

"I should've brought ear plugs," she shouted to Jenna, who was whooping and hollering and clapping her hands. She hadn't forgotten ear plugs. Lacey could just see them nestled into her ears. Someone tapped her on her shoulder and held a pair of orange earplugs under her nose.

Grateful, Lacey pushed them into her ears and looked to thank her savior.

"Annie!" Tears flooded her eyes as she wrapped her friend in a tight hug. "What are you doing here?"

"Just enjoying a show," Jordy interjected, and pointed toward the stage. Lacey looked right as Sam walked out onto the stage and the decibel level in the club rose.

Her heart hurt, like someone had reached inside her chest and was twisting the important organ like a wet rag. She missed him, but it was easier to miss him when he wasn't close enough that she could throw a beer bottle and hit him.

Sam waved bashfully, his favorite guitar hung around his body, and he made his way to the lone stool in the center of the stage.

"Hello," he said as he sat down, "I'm Sam Shoop."

Lacey put her hands over her ears, and saw Annie do the same out of the corner of her eye. Their cheap earplugs were no match for the screaming power of Sam's fans.

Sam picked a few notes on his guitar and the room began to quiet down, and then it settled into a waiting hush.

"I'd like to thank you all for being here tonight. I know this show was very, very short notice." He laughed in that charming, self-deprecating way he had, and Lacey saw a woman about her age burst into tears. "I've been wanting to do a show like this for a while. If I had my way, all my shows would be like this. But I'd either never stop playing shows, or no one would be able to see me play."

Sam made a small adjustment to one of his tuning pegs. "I have a new album coming out—" He was cut off by a wall of sound, and he waited patiently. Or as patiently as Sam could wait. He started talking before the noise died down. "I have a new album coming out next year. We haven't nailed down an exact release date yet, but I can tell you that it's been recorded."

He squirmed on his stool. "This album is, um, special to me. You see, I've been creatively blocked for a long time. I'd sit down with my guitar or at my piano to write and nothing happened. Then I met my wife, my sunshine, my sweet Lacey, and that all changed. Only a few songs on the album are purposefully about her, but she inspired all of them by simply existing."

Sam began picking notes again, and Lacey recognized the skeletal structure of a melody he'd played with at their house.

"The funny thing about me—and anyone who knows me would agree—is that I'm very good at writing songs and making lyrics, but I'm not very good at using my words. I sometimes struggle to tell the people that mean the most to me how I feel. I hurt people that matter to me unintentionally. And that's what this first song is about. It's called 'Morse Code.'"

LACEY WAITED on her old stool at the bar. The All-Nighter had cleared out. Jenna, Grim, and Annie and Jordy had all gone home for the night.

She was waiting for Sam.

He'd played for about an hour, working through the track list for the new album, just him and his guitar or the piano. Sam explained most of the songs, but some he didn't. When he sang "Daisy," he waited until the end of the song to tell the crowd that the love song was about his dog.

Lacey wanted to burst with pride and cry until she flooded the place with her tears because she loved that man so much. "Morse Code" had broken her heart wide open because it was true. Sometimes it was like they were speaking in Morse code but missing the signals.

She wanted to be better. She wanted to make their relationship work.

A gentle tap on her shoulder made her jump. Sam took half a step back. Lacey pressed a hand to her chest.

"What the hell," she gasped, trying to catch her breath.

"Sorry," he said, "I guess this kind of ruins any 'Hello, gorgeous, do you come here often?' pickup line."

Lacey couldn't help herself; she grinned. "Not in a while, but I think I might need to start coming back more often."

Sam took the stool next to hers. His expression was so earnest and broken that she wanted to smother his face in kisses.

"Lacey, I am so, so sorry. I—"

"Sam, it's okay," she soothed, putting her hand on his knee. "We all make mistakes."

"Can I finish?" he implored. "I am so proud of you. You have been so strong and worked so hard to get to where you are. Even though it caught me by surprise, I should have been more supportive. Asked some questions while I figured myself out. I don't know. I just know that I fucked up so bad."

"I don't want to get divorced," Lacey blurted. Relief washed over Sam's face, erasing the anxiety.

"That makes this next part so much easier," he said, and dug awkwardly into his back pocket and pulled out a ring box. At least she thought it was a ring box. It could be earrings. She'd been fooled that way before.

"Lacey Finch, I love you. I love you so much that I've filled up a notebook with songs about how much I love you. I really meant it when I said that marrying you was the easiest decision I ever made." He opened the box and through the tears clouding her eyes, Lacey saw a stunning ring. She started to cry. "This was supposed to be your Christmas present."

"You bought me a ring," she bawled, and flung her arms around his neck.

"And a dining room table. So you don't have to eat at the counter anymore."

That made Lacey cry harder.

"Does all this crying mean that you'll be my wife?" Sam asked, and Lacey laughed.

"I *am* your wife," she reminded him, using a few scratchy bar napkins to dry her face and wipe her nose.

"Yes, you are. But I want you to be my wife because I want to be married to you. I want to spend the rest of my life with you. I want to cook for you, travel with you, and come home to you. Lacey Finch—" Sam rose from his stool and picked up the ring box.

"Don't kneel on the floor, it's so gross!" Lacey shouted, and all the employees who had been doing their closing duties stopped and stared.

Sam chuckled as her face flamed. He stayed standing. "Lacey Finch, please be my very real wife."

Her smile broke through her tears like sunshine on a cloudy day. Lacey nodded as hard as she could. "Yes. Absolutely yes."

EPILOGUE

"LAST CHECK," Sam said, running his finger down the laminated list. "Passport."

Lacey dug it out of her purse. "Check."

"Wallet."

She held up her wallet. "Check."

"Daisy's vet paperwork."

She opened her backpack and touched the folder. "Check."

"Phone charger?"

Lacey dug through her purse, then her backpack.

"Shit." She ran back to retrieve her charger from the hotel nightstand.

They had been on tour for a month, and Graham and Eloise's cheeky wedding present—the laminated packing list—had saved them from forgetting things in four different cities. Sam did his check first, because usually running down the list reminded Lacey of the things she'd forgotten to grab.

Sam loved being on tour with Lacey. When the opportunity had been presented—meaning he'd twisted every arm he could find to get what he wanted—to open for Jenna, he jumped on the chance. It was even better that it wasn't *his* tour, because every night he got to go on stage, do what he loved for forty-five minutes, then watch Jenna and his wife absolutely crush it for two hours.

They hadn't taken an official honeymoon. There hadn't been time. Someday, after Jenna's tour and then his tour, which would start a few weeks after Jenna's ended, wrapped, he would take Lacey on a long, leisurely vacation.

The week they'd had between tour preparation and the start of the tour had been spent in Crane Cove, soaking up all the small-town charm they could. They drank coffee at Stardust, ate Cole's impeccable meat at Cranberry Brothers, and finally got to try the Spanish tapas place.

They agreed that pizza had been the right decision for their first date.

Returning to Crane Cove had felt like an extended wedding shower and reception, all rolled into one. Lacey spent the first few days with her hand extended in front of her body, showing off her sparkling ring to anyone who asked to see it. The ladies of the knitting circle ooh-ed and aww-ed, and surprised Sam with a stack of cards with marriage advice and a recipe box. His favorite piece of advice was "Be kind. Be considerate."

Graham and Eloise hosted a private dinner reception for them at the hotel. Amara even made them a small, simple white wedding cake with yellow daisies for decoration. Sam and Lacey had said no gifts, so naturally their friends ignored them. Graham and Eloise gave them the packing list and a dry erase marker. Connor gave them a journal to record their first year of marriage. Kiki's gift, which Lacey started to open and promptly stopped, was a whip.

Peter, the great sentimentalist, gifted them a collection of poems and love letters between John Keats and Fanny Brawne. To Sam's surprise, Sybil gifted them the same collection, but a different edition.

Sam asked Cole to check in on the house periodically while he and Lacey were away on tour. Cole had mellowed as he progressed into his mid-twenties, and if he guarded the location of Sam's house with half the vigor he guarded his brisket recipe, no one would ever find it. Peter had offered to stay there and house sit when he was scheduled to film a movie nearby, but Sam had heartily declined; he'd seen Peter start too many kitchen fires.

Lacey returned with her phone charger held triumphantly above her head.

"Charger! Check!"

"You are too excited about that." Sam checked off the item. "Sex toys?"

"That's not on the list, but I packed them last night after we cleaned them." Lacey kissed his cheek. "Have I told you that I love you today?"

"Yes, but it never stops feeling good." He kissed her forehead. "I love you, too, sunshine."

His phone dinged in his pocket. Sam waited until Lacey was distracted putting her charger in her backpack to check it. He was a little ashamed to admit that he'd set up news alerts for Jace Kieffer, but if that asshole stepped one toe out of line, Sam was ready to make good on his threat to end his career. But, karma was taking care of Lacey's parasitic ex-boyfriend. His debut single had only gone as high as number nine, and his sophomore song was a complete flop.

Today's little piece of news was benign. Only the lineup for the North Dakota State Fair. Sam pocketed his phone.

Lacey was bent over, adjusting Daisy's harness and leash, and Sam ran a loving hand over the glorious curve of her ass.

"Do you think we have time—"

A polite knock at the door interrupted his attempt to fuck his wife one more time in that particular hotel room.

Lacey twisted her hair into a high, messy bun. "They can't be looking for us yet. We're not even late."

Sam kissed the delicate daisy tattoo behind her ear. He had a similar one in the same place. As soon as they could agree on a design, they were going to get matching tattoos to commemorate their time in Barcelona.

"Do you want to be late, Mrs. Shoop?"

The knock came again.

"It's probably John Paul and Daisy," she said, and went to open the door.

After his stellar performance above and beyond the call of duty in Las Vegas, Sam had hired John Paul to be the head of his security detail for Jenna's tour and into his own tour. John Paul's main job—and definitely his favorite job—was being Daisy's nanny.

Lacey paused with her hand on the doorknob and smiled at Sam over her shoulder. "When we get to Minneapolis tonight, your ass is mine."

She opened the door to greet their dog, who was a wiggly tornado of excited energy to see her mom, and contentment settled over him like a warm, weighted blanket.

This was the life he'd always wanted and had been afraid to reach for. He still had days where the clouds of his low moods refused to part, but they were easier, knowing Lacey's warm sunshine remained on the other side. And he got to help her through her hard days, too.

Sam grabbed their suitcases and wheeled them to the door.

"Should we be early for a change?"

"Everyone else is going to think they're late." Lacey took Daisy's leash from John Paul. "Let's do it."

Sam chuckled and followed his girls to the elevator.

ABOUT THE AUTHOR

Sarah is a Pacific Northwest based romance writer who would call herself "indoorsy". When she isn't traipsing around the country for work, Sarah enjoys buying more books than she can ever read, drinking an irresponsible amount of coffee, and not respecting her bedtime.

Find her on social media @remarkablysarah
www.sarahestep.com